Advance Praise for Highway 7

GW00713277

"Every story in this collection gives
into the darkness. Read all at once
anthology will have you leaving a   f
horror... this is a definite must."
- **Ruby Blotzer,** *Book Reviewer*

"Totally awesome, thrilling, suspenseful, spine tingling. I loved the
twists in the stories which I did not see coming at all. I WANT TO READ
MORE!"
- **Leanne Widenmaier,** *Book Reviewer*

"A masterfully written short story collection, with plenty of grit and
darkness. Perry Prete keeps you in anticipation of that final twist end-
ing!"
- **Dennis Stein,** *Author*

"Perry Prete hijacks your sensibilities and takes you into a nightmare
of strange, disturbing, unnerving, and frightening worlds with his new
anthology."
- **Kristine Barker,** *Author*

"This book contains four short stories that make you feel you entered
the twilight zone. Praise for Perry Prete for these magnificent stories."
- **Arlene Arredondo,** *Book Reviewer*

"4/5 stars"
- **Ilene Bieleski,** *Reviewer at Bookworm's Reviews*

"4/5 stars"
- **Aric Monkman,** *Librarian*

HIGHWAY 7
4 DARK TALES

sands press
Brockville, Ontario

Other Books By Perry Prete

All Good Things
Ethan, a City of Ottawa paramedic, accidentally becomes embroiled in a series of brutal, seemingly unrelated killings. However, Ethan finds a strange connection between them, which he passes on to his lifelong friend, now a detective. Sometimes it takes an outsider to piece together the puzzle.

Ethan comes face to face with the killer.

And this is just the beginning.

The More Things Change - Pinnacle Book Achievement Award
Everyone thought the Second World War ended April 30th, 1945 with Hitler's death.

In 2013, Ethan Tennant, a Paramedic for the City of Ottawa, discovers more than a body on Parliament Hill. He unwittingly unleashes a secret that began almost seventy years ago and still hasn't been revealed. Some people want to keep what he found a secret, others want the world to know. Certain secrets are never meant to be known.

Hilter's dream may not have ended with his death.

The Things That Matter Most
In the summer of 2000, Ethan Tennant, Tom Lister and Galen Hoese work together to catch the killer of young girls during the summer of the new millennia.

Young, innocent girls play in the summer heat, oblivious to the dangers around them, only to fall prey to the worse type of death possible. Parents, neighbours and the police are frustrated by the lack of progress on the case.

The killer is always one step ahead of the police. The killer seems to know more than the police investigating the crimes. It's not until Ethan and his new girlfriend, become involved, that the pieces of the puzzle begin to form a complete picture.

But does anyone really want to see what has remained hidden for so long?

Part One of...?

sands press

A division of 3244601 Canada Inc.
300 Central Avenue West
Brockville, Ontario
K6V 5V2

Toll Free 1-800-563-0911 or 613-498-2398
http://www.sandspress.com

ISBN 978-0-9936753-6-2

Cover concept and artwork by DigiWriting
Original cover concept and artwork by John Tkachuk
Formatting by Kevin Davidson
Publisher Kristine Barker

Ghostbusters lyrics in The Reunion by Ray Parker Jr.

Publisher's Note

For information on bulk purchases of this book or any book published by Sands Press, please call 1.800.563.0911 or email sales@sandspress.com.

1st Printing November 2015

To book an author for your live event, please call: 1.800.563.0911

Submissions

Sands Press is a literary publisher interested in new and established authors wishing to develop and market their product.

As an emerging publisher, we strive to meet the demands placed upon us by the authors and the market. We are currently accepting submissions in most genres. Please research publishers before deciding to submit your project to Sands Press.

Sands Press strives to provide full publishing to all of our clients, however we reserve the right to discuss co-publishing as an option for certain projects.

General Guidelines:

Please provide a brief synopsis of the story, no longer than one page, and include the entire manuscript in DOCX (Word).

Please send your manuscript electronically to:
submissions@sandspress.com.

Please be patient. It can take up to eight (8) weeks before we reply to your submission.

HIGHWAY 7

4 DARK TALES

PERRY PRETE

sands press
Brockville, Ontario

TABLE OF CONTENTS

THE ELEVATOR

QUINN ROHRER

Quinn Rohrer sat at the kitchen table holding a cup of coffee in both hands like a man would hold one in a cold arena while watching a junior hockey game in January in northern Ontario. But Quinn wasn't in an arena, he had no children, and it was July in Toronto. His basement apartment was hot, but he liked it that way. He seldom turned on the air conditioning. He stared with blank eyes at the tiny television that sat high up on the fridge. The network news was on, but he paid little attention to it; it was the background noise he liked. The television had been salvaged from the garbage at the curb. It had been thrown out because it was old, and even had a built-in VHS player beneath the CRT screen. Sure it was dated, but it still worked, and Quinn didn't care how much power it consumed; all his utilities were included in his rent. That was the only good thing about this basement apartment. The landlord was an elderly lady who didn't charge what the apartment was really worth as long as he kept the lawn cut, the leaves raked, and the driveway shovelled.

Quinn got up from the kitchen table, walked down the hall, and, without looking, lowered his head under the furnace duct that ran low across the ceiling. He had hit his head so many times that it was now instinct to bow before the god of Heat and AC that extended itself across his hall ceiling.

Standing in front of the toilet, he began to empty his bladder. The phone rang, and he turned and peed down the side of the toilet and on the wall.

"Shit!"

He zipped up his pants and ran down the hall, bowed before the god, and picked up his cellphone. "Hello?" He wasn't happy.

"Quinn, it's Marty."

Quinn's supervisor at the security company for which he worked was a good friend who always bypassed the guards with more seniority for the overtime shifts. They began working for the company at almost the same time, but Marty was a "Yes Man," something Quinn wasn't. Quinn was good at his job. As good as he needed to be for an office building security guard.

"Got an OT shift if you want it. Evan called in sick. Again!"

"Again? Why the hell do you even give him any shifts?"

"He's full time on the schedule. I can't do a thing about it until the bigwigs decide to fire his sorry ass. He calls in sick again almost every week. What a dick! It's a seven to three. I know you work three to eleven but you're off for the next few days. You get time and a half for eight big hours if you want?"

1

Quinn had left a little wet spot on the front of his underwear by leaving the toilet prematurely. "Do I have time for a quick shower before going in?"

"It's six ten now. Do your best to make it in for seven, Buddy? I'll stop by and bring you a coffee when I'm doing my rounds." Marty hung up and Quinn rushed to the shower.

After a quick shower and shave, Quinn found his uniform from the previous day, held the shirt up to his nose, and inhaled deeply. He detected a slight odour - nothing offensive - but he had nothing else to wear since he had planned on doing laundry before work. He stood in front of the full-length mirror on the back of the bedroom door, stopped what he was doing, and looked at himself. He then pressed out the wrinkles in his shirt with his palms, and didn't like what he saw.

After a two-year college degree in computer programming and completing the first two years of mechanical engineering, he was now a full-time security guard with no seniority or future. Quinn had to drop out of university because he couldn't afford the tuition and living expenses. He stared at himself for a moment, feeling disappointed with what life had dealt him.

Quinn finished dressing, packed a quick lunch and thermos of coffee, crammed everything into his backpack, and rushed out the door. His bike was locked to the main gas line that fed the house. He knew it was a stupid thing to do, but he didn't care. He unlocked his bike, wrapped the chain over his shoulder, and inserted his ear buds. He tapped "play" on his cellphone and an Alan Parsons song began to play. He pushed the bike to get up to speed, jumped on the seat, and rode as quickly as he could downtown.

Quinn arrived at the First Reserve Bank building, where he had been posted for the past two years, just before seven. He locked his bike and made his way from the back loading docks to the service staff lunchroom, where he threw his lunch in the fridge before heading to the front lobby to relieve the night guard. Chad worked permanent nights; he loved nights because he got to work alone. He was wearing his usual dark sunglasses, the top three buttons of his shirt were open, and his clip-on tie hung from the top of the security monitor. Behind the dark glasses, Chad was sleeping, as he was every morning when Quinn relieved him. He had perfected a posture that made it look like he was awake when he was actually sound asleep. It had become a running joke to pull the back of Chad's chair hard and wake him as he thought he was falling backwards.

Quinn walked up slowly and quietly, placing the heel of his steel-toed boots to the ground, then rolling his foot to the floor without making a sound. He continued his cat-like walk until he was behind Chad. His hand floated in the air, reaching for the back of the chair, as Chad spun around and grabbed Quinn's arm. Quinn let out a shriek that would have made a seven-year-old girl proud.

"Jesus Christ Chad. I think I just dropped a deuce in my pants!"

Chad pulled off his dark glasses and wiped the tears from his eyes as he continued to laugh. He had a hard time catching his breath as he stood and watched Quinn trying to reclaim his manhood.

"After months of you scaring the crap out of me, I get you once, and you're pissed. My God, you looked scared. If Marty was here he would've stroked out." Chad continued to laugh. He caught his breath as he logged off the security system and computer. He gathered all of his gear, dropped it into his backpack, and walked away. "Oh my God. I thought you were going to die. Priceless. Just priceless." Chad continued to talk to himself, and his laughter faded as he disappeared down the hall.

"Ass wipe." Quinn pulled out the chair and logged into the security system. He typed in his username, password, and shift, and realized that he had just started the first hour of a sixteen-hour day. A feeling of exhaustion came over him. Quinn poured a cup of coffee from his thermos, shook the container, and knew he would run out of coffee long before the end of the day.

TEENA GRAFFIA

Teena Graffia woke to the sound of the television instead of an alarm clock. The volume was low - almost inaudible - but the large, flat screen on the wall facing her bed lit up the dark room. Teena had opaque curtains and blinds installed over the windows to block out all the light. She wasn't able to sleep with even the smallest amount of light in her bedroom. Unlike most parents, Teena's mother had insisted on closing the bedroom door and never believed in a night-light. Her mother had always told her to face her fears. As Teena grew older, she found it ironic that her mother kept telling her to "face her fears" as if it was some magical phrase to keep the demons at bay. Teena soon learnt that her mother had her own demons.

The television in the bedroom was pre-set to the local morning news program, as it was every morning. Teena tossed the covers back, pulled her long black hair into a ponytail, stepped onto the cool tile bedroom floor, and walked to the ensuite bathroom. The television and overhead light in the bathroom came on when the motion sensor was activated. Like the television in the bedroom, the one in the bathroom was pre-set to the same morning news program. The timer would automatically turn off the television in the bedroom in fifteen minutes. Teena set the shower temperature and let her slip fall to the floor before picking it up and tossing it into the hamper.

Teena opened the glass door, stepped into the shower stall, and stood beneath the rainfall showerhead. The walls of the stall were solid granite, chiselled to look like rock. The floor was brushed black granite and had a fold-down teak bench along the back wall. The stall itself was large enough to be used as a meeting room. The morning financial reports were being broadcast as she washed her hair. She paused for a few moments to hear how the Canadian dollar was trading against the US greenback, the price of gold, stocks on the Toronto and New York Stock Exchanges, and the cost of a barrel of oil.

After showering, Teena sat down at her make up table but applied only enough to smooth out her complexion. Although in her mid-forties, she still looked to be in her thirties, but in a male-dominated field, the professional appearance of a female executive was paramount. She dressed in a solid navy blue suit and crisp button-up white shirt, prepared a fruit and yogurt smoothie, filled her travel mug with black coffee, grabbed her Italian leather briefcase, and left for her job at the First Reserve Bank office tower. After almost twenty years with the bank, Teena had worked her way up from teller to international development manager. Her responsibility was to help promote and develop new projects in the American and European markets.

In the lobby, there were always copies of her three favourite newspapers waiting for her every morning. The cab was parked at the curb outside the building, the same way it was each weekday. She opened the back door, slid into the cab, said "good morning" to her regular driver, and settled in for the thirty-minute drive to the office building.

There was always a bit of casual small talk exchanged between Teena and the cab driver, but usually she sat quietly for the most part, reading the newspaper business section first, then arts and entertainment. The rest of the paper was seldom even glanced at. Today, however, one article on the front page caught her attention. The body of a young girl had been found in a local park, and may be linked to two other possible homicides. The lead detective, Brian Lahey, had no comment on the progress of the investigation. Teena shuddered to think of the horrors that must have gone through the young girls' minds just moments before their deaths. She finished reading the papers, folded them neatly, and placed them on top of her briefcase. Most of the other executives had started to read the daily papers on their tablets, but Teena preferred the old-school method. She patted the newspapers as she looked out the cab windows.

On schedule, the cab pulled up along the curb at the front of the First Reserve Bank building. She paid the fair along with her usual tip, said her goodbyes, and exited the cab. The newspapers were tucked under the same arm with which she carried her briefcase and sipped her coffee as she walked towards the lobby. It had become a habit to stop just before the building, tilt her head, and look up along the facade of the building to the sky. Teena had done this on her first day on the job when she was promoted to the head office, and it had become a comfortable, warm habit. She promised herself that the day the view was no longer exciting, she would find another job.

The feeling was even stronger today than it had been that first day on the job. She loved her work, and like a woman in a nurturing relationship, she fed off her position. It challenged her mentally. Her confidence in her ability as a professional grew with each successful year on the job, although her drive to succeed in business cost her a personal life. Teena spent most of her precious free time alone. Her plan was to work hard until she was fifty, and then retire. And her plan was working; she already had more than enough savings put aside to retire early and not have to worry about finances for the rest of her life.

It was just after seven fifteen when Teena entered the office building. The first set of glass doors to the foyer opened automatically as she approached, then the second set, and the cool air in the building blew across the lobby. Teena's shoes clicked and echoed on the marble floor. Quinn looked up and saw Teena approaching. He smiled. She smiled back.

"Quinn? This isn't your regular shift. What are you doing here?" Teena stopped at the security desk and placed her briefcase and coffee on the counter between them. Teena had always been good at remembering numbers and patterns, and it hasn't taken long for her to commit the security schedule to memory. Quinn was one of the nicer guards who worked the front desk. Regardless of the time of day, he smiled. She wasn't sure if he was smiling at her or just smiled all the time, but she took it as a compliment.

"Picked up an overtime shift. This is going to be a long day: sixteen hours."

Teena had always been friendly with Quinn, even more so than with the other guards. They'd been on a first name basis for months now, against the security company's policy. They only called each other by their first names when no one else was around. She made a point of stopping each morning and chatting with him even if there was another guard on duty, but then it was a more formal encounter.

"Think of the OT pay. More savings for school. The sooner you finish school, the sooner you get to leave here."

"But then who would you chat with in the morning?"

Teena chuckled, pulled the newspapers from underneath her arm, and handed them to Quinn as she did every morning. "Check out the sports sections. Leafs lost another close one. Again!"

Quinn thanked her for the newspapers as she gathered her coffee and briefcase and disappeared down the hall. He switched the image on the preview monitor and watched her walk to the elevators, press the button, and wait. The doors eventually opened, and she entered the elevator as Quinn changed the camera on the monitor again and watched her ride the elevator up to the thirtieth floor.

The First Reserve Bank owned the entire building but only used the top twenty floors. The entirety of their national and international operations was housed in the one location. They then had satellite, regional, or branch offices in most towns and cities across the country. Teena worked on the thirtieth floor, where all international operations were headquartered. The lower ten floors of the building were leased out as office space to various professional companies.

All the building's cameras sent their feeds to large recessed LCD monitors in the front security desk. The cameras were strategically placed to allow an unrestricted view of the loading docks, maintenance areas, lobbies, and hallways of every floor. Each elevator had a single camera hidden in the roof panel of each car. Even though signs were placed around the building indicating that security cameras were located in all public areas of the building, the security guards often got to witness quick, mid-afternoon, "accidental" meetings between bank employees who were unaware that their actions were being viewed, much less recorded.

The security company had a zero tolerance policy for making copies of anything caught on the monitors, but that didn't stop the guards from playing back video clips of events that went on during their shifts. Quinn took his cellphone from his pocket, swiped the screen to the camera app, and took a still of the preview monitor with Teena in full view. He saved the picture in the folder that held all of his other photos of Teena and placed the phone back in his pocket.

He had taken several dozen screen shots of Teena as she walked about the building. Teena was completely unaware that Quinn had been taking pictures of her for months. More and more of his time was spent thinking about Teena; it wasn't an obsession, but more of a curiosity. He had never been attracted to an older woman before. However, she did have all the qualities he looked for in a partner: intelligence, fitness, beauty, and drive. If circumstances were different, he reasoned, he would ask her out in spite of their age difference. Quinn still thought about asking her out; he thought about it more and more lately. But not today; maybe another day.

Quinn switched the preview monitor as Teena exited the elevator and turned left in the vestibule. Each floor of the bank had a glassed-in elevator lobby that made it necessary for the guest to check in before being granted further access. Teena swiped her security card, the light changed from red to green, and she pulled the door open. Quinn and the camera would lose sight of Teena behind the security doors. Quinn kept watching Teena until she was gone, and then continued to stare at the monitor for a few moments. He inserted one ear bud, letting the other dangle loosely, and tapped "play." The next Alan Parsons song began to play, and he went back to surveying the security monitors and reading the newspapers that Teena had left for him.

THE BUILDING

Several times throughout the day, the guards on foot patrol or on break would stop to talk to or relieve the guard on duty at the front lobby. There were always at least seven security guards on duty during the day, and four at night. Two guards were permanently stationed in the loading bays; one in a booth at the entrance, and the other on the docks. Three guards were stationed at each entrance of the building. The "floater," as they called the position, would make rounds and relieve each position for breaks and lunches. At night, there were only the two guards at the loading bays and one in the lobby, with the floater covering breaks and naptime instead of lunch.

Deliveries continued throughout the night, as many of the transport companies preferred the less congested evening and early morning traffic. The front lobby was the position the guards coveted and to which all hoped to be assigned. It wasn't a difficult job, or even stressful, and most of the guards were only working there to pay for school or support themselves after they retired.

Quinn was one of those who wanted to go back to school. He doubted he would ever go back to university, but despised the thought of working security much longer. The only thing he looked forward to each day shift was seeing Teena twice a day.

It had started simply enough. Quinn had said "hi" one morning as Teena walked past, and she had nodded in acknowledgement. Quinn was instantly smitten, the way a sixteen-year-old boy is when he sees an older woman and is suddenly attracted to her for no reason other than hormones. He continued to greet her when he worked the day shift as she walked past alone. If she happened to be with a group, he ignored her and she disregarded him. One day, she smiled back when he offered her a "good morning" and a smile. It wasn't long before she was the one who would offer the morning greeting first.

Then, one morning, she stopped to talk to Quinn. It wasn't much, but it turned out they had a lot in common. She was an avid Toronto Maple Leafs fan, while he hated the Leafs. Their love/hate relationship for the Leafs was always a favourite topic of conversation after a Leafs loss. They would playfully banter back and forth about the games and players. Teena taught Quinn how to read the stocks, which ones to watch, and why. She left her paper one day for Quinn, and that became a routine. If Teena knew she would be arriving for work before the rest of the executives, she would occasionally buy him a coffee.

Teena knew it was innocent flirting; the bank didn't have any policy against what she was doing. She would have the occasional fantasy about Quinn. She thought that was as far as she should take it - after all, Teena was almost fifteen years Quinn's senior - but she enjoyed the attention from the younger man and the thoughts the relationship offered.

Quinn hadn't had a serious relationship since he started university. He had been living with a girl through those two years, and had actually been engaged to her, but after they broke up, he refused to acknowledge that aspect of their relationship. He never discussed the breakup with any of his friends or even his parents. No one knew exactly why they broke up, and after months of badgering Quinn about it, they simply forgot to continue the verbal insults and assaults and it was never spoken of again.

Quinn's parents always assumed that the breakup was the reason he never went back to school. He didn't have to heart to tell his parents or his friends that his fiancée had taken him for what little money he had and maxed out his credit cards. Once Quinn discovered what she had done, he kicked her out. She kept the engagement ring and everything else she had purchased with his money. Quinn had to pay the credit card bills and had nothing left for school afterwards. He was too embarrassed to ask his parents for help. He had always been proud, was always the one who thought he knew women, but after she left he realized he knew nothing about women at all.

The morning business crowd started to flow in just after seven. The typical workday lasted from eight to five with an hour lunch in between. Between seven and seven forty-five, the morning rush was nothing but large groups of men and women in suits who were herded like cows in a pasture. They flowed through the glass doors and passed through security without even looking at whoever was working the security desk; their conversations went on uninterrupted. They simply scanned their ID cards, waiting for the light to change from red to green and for the familiar beep that indicated that they could proceed.

The guards had to watch the monitor and scan the users to make certain that the person standing before them matched the image on the screen. Most of the time it was impossible to clearly see the person who had just scanned their card; they usually continued to walk through with little regard for the security protocols. If a card refused to let the person pass, another executive would scan their card and the two would proceed through security without even offering an explanation to the guard.

As the crowds increased every morning, the line ups grew longer, and the tempers shorter. Quinn watched as the executives spoke on their cellphones, drank their ten-dollar coffees, and ignored him as they passed through the stall. Quinn smiled at them, hoping that even one of the executives would return the polite gesture, but it never happened. Regardless of the moods of the people as they passed through security, Quinn maintained his composure and continued to smile as they passed. "Idiots," he thought to himself. And he knew that when the workers passed, if they took the time to look down upon him, they probably all thought, "What a loser." Everyone except Teena.

The rest of the day proceeded as it did almost every other day: boringly. Quinn had a difficult time staying awake and drifted off to sleep several times. He wasn't nearly as adept as Chad at the "sleeping but awake" look. Quinn would rest his head in his hand when he fell asleep, and then he would snap back to reality when it fell. When the floater came by the relieve him, Quinn went back to the staff room by the loading docks, and took a quick nap instead of eating. He knew it was easy to sneak in a little food while on duty and a lot less of an infraction than getting caught sleeping during the day.

As with most days, the shift went by uneventfully; he had reports to write, documents to complete, and monitors to watch as the bank employees came and left for the day. Basically, a monkey could do his job for a few bananas, he thought. Most days, Quinn felt mentally drained, not from overwork but from not challenging his mind. Other than Teena, wondering how he could leave this job was what occupied his thoughts.

Just before three in the afternoon, the next shift of guards came in to relieve the day crew. Quinn still held seniority, and decided to keep his post at the front lobby so that he would be able to see Teena when she left for the day. He briefed the new shift on the events of the day - there were none - and assigned them their posts. There was a dispute between two guards who didn't get along and didn't want to work together, but both desired the same post. Quinn told them one would work at the post they both wanted for four hours, while the other worked as the "floater," and then they would switch for the balance of the shift. It wasn't what either wanted, but seemed to satisfy them.

As Quinn went back to his duties, he called them both "whiners" under his breath. He reported the shift assignments in the log and went back to the mind-numbing tasks of his job.

In the ninth hour of Quinn's sixteen-hour shift, he called the floater to come and relieve him for an emergency evacuation; guard slang for an emergency bathroom break that expedited the process whenever the guard called for it. There was seldom a problem regarding the other guards complying with the request. They all had them from time to time, so they knew never to question an "emergency evacuation" call. There were so few "emergencies" with which to deal that when they came up, the floater responded enthusiastically.

When his relief, Darryl, arrived from the loading docks, Quinn excused himself and made a hasty exit to the staff washroom. As he sat in the stall, Quinn flipped through his Gmail messages, reading the occasional email but discarding most, then went back to the photo app and the folder that contained all the pictures of Teena.

Quinn opened up a few of the thumbnail pictures, looked at them, and realized that what he was doing could very well be deemed "creepy." He selected the whole file and hit the trashcan icon. The phone asked if he was sure he wanted to throw the pictures away permanently. His thumb rested over the little question box momentarily, then he put pressure on the screen and the folder disappeared. Quinn felt a rush of sadness as he realized that the pictures he had taken over the past few months were gone forever. He knew it was the right thing to do, but he still regretted deleted them. It wasn't so much deleting the photos that he lamented, but the knowledge that he would never have the courage to ask Teena out. He shut down the app, powered down the phone, cleaned up, and flushed the toilet.

The lights in the washroom suddenly went black. The lights above flickered, and then the faint glow of the emergency lighting system filled the room. Quinn quickly pulled up his pants, did up his belt buckle, and radioed the lobby station for a report.

"The entire building went dark. All the systems went down and the generator kicked on. The emergency lights came on as expected," Darryl replied, with obvious panic in his voice.

"I'll be right down." Quinn pushed open the stall door and rushed to the lobby. Several of the building employees were milling about the halls and talking to each other. As Quinn rushed past, they grabbed his arm, swung him around, and asked him what had happened. He pulled away and continued down the hall to the lobby. "Now they want to talk to me. Assholes."

Just as Quinn arrived at the front lobby, the building lights came back on and the emergency lights dimmed, then went off completely. Quinn walked around the desk to see the status board, which indicated that all the systems were normal. Darryl pushed his chair off to the side to give Quinn a view of the security status board. The phones started to ring, and each phone line lit up and flashed to indicate an incoming call from somewhere inside the building. Quinn ignored the phones. Instead, he focused on the board to determine what had caused the blackout.

Darryl started to answer the phones, taking one call at a time. He did more listening than talking, and made notes of the complaints and comments from the callers. He looked over to Quinn, who had his own problems. He was reviewing the building's logs to see if the blackout had been caused by something internal or external. He flipped through the computer records to see if any of the sensors had picked up an anomaly that would have caused the blackout.

Still on the phone with agitated building employees, Darryl slid his personal mobile phone across the desk to Quinn. On the screen was a news alert about a traffic accident that had taken out a transformer and cut power to an entire city block. Quinn asked Darryl to start telling the callers that a traffic accident had caused the blackout, and not to worry. The calls kept coming in for another few minutes before the phones finally started to quiet. Even though it was against policy, Quinn switched the main monitor to the local television satellite feed to watch the news.

As Darryl continued to take calls, Quinn checked the statuses of the four huge diesel generators located in the basement. All the lights were green, indicating that each of the four generators had kicked on as they were designed to and were running smoothly, and providing electricity to operate essential services: lights, main electrical power, and one elevator. He checked the electrical status monitor to ensure that the power they were putting out was enough to handle the load. The generators could only supply enough power to run emergency backup systems, and it would only be a matter of minutes before they started to hit peak demand as some of the building tenants began to switch from electrical outlets to the emergency red outlets to operate what they deemed "emergency" equipment. Every tenant had been briefed on the emergency disaster plan, but that didn't deter some people who couldn't give a rat's ass about anybody but themselves. They all thought their own power needs were more important than anyone else's and, as expected, one of the generators started to peak into the red, indicating that demand was exceeding the output capabilities.

Quinn grabbed a flashlight from the security desk drawer and pointed at Darryl, saying in a strong, "I'm in control" voice, "I'm going down to check on the generators. Switch power to the elevator cameras and see if anyone is trapped inside, and if so call them on the box phones and let them know that we will assign power to each one in order to let them ride down to the lobby. Then call each office disaster manager and get them to start reducing power consumption. We can't switch power to the elevators if those fuck heads upstairs think their laptops supersede the disaster plan. Then call our head office, and give them an update on what's going on. See if they have any idea of when we're going to get power back."

"What if we can't get them to cut power demand?" Darryl asked.

"Simple. I'll cut power to each floor and see if they like it then."

Disasters were one of the few times when, regardless of who the executives were upstairs, they had to listen to security.

*****

Teena was sitting at her desk when the power went out. Her laptop beeped as it switched to battery power, and the screen dimmed. The office door closed automatically, as it should've in the event of a fire alarm or power failure. Teena gazed out at the office floor through her window and saw that the area was dark.

People were standing up and walking to the windows to look out onto the street below. She decided to join them, grabbed the doorknob, turned it, and pulled. Her hand slipped off the door handle and she stumbled backwards. All of the office doors were designed to be opened manually after they closed in the event of an emergency. Teena stepped forward, grabbed the door handle firmly, and pulled hard. The door remained fast and refused to budge. She banged on the window beside the door, catching the attention of the staff on the other side.

"I can't get out," she called.

Several of the staff put their weight against the door as she turned the handle, but again, it held firm.

"Don't worry about me," she yelled through the door. "Check on everyone else on the floor and get back to me after you make sure they're okay."

Teena went back to her chair, sat down behind her desk, and started to shake. She held her hand out, but was unable to keep from quivering, so she cupped her hands together to still them. Memories of her childhood took control of her emotions. In her chair, Teena hugged herself for comfort, not wanting to ever feel the way she had felt as a child again.

*****

Quinn activated the switch on the flashlight and pointed the beam in the direction in which he was headed. He swept the light back and forth, making sure his way was clear. When he arrived at the stairwell at the back of the lobby, he took the steps two at a time, his heavy boots hitting the metal steps and echoing with a clang in the darkness. The emergency lights were still on in the stairwells, but did little more than cast an eerie yellow glow along the walls.

Quinn heard a group of voices bouncing in the emptiness ahead. As he approached the sound, he heard panic in the voice of one of the men. He called out to them, and aimed the flashlight to help them find him. Disjointed arms and shadows of figures made their way up the metals stairs, and the voice of the scared man now turned to sobs.

"This way, guys." Quinn's voice was calm and reassuring. A small group of men and women stopped at the landing just below him and looked up. "Where are you guys heading?"

The woman who was leading the group made her way towards Quinn and stopped a few steps below him. She was out of breath but very calm.

"We were heading to the parking garage. Took the stairs instead of the elevator for exercise." She was panting. "Got disoriented in the darkness. And no one had a flashlight."

Quinn laughed inside but held his composure. "Don't any of you have a flashlight app on your cellphones?"

The men and women in the group all looked at each other, embarrassed that they hadn't thought of this obvious fact and that a security guard had pointed it out.

"The emergency overhead lights illuminate each door, and if you look on the wall beside them, it shows what floor you're on." Quinn shone the flashlight at the wall plaque that indicated their floor number.

Again, the group of executives turned to look at one another in embarrassment. "Well, you should have better lighting," quipped the sobbing man.

Tired of facing their arrogance for years, Quinn replied, "I didn't design this place, I just work here. If you want better lighting, maybe you could donate some of those big bucks you make."

The sobbing man barked back, "Well maybe if you were smart enough you could get a real job!"

"At least I know about the flashlight app on my phone." Quinn pushed his way past the group, making sure his shoulder caught the sobbing man squarely in the chest. He recognized him as the man who had been on his phone that morning during the security checks. He left the group to find their own way back up the flight of stairs to the lobby.

Quinn finally reached the lower level of the garage and pushed the door open. The garage floor was much darker than the stairwell. The few emergency lights on this level were sparse and didn't provide nearly enough light. Quinn was forced to use the flashlight to find his way to the fenced-in secure area where the ventilation shafts and generators were kept. A chain link fence from floor to ceiling ensured the safety of the building's backup generators. Each massive generator was vented into a large silver tube that pumped fresh air in and forced the exhaust out. A set of redundant smaller generators provided power just to the ventilation system for the larger units that fed power to the building. If the smaller generator failed to start or suddenly shut down, the larger generators would turn off as well. The sound of the four diesel generators was deafening. He doubted he could hear the radio on his waist.

Quinn used his master key to unlock the fence, swung the door outwards, and entered the secure area. He checked each generator, making sure that the fuel supply would last the required six hours as dictated by the disaster plan. All of the gauges and lights indicated that everything was running smoothly. He exited the room, locked the gate behind him, and made his way to the stairwell. As he was walking up the stairs to the lobby, his cellphone rang, startling him. He pulled the phone from his shirt pocket and stared at the screen but failed to recognize the number displayed on it. He figured that someone must have misdialed, but answered the phone anyway.

"Quinn here."

"Hi Quinn. Oh I'm so glad I got you. It's Teena."

Quinn felt a little knot form in his stomach. He was excited and nervous to hear her voice. He had never spoken to Teena on the phone before.

"Teena, hi. How did you get my number?"

"I'm like the girl guides. Always prepared. Or is that the boy scouts? I asked one of the guards months ago if he had your cell number in case of an emergency. Anyway, I'm in my office and the electric locks failed. They're supposed to have hours of emergency battery backup power but my office door won't open. I'm really scared, Quinn."

Quinn relished the thought that she had chosen to call him when she was frightened. He hadn't felt needed in a long time, and it was nice to have someone reach out to him for help.

"Don't worry. Turns out it was a car accident that took out a transformer or something, and the power should be back on shortly. The building's backup generators don't provide power for your locks, so you'll have to wait until the main power is back on line."

"I know it's a lot to ask, but if you have time, could you come up and see if you can open my office? I have this phobia thing and I'm really scared shitless right now."

Quinn saw this moment as his chance to be the shinning knight coming to her rescue, which could possibly lead to something more than a morning chat and the exchange of old newspapers.

"I have some stuff to do but I'll get there as soon as I can. Will you be okay until then?" Quinn's voice showed his concern for Teena.

"Thank you. You've made me feel so much better. Hurry if you can."

The line went dead. Quinn looked at the phone screen that faded to black, smiled, and regretted deleting those pictures of Teena. He rushed up the stairs to the front lobby with a renewed sense of urgency to get his job done quicker.

When he arrived at the front lobby security desk, Darryl had already brought three of the four elevators down to the lobby, and the fourth elevator was on its way. He had also called the disaster managers for each floor and read them the riot act regarding abuse of power in an emergency.

"Head office called. Power should be back up in less than twenty minutes. Everything on the disaster protocol checklist has been done. Now we can sit back and enjoy the peace and quiet until the power comes back on and every dick in a suit and tie blames us for it going out." Darryl smiled, pleased that he had completed everything Quinn had asked of him.

"I'm going to run up to the thirtieth floor and check on someone trapped in their office."

"Seriously. You're gonna run up thirty flights of stairs, in the dark, nonetheless, to save some wimp from being locked in the shitter for the next twenty minutes. Are you bucking for a raise?"

"Just trying to help out. I'll be on the radio." Quinn left and made his way to the stairs located in the main elevator lobby. He pushed the door open, aimed the flashlight up to the next floor, and thought, "Why the fuck am I really doing this? Christ, I must be horny or something."

Quinn kept an even pace as he climbed up the steps. By the seventh floor, his thighs were burning, and he was already short of breath. He slowed his ascent but continued to climb the stairs faster than he normally would. By the time he reached the thirtieth floor, he felt a little nauseated, and thought he was going to vomit when he finally stopped. He pushed open the security door and was met with more darkness. He turned left, and was stopped by the glass doors behind which Teena had disappeared that morning. He rattled the door until someone came and pushed it open, granting him access.

Quinn was still panting when the door was opened. In between breaths, he asked if everyone was all right, and one of the office staff told him that Teena's was the only office that locked automatically during power outages.

They led Quinn down the hall to Teena's office. He peered through the glass beside the solid wood office door. Teena was sitting in her office chair, hugging herself, with her eyes closed. Quinn tapped on the glass, startling her. Teena jumped from her chair and ran to the window. Their faces were only inches apart, separated by a thin layer of glass. Teena's eyes were red and swollen from crying, her cheeks moist from the tears. She was still visibly shaking.

Through the window, Quinn asked Teena to ensure that the door handle was unlocked, turn it, and pull hard as he put all of his weight against the door. Teena nodded, and on the count of three, they tried to free the door from the magnetic lock. Teena grabbed the door handle with both hands and pulled with everything she had as Quinn forced his weight against the door. The heavy wood door refused to open, however, giving only slightly around the frame. The magnetic lock at the top of the door held firm.

Quinn stepped back from the door. On the other side, he could hear Teena pulling and screaming for the door to open. Quinn rapped repeatedly on the glass to get Teena's attention. She continued to pull on the handle, her body jerking back and forth, crying hysterically. A small crowd of staff had gathered around Teena's door, watching but not assisting in extricating her from her office cell.

Quinn radioed Darryl in the front lobby to assign power from the generators to the thirtieth floor. He hoped the electrical power would release the magnetic lock on the door and free Teena. Darryl agreed, and said he had to notify the floor managers as to the areas of the building to which he was going to cut power before he could reassign the grid.

Quinn slapped the glass with his open hand and told Teena that it would only be a few more minutes before she was freed, and to return to her desk and wait. He continued to hit the window until she finally understood and stepped away from the door, but made no move to return to her desk. She hugged herself again and held her hand over her mouth. Tears flowed freely, and she shook uncontrollably as she stared at Quinn through the glass.

"Stand back," he ordered the crowd. The gathered office workers blindly stepped away, giving Quinn space. Quinn watched Teena from the other side of the glass; she hadn't moved from her spot, and stared blankly at the door. He turned around and grabbed a metal trashcan from the floor beside a desk. The contents of the can fell to the floor as he raised it up high like a baseball bat and swung with all his might. The pane of glass blew inwards, sending shards flying into the office that narrowly missed Teena as she stood still like a stone. Quinn used the can to break away the sharp glass that was still attached to the frame. He carefully crawled through the small opening, avoiding the glass that remained, and walked over to Teena. She appeared unaware of what Quinn had just done and in a catatonic state, unable to react to his presence.

Quinn quietly, softly, placed his hand on her shoulder. Teena didn't react. Quinn left her side and walked to the door, replicating Teena's actions from only moments before. He grabbed the doorknob, turned it, and yanked hard, but it refused to budge. Standing by the door, he spoke in hushed tones to Darryl over his radio, asking if the power would be assigned to the thirtieth floor soon. Darryl said that he needed a few more minutes, but that once the power came on, the magnetic lock would make a loud metallic sound and release its hold on the door.

Quinn rolled the chair out from behind Teena's desk, placed it directly behind her, and sat her down gently. She continued to hug herself as the tears started to dry, but she still couldn't pull her eyes away from the door. Unsure of what to do, Quinn sat on the corner of the desk and watched over the sedentary woman in the chair. He had always admired this strong-willed executive who had worked her way from teller to upper management at the bank, but still found time to talk to a security guard in the morning on the way to work. What he saw now was a broken woman, scared, lost in her own thoughts and fears. He wondered what she was thinking as Teena continued to stare, unblinking, at the door. He wanted to offer something, anything, but this situation was so foreign to him. Instead, he shooed away the office workers that lingered about, trying to glean a look at what was happening.

Without notice, the electricity came back on, and the magnetic lock re-energized and released its hold on the office door with the tell-tale metallic clank. Teena jumped from her chair, ran out of the office, and stood in the open expanse of the main room. She was panting like an out-of-shape runner. Her fellow office workers stared in disbelief at the view of their superior now crying and shaking from something they thought was so trivial.

Quinn walked out to the main room, placed his arm around her shoulder, and guided Teena back to her office. She struggled at the entrance and began to pull away from Quinn. He entered the office, grabbed a stapler from her desk, opened it flat, and placed it on the ground between the floor and the door, jamming it in place, and preventing the door from closing again. Teena sat back down in her chair, took in a deep breath, wiped her eyes, straightened her suit jacket, and cleared her throat.

"You okay?" Quinn asked.

"Right as rain. Now."

"Good. Maybe I should go and call maintenance to come and clean up this mess." Quinn turned to leave when a child's voice called out to him.

"Please. Stay." Teena's voice sounded scared and alone, and she clearly wanted someone to be with her.

When Quinn turned back to Teena, he could tell she was ashamed. She was looking down at her desk, and couldn't raise her eyes to meet Quinn's. He knew that she was still scared, even now.

DISCOVERY

Quinn escorted his supervisor through the building after word got back to the head office of the power outage and his actions on the thirtieth floor. Quinn followed a few steps behind and to the left of the elderly man dressed in a crisp white shirt and shiny polyester black pants that were cut too short and ended above his ankles. Quinn had to slow his pace considerably so as not to run him over. The old man's gait was noticeably awkward, and he limped with each step. All the security guards had bet that he had broken his hip a century and a half ago and the local witch doctor never set it properly.

The supervisor limped his way through the basement, discussing the progress of repairs with the various technicians who were inspecting the building. He had a metal clipboard that he held tightly in one hand and carried a flashlight in the other. Quinn wondered why he had to escort the old man through the building simply because he had been the guard on duty at the front lobby at the time of the incident. The supervisor ignored Quinn as he spoke on his cellphone and made checkmarks on the inspection certificate. Quinn continued to follow the old man from one area of the building to another as his supervisor followed security procedures. Not once did he acknowledge him or request Quinn's assistance, but protocol dictated that the lobby guard accompany him on all post-emergency rounds.

The supervisor worked his way up from the basement to the thirtieth floor. He exited the elevator and tapped on the window with the metal clipboard to be granted access to the offices where Quinn had caused the damage.

Quinn followed the old man through the maze of halls to Teena's office, where she was still cleaning up the glass. The stapler was still jammed under the door. The supervisor leaned in, knocked on her door, and asked to speak with her. Teena smiled when Quinn stepped into her office behind his supervisor.

"Do you mind if I ask you a few questions about the damages caused to your office by our guard on duty?" Even his voice sounded dry and old.

Teena had time to compose herself again and offered the gentleman a chair. He simply sat without thanking her. He pulled a form out from under the pile of papers held tightly on the clipboard and placed it on top of the other sheets.

"If you're not too busy, I'd like a brief summary of what happened that resulted in the damage to your office." He never looked up from his clipboard, and wrote as he spoke.

"Actually, I'm a little busy clean…" Teena's voice trailed off as the supervisor interrupted her and started asking questions that were clearly aimed at placing the blame on Quinn for his actions. Quinn was stunned by the direction his supervisor was taking.

"Excuse me." Teena raised her voice over that of the old man. He looked up from his clipboard in surprise. Obviously, no one had ever spoken back to him before.

"What your employee did, what Quinn did, was not only appropriate, but it also exhibited chivalry, and was something I needed at the time. If this is about the damage, I'll pay for it. If this is about Quinn breaking the rules or protocols or whatever it is, I'll write a letter of commendation to my boss, who will forward it to your boss, recommending him for a medal or a promotion or a raise or whatever it is your company gives out for going above and beyond. And now, if you'll excuse me, I have to clean up this mess that I caused and get back to work."

The old man pulled the form from the top of his clipboard, folded it, and placed it in his shirt pocket. Teena winked coyly at Quinn while the old man wasn't looking. He smiled back, but the smile faded quickly. Behind her desk, a wood-framed photo of Teena and an older man in a tight embrace, standing on a beach at sunset, sat on the window ledge. Quinn hadn't noticed it when he had been in the office earlier in the day. He looked back at Teena, who was still smiling at him, and he forced himself to smile back.

In the elevator, the old man mumbled something under his breath. Quinn ignored him, however, even when the supervisor turned and spoke directly to him. Quinn went through every encounter he had ever had with Teena in his mind, and couldn't recall a time when she had been anything but polite and friendly. She never once showed any interest in him; never once made an inappropriate move. Quinn wondered if he was reading too much into the wink, the friendly chats in the mornings, and the fact that she had asked the other guards for this cell number. "*In case of emergencies,*" he thought to himself. "*Bullshit!*" he yelled in his head.

The supervisor continued to scold Quinn, who paid no attention to him. The elevator doors opened, and Quinn walked out, saying nothing to the old man and returning to the lobby desk. He relieved the guard who had been covering his duties while he had escorted the supervisor. When the old man finally caught up to Quinn at the lobby desk, he was puffing and holding his bad hip.

He pointed a bony, arthritic finger at Quinn and started yelling. "Don't ever walk away from me when I'm talking to you! You got that, boy?!"

"Whatever." Quinn spun around in his chair, turning his back to the supervisor. A withered old hand grabbed the back of the chair and spun it around until Quinn and the old man were almost touching noses.

"I don't care if you're too good for this job and you'll be gone soon. I won't tolerate disrespect from you or anyone. Got it, you young punk?" Tiny globs of spit hit Quinn in the face as the supervisor yelled at him. Quinn closed his eyes as the old man's breath caught him square in the face.

"Got it. Can I get back to work now?" Quinn pushed back with his heels on the floor and forced the chair to roll backwards. The old man simply packed up what gear he had and limped out the front door.

It was only moments later that the phone beeped and the status light started to blink. Quinn picked up the handset. "Front desk."

"You okay? Did I say something? Did your boss do something?" Teena was on the phone, her voice soft and showing concern.

Not wanting to reveal his true feelings, Quinn lied. "Just pissed I got into trouble. This is the only job I've got, and if I lose it, I'm screwed. Thanks for standing up for me. I appreciate it. One of the other lines is ringing. Gotta go." He placed the receiver back down gently in its cradle and stared at the phone. He hated lying to Teena but he couldn't get that picture of her with the other man out of him mind.

Teena put the phone back in the cradle slowly, knowing full well that Quinn wasn't all right. In the brief time she had known him, Quinn had always been happy when they spoke, and never cut short their conversations. If anything, he always tried to extend them. She left her hand on the telephone handset, hoping he would call back. Her hand rested there for a few moments before she realized she was acting like a fourteen-year-old girl hoping the popular boy would call her. Quinn had saved her today, maybe not in the literal sense, but he had been there when she needed him, and that meant a lot to Teena. She pulled her hand away from the phone and held it to her chin, still secretly wishing he would call back.

Quinn sat at the desk in the front foyer, unmoving and looking down at the phone, wishing he hadn't hung up on Teena. He thought about calling her back and just asking her about the man in the picture, but the more he thought about it, the more incensed he became. Quinn felt betrayed, even lied to. Teena had never mentioned another man, never gave any indication that there could be someone else. He was certain that the attention Teena paid him was sincere. Quinn closed his eyes, put his head down, and, for the first time since he met Teena, realized just how much he liked her.

Several hours later, just before five, the elevators began to open continuously, spilling office workers into the main lobby as they rushed home. As when they arrived in the morning, most of the bank executives had their cellphones stuck to the sides of their respective faces, and ignored Quinn as they swiped their security cards. Today, he disregarded them the way he was ignored. He watched as each face flashed on the screen, but failed to see Teena's image appear. After the last person passed thought the security screening, Quinn entered Teena's name into the system. She was still listed as being in the building, or at least her security card hadn't been used if she had left. He thought about calling, picked up the phone, and laid it back down in the cradle.

There had been a brief burst of activity as everyone left the building for the night, but now Quinn was back to being bored for the rest of his shift. All of his paperwork was done, there were no more forms or occurrence reports to complete, nothing. The time on the security monitor showed five twenty-six: five and half hours left in his shift.

Teena was alone in her office; all the other executives on her floor had left promptly at five. "This is why they'll never get promoted," she thought to herself as she watched them hustle out as the clock struck five. They whisked past her door that was now held firmly open by the stapler jammed beneath it. After Quinn left, she found an old jacket belt in the women's washroom, and borrowed it to wrap around the door handle and secure it to the jacket hook on the wall behind the door. It would now take more than a power failure for her office door to close without her permission.

Teena still felt embarrassed about her emotional breakdown during the power outage. She had been certain that she had overcome her childhood fears, but after today's outburst, she knew she still had some issues with which she had to deal.

Teena still had to finish her presentation that was scheduled for the following morning, and the power outage had put her several hours behind schedule. She looked at the clock on the far wall over the demon door; it was five-thirty. It would be another late night with no dinner. She was getting hungry, and wondered if she should get something soon or wait until she got home. She decided to a compromise with herself; she would get dinner and eat at her desk if she was still working at seven. "Deal!"

*****

Teena's stomach growled and rumbled at her. She placed a hand on it and felt it kick back like a fetus trying to force its way out of the womb. She looked up at the clock above the door; it was now a quarter after seven.

Teena shook the empty can of Red Bull on her desk. She placed it beside the other two empty cans in front of her. The last thing she needed was another energy drink. She wondered if she felt like pizza, or Chinese, then decided that she had a craving for souvlaki and a Greek salad with extra black olives.

A quick call to the Greek restaurant a few blocks away was all that was needed, and her biweekly repeat order would be delivered to the front desk in less than twenty minutes. The owner of the Greek restaurant who took her calls always seemed to be working, just like her. He never had to ask for her name, or where the order was to be delivered, a sure sign that she ordered far too often. Teena wondered if he ever took a day off, or if he even had a social life. And she wondered if he was as lonely as she was. This time she doubled the order, hoping that

Quinn liked Greek food.

She picked up the phone and dialled the front desk. Quinn answered on the first ring. "Security."

"How's my saviour tonight?" Teena chucked a little.

Quinn wanted to come back with something comical but he hated playing head games, so he opted for the direct approach. "Better now."

"I have an order coming in from Milos Restaurant. It should be here in about twenty minutes. I remembered what you said about working a double shift today and since you were my dashing hero, I thought I would treat you to dinner. Hope you like Greek?"

Quinn smiled. "I love Greek. Thanks. But you didn't have to."

"Didn't have to, but I wanted to. It's the least I can do. I want to apologize for what I did, and if I got you in trouble. You seemed a little pissed when you left my office."

"I got in a little shit. No biggie. Don't worry about it," Quinn said softly. He held his head low, not wanting anyone to overhear his conversation.

"Either way, it's my fault. I have some issues to work out. One day, maybe, I'll tell you all about them. And believe me, I have a lot of baggage."

Teena chuckled loudly, hoping it would help Quinn relax. She heard laughter on the other end of the line, and smiled broadly even though Quinn couldn't see her. Teena hoped that whatever it was that had caused Quinn to react the way he had in her office was no longer important. She realized at that very moment that she did have feelings for Quinn, although what exactly those feeling were remained a mystery, even to her. But Teena did hope that she would have the chance to explore them further.

"I'll come down and wait at the front desk if you don't mind." Teena prayed that Quinn would agree.

"That'd be nice. I could use the company."

Teena dropped the phone, grabbed her purse, and raced for the elevator. She repeatedly pressed the down button impatiently. She wasn't sure why, but her stomach was in knots and her palms were sweaty. She looked up at the elevator display and stomped back and forth as if she was waiting for someone to exit the only bathroom stall with a full bladder. The elevator seemed to be held up on one of the floors above, so she turned to the bank of elevators on the opposite side of the foyer and pressed the down button again.

Teena stood in the middle of the foyer and looked back and forth at both displays, waiting for one of them to stop at her floor. She watched as the first elevator she selected cleared the floor and began the descent to the thirtieth floor. With a muted "ding" the doors opened, and she repeatedly pressed the "L" button, then stood back to watch the display count down from thirty.

The elevator travelled nonstop from her floor to the lobby. The silver doors slid apart and Teena stepped forward, paused, collected her composure, and then casually walked to the security desk. As she approached, Quinn had his back to her, and was typing, his attention on whatever was on the screen in front of him. She pulled her security pass from her purse and quietly swiped it over the scanner. Teena's picture came up on one of the screens facing Quinn.

Quinn turned with a broad smile on his face. He stood as Teena walked around the desk to join him. They were only inches apart. Teena had never realized that Quinn towered over her small frame. She felt the nervousness return, and kept her hands behind her as she wiped her sweaty palms on the backs of her thighs. She wanted nothing more than for Quinn to reach down, wrap his arms around her, and kiss her.

Quinn stood looking down at Teena and inhaled her perfume. He had never noticed her fragrance before, but he loved the gentle floral scent that flowed about her. He should have been looking into her eyes, but instead, he found it hard not to focus on her lips. Quinn had to hold back his desire to grab Teena, pull her in tightly, and kiss her. Scenarios of what he wanted to experience with Teena flashed in his mind.

What should have been an awkward silence was more of an unmoving intimacy. Teena finally let out a forced cough to break the moment. Quinn smiled, turned, and sat down. Teena sat on the corner of the security desk and shuffled close to him. She laid her purse down behind her.

For the next twenty minutes, Quinn and Teena chatted. They laughed at comments that weren't funny, and she reached out and touched his arm several times. Each time Teena touched Quinn, his heart would begin to race, and he could feel the excitement building within him.

The large glass door to the lobby was pulled open, the status light on the security desk lit up, and both Quinn and Teena turned to see the deliveryman walking up to the security desk. Quinn recognized him from his frequent visits to the building, and wondered if each time he came to deliver a meal, it was for Teena.

The young man laid the bag on the upper section of the security desk, ripped the bill rom the brown paper bag, and out of habit, knew to present it to Teena. She smiled politely at him and, without looking at the amount, handed him a twenty and told him to keep the change. From past orders, Teena knew the amount for the two dinners and salad would be less than fifteen, and the rest was his tip. He swiped the twenty from her hand, turned, and left the lobby without saying a word.

Against company policy, Quinn pulled one of the chairs up to the desk and invited Teena to join him. Quinn and Teena sat side-by-side, eating, chatting, and getting to know each other better. Casting aside job titles, ages, and social statuses, the two of them laughed and joked about their respective actions in her office. The relief security guard stopped by while they were eating, stole a piece of lamb from Quinn's souvlaki, and left. Over the course of dinner, Teena's chair managed to slide closer to Quinn's. He noticed what she was doing and made certain his chair stayed in place. By the end of the dinner, the two chairs where almost touching.

Teena's cellphone let out a single chirp, which she ignored. As they continued to talk and eat, the chirping persisted. Teena pulled the cellphone from her purse, unlocked it, and looked at the screen. "Work email. Sorry." Teena pressed a few keys, then placed the phone on the counter beside her salad.

"Does that happen a lot?"

"What? Email? I specialize in international development. With the time changes, I get emails and texts at all hours of the night. It makes it hard to have any type of social life." Teena pushed the phone farther away from her meal.

"Why don't you work afternoons instead of working all day, and then take calls all night?" Quinn was curious.

"I have to work with the staff here and also with the staff in our merging markets. Most of the people in this position only last a few years before moving up the corporate ladder. It's a small price to pay to get ahead."

"Is it really worth it? I mean to devote so much time to the company and lose so much of yourself just for a job."

Teena smiled, took a bite of salad, and spoke while she was chewing. "I'm the youngest person ever to hold this position in the company, and a woman to boot. Hopefully in a year, maybe less, I'll get the call to go work in Europe. I'd love to go to London." She finished eating. "What about you? We've been talking mostly about me all night."

"My life hasn't been so great. My parents died before I was fifteen. Things were okay at home before they died, but after I had to move in with my aunt and uncle. They were great, older, never had kids of their own. I got into some trouble, left my aunt and uncle within the year, and moved in with a few buddies from high school. I've had to make do ever since. I get along better with my aunt and uncle now. Took a few odd jobs, decided to go back to school, and ran out of money while I was in university, so I took a sabbatical and ended up working here. This is just so I can save up some money to go back to school and finish engineering. I figure I should…"

Quinn was cut short by Teena's phone. The phone buzzed and a picture of the caller was displayed on the screen. It was the same man who was in the picture behind Teena's desk. The image being displayed was a close-up of the man, smiling and looking directly into the camera. Quinn thought that it looked like the picture that came in every new photo frame you bought.

Teena smiled broadly, grabbed the phone, gave Quinn the "one minute" sign, and stepped away from the desk. Quinn noticed that Teena was laughing out loud, giggling, and speaking softly. The clicking of her heels echoed in the vast expanse of the granite foyer as she walked about with the phone pressed to her ear.

The one minute Teena had promised became thirty as Quinn finished Teena's salad, threw the Styrofoam containers away, and cleaned up his work area. Occasionally, Quinn would look up and watch Teena as she walked from one side of the foyer to the opposite side and back again, moving the phone from one ear to the other as she talked. She would look over, notice Quinn watching her, and smile back.

Finally, at the far end of the foyer, Teena sighed heavily, tapped the phone, and pocketed it. Her shoes clicked audibly on the floor as she almost skipped her way back to the security desk. She was smiling broadly as she took the chair beside Quinn.

"I am so sorry." Teena saw that the food containers were stuffed under the desk in the waste paper basket. "You cleaned up, too. Oh God, I owe you another dinner, don't I? I feel so bad for spending so much time on the phone."

"It's okay. You have things to do, and besides, you're still working." Quinn hoped that Teena would offer a bit of information about who the caller was. He didn't want to experience a repeat of one of his previous relationships where he was kept in the dark about the girl's other sideline activities.

Teena was thrilled that Quinn was being so understanding. "That was a personal call and I shouldn't have ignored you like that. I'm sorry it…" The lights in the lobby went black, flickered on and off a few times, then came back on. The security monitors and clocks remained active and didn't flicker or turn off.

"How come those television screens didn't turn off?" Teena asked as she pointed at the security console.

"The entire security system is supposed to be on a separate, stand-alone power supply. 'Supposed to be' are the key words. They fail all the time. Not sure why, but they keep saying they'll fix it."

The power failed again, causing the foyer lights to burn brightly and then suddenly turn black again and again. This time the security monitors failed and went dark, as well. Teena jumped in her seat and rolled in closer to Quinn. "Christ that scares the shit outta me. When's it gonna stop?"

Quinn smiled at Teena as she cowered in her chair and looked up at the ceiling lights like she was gazing at the night sky, expecting lightning and thunder to come crashing down in the lobby.

"Until they get that transformer fixed, we can expect brownouts for a while. I wouldn't worry about them. If it's serious and lasts for more than a few seconds, the generators will kick in."

"I guess I shouldn't be such a child and learn to get over my fear, huh?"

"It's cute. Just don't let it get too annoying," Quinn teased good-naturedly.

Teena stood, pulled the phone from her pocket, and stuffed it in her purse. "Damn phone battery dies so fast. Next time, I'm getting a phone with a replaceable battery." She zipped up her purse and slung it over her shoulder. Bending down, she gave Quinn a slow kiss on the cheek, with her eyes closed. She lingered for more than a few seconds before she pulled back. She began to walk away, but after a few steps, she turned to see him again. "Bye."

Quinn watched her until she rounded the corner and he heard the elevator bell chime its arrival and the doors close. Normally he wouldn't even notice the sound, but with the building vacant except for a few guards and some lonely office workers still on the upper floors, everything seemed louder than it ever had in the past. He turned in his chair and went back to the job of watching his monitors, focusing on one in particular: that which showed Teena standing in the elevator as it rose to her floor.

The lobby lights remained bright, and Quinn hoped they would stay on this time. The aroma from the Styrofoam containers under the desk began to nauseate him. He kicked the can, and it slid to the back wall and made a loud "glang" sound. At that exact moment, the entire building went dark. Quinn's monitors flickered, and then went black. The lobby was dark, and even the lights from across the street were out. He waited for the building's redundant backup generators to kick on. Nothing! The lobby lights began to glow, trying desperately to force themselves back to life as the electrical current started to flow, then faltered. Darkness overcame the whole building. Quinn looked down at his console. The battery backup system, independent of the building's generators, should have kept the security panel active. Frustrated, he tapped the monitors in a vain attempt to resuscitate the screens.

The portable radios began to crackle with voices. Each of the guards was attempting to talk over the others as soon as the air cleared. They were calling for Quinn to direct them and provide guidance. Quinn held the portable radio in front of his face and keyed the microphone.

"K, everybody, I need silence please. Shipping, go and lock all the entrances and exits for delivery trucks. I don't want anyone coming in. If they're already here, they stay until the power is back on. Check all the building exits and make sure they open from the inside only and are still locked from the outside. Grab emergency flashlights, make sure they have a good charge, and take two if you feel you need the extra light. Same goes for the portable radios. If you think the charge is low on the batteries, put in a new one. I'm calling the utility company and the engineers back to fix those fucking generators. Does anyone know the count of people still in the building?"

The guards at the loading docks gave an all clear; no delivery trucks had been in for the past hour. The float guard said he thought the only people still in the building were the cleaning staff. Quinn asked him to check the login sheets and then go floor to floor and make sure everybody was accounted for.

Quinn picked up the phone, pushed line one, and tried to dial out. Nothing! No tone, and no busy signal. He radioed the other guards to alert them that the main telephone system was down and asked them to check to see if their cellphones had a signal.

Just as Quinn put his radio down, his own cellphone began to vibrate in his pocket. "At least the cellphones still work," he thought. Teena's number came up on his call display. He slid the button over to green to answer. He had forgotten about Teena during the power failure. He hoped she had made it to her floor and gotten out of the elevator.

"Hey, how're you making out?" Quinn felt true concern for Teena, knowing how she had reacted to being locked in her office.

"Quinn? I'm still in the elevator." Teena was panting; her voice cracked, and the fear in it was real. Quinn could sense Teena holding back her panic.

"Teena?" Quinn spoke softly and quietly, wanting Teena to know that he was there for her. "I need you to listen to me, okay?"

"Can you come and get me please? Now! It's dark, I can't see anything, and my phone's almost dead." Teena was pausing between every few words to breath. The panic in her voice was now evident.

"There's supposed to be a small light in the elevator. Is that not working?"

She whispered, "No."

"Okay. We've already called the engineers to fix the generators, and we've got a call in to the city to see when the power will be back on. I'm not going anywhere, but if your phone battery is almost dead, we shouldn't talk too long so you can preserve the power."

"No, I want to stay on the phone with you. Don't you hang up on me! Don't do it. Please." Teena was begging, pleading with Quinn not to hang up on her. Her phone began to beep as she continued to talk.

"What floor did the elevator stop at? Do you remember the number?"

"I don't remember. I don't remember. Quinn, my phone is beeping. It's dying. I'll be all alone. Oh God, I can't take it. You have to get me out, now." Teena's voice cracked.

The phone shook in Teena's hand as she spoke. She could feel moisture forming on her forehead and in the palms of her hands. She rubbed her free hand on her pants to dry it as she paced around the elevator. The tiny space already felt as if it was closing in on her.

"I'll check each floor one by one until I find you. I'll be right up and I won't leave you once I get there. You understand? Hang up to save your battery, okay?"

"You're coming to get me? You won't leave me?"

"Once I find you, I won't leave you. Now turn off your phone and save your battery. Only use it if you really have to."

As Teena reluctantly ended the call, she noticed the time was eighty forty-five, powered down her phone, and clasped it in both hands as she continued to walk in circles in the elevator, using the railing as a guide. Sweat started to bead on her forehead, roll down her cheeks, and drip off the end of her nose. Teena began to talk to herself. Her voice cracked at first, but she forced herself to calm down, and her voice became strong and assertive. She started to convince herself that everything would be all right.

Teena continued to pace in circles. She held her right hand out to the side and slid it along the wall. As her voice calmed, so did her pace. She told herself that she was going to be fine, that Quinn would be along shortly, and that this incident was nothing more than a test. She reminded herself that the events of her childhood were nothing more than character builders, and that she was better than anything from her past. She had overcome most of the childhood trauma, and this event was just another trial, she told herself.

Teena paused, held out her hand, found one of the corners, turned, and leaned against the wall. She placed both hands out along the rails, took in a deep breath, held it, and then let it out slowly. She repeated this breathing exercise several times until she felt her pulse slow and her breathing rate decline. She wanted so badly to turn her phone back on and use the flashlight app just to see the elevator. She had been in the exact elevator compartment hundreds of times, no, thousands, she told herself; surely if she thought hard enough she could envision every detail of the box.

Even in the darkness, Teena closed her eyes, and pretended that the elevator doors had just opened and she had walked in. In her mind's eye, the elevator was empty. She turned, faced the closed silver doors, and pressed the button for the thirtieth floor. She stared at the doors. The doors weren't just silver, they had a pattern on them. There was a brushed circular pattern on the doors. She hadn't noticed the pattern before. What else had she missed? Her mind's eye moved from the doors to the tiny black screen above the rows and rows of buttons of the control panel. The red number on the black background started at one and slowly increased.

Teena thought intently and focused her mind. Was there a telephone inside the elevator? Below the panel of buttons, there was a small silver door. Yes, there was something there. She slid along the wall to the front of the cab and ran her hands down the control panel until she found the small metal door that surely held the emergency telephone. Pulling on the flush knob, Teena opened the door and reached into the space. She found the telephone handset, felt a sense of relief, and lifted it from the cradle. She put the cradle to her ear but failed to hear a dial tone. In the dark, she found the coiled cable on the base of the handset. She followed it down and found that it dangled freely. Her fingers ran down the cable to the bottom, where she found frayed ends. She placed the handset back in the cradle and slammed the metal door shut.

Frustrated, Teena turned her memory back to the walls. Fake wood-grain laminate panels adorned the two sides and the back wall. A flat silver railing ran along the length of the wood-grain panels. She looked down. The floor was polished black granite. Not granite. No. Think. Not granite. She slid her foot in the darkness and felt the space between the black porcelain tiles. She continued to look at the floor and didn't notice anything out of the ordinary. Teena looked up to the ceiling of the elevator and saw a polished silver grate diffusor covering the lights. She focused harder, looked beyond the grates, and saw the dark outline of something. In the darkness, Teena tilted her head upwards, squinted, and saw the outline of what she thought was an access port. She saw the outline behind the chrome grate and followed it until she was certain it was a service door. And, if someone could get in, someone could also get out. It was an option to consider if the situation required extreme action.

Teena was confident that she had scanned the entire elevator in her mind. Even in the blackness, she was surprised at how much she remembered of a tiny room she didn't consider important.

How much time had passed since she began to scan the interior of her new accommodations? Teena didn't have a clue, and she desperately wanted to check her phone, but didn't want to lose the battery power it would take just to see the time. Just the thought of being trapped again, for the second time in a single day, make her shiver. She rubbed her arms and felt goose bumps covering her skin. Her only source of communication could lose power at any minute. She became aware that her breathing had become heavy in her chest, and the rate had increased. Panic began to overtake her again. She hugged herself, wrapping her arms tightly around her chest.

Teena couldn't see anything in the elevator cab, but forced her eyes tightly shut and turned her face to the back wall. Her breathing echoed off the wall and the hot moist air bounced back onto her face. She forced herself yet again to calm down.

A loud metallic clank bounced off of the roof of the elevator cab directly above her head and shocked her out of her panic attack. Looking up, she hoped to see a glimmer of light, the access panel opening, and someone there to rescue her. She was certain that the noise had occurred on the top of the elevator cab, but realized that she had no way of knowing if it had come from directly above her or somewhere higher up in the elevator shaft.

"Hello!" she yelled as loudly as she could. She cupped her hands around her mouth and screamed again, "Hello!"

There was no response. She stopped moving and remained calm, not making any noise. From above, she thought she could hear Quinn laughing. She focused her attention and listened more intently to see if she could distinguish the noise coming from outside the cab. She pointed her ear upwards. There it was again. Teena could definitely make out laughter, and she was certain it was Quinn's voice.

"Quinn. I'm in here." Teena paused and waited for his response. She stood upright on her tiptoes in the cab, grabbed the handrails, craned her neck, and yelled again, "Quinn."

She waited for a few moments, and then yelled even louder, "Quiiiiin."

Teena's yells were met with silence. She went to the next corner of the cab and yelled again. Nothing but silence, deafening silence. Teena then went to the silver doors with the brushed circular pattern on them and yelled through the crack. Silence. She remained at the door and attempted to peer through the crack to glimpse any light or movement. The laughter she thought she had heard was now gone. Surely it must have been noise from above her elevator that echoed in the shaft and made her think it was Quinn laughing.

She found her way back to the corner, sat down on the floor, and pulled her knees in tightly to her chest. As she pulled the phone from her purse, she desperately wanted to power it up and call Quinn. Her thumb rested lightly on the power button, but she resisted the urge to push it down and power up the phone.

Quinn ran up the stairs, holding the light in front of him and illuminating the stairwell. He took two stairs at a time, and the radio on his belt swung wildly as he navigated the passageway. He used the railing for support as his breathing became laboured and his lungs began to burn. On the fourteenth floor, he paused on the landing and bent over with his hands to his knees, trying to catch his breath. He straightened up. Feeling the lactic acid building up in his thighs, he tried to rub the pain away.

Quinn checked his radio; it was still on, volume set to max. Swiping up on the screen of his cellphone, he checked the remaining power in the battery. It still had fifty-three percent. He pocketed the phone, opened the door, and entered the main hall of the fourteenth floor. Like the rest of the building, the hall was dark, with only the emergency lighting system on a stand-alone battery system providing some light to guide the occupants towards the exits. Even with the emergency lighting system, Quinn still needed to use his hand-held flashlight. He shone the flashlight to his right then left, found the elevator doors, and walked to them. On one side of the wall, two silver doors stood in contrast to the darkness. On the opposite side of the hall, there were two more silver elevator doors. Out of habit, he pushed the down arrow button on the control panel between the two doors. The button didn't light up, so Quinn pressed the button with the up arrow. It, too, failed to illuminate.

Quinn set the flashlight down, aiming it at the silver doors, pulled the elevator emergency security key from his breast pocket, found the small circular opening at the base of one of the doors, and inserted the "T" shaped key. He turned the key and unlocked the slider bar that allowed the outer doors to open. He inserted his fingers between the two doors and began to pull them apart. Once the doors were fully opened, he braced one side open with his leg and pushed his back against the other side. He pulled the second flashlight from his belt, pushed the power button, and aimed it down the elevator shaft. The beam simply blended into the blackness and failed to find an end. He turned the light upwards and scanned the foreign-looking structure of I-beams bolted to the white concrete walls, dangling cables, and counter weights.

Up above, the beam lit up the floor of the elevator cab. The perspective of the narrowing shaft, the dim light, the criss-crossing beams, and the tangles of cables made the distance difficult to gauge. He called out Teena's name over and over, then paused and waited for a response. He heard nothing. He had three more elevator shafts to inspect before he had to decide to proceed up or go back down.

Quinn used the same key to open the elevator doors beside the ones he had just inspected and repeated the process of attempting to locate each elevator. The other three elevator cabs were each on the lower floors. Quinn figured that since Teena had been in the elevator just before the power went out, the first shaft he inspected certainly had to be the one in which she was located.

Once he had packed up his gear, Quinn entered the stairwell again and began his assent to the elevator above. He radioed one of the other guards and asked him to meet him and help with extricating Teena from the elevator. Quinn no longer had the energy to take the stairs two at a time; instead, he controlled his pace. It didn't take long for his thighs to start to burn again and his breathing to become laboured.

Teena rocked back and forth, curled in the corner of the elevator cab. She hid her face between her knees and sobbed quietly. It was a struggle for her to maintain some form of composure instead of just letting her emotions take over. Her lower jaw was clenched tightly, and the pressure building in the joint in front of her ears was causing them to ache. Teena's fingers were interlaced around her knees and were now going numb from digging into the backs of her hands. Pain helped take away the thoughts. Teena had to deflect the stress she was feeling, and this method was the one she had used when she was a child.

The basement wall was gritty, dusty, and cold. It was always cold. She dug deep into the earthen floor with her heels, back and forth, back and forth. It was something to pass the time, and each time she was down here she dug with her heels. She would laugh at how the constant digging with her heels would scrape away the callouses from her feet, and on those summer nights when she lay in bed, she would glide her feet over the silky sheets.

Teena scratched at the stone wall with her right index finger. Slowly, she would scrape at the stone, hoping it would miraculously collapse and free her. She turned and looked up in the direction of the wooden steps. She knew where they were, even in the total blackness. A sliver of light broke through beneath the door but didn't provide any real illumination in the basement where she was placed whenever her mother thought she deserved to be punished, or just wanted some time alone. Teena realized that no matter what she did, when she did it, or why, she could end up in the basement for days, alone, with no food or water.

Teena became aware of where everything was in the basement once her eyes adjusted to the lack of light. She began to move around slowly. She still had to hold her hands out in front of her to prevent herself from bumping into things. Those times when her mother would leave her in the basement for days, Teena had to use a deep hole she had dug as a toilet and toss some of the loose soil on top to cover the stench. Teena was surprised that she had become accustomed to the smell over time, a smell she hoped she would never have to experience again.

Teena heard the door open and slam shut above her head. There were two distinct sets of footfalls that walked past the wooden door to the basement. She heard some quiet conversation, laughter, and the sound of something heavy landing on her mother's bed. There was more laughter, voices too quiet to distinguish, and ultimately the sound with which she had eventually become familiar. The springs on her mother's old bed squeaked and the headboard bounced repeatedly against the wall. There would be squeals of excitement, more laughter, and some talking. The toilet would flush, and water would run through the pipes down to the basement. Depending on the visitor, the guest would leave immediately or, on the rare occasion, he would stay for a while.

It was only after the guest had left that her mother simply unlatched the basement door and pulled it open. Teena would take her time exiting the basement and would head directly for the tub where she would wash herself clean. When the bath water cooled, she would drain some and add fresh, scalding hot water. It was the only way she felt clean after spending time in the dark dungeon of a basement. Teena had learnt long ago never to discuss the matters that took place while she was sequestered to the basement. The one time she had asked her mother why she had to be in the basement when her friends stopped by, Teena received a beating so harsh that she stayed home from school for weeks until the bruises were no longer visible.

On her sixteenth birthday, her mother promised to show her what she did while Teena was locked away. Her mother told her she could quit school and work with her to help bring in the needed money. Teena agreed but told her she wanted to continue to go to school. Her mother reluctantly acquiesced. On the day she turned sixteen, Teena packed her school bag with her books and whatever clothes she could fit in, left for school, and never went back. She promised herself she would never, ever go back to that house again.

Years later, she found a small article on the Internet about a woman beaten to death at the address with the dark dungeon basement. There were no tears, no remorse; she may have even smiled when she read the article. Someone did to her mother what she was too weak to do herself. She didn't save the article, or print a copy of it. Teena just closed the Internet browser and continued doing what she had been doing.

The sound of her nails scratching at the wood laminate wall broke Teena's thoughts of the past. Even in the darkness, she opened her eyes to the noise. She pulled her hand away and clasped it tightly around her knees again. She was crying and could feel the tears run down her cheek, drip off her chin, and land on her slacks.

On the thirty-second floor, Quinn used his elevator access key to open the silver doors and scan all four shafts. Peering down the shaft, he found the elevator cab for which he was looking. Quinn counted the floors from where he was. Teena's elevator had been only one floor away from its destination when it had stopped.

From the open doors, Quinn yelled out Teena's name over and over again. He paused and waited for a response. He was met with silence. Reaching into his pocket, he pulled out his cellphone and dialled Teena's phone. The phone rang several times and then went directly to voice-mail.

"Damn!" He waited for the message to finish. "Teena, when you get this message, call me on my cell." He wished he had never told Teena to shut off her phone. Quinn pocketed his cellphone, let the elevator doors close behind him, and ran to the stairwell, then bolted down the stairs to where he was positive Teena was trapped.

In the blackness, Teena spun around towards the elevator doors as she heard Quinn calling out to her. His voice echoed in the metal box. Teena continued to turn in the direction of the voice as it bounced off the walls and then faded into nothingness. She was convinced it was Quinn's voice.

"Quinn. Quinn." Teena took two steps forward and slammed into the elevator doors, but still continued to yell his name. She pounded her open hand repeatedly on the metal doors, hoping Quinn would hear her. Teena stopped momentarily, waiting for Quinn to answer her pleas. She stood there in the darkness and heard only silence. There was a whisper, a sound, something; she was certain of it. She screamed, louder than she thought she could, "Quinn!"

On the other side of the door she heard laughter. It was Quinn's voice again. He was laughing at her. "Quinn, is that you? I'm really scared. Can you get me outta here?" She was pleading. "Please Quinn, answer me."

From the other side of the elevator doors, the laughter became louder, and then stopped abruptly. She heard Quinn speaking but couldn't understand what he was saying; then the words became clear.

"…tease me, lead me on, while you have a boyfriend. Then you have the nerve to talk to him in front of me. You deserve everything that happens to you." Quinn's voice was stern and very angry.

Teena stepped back and pressed her back against the wall, her hands grasping the railings for support. Again, she started to shake, and her knees buckled, almost sending her to the floor. Teena heard Quinn yell at her again. She spun around, directed her back to the elevator doors, pushed her face into the corner, and covered her ears with her hands.

With her ears covered, Teena closed her mind to the place she was in and tried to recall how she had calmed herself as a child. She let her mind drift back. Back to the days in the basement, back to when she was a young girl. She could feel the soil on her bare feet, the dampness of the stone foundation on her skin.

She began to smell the flower gardens she used to tend with her grandmother by her side. Her grandmother had taught her how to prune the plants, and cut off the dead branches to help the healthy ones grow. Together they would pick flowers, and then bring them into the house where the two of them would spend hours making arrangements and placing bouquets in crystal vases in every room. Her grandmother had made her mix a teaspoon of honey with the water in each vase. "The sugar helps the flower live longer and makes the colour brighter," her grandmother used to say. Teena wasn't sure it actually worked but she did as she was told. The scent of floral arrangements would fill her grandmother's house. Sometimes the scent was overwhelming, but in a beautiful way.

Each morning before her grandmother woke she would walk about the house, collecting the leaves or petals that had fallen off the stems, and trimming the dying blooms to let the stronger ones live longer. Teena felt horrible cutting short the lives of the flowers that could still bring colour and aroma to the rooms, even if it was only for a day or two longer. She collected the cut blossoms and placed them in a wicker basket, and then put the basket on the back of the toilet tank in her bathroom. It was her way of giving the flowers a few more days of joy before they wilted and dried up. Without her grandmother knowing, sometimes she would put some of the dried flowers and leaves in her pillowcase, so that she could fall asleep to their fragrance.

After her grandmother died, her mother took to locking her in the basement when she needed her time alone. Those memories stayed with her throughout her life. There were few memories she held dear from when she was living with her mother. Teena was never told who her father was and couldn't recall ever meeting him. For all she knew, he was probably one of the many men who frequently visited her mother. Unless she performed a DNA test on every visitor, there was no way of knowing who her father was. Even as a young girl, her mother used to tell Teena that she wished she had aborted her pregnancy.

A heavy thud on the outside of the elevator broke her concentration. She turned to look but only saw blackness staring back at her. She waited, thinking it was Quinn banging on the elevator, still mad for some reason. A minute passed, then two, and Teena hoped she wouldn't hear anything more. There was no reason for Quinn to be upset. Teena knew she would have to speak with Quinn about what he had said and clarify that the man with whom she had been speaking was her cousin. The only cousin she ever knew she had. They grew close, and became like brother and sister.

For a few moments, she was met with silence. Teena rationalized that it must have been the electricity trying to come back on and sending a jolt to the elevator motors. If electricity even worked that way. She chuckled at herself for making up things. Teena's childhood fear was real, deep within her, and taking over. She would fight that fear every step of the way.

Teena jumped as the elevator dropped a few feet and then stopped suddenly. She stumbled backwards, reaching blindly, lost her footing, and struck her head on the wall. Teena's head started to spin, she saw stars dancing, nausea overcame her, and she felt a little vomit rise up in the back of her throat. She swallowed hard to keep the vomit from coming up. The acid in her throat burned and she desperately wanted some water to clear the taste. She inhaled deeply through her nose to calm her stomach. One slow breath in followed by another and yet another helped to quell the nausea. Finally, the nausea abated entirely. As Teena was about to stand, the elevator dropped a few feet and stopped again, sending her back to the floor. She screamed so loudly her ears began to ring.

"Stop it!" she yelled. Teena looked up at the ceiling, knowing it was there in the darkness, and yelled again, "Stop it!" Tears flowed freely. She began to sob uncontrollably as she continued screaming. Eventually, her screams turned to sobs as she cried and whispered, "Stop it!"

It started softly at first, but then Teena could definitely make out the sounds of footfalls above her on the roof of the elevator. She held her breath and followed the footsteps as they walked around the roof. She listened as the person above her tried to mask their steps, but the sound reverberated in the small metal box. The sounds of footsteps ceased, but then she heard metallic sounds as though a man was taking a pee on the roof of the box. As the liquid continued to bounce off the roof, Teena heard laughter again. She focused and now was certain it was Quinn. The laughter continued.

"Stop it! Why are you doing this?" She paused, took in a deep breath and screamed, "Stooooop!" Teena was exhausted. She started to pant and felt the tears coming again. She realized that her days trapped in her mother's basement paled in comparison to this ordeal. She was truly afraid.

The tears dried up, her sobbing ceased, and eventually Teena fell asleep curled up on the elevator floor. Her head was leaning against the wall, and her hands were clasped firmly around her knees as she slept. Eventually, her hands released their grip and fell to the floor. Her legs relaxed and fell flat. Teena coughed, covered her mouth, and coughed again. She tasted something in her throat. It wasn't bile this time. It was something thick, making her cough a third time. She opened her eyes, but in the darkness she couldn't see anything. Her eyes started to sting. She immediately recognized the taste of smoke.

Teena stood and felt the heat increase and the smoke thicken in her throat. She dropped back down and crawled around in an attempt to find the doors. Wood panels eventually gave way to the stainless steel of the entrance doors. Her fingers found the crack where the two doors joined and she pried her fingers between them. Teena mustered all her strength and pulled in opposite directions. She moaned as she pulled harder, but her lungs filled with more smoke. She coughed and spit and could taste the thick, charred smoke. The doors began to separate, so she pushed her fingers farther between the doors, breaking off her nails. When the doors were almost a foot apart, the inner rubber seal began to give way and a furnace blast of heat broke through, forcing her back. The elevator door slammed shut as she fell backwards. She dug her heels into the floor and made her way to the back of the box.

Teena pulled at her blouse sleeve until it ripped at the shoulder seam. She yanked it free and wrapped it around her mouth, tying it securely behind her head. She kept her eyes shut tightly as she patted the floor until she found her purse, retrieved her cellphone, and powered it on. It took an eternity for the familiar tone to be heard that indicated that the phone was finally ready for use. The smoke stung her eyes, but she forced them open so she could dial 911. She put the phone to her ear and heard a busy tone. "Fuck!" She hit end, then send again. This time the phone connected and a female operator answered, "911. What is your emergency?"

"I'm trapped in an elevator and the building is on fire. The elevator is filling with smoke."

"I have your cell co-ordinates but I can't determine your exact location. What building are you in?"

"First Reserve Bank." Even with her light blouse covering her mouth, the smoke entered her lungs, and she coughed, spitting up black phlegm.

"Fire, police, and EMS have already been dispatched and are on their way. Are there several banks of elevators so we can direct rescue to your location?"

"Just the four off the main lobby." Teena heard her phone beeping.

"Stay on the phone with me until rescue arrives," the dispatcher said.

"My phone is dying. I don't know how much longer it'll last. Please stay with me." Teena was pleading with the dispatcher, who remained calm.

"I'll stay with you as long as want me to."

"I can't see anything and the elevator is almost full of smoke. And I can't breathe."

"Lay flat with your face to the floor. Breathe slowly. Do you have something to cover your mouth with?" The dispatcher's voice was firm and showed no signs of panic.

"I tore my sleeve off." Teena coughed repeatedly, then caught her breath. "And it's covering my mouth and nose but I still can't breathe."

"The fire department should be there shortly. Do you know where the fire started?" the dispatcher asked.

"The building I'm in experienced several power outages today." She took in a deep breath and coughed. Her lungs were burning, and she could feel the heat inside the compartment increasing every minute. She had no idea from where the smoke was coming, but she figured it had to be directly around the elevator.

Like a bolt of lightning striking her, Teena realized it was Quinn. He wasn't taking a pee on the roof of the elevator, he was pouring gasoline on it.

"Are you still there?" Teena screamed into her phone, which beeped again.

"I'm not leaving you." The phone beeped. There was little battery life left.

"It's Quinn."

The phone beeped. "Who is Quinn?" Beep.

Beep. "The security guard…" Beep. "It's Quinn." Before she could finish, the light on her phone went black. The battery lost all power and died. Teena held the phone before her and saw no light. She threw the phone against the wall and heard it bounce. "Fuck."

The heat inside the elevator started to become unbearable. Her back was beginning to sweat, as the smoke had made its way all the way to the floor. Each breath became more and more laboured. Her eyes stung and the tears started. Her coughing was relentless. Each breath drew in more smoke than oxygen. Teena started to hold her breath and only breathe when she couldn't hold it any longer.

Teena crawled to the corner, hoping the smoke wouldn't migrate there and be as thick as it was in the centre. She pushed her face into the corner so hard it sent sharp spasms to her brain. She took in a deep breath. The smoke was so hot that it burnt her lungs. She knew her time was limited.

Somewhere in the smoke-filled blackness, the sound of something metallic striking the doors reached her ears. She took in a deep breath of hot smoke. The firefighters are here, she thought.

Teena's head started to spin. She couldn't think, and she couldn't breathe. Her eyes felt heavy and she fought to keep them open, but lost the battle as they slowly closed. Her heart was beating hard in her chest, fearful of what was about to happen. Nothing made sense. The heat was too much. Teena simply gave up and collapsed. Her heart stopped, her lungs so full with hot black smoke that they couldn't sustain life any longer and simply ceased to work.

The elevator door opened and Quinn and Darryl stood looking at Teena lying on her stomach in the corner of the elevator. Quinn stepped in, held her head gently, and turned Teena over. She was unconscious, breathing but covered in sweat. He looked around the inside of the elevator compartment for any clue as to why she had passed out. Everything looked as it should.

"What's wrong with her?" Darryl asked.

"You got me." Quinn was puzzled. "She's still breathing. I think she passed out or something."

"How long was she trapped in the elevator for?"

Quinn shrugged his shoulders. "Only a few minutes. She called me on my cell and told me she was trapped. I raced up, found where she was, and called you for help. Probably five, ten minutes at the most."

Quinn scooped Teena up in his arms and carried her out of the elevator.

"I'll call 911 for an ambulance," Darryl offered.

THE END

THE REUNION

THE INVITATION

Stan Sanburg sat on the balcony of his apartment reading the invitation he had received in the mail. It was a simple note, his mother's handwriting on a plain white card:

You are cordially invited to attend
this year's Sanburg family reunion at the family home
beginning any time on Saturday July 4th and finishing sometime on Sunday July 5th

Below the invitation details, his mother had added a special note to her only child:

Please try to make it this year. It's been far too long. Love Mom.

He sat there looking at the card, wondering if he should attend this year. Stan had always made excuses for not going, but with each of the past five years, the excuses had been weaker and less convincing. He reached for his glass of wine, took a sip, and spat it back into the glass. He really wanted a beer and had no idea why he had poured wine. He got up, dumped the wine in the kitchen sink, rinsed the glass, and put it in the strainer. Pulling the bottle of beer from the fridge, he twisted the cap and blindly tossed it into the sink. The cap missed the mark, and ricocheted off the back wall and onto the floor. He thought about picking it up, and came to regret not doing so later that day when he stepped on it.

Stan was sitting back on the balcony, beer in hand, staring at the invitation. He knew the date of the reunion; it was always the first weekend in July, every year. He rolled the cold bottle over his forehead as he continued to look at the invitation. The condensation on the bottle only mixed with the sweat, but it did cool him down slightly. He sloughed in the cheap plastic lawn chair and rested the bottle of beer on his bare stomach.

It was the last week of June, the weather was extremely hot, and his air conditioning unit had stopped working a few weeks earlier. He had brought the A/C unit in to get repaired, but now he wished he had simply purchased a new one. He rationalized that his job kept him away from home travelling most of the week, and the need for a new air conditioner wasn't justified. Now he wished he was working and staying in some nice hotel with room service, a large flat screen television, and A/C cold enough to hang meat.

"Hey neighbour," a voice called out to him.

Stan slowly turned to the left to see his neighbour standing on her balcony only a few feet away from where he sat. She was alone, smiling, and wearing a bikini with an open cotton shirt and flip-flops. He had seen her many times in the hall and elevator, and there was always the obligatory head nod and uncomfortable "Hi." Coming from the country, he was now ashamed he had never made an attempt to be friendlier or at least introduce himself.

"Hey." Stan turned back to studying his mother's invitation.

"I know this sounds corny, but you look hot. I mean as in temperature hot. Wanna come over? I'm having a bit of a party, then we're heading to the pool downstairs." She gestured inside her apartment. Stan hadn't noticed the music or the loud conversations earlier.

"Thanks, I'm good."

"Oh, come on. I saw them take your air conditioner away. You're cooking out here, my apartment is about thirty degrees cooler, we have beer and coolers on ice, and it gives you a good excuse to meet the rest of the people on the floor. Do you have something better to do on a hot Saturday afternoon?"

Stan thought about accepting for a moment. "Next time," he said politely.

"Aimee." She extended her hand as she leaned across the balconies.

Stan smiled, stood, and dried his hand from the wet bottle of beer on his shorts. He leaned across. "Stan."

As Stan leaned forward, Aimee noticed the odd chain and pendant around his neck. "Nice to meet you, neighbour Stan. Interesting thingamajig around your neck. What's it supposed to be?"

Stan stood back on his balcony, touched the yellowed wolf tooth suspended on a gold chain around his neck, and said, "It's nothing, just something I got as a kid. I used to have a lot of nightmares and my dad got this for me and told me never to take it off."

"Does it work?" Aimee asked. She was still leaning forward on the railing, showing her cleavage.

Stan knew she was flirting, but he wasn't interested in anything more than being a good neighbour. "So far. Haven't had one in almost ten years."

"Well, Stan who doesn't have nightmares anymore, if I ever get scared, I know who to call."

"Ghostbusters?"

"Funny man. Last chance. Coming over?"

"Rain check."

"I'll hold you to that." Aimee pointed at him, spun around, and went back inside to join the party.

Stan knew his comment wasn't that funny. It wasn't funny at all. He sat back down and for the first time actually noticed the music. He rested the beer on his stomach. Holding on to the bottle had warmed up the beer fast. He went back inside to get a cold beer.

"Fuck," Stan yelled as he stepped on the beer cap he had left on the floor.

*****

Stan lay in bed naked; the covers had long since been kicked off. The heat had not subsided and the humidity had increased throughout the day, making the night air thick and sticky. He drifted in and out of sleep, unable to get comfortable.

A large plastic fan was placed on the dresser at the far side of the bedroom and oscillated the cool breeze past him every few seconds. The ceiling fan directly above his bed spun at the highest speed and made a constant "whoop – whoop" sound. At first the noise was annoying and he wanted the fan replaced, but he soon found that the rhythmic sound was hypnotic and had a calming effect on him.

Stan's skin was wet from sweat and he hoped the fans would cool him down, but they did little to help with the high humidity. He thought about Aimee and wished he had accepted her invitation to join the party. He was twenty-seven and acting like an old man, shunning human contact. Meeting new people who were living in the building would've been nice. He had been living in the same apartment for almost two years and didn't know one of the other tenants by their first name.

That could change with Aimee, he thought.

Stan shook that idea from his mind. The last thing he wanted or needed at this time was a relationship. He sat on the edge of the bed, lifted his right foot, and rubbed the spot where he had stepped on the beer cap earlier in the day. "Damn that hurts," he exclaimed as he tried to rub out the pain.

Stan limped to the bathroom, turned on the light, opened the medicine cabinet, and took two Advil. He turned on the cold tap and drank from the spout. He kept the water running as he stood. Eyes closed, he cupped a handful of cold water and splashed it on his face. He opened his eyes, and saw the face of the beast. "Christ," he yelled as he fell backward against the bathroom door.

In the mirror, he only saw himself now. Not the beast of his nightmares. He stepped closer to the sink and looked deep into his own eyes. He didn't like what he saw and swung his fist at the mirror. The glass cracked and shattered into a hundred shards. Stan was now looking back at a distorted version of himself. He glanced down at his right hand and felt the pain of several small lacerations that cut deep into the skin.

"Idiot," he said to the distorted version of himself in the mirror.

The next hour was spent cleaning up the glass from the floor and sink and pulling the loose glass from the medicine cabinet frame. He was sitting on the couch applying a few bandages to his knuckles when he came to the realization that he had to go to the reunion the next weekend.

Stan fell backwards on the couch, closed his eyes, and remembered that day almost ten years ago. He rubbed his injured hand as his mind became fuzzy and he drifted off. He had tried to forget that day, but it kept coming back, reminding him of who he really was.

Rosalyn and Stan were both in their third year of high school, and the friendship that had started when they were young friends years earlier had finally turned into an adult relationship. Stan remembered that the longer they were together, the stronger their bond became. Summer vacation had long passed. Fall was now taking hold and bringing in the cooler temperatures. After high school, Rosalyn wanted to go to college, but Stan wanted to start working with his father and eventually take over the family home. It was something that his parents had talked about for as far back as he could remember.

Since they started dating, it became common for Rosalyn to stop by the Sanburg home and stay late, sometimes even sleeping over - in a separate bedroom, of course.

The leaves had started to turn. Colours of yellow, red, and orange took command of the green foliage on the trees, or forced those leaves that failed to change to fall to the ground prematurely. Fall was Stan's favourite time of the year. He was always uncomfortable in the summer heat.

Mid-term exams had started and Rosalyn was spending more time studying with Stan at his parents' house. That night, it was just after eleven when they decided to call it quits. The night was unseasonably warm, with a full moon in the clear sky. Stan wanted to drive Rosalyn home, but she wanted to walk. Rosalyn had come straight from school and didn't have a jacket for the walk home. He draped his mother's jacket over her shoulders and grabbed two flashlights from the hall desk. He told his parents he was walking Rosalyn home and would be back in a little over an hour.

Rosalyn and Stan held hands and spoke little. Their pace would take more than the usual time to make it to Rosalyn's house. Fingers started to twist and fight for position in the handhold, and they giggled. Stan recalled that this simple finger fight for supremacy was one of their secrets they shared with no one.

"Do you think Mrs. Bleavans will go overboard with the science exam again?" Rosalyn asked.

"She's famous for her long-winded, convoluted questions that only Mensa candidates can decipher. I swear, she takes pride in seeing how many kids she can fail." Stan twisted his left index finger and middle finger into a tight hold around Rosalyn's thumb. She squirmed her way free and fought back with a barrage of finger over finger assault.

"If I fail her exam, it'll bring down my average and make getting into my university of choice next to impossible."

"You have the best science mind I know," Stan reminded Rosalyn. "Take your time, read the question, deduce her logic - not what you think, imagine what the old bat is thinking - and go from there."

Rosalyn got a strangle hold on Stan's baby finger and twisted. He let out a yelp that made her laugh. "If you know how she thinks, how come you don't do better in her class?" she asked.

"I hate, I mean really hate, science. I like the one-on-one approach and work-ing with my hands. The only thing I want to do is go work with my dad. He's the best farm equipment salesman in the whole united counties. No one can sell the way he does. I can watch him work all day. He's a master at reading people and getting them into just the right piece of equipment." Stan tried to release his baby finger but Rosalyn held firm and pulled hard, causing his finger to snap each time he tried to free himself.

"You don't want to leave and move to the city? I mean really, what kind of life can we have here if we stay?"

Stan stopped and looked at Rosalyn as she stood under the trees. Moon-light rippled through the half-naked trees and illuminated her face. "What do you mean by that?" he asked.

"What?" Rosalyn looked truly surprised.

"You said, 'what kind of life can we have?'" he told her.

Rosalyn laughed loudly, let go of Stan's left hand, and cradled his face in both of her own. "We grew up together, I know you better than I know myself; of course I imagine our lives together. Don't you?"

Stan leaned in close and kissed her. "Did you just propose to me?"

"Sorta. I promised myself to you. How's that?"

"I'll take it. So that makes us, what?"

"We don't need a title; besides, I fully expect you to take my last name when we get married." Rosalyn laughed, grabbed Stan's hand again, and began the fin-ger fight anew.

"Stan Vernon. Yeah, I can get used to that. Does that mean I can be a stay at home husband and have you buy me shiny things and treat me like a prince?"

"Don't bet on it." Rosalyn twisted four of Stan's fingers into a tight spiral and pulled, causing him to yelp again. "Just remember, I can always kick your ass." She leaned in close and rested her head on his shoulder, then moved her hand up to his elbow and squeezed his arm into her. "I love you," she whispered, barely audible.

It was the first time Rosalyn had ever told Stan how she felt. He had known she loved him, but she had never said it before.

"Back at ya."

Hours later, Stan's father woke up to go to the bathroom and noticed that Stan's bedroom light was still on. He walked over as he rubbed the sleep from his eyes. Placing his hand on the door, he slowly slid it open wide, only to find the room empty. Mr. Sanburg walked downstairs to discover all the lights still on, the front door unlocked, and Stan's shoes and jacket missing.

He went to the kitchen and called the Vernon residence.

"Have Stan and Rosalyn shown up yet?" he asked in a panic.

"I just assumed she was staying at your house again tonight," Mrs. Vernon told him.

"Get in the car, drive to our place, I'll do the same, and we'll meet in the middle somewhere." He slammed the phone down and ran upstairs to wake his wife and tell her to call the Vernons if Stan and Rosalyn showed up while he was out looking for them.

Mrs. Sanburg bolted from the bed. Call it a mother's intuition, call it what you will; she knew something was wrong - horribly wrong.

Mr. Sanburg climbed into the pickup truck, started the engine, and lit the high beams so he wouldn't miss anything. The moon was bright tonight, he thought to himself - a fall harvest moon. His stomach was sour, and he felt the burning taste of bile at the back of his throat. He was scared, not for himself, but for his son and his girlfriend.

He floored the accelerator and turned left out of the driveway, the back tires sliding on the gravel road. Even with the high beams on and the bright moon, it still wasn't enough to illuminate the tree-lined roads well enough to find the kids even if they were only a few feet off the road. Mr. Sanburg slowed the speed of the truck so he could look on both shoulders of the road.

Mr. Sanburg kept pressing the horn, hoping they would hear it and make themselves known in case they were hiding. His head went from side to side, but he saw only dark brush on either side of the road. "*No bodies are good,*" he thought to himself. "*No bodies, Christ, what if they were hit by a car and taken to the hospital?*" Scenarios kept running through his mind, each one worse than the last. "*Fuck, I should've called the police and the hospitals before leaving.*"

Mr. Sanburg suddenly slammed on the brakes, and the truck slid sideways on the gravel road. He lost control of the truck, sending the back end into a culvert, then coming to an abrupt stop against a tree and denting the box panel. He shook his head, felt the blood trickle down from a small cut, engaged the four-wheel drive, and pressed hard on the gas. The truck dug into the gravel road and pulled itself out of the culvert. Mr. Sanburg turned the truck around and drove a hundred feet or so to where he thought he had seen something. Driving slowly, he saw the lights bounce off the reflective material on Stan's sneakers. Only his legs were sticking out of the brush on the north side of the road.

Mr. Sanburg stopped the truck so that it blocked both lanes on the dirt road, with the lights aimed at the area where his son lay. He jammed the gear selector into park and jumped from the truck. He pulled the thick brush away from his son to find him bloodied and unconscious. He held his head and slowly turned him over so that Stan was on his back. He placed his hand on his son's chest and felt it rise and fall with each breath. There were four horizontal gashes across his left cheek, and his jacket was torn across the chest and the back. Mr. Sanburg did a quick body exam to make sure nothing was broken before carefully carrying him out of the brush and onto the road. He laid his son in front of the truck, covered him with his jacket, then grabbed a flashlight from the truck and went into the woods to look for Rosalyn.

The flashlight swept back and forth, but in the dense brush he could only see a few feet in front of him. He called Rosalyn's name repeatedly, hoping - praying - for a response, but heard nothing. Mr. Sanburg tried to rush his search, but tripped and fell forward, landing in the damp underbrush. He lost his grip on the flashlight and it went tumbling into the woods. He saw the light beam and crawled on his hands and knees towards it.

Suddenly, Mr. Sanburg froze. He heard the panting of a wolf or a bear behind him, within a few feet. The air was cool but he could still feel the hot breath over him. The panting turned to a deep throaty growl. It rumbled the air around him, which was filled with a foul stench of rotting flesh. Mr. Sanburg thought he knew every animal in these woods, but he wasn't familiar with the sounds coming from whatever was behind him. Mr. Sanburg slowly turned his head to see what was stalking him, when a car horn blew from the road. He turned to the road, then back to the beast, but he heard it run off before he could see it.

Mr. Sanburg found the flashlight and made his way back to the road to find a police officer caring for Stan and Mrs. Vernon yelling for her daughter.

Stan woke up a few minutes later, stood, and made his way to the bookshelf. He dug through the old books and found his high school yearbook. The page he was looking for was dog-eared. It was the only page he ever looked at. Stan knew exactly where to look: which row, which column. Just to the left of his picture was that of Rosalyn Vernon. He reached out and touched her face in the picture. She had been then and still was the standard by which he measured all other women.

The nightmares began the night Rosalyn disappeared - the night he saw the beast. Stan was more than devastated; he was unable to function. Both of his parents knew the circumstances by which Rosalyn had left, but neither of them would ever tell Stan's secret.

Stan hadn't seen another girl since Rosalyn; he couldn't, not after the way she left. He couldn't help but feel responsible for what had happened. He closed his high school yearbook and carefully placed it back on the shelf. Sitting on the couch, he clutched the ancient Indian talisman around his neck that was meant to keep the evil spirits away. It had hung there since shortly after that night. Now, for the first time since his father had put it around his neck, he had seen the beast. And it scared him, frightened him to his very soul. Stan moved away from home because he was so afraid of seeing the beast. He moved away from the only home he had ever known; the home of his father, his grandfather, and every Sanburg for generations. Stan was the last Sanburg. He felt cursed. Maybe there was a family curse.

It was late, but Stan wanted to call his mother and tell her what he had decided. He picked up his cellphone and dialled the number. He knew there was only one phone in the house, and it would take time to get to the phone in the den on the main floor. The phone continued to ring until a very tired and confused Mrs. Sanburg answered it.

"Hello."

"Mom," Stan said softly.

"Honey, what's the matter? Why are you calling so late?"

"I'll see you for the reunion."

"You're coming?"

"I'll be there."

"Your dad will be so pleased to see you."

"Go back to bed, Mom. We can chat next week."

"That's great news, honey. I can't wait to see you. The house hasn't been the same since you left."

"Go to bed, Mom."

"Yes, dear. Oh Stanley, I can't wait."

"Good night, Mom."

*****

The Saturday morning of the reunion, Stan packed his bag and sat on the end of the bed. He picked at the scab on his right hand. He had replaced the glass in the bathroom without telling the landlord. Looking down at his hand, he figured the wounds would leave scars if he kept picking at them. *"Just what I need, more scars,"* he thought.

His stomach was in knots; he almost threw up a couple of times. Above his head, the fan beat out the familiar "whoop – whoop" of the unbalanced blades. Though his shirt, he rubbed the wolf tooth on the chain. The memory of the day he received the Tlinglit charm played over in his head as it had a thousand times over the years.

It was late one night, months after Rosalyn disappeared. A friend of Stan's father stopped by the house after his mother had gone to bed. His father introduced him as a member of the Tlingit Indians, part of the Goch or wolf tribe. Stan couldn't recall his name, only how passionate he was about the circumstances of Stan's story. Stan recounted the events of the night that would end up scarring him for the rest of his life to his father's friend.

His father's friend paused for a moment, then recalled a story told to him when he was younger. "You were touched by the Kushtaka. The Kushtaka will trick you to come close, then it will steal the souls of the young and keep them for itself. The Kushtaka will keep the souls here," he tapped Stan's chest over his heart, "and here." With his right index finger, he touched Stan's forehead. "The evil spirit Kushtaka will never take you as long as you wear the tooth of the wolf. The wolf will scare away the Kushtaka."

The man pulled out a tooth, a long fang, from his pants pocket. "Hold it here." He showed Stan how to hold the tooth at the very tip. "Don't let go," he ordered. From his other pocket, he retrieved a long strand of thin leather fashioned like a shoelace. "Hold tight. The leather traps the spell in the tooth and keeps you safe. If you drop the tooth during the ceremony, it cannot be tried again. You must hold tight. Do you understand?"

Stan nodded his head. He pinched the tooth hard with his index and thumb and, with his other hand, gripped those fingers tightly. The tips of his fingers turned red as his father's friend spoke softly, eyes closed, and recited a spell in his native language that could very well have simply been a nursery rhyme or a recipe for venison. Whatever was said, however strange the ceremony, Stan had been afraid of what had happened to Rosalyn and what might happen again if he let go of the tooth.

When the man was finished wrapping the tooth, he turned to Stan's father and asked if he had a necklace from which to hang the charm. His father took off the thick gold chain around his own neck and handed it to the man. He told Stan to release his hold on the tooth, then secured it to the chain.

"Never remove this." The man looked directly into Stan's eyes. He was deadly serious, and Stan understood. He motioned for Stan to bow his head. Stan hung his head low as the Tlinglit man his father sought out placed the chain around his neck. When Stan looked up, the man said to him again, "Never, ever take this off. The Kushtaka is here," he tapped Stan on the chest, "and will return if you remove it. Do you understand?" Stan nodded. "Do you understand?" the man repeated gruffly.

"Yes sir, I understand. Never ever take it off. I promise."

*****

Stan wasn't comfortable with what his father had arranged and never believed in the Indian superstitions, but the Sanburgs had been part of the land and lived alongside the Native Indians long enough to respect their ways even if they didn't believe them.

Stan stood, grabbed his bag, turned off all the lights, and locked the apartment. As he walked towards the elevator, Aimee exited the lift and saw Stan coming towards her.

"Hey, Ghostbuster."

"Hey, Bikini Aimee." Stan regretted saying it even before it came out.

Aimee blushed slightly. "I was going to call you this weekend and see if I could take you out for a drink, but it looks like you're leaving."

Stan looked down at his small overnight bag. "Weekend at the parents' place." He sighed heavily.

Aimee leaned against the wall beside the elevator. "Well, if you don't want to go, I could call the rest of the guys on the floor and have another party. Would that make you want to stay?"

"Believe me, if I hadn't promised my mother I would go, you wouldn't have to throw another party to make me stay."

"How come you don't want to go?" Aimee asked.

"It's where I started having those nightmares I was telling you about. I'd prefer to stay home and have you buy me a drink, but family comes first." Stan flicked his eyebrows up and down.

Aimee stepped in closer and placed her hand on Stan's chest, felt the wolf tooth pendant, and said, "Just make sure you wear this charm thingy so you don't have any more nightmares, K."

Stan smiled back. It had been far too long since a woman had touched him that way. "K."

"So we can do drinks when you get back?" Aimee asked as she walked down the hall to her apartment.

"Yeah, we can do drinks when I get back."

"Catch you later, Ghostbuster," Aimee shouted as she closed her apartment door.

Stan pushed the button for the elevator and waited. "Ghostbuster," he said softly to himself, then laughed. "Who ya gonna call? Ghostbusters."

The elevator doors opened and Stan stepped inside. "Shit, that song is gonna be stuck in my head all day." Stan stuck his head between the closing doors and looked down the hall to Aimee's apartment. He laughed again, muttering, "Ghostbusters."

THE DRIVE

Stan was driving east into the morning sun; both windows were down, the air conditioner on high, and the radio turned off. As he had predicted, the Ghostbusters song was stuck in his head. He tapped the steering wheel with his fingers as he drove along the highway.

It had been years since Stan had been down these roads but he remembered them like he had only been gone a week. The trees had grown, but there weren't many new homes; in fact, he only counted two of them.

Stan turned off the highway and on to a dirt road. His brand new black Cadillac CTS bottomed out in a deep pothole on the passenger side and jostled him in his seat. "Shit, I should've bought the SUV," he said out loud. Dust kicked up from the tires, filled the car, and covered his dashboard, leaving a gritty, powdery film across the glossy black surface. He pulled up on the switches and the two power windows rolled up. He quickly forgot about the dusty road and the pothole, and started to hum the tune to Ghostbusters; soon he was singing at the top of his lungs.

"…something strange
In your neighbourhood
Who ya gonna call?
Ghostbusters
Da da something weird
And it don't look good
Who ya gonna call?
Stanley
I ain't afraid of no ghosts
I ain't afraid of no Indian spirit
Blah blah your head
Who ya gonna call?
Stanley
If you're seeing things
Something something your head
Who ya gonna call?
Stan the Ghostbuster
An invisible man
Sleeping in your bed

Who ya gonna call?
Not the Ghostbusters, call Stan
Something something something
I forget most of the words.
Ghostbusters
I ain't afraid of no ghosts
I hear it likes the girls"

Stan stopped short when he sang the line "likes the girls." It wasn't fun any-more. Nausea quickly overtook him. He slammed on the brakes, pulled over, jammed the car into park, opened his driver's door, and vomited beside the car. His stomach heaved up and down, forcing his body to move in waves against his will. He made sounds that normally, if he heard them, would make him want to throw up. But he was now the one making those sounds. He tried to close his eyes but he couldn't. The vomit came up and forced its way out of his mouth and nose. He didn't have much to eat for breakfast, and what little came up burnt his throat and nostrils.

Stan looked down in the dirt to see a small puddle of what looked like toast, coffee, and something that he couldn't even describe. If he didn't leave imme-diately, the smell of what he had just thrown up would make him start heaving again. Wiping his mouth with the back of his arm, Stan wanted - needed - some water to rinse and get rid of the foul taste. He took the energy drink can from the cup holder and shook it. Empty. The can had been there for a few days, but any liquid would do. He regretted not bringing a bottle of water or a coffee.

He slammed the driver's door, put the car in gear, and sped away, hoping the corner store he went to as a child was still there. Stan rolled down his window and had to spit every few minutes to clear his mouth, but he still desperately needed some water.

Up ahead, four houses sat on the corners where two roads crossed. Before he left home, one of them had belonged to the MacLeans, who also owed the house directly across the street and had converted it into a general store and lunch counter. Despite the fact that there were a dozen miles between most homes in this part of the county, the store was always busy, the food always fresh, and the coffee as bad as anyone could ever hope to taste. Bad coffee aside, it had been his favourite hangout as a child growing up in the middle of nowhere.

As Stan approached, he noticed the dirt parking lot was full. Each one of the vehicles in front of the general store was a pickup, and each pickup was at least twenty years old. People around these parts seldom purchased cars, and the only time they bought a new one was when they literally put the old truck out to pasture and let it rust away until it was back to being part of the earth. He pulled in between two light blue seventies-era pickups. Both trucks had their windows rolled down and their keys still in the ignition. He put the car in park, killed the engine, and walked to the diner side of the store, but not before pointing his key fob at the car and locking the vehicle.

The front doors of the general store were open and Stan heard laughter coming from inside. He already knew what they were laughing at. As a teenager, he and his friends always made fun of tourists, too.

"All right. I admit it. It's been a few years since I've been home and you get into some bad city habits," Stan yelled out.

Mitchel O'Brien stopped laughing, got up from the counter stool, and looked at Stan long and hard. "You old son-of-a-bitch." Mitchel walked over to his old high school friend and gave him a big hug. "You old son-of-a-bitch," he repeated. "Look who's back: Stan the Man himself." Mitchel yelled so that everyone at the lunch counter could hear the announcement. "He actually locked his car before coming in the store. Big city guy now."

Mitchel pushed back from Stan and realized that the last time he had seen his old friend, he had been mad at him. "Hey, you still owe me money," he shouted.

"For what, Rusty?" Stan was surprised his friend remembered the old debt. Stan and the rest of his high school friends used to call Mitchel "Rusty" not because he had red hair, but because the car he drove back then had more rust holes than solid body panels.

"You lost that bet, remember, about, oh shit. I can't even remember myself. Anyways, no one calls me Rusty anymore 'cept you. I got myself a new truck. No rust hardly at all. A 1987 Ford. Not even thirty years old yet." Mitchel let out a hearty laugh and gave his old friend another hug. "Man it is good to see you, Stan, but man, you need a tic-tac or something cause boy, that's pretty strong." Mitchel waved his hand in front of his face to clear the air.

Stan smiled back; he wanted to laugh too, but held back for fear his breath would assault his friend. He covered his mouth with his hand. "Got a little car sick on the way up here. Forgot how bumpy these roads can be."

Stan excused himself from his old friend and went to the counter. The waitress at the far end walked over to him as she wiped her hands on her apron. She picked up a few used coffee cups along the way and placed them in the plastic bin under the counter before she got to Stan.

"What can I get you?" she asked without even looking at Stan.

"Bottle of water, please."

Without looking up, the waitress said sarcastically, "We don't have bottles of water, would you like a glass of water?" She then took a moment to look at her customer and her expression changed from annoyance to excitement.

"Stan Sanburg. Stan Sanburg." Wanda MacLean hopped up and down behind the counter, then ran to the far end, through the opening, and back down behind the customers to jump into Stan's arms. Wanda kissed him hard on the lips and threw her arms around his neck. "Oh my God, Stan. I didn't think I'd ever see you again."

Stan let Wanda down slowly, and put his arms out to the sides. "Here I am."

"Sit, sit. Let me get you that water." Stan sat on the counter stool. Wanda and Stan had been close, brother and sister close, before he met Rosalyn. Mitchel left his coffee where he had been sitting and moved beside Stan.

"You want a refill on that coffee, Mitch?" Wanda yelled out.

"Can only drink so much of your black tar coffee, hon," Mitchel replied.

"Coffee still sucks here?" Stan asked.

"It's like their signature dish. It's the only coffee we know. If I had a coffee from one of those city coffee chains, I'd probably think that coffee was the worst thing I've ever had. It's what you're used to."

Stan laughed with his old friend. Time had slipped away, but in a matter of minutes, Mitchel, Wanda, and Stan had become reacquainted. Stan felt comfortable, at home, despite the fact that he had been away for five years.

Wanda put the glass of ice water down on the counter in front of Stan.

"In town for your family reunion?" Wanda asked.

"They have it every year. Same weekend," he replied as he drank half the glass of water. "Thought I'd give it a chance this year, see if they got any better."

Wanda topped up his water glass. "Trailers and campers have been stopping through here since last night, coming in and getting a quick bite, supplies, and beer. I tell ya, the Sanburg family reunion probably puts more money into the town economy than some businesses."

Wanda asked Stan if he wanted anything to eat. With his empty stomach rumbling from losing its contents on the gravel road, Stan decided a quick lunch and some catching up couldn't hurt. He was going to ask for a salad - a big city thing to order, he thought - but changed his mind and asked for bacon, eggs, and white toast. He was, after all, on a mini vacation.

Mitchel and Stan sat side by side at the counter, Stan sipping his ice water, Mitchel deciding whether he wanted another cup of tar or not. Stan listened while Mitchel talked about how little things change. Sons grow up, take over the family farm, and those that don't decide to move into the city. Stan felt that Mitchel pointed that out especially for him. A few new homes get built, but mostly the old ones get renovated. Time seemed to have forgotten country life. Mitchel was proud to point out that he still didn't have a cellphone - still had a rotary phone on the wall in the kitchen. It was the same phone that had been in the house when he was a kid before his father passed away. Mitchel's children each had a cellphone, and a tablet, and a TV in their rooms, and a laptop. It was something he fought against, but even he had to admit that times change and you either change with them or get left in the dust.

Shortly after, Wanda placed Stan's order before him. It had been years since Stan had a meal from his hometown, and he was looking forward to devouring it. Stan was wiping the runny egg yolk off his plate with the last bit of toast when he felt a presence behind him. Mitchel stopped talking, and Wanda fell silent and looked over Stan's head.

Stan put the toast down and slowly spun around on the stool. His head snapped to the side as his left cheek felt the burn of an open-palmed slap to the face. He was looking down at the floor and saw a few drops of blood fall between his shoes. He blindly reached behind him and grabbed his napkin to wipe the blood from his mouth. He saw the shoes of a woman standing before him, unmoving. Stan didn't have to look up to know who they belonged to or why she had hit him. He had hoped to avoid seeing her, and in all the reminiscing, had simply forgotten about the possibility of bumping into her.

"Can't even face me, you fucking bastard." The voice was gruff, stern, and full of anger.

Slowly, Stan raised his head to look at Rosalyn's mother. He knew what was coming, and felt the impact of another slap. He fell off the stool and landed on the floor. Mitchel stood to help his friend and Stan put up his hand to stop him. He knew Mitchel had to live in town with Mrs. Vernon, and didn't want to come between the two of them.

Stan braced himself on the stool and pulled himself up. For the first time in almost ten years, Stan stood face to face with her. He didn't say a word, his cracked lip still bleeding. He squared his shoulders, used the napkin again to dab up the blood, and sighed deeply.

Mrs. Vernon's arm raised for yet another attack. Stan stood still, ready to feel the wrath of her anger, when a hand reached around and stopped the swing in mid-stroke.

"That's enough," Wanda screamed. "I know you're mad at Stan for what happened to Rosalyn, but for Christ's sake, that was a decade ago. If you have matters with Stan, take them outside and out of my restaurant."

Mrs. Vernon pulled her arm from Wanda's grip. She pointed her finger at Stan. "You're the one responsible for my daughter's death. She loved you, Stan. We loved you, Stan. And you have the nerve to show up here as if nothing has happened just because a few years have gone by. If your parents had any decency, they would've moved out of that home and away from here. They're as much responsible as you." Mrs. Vernon stepped forward, stopping only inches away from Stan's face. "You never should've come back here. You don't belong anymore."

"I don't belong anywhere, Mrs. Vernon," Stan said softly, almost whispering.

Wanda shoved her arm between the two individuals, separating them. She pointed to the exit. "Take it outside."

Silently, Stan reached into his pocket, pulled out a twenty-dollar bill, and tossed it onto the counter. He walked slowly out to his car, unlocked the door, sat inside, and broke down. He sobbed into his hands, now thinking that his trip was a horrendous idea and that nothing good was going to come by returning home. He stopped crying, wiped his eyes dry, looked in the rear view mirror, and saw that his lip and chin were still bloodied. Stan failed to notice the heat inside the car that was quickly becoming unbearable, and that his back was sticking to the leather upholstery.

Fifteen minutes passed in the car before he felt it was safe to return to the restaurant. In spite of the fight he had with Mrs. Vernon, he really had to pee and wash his face before arriving at his parents' house. Stan had seen Mrs. Vernon leave the diner and hoped she had driven away, as well. He decided to wait another few minutes before re-entering the store.

Stan opened the car door and waited. No one attacked him, and he jokingly thought, "*No gun shots either, that's a good sign.*" He exited the car and was about the lock it with his remote. "Fuck this," he said out loud.

Stan walked into the restaurant, past Wanda, and directly to the men's washroom. Looking in the mirror, he realized that the damage wasn't as bad as he had thought it would be. His cut was inside the lip so no one would notice, and there was no swelling to speak of. His mother would've been worried to death and called Mrs. Vernon to chastise her for taking her anger out on Stan. "*Best let the women folk be,*" he thought.

He splashed water on his face, looked in the mirror, and expected to see a monster. Stan didn't see that monster that Mrs. Vernon saw. Instead, he saw himself. He looked no different than he had that morning or the last week. He saw what he had seen for his entire life. He was who he was. What happened was ten years ago. He had paid the price and hadn't been home since. He now knew coming back was indeed the right thing to do.

Stan finished in the washroom and walked down to the end of the counter where Wanda was serving another customer.

"Sorry for that," Stan apologized.

"That? That was nothing. You seem to've forgotten how things go on Friday nights after the game. Besides, Mrs. Vernon is a pompous bitch and you should've popped her one back."

They both chuckled at her comment. The support made Stan feel welcome again.

"Can I get a coffee to go?"

"Seriously? You want one of our coffees?" Wanda was surprised by Stan's request.

"Yeah, I need something stronger than water after that."

"We don't have take-out cups. Go buy a travel mug and the fill up of coffee is free." Wanda pointed through the doors to the general store section of the building.

Stan thanked her, went and bought the cheapest travel mug he could find, and had it filled with coffee. As Wanda filled his mug, he realized that it might've been a mistake; the coffee was indeed as black as tar.

Stan left a tip. "Thanks," he said.

"For the coffee? You won't thank me if you drink all of that."

"Not for the coffee. For, well, you know."

Wanda smirked. "That was fun; besides, she deserved it."

"I'll stop by before I leave for the city."

"You do that, Mr. Sanburg," Wanda ordered.

Stan left the restaurant and took a sip of his coffee. It was as bad as he remembered, but at least it shook the cobwebs from his mind. He got in the car, started the engine, pulled out of the parking lot, and headed for his childhood home.

SATURDAY AFTERNOON

The large stone farm house sat in the middle of the forest, miles from any town or city, far from any paved roads, surrounded by dense woods and brush. The house had been the Sanburg family home for more than four generations, and over that time the land the house sat on had never been developed or turned into farmland. It had simply remained an undisturbed forest, possibly as far back as anyone in the region could remember. Hundreds of years earlier, the grounds had been home to tribes of Native American Indians who had been driven from the lands when European settlers arrived. A small river ran along the back of the old property and meandered through the land to a small lake on the eastern side.

Over the generations, many of the Sanburgs had been born and raised there, and then left the family home for the city hours away. Only the parents of the last generation of children continued to live in the house to keep the ancient dwelling in liveable condition and the tradition alive. Recently, the house had become more of a gathering place for the extended family. Each summer, the Sanburg clan would return to the house for a weekend family reunion, and some of the older family members would take it upon themselves to do a little maintenance on the historical building. It was something they felt they owed to what was referred to as "the old matriarch home."

It had been more than five years since Stan had been home, and although he missed his family and the reunions, he had always hated - detested - the house he grew up in. He was never sure why he hated living there. He thought that perhaps it was the same reason he did so well as a realtor. He always knew when his clients entered a home and felt at one with the house. The hairs on the back of his neck stood erect, goose bumps covered his arms, and he felt that chill he still remembered from when he was a child.

Stan sipped his coffee to chase away the nervousness he felt about seeing his parents again, and carefully placed the travel mug in the cup holder, taking his eyes off the road. The car hit another pothole, causing the hot liquid to jump out of the small hole in the lid and splatter the centre console with black liquid drops.

"Shit." He flipped the lid down, locking it in place, wiped the coffee droplets from the console, and licked his finger clean. He tasted a mixture of coffee and car cleaner. He gagged a bit, but it was worth the taste to avoid having dried coffee stains on his new black leather interior.

Stan kept the lid locked for the remainder of the trip, and spit several times out the window in an attempt to rid his taste buds of the disgusting mixture. He then noticed that the layer of dust that covered the dash was thicker that it had been earlier as he drove down the long winding dirt road. He blindly reached into the door pocket, pulled out a dust wipe, and started to dab up the loose road dust he had collected when the windows were down.

The scenery started to look familiar. He recognized some of the neighbours' farmhouses from his childhood. That comfortable feeling he looked for in his clients when they found their home still did not stir inside him as he approached the driveway leading to his house. He turned from one dirt road to another. The trees had started to overtake the driveway and had created a canopy of oak and pine branches. Many of the new tree branches had begun to reach out from the edges of the dirt driveway and poked at Stan's Cadillac. He worked hard to keep the car interior and exterior meticulously clean, and the dirt roads, dust, and now the scratches to the paint added to the already horrible day.

"Ah, fuck!" Stan had worked extremely diligently to become the best sales agent in the district, and his reward to himself was the car of his childhood dreams, a Cadillac. He remembered the stories his grandfather had told him time and time again: that people who drive a Cadillac had reached the pinnacle of success. Stan felt he had reached his pinnacle, and had wanted that Cadillac more than he wanted a new home. He felt that comfort as soon as he sat behind the wheel. It was his home. The thought that the tree branches that grew out from the driveway of his youth were now marking the symbol of his success pissed him off greatly.

The canopy of tree branches caused the automatic lights to turn on and il-luminate the road ahead. Stan made a small turn to the right and saw children running around the front yard. As he completed the turn, they came into full view: more than two dozen people sat at old wooden picnic tables, others stood in front of the barbeque and cooked burgers and hot dogs, some of the adults had gathered and were holding cans of beer and smoking cigarettes away from the kids. Along the left, cars and pickups lined the yard on the makeshift parking lot. Stan parked away from the other cars and trucks, hoping that the distance would prevent any further damage to his new car. He recognized his father's old pickup and decided to park beside it. The dent on the passenger side of the box was still there.

"Look at little Stanley driving his big Caddy!" Stan heard someone yell out as he exited his car and hit the trunk release button. He turned to the crowd and calmly waved, not sure who had made the sarcastic comment. He didn't want the others to see him inspect the paint on the driver's side of his car, so he casually glanced at the shiny black surface as he slowly walked to the trunk and ran his fingers along the finish. There were only surface scratches that he was sure could be buffed out. He lifted the trunk lid and pulled out his weekend bag. A gentle tap and the trunk lid closed on its own.

"Hey Stanley, nice car," his cousin Brian called out while holding up a can of beer. Stan hated being called Stanley, even as a young boy. After he moved way, he filled out all legal forms as "Stan" and not "Stanley." He refused to acknowledge all references to "Stanley," but now all of his childhood torment came flooding back. Brian kept harassing him as Stan walked toward the front entrance. Stan smiled, waved back, and thought that Brian probably could've afforded a Cadillac if he didn't drink so much. *"Probably smokes pot, too,"* he thought.

The front door was open and Stan stopped in the foyer as more children ran from room to room, yelling and shrieking. The heat and humidity in the house helped the memories flood back as he saw himself and his brother doing the same thing. Stan stood in the foyer, taking it all in. The past ten years seemed to fly by as he surveyed the house: the living room to his right, the den to the left, and the stairs on the right side of the hall that led to the second story. To the left of the stairs bright lights, delicious smells, and the wonderful, familiar, metallic sounds of pots and pans and chatter that can only come from the kitchen burst forth.

"Stanley!" a woman's voice yelled out. Stan looked up the stairs to see his mother rushing down as quickly as her age would allow. He didn't mind when his mother called him by his full name. His mother wrapped her arms around his neck and hugged him tightly. She kissed him on the cheek, placed her hand on the back of his head, and ran her fingers through his hair.

"Your hair is getting so long, honey. When did you start letting your hair grow?" she asked.

Stan shook his head to make her stop examining his hair. "It's more comfortable like this. Besides, I like it long." Stan had dark black hair that he brushed back and away from his face. "And," he said, "it's getting a bit thin on top."

His mother pulled his weekend bag from his hand and yelled for one of the children to take it upstairs. She grabbed Stan's hand and led him to the kitchen.

"Stanley!" several women screamed as they turned to see Stan enter the 1950s kitchen. He stood immobile as his aunts gathered around and took turns hugging him. He smiled politely, and, looking over the elderly women, he saw the kitchen of his youth. Nothing had changed. He imagined that the cabinets most likely still held the same products in the same locations. After the hugs and the cheek squeezing had finished, he casually walked to the fridge, pulled out a cold drink, and popped the lid. Leaning back against the porcelain sink, he took a long slow drink and wiped his mouth with the back of his hand. The house still had no central air conditioning. His mother opted for a vintage solid still fan that his father had mounted high up in the corner to prevent the children from sticking their fingers into the steel blades. Fans from that decade weren't made of plastic but of coated metal, and sported nothing more than a few decorative wire bars to remind you that sticking your fingers into the blades was dangerous. Unlike today, when no one takes responsibility for their own actions, he only had to stick his finger in the fan once as a child to learn his lesson, Stan remembered. He still had the scar on the side of his index finger as a war wound.

His mother and aunts asked him about his job, city living, and when he was going to move back home. Stan smiled, choosing not to tell them he never planned on moving home. It took an incredible amount of courage just to make the weekend reunion.

"Have you seen your dad yet?" his mother asked.

Stan took a drink from the can, shook his head from side to side, and remained silent.

"You really should go find him. He's been waiting for you to get here all day."

"I will, soon. Just want to get settled in first."

Several pies, cakes, roasts, and chickens were laid out on the kitchen table, ready to be devoured outside on the picnic tables. Stan grabbed a plate from the cabinet - he was right, their location hadn't changed - and cut himself a piece of sugar pie. As he continued to stand at the counter, the women quizzed him about his new car they'd heard so much about, his relationships, and almost every aspect of his life. He laughed at the questions about his love life and gave secret looks to his mother as his aunts continued their interrogation.

"Just haven't found the right one yet. When I do, ladies, you'll be the first to know." Stan pointed his fork at his aunts to emphasize his point.

One of the aunts spoke up. "What about that nice girl you were seeing when you first started high school. She was sweet. And if I remember, she was smashing."

Stan laughed. "Smashing. Who says 'smashing' anymore? And yes, Rosalyn was totally smashing. But, she left." He stopped abruptly, hoping his aunts would do the same.

His mother knew about the circumstances behind Rosalyn's disappearance and what was really going on in his life. It was their secret, one that neither would divulge.

Stan finished his pie, put his plate in the sink, and kissed his mother before he headed outside to see his relatives, something he dreaded. He stepped through the front door onto the stone entrance and looked out at the front yard to see his cousins, their spouses, nieces, and nephews enjoying the summer heat.

Stan walked about the front yard, shaking hands with distant cousins, chatting about life, and answering questions about how he could afford his childhood dream car. He simply told everyone he was really quite good at selling real estate. Stan finished his can of pop, tossed it into the large blue barrel used as a recycling box, and continued to walk around. He prepared a plate of tossed salad, some questionably warm potato salad that had been out too long in the hot afternoon sun, and cold beans, and sat at the edge of the picnic table. Just before he started eating, a large figure sat beside him and cast him in shadow.

"Stanley." His father stared straight ahead.

"Dad, please, I've told you since I was ten that I prefer 'Stan.' 'Stanley' is great if you're a snot-nosed five-year-old."

The elder Sanburg leaned in and gave his son a kiss on the cheek where Mrs. Vernon had slapped him earlier. "Miss you, boy. It's been too long."

Stan felt a bit of a sting on his cheek, touched his face, and was reminded of when he was a boy and his mother and father used to kiss his boo-boos to make them feel better. "*Son-of-a-bitch, it works,*" he told himself. He thought briefly about wiping the moisture from his cheek but decided against it. He smiled back at his dad. "It has. How's the house?" He pointed towards it with his head.

"Frankly, I'm a little worried. No one wants to live in an old stone house anymore. She's a solid building, but she's hard to heat in the winter and hard to cool in the summer. If you don't take over the house when your mom and I pass, it'll be the first time in over a hundred years since the house was built that a Sanburg hasn't lived in it." His father kept his head down as he spoke, sad in the knowledge that times had changed and left him behind.

Stan put his arm around his father's shoulders and pulled him in tight. "I haven't made up my mind yet, and besides, you and Ma are gonna be around for a long time. I don't have to decide right away. And there's a lot of people here you could ask if they want the house." Stan scanned the yard as dozens of people scurried about.

"They aren't Sanburgs. They're from your mother's side of the family, and the house has always had a Sanburg living in it. I love them as much as anyone can, but I want blood to be in charge of the home. And you're the last one. Your mother would've loved to have had more kids, but she couldn't. Or I couldn't. It doesn't matter. What matters is you living here. I can't imagine someone buying the house and tearing it down and turning it into condos."

Stan laughed loudly. "Dad, I seriously doubt they would tear down a beautiful old house with stone work like this, and look at that woodwork. That craftsmanship is something you can't duplicate nowadays unless you spend big bucks. This house is worth a mint even in its present condition. It just may need, well, wiring, insulation, heating system, cooling system, new roof, new windows, plumbing, and - we have too many unwanted guests living here."

Mr. Sanburg looked around, shocked that his son would have brought up the subject. He hoped that no one heard Stan mention the unwanted guests.

"I've asked you never to mention that." His father had a stern look on his face.

Stan stood up from the picnic table. "Not talking about something doesn't make it go away." He tossed his half-finished plate of food in the garbage and walked into the house.

SATURDAY NIGHT

Hours later the sun had set, the roast chickens had been devoured, what little was left of the sides and desserts had been placed in plastic containers, and what couldn't fit in the fridge had been packed in coolers with ice and divided up between the families. Trailers and campers had closed their doors to prevent mosquitoes from coming inside for the night. Shorts had been replaced with long pants, and T-shirts with jackets, as everyone sat around fires that roared high into the night sky. Tiny sparks floated up and meandered, hoping they would drift high enough to be with the stars.

Stan sat between his cousin Brian and his wife Meredith. Their two children, Lisa and Judy, were fast asleep on their favourite uncle's lap. A full day of running around outside with other cousins whom they hadn't seen since last year's family reunion, and eating too many sugary desserts, had taken their toll on most of the children. Stan stroked his nieces' hair as he caught up with Brian and Meredith. Even though Brian and Stan had been close as children, playing in the same yard, doing pretty much the same things that Lisa and Judy had done all day, they now only saw each other at the reunions, and Stan had missed the last five.

"Is selling houses that profitable?" Brian asked.

"Selling commercial property is more profitable. I travel around the whole eastern township selling buildings, warehouses, businesses, and retail properties. It's a lot of fun, you meet a lot of people, and my goal is to retire early."

Meredith covered Lisa with her sweater as she slept. "Aren't you lonely?"

Stan smiled a fake smile. "Nah, I'm too busy to be lonely. My boss says I've had the best sales figures in this half of the country and I could make partner in a few years. Then I might think about settling down."

"Seems lonely," Meredith said quietly, almost not wanting Stan to hear her.

It was lonely. Stan was isolated, but keeping busy was his way of avoiding thinking about things that had been, things that could've been. He did want things to be different, but he accepted his fate and made the best of it.

"Like I said, too busy to be lonely." Stan smiled at Meredith. She understood that he wanted to drop the conversation.

Stan adjusted his jacket and the gold chain around his neck became visible. He quickly stuck the chain back under his shirt.

"Are you still wearing that thing?" Brian asked, almost jokingly.

"Yeah." Stan was embarrassed.

"What thing?" Meredith broke in.

"Stan's been wearing this good luck charm thing since high school. I think he got it at Wal-Mart or some place." Brian laughed loudly. "Show her, Stan."

"It's an Indian charm, not a good luck charm. It's meant to drive away the spirit sucker Kushtaka." Stan quickly flashed the wolf tooth wrapped in its leather band, then tucked the charm back in his shirt and zipped up his jacket to the top. Unknown to Stan, however, the zipper caught the decades-old leather and ripped a strand. The wolf tooth fell from the chain, but was held at Stan's waist where his shirt was tucked into his pants.

"Does it keep all the boogie men away, too?" Brian held out his hands and waved his fingers up and down.

"So far, so good."

"Stop teasing him," Meredith ordered Brian. Brian shrunk in his chair and changed the topic of conversation.

The three of them continued to make small talk about work, life, children, and all the things that adults discuss to make them feel as if they have finally grown up. Stan kept up the charade with Brian, enjoying talking to his boyhood friend with whom he had lost touch so many years ago. As Brian spoke, Stan wondered if he could ever be like him: a parent, a husband, responsible. Stan thought maybe he would get a puppy and see if he could handle the responsibility. Brian continued to bestow the virtues of parenthood, and Stan decided a puppy was too much; he would start with a ficus - no, maybe a cactus.

Most of the children had gone to bed in their respective campers, and talk of going into town to visit the new country bar was making its way around the parents. Brian picked up Judy, and Meredith hoisted the younger Lisa. Neither woke as they hung like rag dolls over their parents' shoulders.

"Are you coming with us to the new bar?" Meredith asked Stan. "Everyone is going."

"Nah, I'm gonna stay behind. Besides, someone has to take care of the kids while the mommies and daddies have their play time." He held out his arms to take the two girls. "It's getting chilly out; I'll take the girls upstairs and put them in my bed. Then I'll stay out here and watch over the rest of the kids to make sure everything is okay."

"You sure? Even your mom and dad are coming." Brian was trying to coax Stan into joining them.

"Gimme." Stan held out his arms to take Lisa and Judy. Brian and Meredith surrendered their children willingly and ran to their trailer to change and join the rest of the family in town.

"And I thought I was the irresponsible one?" Stan held his two nieces up high and walked in through the open front door, kicking it closed with his foot and making his way upstairs to his childhood bedroom. He pushed the heavy wooden door open with his back. The weight of the door reminded him of how the rest of the house was built. Laying the two girls down on his bed, he covered them with a light blanket, went to his closet, and found Pooh. Stan held the plush Pooh Bear in front of him. "Hello, old friend. Protect my two nieces the way you protected me on those dark nights," he said in a whisper. Stan laid the bear between the two girls, kissed them on their heads, and went back outside to play night watchman.

*****

Stan sat by the last remaining fire pit, his laptop open, the light of the screen casting his face in an eerie glow. He kept tossing more wood onto the fire, hoping it would keep the night at bay. His back could feel the cool air, but his face dripped with sweat from the heat of the fire that burned high into the night. His intention was to finish the paperwork on the commercial retail space he was selling, but instead, he was playing chess against the computer. He had forgotten how bad the Internet service was out here in the land of lost time. Even his cellphone only had one bar, so using it as a Wi-Fi hot spot wasn't going to work well.

The computer won the first two games, and he was losing badly on the third. Between each game, Stan walked around and checked on each trailer to make sure the children were still sleeping, and hadn't woken up and wandered off into the bush. He would glance up occasionally at his bedroom window, as if seeing the window made everything all right.

Stan finished his can of Diet Dr. Pepper and walked to the edge of the woods to relieve himself. He didn't want to go inside to use the bathroom and leave the children unattended. Walking back to the fire, he glanced quickly up at the bedroom window where the girls lay sleeping and thought he saw a distorted figure pass in front. He stopped short. His eyes never left the window. For more than a minute he stood, not breathing, unmoving, eyes locked on the bedroom window of his youth, waiting to see if what he thought he saw was real. Nothing happened. He slowly took a deep breath, then let it out. It must have been a shadow from the fire, he rationalized.

As Stan walked back to the fire, he kept his focus on that one window. Each blind step was calculated and precise as he found his way back to his seat. He slid his feet in the damp grass to avoid tripping over toys that had been left out or fallen branches from the trees.

In the corner of the window, a dark shadow appeared for just a second, then disappeared. Stan stopped short. He stared at the window; the shadow came fully into frame in the four panes, stopped, and the shape appeared. He felt vomit rise in his throat, tasted the bile, and forced it back down. Everything inside of him wanted to run upstairs to see if he was right, but his body refused to co-operate.

The shadow moved again, turned, and looked out the window directly at

Stan. Stan's focus zoomed in and locked on the shadow's face. Immediately, Stan knew. His pulse quickened, adrenaline surged, he clenched his teeth, and anger overcame any fear.

"Noooooooo!" Years of pent up rage and frustration welled up inside him. Every neuron fired simultaneously, his muscles twitched, and his heart beat so hard within his chest he thought it would burst forth.

Stan ran through the wet grass. His feet slipped but he caught himself each time and ran up the stone steps, pushed open the front door, and sent it smashing into the wall then bouncing closed behind him. He raced through the front foyer to the den. He found his father's desk and pulled at the drawer that held what he needed, but it refused to open. "*Of course it was locked, you idiot, there's always kids around,*" he berated himself. He grabbed the top of the desk and toppled it to the floor, then kicked at the back wooden panel of the piece of furniture until the wood cracked. He pried his fingers into the crack and peeled back a large piece of wood. He then reached blindly inside until he felt the cold steel of his father's revolver that he kept locked in his desk.

"*This isn't going to happen again,*" he thought to himself. "*No fucking way is this happening.*"

Stan ran up the stairs, fully expecting to meet the figure that cast the shadow in his bedroom. He took the stairs two at a time, topped the landing, turned and fell into the wall, righted himself, and pushed the heavy wooden door to his bedroom open. He held the gun high, pointing it in front of him. He scanned the room: nothing. He entered the room slowly, and saw the two girls still sleeping on the bed. After opening the closet, he ripped down whatever clothes were hanging inside and threw them to the floor.

Stan heard a sound behind him, spun on his heels, and pointed the gun at Lisa, who was stirring under the blankets.

"Uncle Stanley. What are you doing?" With only the moonlight coming in through the window, Lisa didn't see her uncle pointing a gun at her, she just saw him pulling clothes down from the bar in the closet.

Stan held a finger to his pursed lips, asking his niece to keep silent. Just then, Judy began to wake up and started to rub her eyes.

"Sweetie, shhh." Stan requested that his two nieces keep quiet. Not wanting to scare them any further, he held the gun low against his leg.

Stan turned his attention back to his task of finding whatever was in the room. He turned back to the closet, checking deep into the corners. Finding nothing, he closed the closet door and walked slowly towards the bed the two girls were on. He lowered himself to one knee and carefully peered under the bed. It was dark and impossible to see anything, so he used his free arm to sweep from side to side. Stan found nothing, stood up, and saw that he had terrified the two girls. He tucked the gun in the small of his back and sat on the bed between them.

"Did you two see anything in the room, anything at all?" he asked them softly, quietly.

"Nope," Judy replied. Lisa shook her head from side to side.

Stan sighed, thinking that his childhood fears had taken control of him again. He placed his hand on Judy's head and stroked her hair. "K. Thanks, girls."

"What did you see, Uncle Stanley?"

"I thought I saw someone run through the bedroom and I got scared."

The two girls laughed out loud. "Uncle Stanley is a scaredy-cat!" proclaimed Lisa.

"You betcha I'm a scaredy-cat when it comes to my two girls. Sorry I woke you. Go back to sleep and dream of nice things." Stan kissed each niece on the top of the head and watched as they snuggled up on his bed.

As Stan pulled the blanket up high, he heard glass shatter down the hall. Startled, he turned on his heels and looked out into the hall. The moonlight broke through the far window and cast a dark shadowy figure against the wall as the thing lumbered towards the bedroom.

Judy and Lisa sprang up and stared out the bedroom door. They couldn't see anything except a moving shadow, and the sound of claws slowly being dragged against the hardwood floor kept their attention focused on the hall. No one dared make a noise, and their gazes never wavered from the tall, misshapen shadow figure as it progressed closer to the bedroom.

"Uncle Stan. I'm a scaredy-cat now," Lisa whispered.

Stan pushed the children back into the bedroom and turned back to the door, slamming it closed, but not before he caught a scent that almost caused him to vomit. The scent reminded him of road kill left out in the sun too long. His mind went back in time and he remembered that smell, and the memories that accompanied it. He felt his pulse quicken, and his breathing became heavy. Stan wanted to leave; he wanted to run away and never come back.

He put his shoulder and all of his weight against the door as he fumbled for the antique lock key to secure it. Once the bolt was in place, he pulled the brass key from the lock and pocketed it.

A forceful bump on the opposite side of the door sent Stan flying to the floor. The gun he had tucked in the small of his back fell and slid across the floor under the bedside table. Stan sprang up and put his back against the door. On the other side of the thick wood barrier, he heard a low growl of something indistinguishable. It was deep, throaty, and wet. Even with the door between them, the stench was overwhelming. Hearing the growl, the girls started to cry and scream. Whatever it was on the other side hit the door again. Stan was certain the old wood door would hold for a long time, but he wasn't so sure of the brass door lock. With enough force, it might break free of the wood and allow the thing to enter the room, he worried.

"Uncle Stanley, make it stop," Lisa screamed as she stood, frozen in place.

"I'm trying, honey." Stan knew it wouldn't stop. He knew from experience that once it made its appearance, only the light of day or getting what it came for would make it go away. And Stan wasn't about to let that thing get anything tonight.

Stan faced the door, placed both hands up high, and braced his feet back so that all of his weight was against it. He hoped he could keep whatever was in the hall out until his parents returned and scared it away. He closed his eyes and put his head down as another hit to the door shook him. Stan held his ground and refused to give in again. Once more, the thing in the hall hit the door with such force that Stan's feet slipped out from under him and he fell flat, face first to the ground. He felt his nose fracture as he hit the hardwood floor and tasted blood in his mouth. He pushed himself back up, spit blood onto the door, and re-assumed his position. Stan felt vibrations in his palms through the door as claws scratched at the wood and dug tiny channels into the thick, solid panel. The scratching was constant. Eventually, even the thickest wood would weaken from the non-stop clawing.

"Judy," Stan screamed.

"Don't yell at me, Uncle Stan." Judy was cowering on the bed, the blanket pulled up high around her neck.

Stan softened his voice, breathing in hard through his nose and feeling the blood drain into his mouth. He spit again and in a calm voice asked, "Judy, honey, can you find Uncle Stan's gun please?"

"Mom and Dad said guns are bad. Only bad men have guns," she argued.

"Mom and Dad are right, honey, but sometimes even good men need guns. Police have guns to keep the bad men away, right? I'm a good man trying to keep the bad man on the other side of the door away." Stan wasn't looking at Judy, he was looking down at the floor, watching the shadow of the bad thing move about as it continued to claw at the door.

Judy refused to move, preferring the protection of the blanket to helping her uncle. No one noticed Lisa, who had heard her uncle's request to find his gun and located it under the bedside table. Lisa held the gun with two hands and began to walk towards the door.

Lisa was only feet from the door when the thing in the hall let out an ear-piercing growl in frustration, causing her to squeeze the revolver's trigger. Wood splintered beside Stan's left hand as the bullet penetrated only an inch or so into the door. The room filled with gunpowder smoke, and Stan pulled his hand back and fell again to the floor. He was now looking under the door, and in the dim light he could make out the foot of whatever it was trying to make its way into the bedroom. Stan completely forgot that Lisa had almost shot him, as he was focused on the matted hairy foot of the humanoid monster now only inches away from him. The smell was intense, putrid, and Stan was hit with another wave of nausea.

Stan turned and sat against the door. Lisa had dropped the gun after she fired it and stood crying. It was almost beautiful. The tears shone like tiny diamonds on her cheeks as the moonlight reflected off them. Stan held out his arms and Lisa fell into him. She was sobbing and Stan could feel her chest heave as she cried.

"Don't worry, honey. Nobody got hurt and you found Uncle Stan's gun. You're a good girl. A brave girl." Stan lifted her up and back so he could see her face. "You're very brave. You need to stand and go protect your sister now, okay?"

Lisa nodded her head. "K."

Stan put her down on the floor. "Watch your feet, honey. There're splinters everywhere. You might hurt yourself."

Suddenly, it hit him.

Stan picked up the gun from the floor, then laid flat at the base of the door. The smell assaulted him again as he positioned the barrel of the revolver under the door, less than an inch from the foot of the beast. He pulled the trigger, once, twice, three times in rapid succession. The bullets entered the foot of the beast, fracturing bones and tearing through soft tissue. Stan's ears rang and smoke filled the air around him. The smell of gunpowder masked the putrid odour of the beast only momentarily.

From the other side of the door, the beast screamed in agony and fell backwards onto the floor. With only an inch slot to look under, Stan saw the beast rolling about. He had two shots left. Placing the revolver back under the door, he aimed at the largest bulk of fur closest to him. He pulled the trigger once more. The beast rolled away from the door and screamed as the bullet penetrated its side. The howl was unlike anything Stan had ever heard. The beast was hurt badly, and the way it was howling in pain, Stan almost felt sorry for it.

He waited and watched under the door for several minutes as the beast continued to wail in agony. Lisa and Judy, both on the bed with the blanket pulled up high, were crying loudly to drown out the sounds of pain coming from the other side of the door. They cried not because they were afraid any more, but because they felt compassion for the beast. Compassion, which Stan knew the beast certainly didn't have when it took Rosalyn.

Stan lay on the floor and pressed his head down to see what he could from beneath the door. Only a small part of the beast was visible. What he could see looked humanoid - like a man covered in thick dark brown fur - but the foot he shot was more like that of a bear.

Something pinched him at the waist and he winced. He twisted and adjusted himself to see if a splinter of wood had fallen down his pants. Still looking under the door, he stuck his hand up his shirt at the waist and felt around. Panic overtook him when he touched the tooth that had fallen from his chain.

Stan bolted upright, never letting go of the charm, and in the dim light he inspected it. The leather that wrapped around the wolf's tooth was unbroken. "*The spell should still be intact. It has to be,*" he determined. "*I was still touching it. Just the piece that held it on to the chain broke.*" Stan removed the chain from around his neck, and with the two broken ends of leather, tied a knot around the chain. "*This has to work,*" he thought, and slipped the chain back in place.

He lay back down on the floor, but he had lost sight of the beast when he was re-attaching the tooth to the chain. He closed his eyes and prayed to his father's friend who had put the original spell on the tooth to keep him safe. The children continued to cry as Stan prayed.

The crying and the howling the beast was making slowed and became less intense. It then turned to almost human sobbing. With his eyes closed, Stan hoped the beast was dying or close to death.

"Hey, what's going on up there?"

"Uncle Stan, are you up there?"

Voices from outside broke Stan's trance.

There was yelling and screaming coming from the front yard, as the commotion in the bedroom had woken up the children who were sleeping in the trailers. Getting up, Stan checked the lock on the door, and pulled the handle a few times to make sure that it was still providing a solid barrier between the beast out in the hall and the children inside.

Stan went to the window and saw about a dozen children looking up at him.

"The front door was locked, Uncle Stan. We couldn't get inside," one of the boys said.

"Everything should be fine now. Please, make sure everyone goes back to bed and lock the trailer doors and don't open them until your parents come home."

"Uncle Stan, I don't - "

Stan raised his voice. "Just do it."

The children had never heard Uncle Stan raise his voice before. They silently dispersed, and went back to their trailers and did as they were told.

Stan went back to the door, lay down, and pressed himself closer to the floor. He tried to see the beast from under the door, but it was gone. He still heard the sobbing, but now there was also laboured breathing. "*It must have moved,*" he thought.

"Girls, go into the closet and cover yourselves with the clothing, and don't come out until I call for you, K? Come here." Judy and Lisa carefully walked closer to their uncle. Stan removed the chain from around his neck and gave it to Judy. "You're the big sister so you have to take care of Lisa. This will protect you and your sister from anything bad. Keep it tight in your hand and whatever you do, don't let it go. K?"

Stan turned to Lisa. "Judy will take care of you but you have to take care of the key." Stan held the brass key for the bedroom door in front of Lisa. "You have to keep the door locked until I give you the magic password. Can you do that?"

Lisa nodded her head up and down as tears flowed. "What's the magic password?"

Stan thought for a moment. "Uncle Stanley's a scaredy-cat. Say it, Lisa."

Lisa said softly, "Uncle Stanley's a scaredy-cat," and grabbed the key that was held out in front of her.

Stan had saved one bullet in the revolver. He cocked the hammer back as Lisa unlocked the bedroom door. Slowly, at a snail's pace, he pulled the door open and peered one way down the hall, then the other. Directly in front of the door he saw a small pool of blood, and a few tufts of dark fur lay scattered about. A trail of blood led down the hall. Stan opened the door wide and, the revolver leading the way, he stepped out and closed the door.

Behind the door, Lisa inserted the key and locked it from the inside, then grasped the key with both hands. Judy held the good luck charm close to her chest and led her sister to the closet.

The moon had shifted in the late night sky and the hallway was more in shadow, which made it difficult for Stan to see much. From his childhood days, he knew where the wall switch was. The revolver was pointed in the direction of the blood trail, and with his free hand he fumbled for the switch. His fingers found it and turned the single overhead light on.

Stan closed the hammer on the revolver and ran to the body lying on the floor.

The naked girl was curled up against the wall with a severe injury to her right foot and a bullet wound in the right side of her chest. Her body was covered in a slippery, thick goo. She was shivering, her breathing was laboured, and her eyes were closed. Stan put his hand to her cheek and gently, slowly, turned her face to see it. His heart stopped as soon as he recognized her. It had been more than ten years since he had last seen her when he was walking her home that night. She was older now, but it was definitely her.

"Rosalyn," Stan softly whispered.

Rosalyn opened her eyes and gave a weak smile. "Stan? Is it gone?" she asked.

"It's gone." Stan pulled her in close, wiped the goo from her face, and kissed her on the cheek. "Come on. Let's get you to the hospital."

Stan looked down the hall to his bedroom and yelled, "Uncle Stanley's a scaredy-cat. Uncle Stanley's a scaredy-cat."

He heard the sound of metal clicking and of hinges creaking as the door slowly opened and the faces of his nieces peered around the edge of the frame. Both were still crying as they saw their uncle and stepped into the hall. The two girls, each providing strength to the other, walked hand in hand to where Stan sat cradling Rosalyn and stood over the adults.

"Is that the monster, Uncle Stanley?" asked Lisa as she pointed to Rosalyn.

Stan chuckled. "No, honey, this is Rosalyn. She was hurt by the monster and we have to get her some help. Can you find a phone and call 911?"

"Yeah."

"You guys did really good," Stan complimented his two nieces.

"I know," Judy replied, grabbed her sister's hand, and ran down the stairs to the den to call 911.

Stan pulled off his jacket and wrapped it around Rosalyn, then scooped her up in his arms. Rosalyn blindly reached down and found Stan's hand, locked her fingers around his, and twisted them. Stan pulled her in closer, closed his eyes for a moment, and felt the last decade melt away.

Stan then carried her downstairs to wait for the police and ambulance. He laid her on the couch, covered her with an afghan, and propped her head up with a few pillows.

Lisa came over to where Stan sat with Rosalyn with a tea towel she had found in the kitchen in hand, and passed it to her uncle. "For her foot," she said, and ran off.

Stan gently wrapped Rosalyn's foot and asked, "Can you talk?"

Rosalyn nodded.

"Where've you been?"

"It took me that night. I was inside it, around it, trapped. I didn't have a body, I could see what was happening but I couldn't do anything. It was like being para-lyzed. How long have I been gone?"

"Ten years."

"Ten…" Rosalyn's eyes widened and she broke down and began to cry. Stan held her tightly as he heard the siren in the distance.

Ghostbusters lyrics by Ray Parker Jr.

SOCIAL STUDIES

1

On the first day of school, the professor stood at the front of the classroom and watched her new university students as they walked past her desk and found a seat in her Social Studies class. This year was not her first teaching, but on the first day of class each year, she was always amazed at how, regardless of where she taught, the students all seemed to understand the unwritten laws of school. They fumbled about, jockeying for positions in the hierarchy of seating locations that only the young adults themselves understood. The professor watched as they took their seats: the jocks - typically, those who tried to avoid eye contact or being singled out to answer questions - at the back, and the nerds or those who wanted to participate at the front. The arrangement of those who took the desks in between still confused her. Perhaps it was more of a first come, first seat.

Mrs. Helms had been teaching for almost ten years but looked much younger than her age. She kept in shape by running and working out several times a week. Being a young, good-looking female professor in a room full of testosterone-charged young men barely out of their teens and now in the midst of becoming men often caused problems. And her youthful appearance had more than once made the female students feel uncomfortable in the knowledge that their male classmates would focus on their professor for the beginning of the semester instead of themselves.

Once everyone had taken their seats for the semester, she walked from behind her desk and sat on the corner, pulling her skirt down and making sure to keep her legs crossed. She knew that even the nerds at the front of each row would try to sneak a peek, both boys and girls. She made a mental note to start wearing pants regardless of the weather.

She sat patiently, waiting for everyone to calm down, and knowing full well that asking for silence was not a great way to start a new year. Instead, her preferred method was to give the students the benefit of the doubt, assume that they had some level of intelligence, and trust that they would stop their chatting on their own.

Her tactic worked. Within a few minutes, even the jocks at the back who refused to sit straight in their seats but preferred to rest facing their friends had stopped talking and were silently waiting for her to say something.

She stood up. "Welcome to Social Studies 101. I'm Mrs. Helms. I'll be here to guide you through the semester, but for the most part, you will direct yourselves through this course."

"I'd like to guide you," a voice yelled from the back.

"Wow, you must be really popular with the ladies with comments like that," Mrs. Helms replied.

The class broke out in a chuckle, and the identity of the boy who had anonymously made the comment was discovered as one of the jocks put his head down in embarrassment. A few in the class turned to gawk at their new classmate, who promptly glared back at them to show that he was still above them in the pecking order.

"Anyway." Mrs. Helms paused. The class turned their attention back to their professor. "Today, and today only, I will take attendance. If you choose not to show up after today, I have no problem failing each and every one of you. Since there isn't an empty seat in the class right now, I'll know who's not here soon enough, so don't try to snow me." Mrs. Helms took attendance and placed the sheet inside one of her desk drawers. She walked around, leaned against the desk, and faced the class.

"This is not - I repeat, not - an easy class. Some of you may have been confused by the class title and thought that you would be learning how to use Twitter, Instagram, and Facebook. This class will make you work hard because a lot of it is self-taught and self-study." Mrs. Helms walked up and down the aisles, and then took her seat behind her desk. "This is how Social Studies works." She pulled a newspaper from a drawer and showed it to the class. "This is your source material. No text books; you will read just the newspaper."

"What's a newspaper?" the same voice from earlier barked.

This time, no one chuckled or paid him any attention. His head lowered.

"Good question, Mr.?"

"Taggart."

"Good question, Mr. Taggart. For us older folks, this," she waved the paper in the air, "is how we used to get our information. Today, this is online. But, in my opinion, the online version lacks any tactile experience, and that, unfortunately, is something that you all lack as well. The tactile experience is what we will learn in this class. A tablet or computer is missing a lot. It's quicker, and you can access newspapers from all over the world to research a topic, but believe me when I say that the look, feel, and smell of a physical newspaper will only add to the experience."

The same voice from the back called out, "I'm all for feeling things." This time the class did laugh out loud.

"Well, Mr. Taggart, you are now my star student. Come up here, please."

A chorus of "ooos" and "ahhs" followed the young man as he stood and walked to the front of the class, and then sat on the same corner of the desk that Mrs. Helms had just vacated. Mr. Taggart was an imposing figure for a first-year university student. He stood just shy of six feet tall, weighed close to two hundred pounds, and was very good-looking with his thick, dirty-blond hair.

Mrs. Helms stood, handed Mr. Taggart the newspaper, and asked him to find an article that he found interesting. "And don't think this is a joke. Whichever article you pick will be your assignment for the year."

"I don't get it," Mr. Taggart stated. "Wadda ya mean?"

"Each of you has until the next class to bring in one article from a current printed newspaper that you want to follow up on. Like a detective, you will investigate the story through to the end of the semester, and see how one story can affect many people on different levels. Just because the media drops the story doesn't mean that it is over. You will attempt to discover why the press decided to report on it, why it made the news, who the people behind it were, what the consequences of their actions or lack of actions were; the stuff that happens after the media decides to stop reporting. You will follow the trends on social media and in the newspaper, and you will see how fast a story can be spread by tweeting it. By following the story on all the social media sites and in the newspaper, you'll see how each one takes a different perspective. You may not agree with Facebook or Twitter, but maybe the old-school paper is more mainstream than you realize. Got it?"

There was a chorus of "yea" and "sure" from the students.

"Why do we have to make our choice now and why can't we change later?" asked one of the students sitting in the very front row.

"Good question. In life, there are no do-overs. A choice we make today affects us for the rest of our lives. Being forced to make a decision today and having to stick with it for the rest of the semester teaches you the importance of every decision you make. In this case, your choice will determine what you work on for your class assignment, and the grade is subjective. I'll look at how you adjust your assignment over the course of the next few months as trends change, and those changes may affect your view on whatever topic you choose."

"I don't get it," the same student proclaimed.

"Let's say you pick a political issue, like an election. You may say that one candidate is better or worse than another at the outset, but as the race evolves, you may change your mind. So, I'll be looking for the timeline in your assignment. Twitter, Facebook, or the news media may affect your view on the party he or she represents, or the candidate may do something or say something to change your opinion." She paused to catch her breath. "And, if you change your mind or stay the course, I want to know why."

Mrs. Helms walked up and down the aisles. "There is only one major stipulation." Her voice raised in volume to emphasize her point. "You cannot pick a story about pop culture; in other words, no singers, no actors, no music, no movies, no videos, no sports, no video games. Does everyone understand?"

There was a collective moan from the class. Mr. Taggart spoke for his classmates. "That's pretty much most of our lives."

"There's more to life than that stuff. Believe me when I tell you that eventually, most of you won't even care about those things, and that in a few years you will be wondering what the kids are listening to the way we wonder what you all listen to."

"You sound like my mother," Mr. Taggart added.

Mrs. Helms smiled. "And I assume you will honour me with the same respect you afford her?"

"For sure, Mrs. H."

She smiled at Mr. Taggart. "Go ahead and pick your article, and remember the rules."

Mr. Taggart opened the newspaper, held it high, and seemed unfamiliar with how to handle the old-school media format. He looked at Mrs. Helms, silently asking if he could sit at her desk. She gestured to her seat. He sat in her chair, flipped through the paper, and slowly reviewed the articles, taking his time before selecting one. He pointed to it, indicating that his decision was made.

Mrs. Helms stood behind Mr. Taggart and reviewed his selection. "Good choice, Mr. Taggart." He smiled cockily at the class.

Mrs. Helms read the story about electric cars aloud. She then asked the class to discuss the merits of the article: why it was important to the public, the future, and the environment. Active discussions about whether or not electric cars would ever be mainstream, if the old batteries caused more pollution in landfills than the emissions from gas engines, and so on ensued. "Now that the class has helped you with a lot of what you need to research, I expect you to have a running head start, Mr. Taggart."

"Mike."

"Thank you, Mike. You still have to call me Mrs. Helms, however." A few chuckles rose from the class.

Mrs. Helms passed out a sheet of paper to each student that detailed the criteria for the year's assignment. She spoke as she handed out the instruction sheet and walked the aisles. "There is only one class assignment. There will only be one grade. No rewrites. I will review each assignment and that will determine your grade. Every class, we will discuss one person's progress, or have a group discussion on how to proceed. Bring all of your work with you to every class. And," she stopped at the back of the class, and all of the students turned to face her, "remember, you must choose your article from a printed newspaper. Do not, I repeat, do not use an electronic paper to choose your topic. You have to bring in the article that you cut from the paper. You can do your research online, but you must find your article in a print paper. I want to see your choice next class." She waved her hands across the class as some of the students moaned, while others put their foreheads to their desk. "Any questions?"

The class went silent.

Mike Taggart stood up and walked past Mrs. Helms towards his seat. "I stole the whole paper, Mrs. H, in case there's something I missed." He floated the newspaper over the heads of some of the students around his desk.

"Mr. Taggart."

He turned to face Mrs. Helms.

"Sorry."

Mrs. Helms divided the class into four study groups, making sure each group had an equal number of students with an even gender representation. She spoke to each faction, explaining the rules of the study group. Each person was responsible for his or her own final report. The students could bounce ideas off members of their respective group, but doing work for each other was forbidden.

The rest of the class was spent discussing the merits of electronic media versus print. Each person voiced his or her preference. Mrs. Helms kept a close watch on each student who participated and those who remained silent. Hers was a class that required participation, and she didn't want to have any students fall behind on the first week of school.

The bell rang, and the students replaced their desks, grabbed their backpacks, and started filing out the door. Mike Taggart stopped at the professor's desk after everyone else had already left. "I just wanted to thank you, Mrs. H."

"For what, Mike?"

"You know," he said as he held his head low.

"I know, Mike."

Mike walked out of the classroom.

2

Rose Metzel sat barefoot on her bed in leggings and an oversized sweatshirt. The bedroom door was closed, and her ear buds blocked all noise except for the music that played loudly as she flipped through the newspapers. Sheets of newspaper covered the bed, crinkling under her as she moved. Of all the things to do during the first week of the first year of university, having to go to the convenience store and buy several newspapers on the way home was not what she had expected. It was silly, she thought, to have to pay for newspapers that she could download for free on her tablet.

Rose found it hard to focus on only one article at a time with so many stories to view at once. She smelt her hands, and thought that the papers made them smell like stale fish. The constant page turning had made her fingers turn black from the ink. She rubbed her fingers on her leggings, transferring the ink to her pants. Her long, wavy black hair kept getting in her face as she leaned forward. She spun her head to the left, and her hair came to rest on her right shoulder. Rose pulled her hair tight and curled it up high into a bun on the top of her head. *"This is shit!"* she thought. Her neck was stiff and sore from leaning forward for so long. It was easier to hold her tablet upright.

Rose had been pulling straight A's in high school the previous year and wanted to maintain that average to get into medical school. It wasn't because both of her parents were doctors; Rose truly loved the idea of medicine. Having to flip through newspapers for a class in Social Studies was not what she had thought she would have to do.

Rose was upset about getting Mrs. Helms for Social Studies and about the class assignment for the year. One assignment; one singular, solitary assignment. Get it right or fail. No exams, no studies, just create a paper based on a single story that was chosen during the first week of school and would remain their choice for the rest of the semester.

"Honey! Dinner!" Rose's mother yelled from downstairs. Her mother waited and, receiving no answer, called a little louder, "Dinner!"

Rose was familiar with the evening yelling ritual. She yanked the buds from her ears and rolled off the bed, the papers ripping and crackling as she moved, some falling to the floor. She loosened her hair, letting it flow naturally down her back, and bounded down the stairs to the dinner table. Her father and mother had already taken their seats, but her older brother's chair sat vacant, since he had left for his third year of university across the country a few weeks ago. Her father made it mandatory that all family dinners were at the table, and that all electronics and televisions were off; they didn't even answer the phone while eating. Due to their substantial age differences, Rose thought it ironic as she sat there digging into her meal that her dad and professor both had the same views about electronic media.

"First day of school and they have you stuck upstairs with homework already?" Rose's mother asked. Rose was her mother, just thirty-one years her junior. Her parents had met in medical school, wed after graduation, become pregnant with Adam almost immediately, and then had Rose three years later. Her father was a surgeon, and her mother practiced family medicine. They both made a point of being home for dinner every night; family came first.

"It's a stupid assignment. I have to pick a story from the newspaper, cut it out, and follow the social ramifications of why the story is relevant in the print media, on social networks, and on TV. It's lame."

Her father pointed his empty fork at her. "Actually, that's a very good study guide. It's perfect for your studies in medicine eventually."

Rose looked at her father like he was stoned on meth. "Dad! Seriously?"

"Think about it, honey. If you have a patient with a condition that you can't diagnosis, you follow the progress, take notes, investigate the family history and patient's history, research the presenting signs and symptoms, and make a diagnosis. It's perfect for your career, hon."

Rose finishing chewing, swallowed, and pointed her fork at her father. Fork pointing had become a family trait used to emphasize a position. "Medicine is about treating patients, surgery, and healing."

"Medicine is about investigating first, surgery last. You have to diagnosis the disease and that's done through investigation and research. Research is reading books, searching the Internet, and lots of investigation with the patient and family."

"Your dad's right, hon. Even in family practice, you have to listen to the patient before treating them, and it can involve research. This project sounds like a perfect learning tool for med school," her mother added.

Rose continued to eat and argue with her parents about her future career and about school. Deep down she knew that they were right, but their dinner arguments were a part of their lives. Especially when Adam was home. Now that he had left for school, Rose felt it was her responsibility to continue the tradition.

Rose finished her plate, went to the kitchen for a small second helping of mashed potatoes, and returned to the table. They continued the banter, each person making their point before a counter point was made. The topic changed several times, and it was always light-hearted. On the rare occasions when Rose wasn't able to attend the family dinner, she always missed the conversations. Debating with two well-educated doctors wasn't always easy, but she found it stimulating.

After dinner, Rose and her parents cleaned up, loaded the dishwasher, and sat back down at the table for another tradition of tea and shortbread cookies. Her father had carried over this tradition from his family before they emigrated from Europe. The three of them sat in their usual spots at the dinner table for dessert, and the talk over tea was always more casual and relaxed, never confrontational.

Rose finished her tea, put her cup in the dishwasher, and ran back upstairs to her room. Feeling technologically deprived, she placed her buds back in her ears and cranked the music. Her head began to bob to the rhythms, and her long hair bounced about her head. She was picking up the newspapers that had fallen to the floor and tossing them back onto the bed when an article caught her eye. Rose picked up the paper and read the headline: "**Latest murder victim may be linked to other homicides.**"

Rose couldn't recall reading anything online about a killing in the past few weeks, and there hadn't been anything in the other papers. She sat on the floor, her back pressed tightly against the bed, and held the paper out before her.

Latest Murder Victim May be Linked to Other Homicides
By: Emily Nelson

Three young boys riding along the Butler Creek path made a gruesome find last Saturday.

The boys, aged eleven to thirteen, whose names haven't been released by police, found the decomposing body of a young woman. The body was found without clothes and buried in a shallow grave. It appears as though animals had dug up part of the body, which was visible from the path when the boys rode past.

Police were called in, secured the area, and began an investigation. When questioned, police refused to offer any details about the body or the identity of the victim.

Friends of Angela Blunt have already begun posting condolences to the family on her Facebook page.

Unnamed sources claim that evidence found on the body is similar to that found on two other women killed under eerily similar circumstances. All three women were found naked, in a shallow grave. Most of their hair had been cut short, and ligature used to kill them. Police are refusing to provide any more details regarding what else they may have discovered, or if the three dead women may have been murdered by the same person.

Rose tore the page from the paper and read the article again. Rummaging through her school backpack, she found a purple highlighter. She reread the article, highlighting the sections she found important. Once she determined which sections were significant, she booted up her laptop and did a Google search for anything relating to the story she had just read.

The Google search revealed over twenty-three million hits on female bodies found all over North America. She thought for a moment, and then refined the search to "murders female Ottawa." The number of hits declined dramatically to three hundred thousand. Rose clicked on the first of the results, read it, and discounted it. This process continued over and over again and yielded no new information. Finally, she scanned each hit and only opened the ones that came from a local newspaper. Still, nothing new was discovered. The only link she found was to the same story she had torn from the paper.

After hours of scouring for more information, her back hurt, her neck was stiff, and the laptop battery was getting low. Rose decided it was time to get ready for bed. She cleaned up the loose pages of newspaper that were scattered about her bedroom, powered down her laptop, and plugged it in to charge overnight.

Rose finished her night time rituals, stripped down, put on her father's old dress shirt she wore as a nightshirt, and crawled into bed. She fluffed up her pillow as her mind raced with thoughts of the story she had chosen. She realized that she hadn't even known about the dead girl until she'd read the paper. None of her social circles had made any mention of the murder or any of the circumstances behind it. Now she knew why her professor made them pick their story assignment from a newspaper. Her news came from Facebook and Twitter. Her world was secluded and restricted. Rose got to choose what information came in, and everything was filtered according to what she wanted to know. A traditional newspaper reported on all the news of the day and followed up on previously reported stories. Newspapers on the Internet had a tendency to be less complete than their print counterparts unless you paid for the full electronic version of the paper. She understood the point her professor was trying to convey.

Rose closed her eyes, turned over, tucked her arm under the pillow, and drifted off to sleep. Rose went to sleep knowing she had found her story.

3

Rose woke up to the sound of her parents taking turns in the bathroom. She picked up her phone, swiped up, and saw that it was before six in the morning. She pulled the pillow tightly over her head and tried to drown out the noise. The sounds were now muffled but still loud enough to keep her up. She let out a deep growl that echoed under the pillow. She flipped the pillow back under her head and let out another growl that she hoped her parents would hear. They didn't, but it still felt good to vent.

Rose pulled the blankets back, slid her feet to the floor, and heard a crinkle beneath her in the dark. She made fists with her toes and curled the newspaper between them. It tickled her feet and she smiled gently. Sitting on the side of the bed, she checked her email and text messages on her phone. Most of the texts were from friends complaining about the first day of university, and the difficulties of finding classrooms and managing homework. A few friends who were also in the Social Studies class were whining about having to buy newspapers. They felt embarrassed about reading through media that belonged to their grandparents. Rose curled her toes, felt the tickle, and smiled. Her friend Jenny complained that anybody who was anybody wouldn't read the newspaper. Rose sent Jenny a short text:

"*Yo bitch had a slam with the old school paper found my story. U?*"

Rose waited, but Jenny failed to respond immediately so she walked out into the hall. Her mother passed by and gave her a peck on the cheek and a quick "Morning hon" as she walked past. The bathroom door was locked, indicating that her dad was still inside. She didn't have to pee badly enough to try the downstairs bathroom.

Zombie-like, Rose returned to the bedroom, closed the door behind her, and fell face first onto her bed. She decided to wait for the noise to subside before trying the bathroom door again. Her eyes were closed, her mind in a fog, and her thoughts drifted back to the newspaper article: dead girl, murdered, details, how did she die? The article provided few details, where could she find out more about what happened, how did she die, what was it like? Having two parents in the medical field, she had been exposed to anatomy all her life, so she was acutely aware of what happens when the body dies. Her mind filled with emotions as she imagined someone's hands around her throat, squeezing tightly. Her apprehension increased as she thought of her airway being constricted, the pressure building inside her throat, her lungs beginning to burn, wanting air. She couldn't exhale; she couldn't inhale. The pressure in her eyes increased, and tiny blood vessels exploded. She wanted to speak, to scream, but she couldn't.

Rose jumped up from the bed. She was dripping with sweat. Had she fallen back to sleep and dreamt the whole scenario? She sat on the edge of her bed and started to cry. Is this what the dead girl went through before she died? Is this what death was? Rose wiped the hair back from her face and felt the moisture at the back of her neck. She sat upright, wiped her nose with the back of her hand, and then cleaned her hand on her nightshirt.

The noises from the hallway had disappeared. Rose made her way to the bathroom, started the shower, disrobed, and stood under the stream. She tilted her head back and let the hot water run across her face. She felt as if she could have stayed there forever. It was safe and warm. After shaving her legs, she washed her hair, shut off the shower, and made her way back to her bedroom. Rose felt insecure and scared. Locking the door behind her, she leaned against it. She now regretted her choice for the Social Studies assignment. Was it dread or excitement, she wondered?

On the end table, her phone was beeping and the red light was flashing. Rose swiped up to bring the screen to life. She jumped when she saw the time displayed on the phone, and ignored the messages. She knew she must have fallen back to sleep - school started in less than thirty minutes.

Rose pulled her hair back into a ponytail, which she despised doing. She loved her thick, long, wavy black hair, and the way it framed her face. Pulling it back in public meant people could see her ears. She hated her ears. She never wore earrings; that would bring attention to her ears. Her hair was wet, and she knew that it would still be damp at the end of the day.

Five minutes of makeup, yesterday's jeans, a clean top, socks, and her favourite boots, and she ran downstairs. Everyone was gone, and the house was empty and quiet. She grabbed an apple while the Tassimo made her a chai tea latte to go in a travel mug. After pulling her keys from her purse, she tossed her backpack to the passenger seat, started the car, and backed out of the driveway. The time on the radio showed that she had less than ten minutes. She munched on the apple and drank the tea as she drove.

Rose pulled into the parking lot, killed the engine, and ran to class. Her professor stood at the door and was preparing to close it as she ducked past, looking up at him and smiling sheepishly. She found the seat she had chosen the day before, placed her backpack between her feet, and pulled out her textbook and tablet. She listened as the professor started the class, but her mind promptly wandered back to the dead girl.

Rose was almost upset with herself that she hadn't been aware of the murder. A young girl had been killed, and all she was concerned about was her circle of friends on Facebook. Her mother was right: there really were more important things in life than using social media to spy on your friends' lives. The majority of her time - before school, in school, after school, at work, and at home - was spent on some form of social media.

The professor spoke at the front of the class, walked up and down the aisles, and scribbled on the blackboard. Rose looked at the professor but didn't absorb anything of what was said in class. The professor pulled out a book and told the class to turn to the first chapter. Some of the students opened books, while others had downloaded the textbooks on to their tablets. Rose looked around the class and did a quick survey. Most of the students were using tablets; only a few diehards were using books. "*Probably too poor to buy a pad*," she thought to herself.

"Excuse me, sir," Rose said suddenly, raising her hand.

"Yes." The professor pointed at Rose.

"My tablet is dead. I know I plugged it in last night. Sorry."

The professor tapped a few books on the corner of his desk. "The last time I checked, you didn't have to recharge a book. Come on up."

"Thanks."

Rose stood, walked to the professor's desk, retrieved a copy of the textbook, and sat back down. She turned to the first chapter. As she opened the book, she noticed a musty smell. She lowered her head slightly and inhaled. It wasn't musty; it was something else that she couldn't quite put her finger on. With her eyes closed, she inhaled deeply, and the scent filled her nose and travelled down into her lungs. She loved the smell. It was a combination of the ink, the paper, the moisture in the paper; she wasn't sure. Rose felt a warmth creep up on her. It was unlike anything she had experienced before, even though she had read books all her life. That smell had most likely been in all the other books, but she had never noticed it before. Maybe it was a smell that reminded her of her childhood, when she used to play with the hardbound books and pretend to read Dr. Seuss.

The clock indicated the end of the class. The professor had been in mid-sentence, but the students powered down their tablets, closed their books, packed up their bags, and walked out without so much as a word of acknowledgement.

Rose stayed behind and walked up to the professor who was now sitting down at his desk. "Is it okay if I use the book for the rest of the semester?"

Looking up in surprise, the professor saw who it was. "Rose, right?"

She nodded.

"Is your tablet broken?"

"No. It's just that I find it easier to read."

Even more surprised, the professor smiled gently. "Sure. I'll get you to sign the book list tomorrow."

Rose thanked him and was walking out of the class when he spoke up again, saying, "It's really nice to see someone younger appreciate the benefits of a book."

Rose turned to him. "If it was only a little lighter to carry around," she joked. She hoisted her bag over her shoulder and walked into the hallway with the rest of the students who were changing classes. The hallway of a university building is a lot like rush hour on the freeway. Traffic flows in two directions, and students jostle for a position, readying to make a turn through a break in the oncoming flow. Sometimes collisions occur - some intentional, some not - and words get exchanged. Today, Rose took the slow lane. Even though this was her first year at university, she was adept at seeing things from a different perspective, and she already knew the traffic patterns and where it was the heaviest and the lightest. More importantly, she knew her destination. Unlike other newbies who walked around looking at the room numbers, scouring about like squirrels to make it to class on time, Rose took her time. Friends waved or said "hey," but she pretended not to notice. Her phone even chimed several times with text messages that she ignored.

Regardless of what happened around her, Rose was oblivious to her surroundings. Her mind played scenario after scenario, speculating about how the girl died, what she went through, and, more importantly, who did it. Again, she felt embarrassed by the fact that in her own little world, she had known nothing about it until the information was forced upon her.

Rose instinctively knew where to go. She was operating on autopilot. She walked into her next class, took her seat, and faced forward. Her phone chimed again, and at the same time she felt her hair being pulled back gently over her shoulder. She ignored her phone, looking back over her shoulder instead.

"Hey gorgeous." Taylor Templeton leaned forward over his desk, reaching close enough to kiss her. Taylor and Rose had been going out since the seventh grade. There had never been anyone else; no other person had even come close to making either look at another.

Taylor and Rose had grown up together. They had been like best friends, or brother and sister, until the seventh grade when Taylor had kissed Rose behind the portable classroom after school. Regardless of their ages at the time, their lives had changed. And even now, they both independently wanted a career in medicine; Rose a surgeon, Taylor a psychiatrist.

Rose pulled her hair back over her shoulder. All thoughts of the murdered girl left her mind when she saw Taylor. "Hey yourself." Another student walked past them, and his bag brushed Rose's shoulder. "Sorry," he mumbled. Rose acknowledged the apology and immediately returned her attention to Taylor.

"I texted you when you walked in. You didn't even see me," he said.

"I've been kinda out of it lately. Did you hear about Mrs. Helms' Social Studies class assignment this year?"

"Yeah. Glad I didn't take that. You pick your story yet?"

Rose went on to explain her choice and what it was doing to her; how she had become so focused on this one story in such a short time. The thought of a person holding the power of life or death over another person fascinated her. Even Rose had to admit that she was freaked out by how much it consumed her.

"I haven't started my studies yet, but I'm glad you came to see me, Ms. Metz." When Taylor joked with Rose, he always called her Ms. Metz. "I wouldn't worry about it. In my opinion, what you're feeling is not obsession, but guilt. You feel guilty that in your secluded life, you didn't even know that this girl was killed not far from where you live. It hit close to home, and you feel bad. Not only for her, but for yourself for living in bubble." Taylor smiled at her. "In my uneducated opinion."

Rose smiled back and reached over to pull his thinning blond bangs down over his forehead. Even at his young age, Taylor's hairline was already starting to recede. Since leaving high school, he had been letting his bangs grow and fall forward, giving the impression that his hairline wasn't so far back. A young man's comb over, he thought. Rose knew his thinning hair bothered him. She fixed his bangs often to make sure others wouldn't notice his hairline. Rose loved his young boy looks, his not-too-muscular physique, and how he stood so much taller than she did. Rose was just over five feet tall, while Taylor was a foot taller and sixty pounds heavier.

"You're probably right. I feel so bad for her. And her parents and friends. My God! I can't imagine anything like that happening to anyone I love. I've never had to deal with death before."

The classroom started to settle and the professor began his lesson.

"Get used to it, sweetie. Death is part of being a doctor. You'll have to learn to deal with it sooner or later."

Taylor sat back in his seat. Rose turned around and realized she hadn't ever had to deal with death, not even of a pet. Her father never allowed animals in the house. She felt a wave of anxiety spread over her as she wondered if she had made a mistake by deciding to become a doctor. She hadn't even factored death into the equation. It was time to face reality.

Rose heard the faint chime of her phone again. She pulled it from her front pocket, held it close to her, and blindly swiped up to bring the screen to life. She carefully looked down, saw the new text message, tapped it, looked up, and waited for a few moments. When the professor had his back to the class she read the message: "*My parents doing date nite this week. Laundry? XX.*"

Without looking behind her, she simply nodded her head in agreement.

"It's a date then," Taylor whispered.

*****

Rose and Taylor had talked about attending grad school together, but knew that the likelihood that they would both be accepted to the same school was remote. It was a possibility, but one that they would deal with if and when it presented itself. Rose knew that a tall, good-looking man like Taylor would attract a lot of women. She was confident that Taylor wouldn't stray if they were attending different schools, but she wasn't as sure of her own ability to stay faithful. This secret she kept hidden from Taylor and her parents, and was something she didn't even like to think about.

After her traditional dinner and tea and shortbread cookies with her parents, Rose went upstairs to work on her homework.

Rose had picked up a few newspapers on her way home. She read each one from front to back. This time, the ink transfer on her fingertips didn't bother her, and she started to enjoy the smell of the newsprint. She even liked the sound the pages made as she turned them. It was a new sensory experience that she thought she would continue to enjoy even after the class assignment was over.

The first newspaper revealed nothing new. Neither did the second or third.

One of the Sun newspapers had a small article buried in the midsection about the family of the victim and stated that no new evidence had been uncovered. Rose went on her laptop and Googled everything she could think of about serial killers who strangled their victims. She found references to Dennis Rader, convicted of the BTK killings; the Boston Strangler, Albert DeSalvo; the Hillside Stranglers, Angelo Buono and Kenneth Bianchi; the Green River Killer, Gary Ridgway; Antonio Rodriguez, known as the Kensington Strangler; and the Queen of Stranglers, Marie Ret.

Rose was most taken by the young female serial killer of the bunch, Marie Ret of Paris, France. Marie was the leader of a band of Parisian garrotters and robbers. Rose was fascinated by the idea of a woman serial killer. Marie had been in control of several men at a time when women did not have many rights. The story of a woman who controlled men, murdering and robbing people, captivated Rose. She read everything she could that night on Marie Ret. Rose wondered if Marie Ret would have found the young victim, Angel Blunt, to her liking. Was Angela the type of victim she sought out? Rose let her mind wander. If she had been Marie Ret, would she have been strong enough to control men and kill her victims? Rose laughed at herself and searched for more details on the life of the female serial killer from France. What little information there was, she printed and set aside for later.

It was still early. Rose's eyes had begun to blur, but there was still enough light out for a drive to clear her head. Rose asked permission to use the car, grabbed the keys and her phone, and told her parents that she was heading to Butler Creek for a walk in the park and that her cell phone would be on. She told them she

would be back within the hour. She expected her parents to forbid her from going to Butler Creek, but apparently they knew nothing about the murder or they
would have objected to her going out alone.

Rose pulled a light nylon jacket from the closet as she left the house. Not long
after, she pulled into the empty parking lot at Butler Creek, stopped under the
over-hanging light, killed the engine, and sat silently looking outside. She decided
to walk the paths and see where Angela Blunt had been murdered. She felt a tingle
inside her belly at the thought of being where the other girl had died.

Rose zipped her jacket up high, locked the car, and found the path. As she
walked, she swiped her finger over the screen on her phone, brought up her Twitter page, and searched for anything regarding Angela Blunt. Nothing. She looked
up Angela's Facebook tribute page, found it, "Liked" it, and left a short note of
condolences. By the time she looked up from her phone, she had made it to the
place where it had all happened. She felt a sudden chill as she realized that she
may have seen the killer, or anybody, on the way to the park, but she couldn't
recall if she had even passed anyone. Had Angela Blunt done the same? Had she
been on her phone, looking down, not seeing anyone, no one seeing her? Was
Angela invisible to everyone she passed because she was staring at her phone?
Did the people she passed ignore her because she was looking down and didn't
acknowledge them? Rose's mind raced with various scenarios.

It was dark by the time Rose arrived at the park, which was only lit by the
few light standards placed every few hundred feet along the path. She used the
flashlight app on her phone to illuminate the areas on either side of the path. It
didn't take long for her to find a shrine around the base of a tree where the body
had been found a few days earlier. The police barricade tape had long since been
taken down, the area thoroughly examined by the investigative team. The shallow grave had been examined, filled, and levelled to avoid allowing the curious to
do, well, whatever the curious would do. *"Maybe for doing what I'm doing now,"* Rose
thought to herself.

Rose felt a wave of nausea pass over her and gulped hard to hold it down.
She pocketed her phone, ran back to the car, and sat in the driver's seat, ashamed
of what she had just done. Curiosity had taken control over her common sense
and she had violated the dead girl's memory by gawking at the sight of the location of her death.

The next few days of school passed by without Rose really knowing what she
was doing. If anyone could be said to be in a zombie-like state, it was she. For
three nights after school, she ignored her homework, choosing instead to go back
to the Butler Creek park and sit under the same tree. The feeling that she was des-
ecrating Angela's memory by going back to the spot had long since passed, and
been replaced by the sense that she was honouring her memory by keeping vigil.

Taylor had noticed Rose becoming more distant, and failing to return his texts and Facebook messages as promptly as she used to. Rose tried to make him believe that she wasn't really feeling like herself. She wasn't lying. Rose couldn't get over the sense that she and Angela were connected, and that she was responsible for not being there for her when she had been attacked.

Rose had brushed off Taylor once again, choosing instead to spend another night with Angela at the base of tree. She pulled her legs up to her chest and felt the temperature drop as the sun dipped below the tree line. The sky above the trees burned brightly in hues of yellow and orange. Below the trees, it was midnight black. She sat alone in the spot where Angela Blunt had been murdered, and the thought gave her comfort, almost as if she was there for the girl she had never known or met.

Her phone continued to beep with incoming texts and Facebook messages. Rose turned off the phone, not wanting to be disturbed any further. She pocketed the device, hugged her knees tighter to her chest, and rested her head back against the tree trunk. It wouldn't take long before the night sky would be as dark as it was in the park. Rose closed her eyes and let her mind drift into sleep.

Rose woke several hours later, the darkness thick and cool around her. There was a single light standard with a low-wattage bulb nearby that did little to illuminate the path and the area around it. Rose stood, stretched, and pulled her phone from her pocket. When she powered it back on, she saw that she had received over a dozen messages and almost three hours had passed.

The sound of footsteps in damp grass startled her and heightened her senses. Rose spun around, looking left and then right for whatever was making the noise. In the darkness, she was unable to see who or what was walking close to her. Silently, she stood and peered around the tree in the direction from which she thought the noise was coming. She spied a figure - female, she thought - who was walking alone and frantically looking behind her. Rose watched in silence as the girl walked quickly through the park towards her. The sound of the footfalls doubled, but the girl's pace hadn't quickened. Rose looked past the girl and saw a dark figure ducking in and out of the shadows. This figure was taller, too large for a female, she thought, and definitely attempting to keep his identity a secret. Rose could make out that the second figure was wearing a bulky hoodie pulled over his head, and was leaning forward as he walked.

Rose watched as the second figure found his prey and focused attention on her. The female kept looking behind at the second figure, who didn't even bother to hide now. The male quickened his pace almost to a sprint as he broke from cover and made a direct line to intercept his prey.

The female darted in the opposite direction, away from where Rose was hidden behind the tree. Her stalker tuned sharply on the grass, lost his footing, fell to the ground, got up, and began a full out run at the girl. Rose took the opportunity to run in the direction from which the two had just come. She fell headlong behind a bush and started to sob. She covered her mouth; she was scared for her life. She could feel the snot and tears wetting her hand. At first she didn't want to watch, but then something inside her compelled her to look up. Laying low under the bush, she turned around to see the girl dart back in the direction from which Rose had just come, the man now only a few feet behind her.

The man lunged at his prey and knocked her to the ground. She was on her stomach and he was straddling her, pushing her face into the grass. Low grunts from the girl went nowhere in the night as the man reached inside his hoodie and pulled out a strand of bright yellow nylon rope. The girl kicked her legs, her shoes scratching the soil as she tried to gain some footing, and her arms attempted to reach up and behind to inflict damage to the man on top of her.

For a moment, Rose thought about going to the girl's aid. She considered kicking the attacker off and then running for her life, but she froze. She couldn't move. Maybe it was her instinct to stay alive, or maybe it was cowardice. She didn't know what it was, but she hated herself for not acting.

The girl got enough traction and momentum from digging into the grass with her feet to buck upwards and throw the man to the side and off of her. He landed hard on the grass and rolled once, giving the girl enough time to right herself and start to run away. The man got to his feet, took a few long strides, and tackled her again. This time, he was on top with his knees on her shoulders, facing her, and he swung a heavy right cross to her left cheek. The girl went limp.

The man reached inside his hoodie pocket, failed to find what he was looking for, and panicked. He patted the pockets on his hoodie, felt his pant pockets, and looked to his left, right, and behind. Frustrated, he reached down, unclasped his belt buckle, and pulled the leather strap through his belt loops. He paused, looked at the unconscious girl between his legs, saw the blood oozing from the cut under her left eye, leaned forward, and licked the blood from her face.

He had just tasted blood for the first time. It was warm and metallic-tasting. His tongue rolled inside his mouth, mixing the blood with saliva, before he swallowed it all. He bent down a second time to clean off all the blood, licking around the wound, over her eye, across her mouth. He felt his excitement grow and couldn't hold back. This feeling was a new sensation and he loved every moment of it. He leaned forward again, kissing the girl, sticking his tongue in her mouth, turning his head slowly, passionately, and felt himself explode. He sat upright and moaned. The hood fell backwards off his head, and in the dim light Rose could make out the side profile of his face.

Rose stared at the man, memorizing his features. She hoped she would be able to recognize him if she ever saw him again, or could help an artist make a composite of his features. His short dark hair was combed back and away from his face. He had a distinctive, unmistakable nose; it turned up at the end, like someone was pushing it. He clenched his jaw when he put his head back, and Rose could make out his thin lips. He quickly straightened up again and pulled the hood back over his head.

Rose closed her eyes and memorized his features. She thought hard about the man's physical qualities, drawing a picture of him in her mind and hoping it would last. Rose opened her eyes to the sight of the man wrapping his belt around the unconscious girl's neck. The man pulled the two ends of the belt together and paused for a moment. Rose held her breath, hoping this terror wasn't real, and readying herself to pounce on the man if he went through with his plans. It seemed like forever passed as he held the two ends of the belt in his hands; then slowly, methodically, he began to twist the belt together. He turned his hands, and the leather wrapped around his fist and tightened around the girl's neck. The man kept constricting until the belt was so taut that it lifted the girl's head off the ground. There was an eerie silence in the air; no noise emanated from the unconscious woman or the man. There was only the gentle rustle of the breeze through the leaves.

Rose got up on all fours, ready to pounce. She saw that the man was balancing himself as he stood and held the girl suspended by her neck, her arms dangling at her sides. Rose coiled her legs. *"On three,"* she thought, and counted in her head, *"One, two, three."* Rose sprang into action, slipped on the grass, and fell flat on her chest.

Hearing the noise behind the bush, the man panicked and released his grip on the belt, pulling it free from around the girl's neck. He jumped to his feet and bolted in the direction from which he had come.

Rose saw the figure run up the hill and disappear into the night as she stood behind the bush. She knew she could never catch him, and didn't think she had it in her to give chase. Turning towards the girl still lying motionless in the grass, Rose realized that she had waited too long to act.

Rose stood in shock as she gazed at the girl on the grass. She wanted to go to her, but her body had turned to stone. She slid one foot forward on the grass and then the other, and was finally standing beside her. The girl's face was turned away from her. Rose knelt down and, with a shaking hand, turned the girl's face towards her.

Rose fell backwards and landed on her butt, tears streaming down her face. She kicked her heels into the dirt, trying to get away from the dead body of Angela Blunt.

Rose kicked her legs so hard that she finally woke herself up. She was still sitting at the base of the tree.

4

That night, Rose cried in bed as she tried to shake the image of Angela Blunt lying dead before her from her mind. She didn't get any sleep, and felt exhausted when her phone alarm went off. She fumbled out of bed, made her way to the bathroom, and sat in the tub with the shower raining down on top of her. It was only when the hot water ran out and the water temperature started to cool that she decided it was time to get out.

Rose passed her parents on the way out the door, having decided to skip breakfast and try to make it to school on time. A familiar car that made her smile and forget about the dream the night before was parked in front of her house. She climbed into the passenger seat, gave Taylor a kiss on the cheek, clipped the seatbelt on, and tilted her head back on the headrest.

"Things getting back to normal?" Taylor asked as he stared forward.

"I'm sorry. I've totally ignored you, huh?" Rose looked across at Taylor as he drove. She put her hand on his lap and rubbed. She smiled at him, and after the length of their relationship, Taylor instinctively knew what she was doing. Without taking his eyes off the road, Taylor smiled back. Rose took her hand from his thigh and rubbed his right cheek where she had kissed him earlier. The rest of the drive to school was silent as they sat close to each other in the front seat.

Taylor parked in the student parking lot and locked the car, and they walked hand-in-hand to the front door of the school. They kissed and began to go their separate ways.

"Laundry tonight?" Taylor called back over his shoulder.

"Wouldn't miss it." Rose was beaming.

*****

Taylor straddled Rose in his bed, panting and trying to catch his breath. He looked down at her; she, too, was glistening with sweat. She licked the sweat from her lips and brushed the wet hair from her face. She was having a difficult time catching her breath as well.

"Wow. What's gotten into you?" Taylor asked. He paused to breath. "Whatever it is, I love it." Tiny beads of sweat dripped off of Taylor's nose and onto Rose's bare chest. In the dim light of Taylor's bedroom, the sweat glistened on Rose's skin like baby oil. "I never get tired of seeing you from this angle." His wet, thinning blonde hair stuck to his forehead.

"You liked it?" Rose asked. She reached up and brushed aside some of the wet hair from Taylor's eyes.

Taylor nodded his head in agreement while breathing heavily. "K. What's up?"

"You're gonna make a fucking great shrink. You know exactly what to say to me. I just hope you don't use those skills to get women in bed when you move away to med school." Rose laughed.

"Never gonna happen."

Taylor rolled over onto his side of the bed. Rose pulled Taylor's left arm up, put her head on his chest, and wrapped his arm around her. She rubbed his wet chest and twirled the few chest hairs he had.

"I'm glad you called me over to help with laundry."

"My parents have a date night. I don't know why they don't just tell me they're going to a motel to fuck their brains out, or give me the car and fifty bucks to take you so they can do it here." Rose was well aware of Taylor's parents' date nights. They hadn't changed in years, and they honestly believed that she and Taylor thought they were going to have dinner and see a movie.

"Can I ask you a question?" Rose continued to play with Taylor's chest hair.

"Sure. Anything."

"Are you bored with this?"

"This?" Taylor pulled his arm out from under Rose's head. "Seriously. After what we just did, you're asking if I'm bored."

"Well, you know you're the only person I've ever been with." Rose's voice was soft and almost muted.

"And you're the only person I've ever been with. I've never even thought of another woman. Well, not unless you count Marilyn Munroe. No man will ever be able to resist her." He laughed out loud. Rose didn't even chuckle. "Oh come on. That was funny. K. Seriously. What's up?"

"I've been thinking about trying some new things."

Taylor bolted upright and his face lit up. "You mean more than what we did tonight?" Then his face fell. "Wait, is this because I'm boring? I'll try harder next time."

Rose sat up in bed facing Taylor. She thought it was cute how he was always trying to please her. "No, I mean kinky. Really kinky."

"You don't want another guy, do you? Because if that's what it takes to make you happy, I'll do it."

Rose grabbed his hands and held them tightly. "Don't freak, K?" She paused, and took a deep breath. "I want you to choke me."

Taylor pulled his hands away, terrified at what Rose was asking. "Are you fucking nuts?"

"I read about it before coming over. Seriously, it's not that weird. A lot of women like it." Rose was trying to calm Taylor, who was visibly shaken. "What's the matter?"

"You're just freaking me out."

"Stop for a minute and think about this. You're the one who wants to become the shrink. Analyze it."

Rose had known for years how to control Taylor. By making him think like a psychiatrist, she could convince Taylor to rationalize almost anything.

"Okay. Wait a sec. Choking is a sign of dominance." He stuck out his lower lip and cocked his head to the side. "Regardless of what a woman's views are on equality, some like to be dominated. Sometimes people in positions of authority like to take a submissive role to clear their heads. There's also the danger and risk aspect. If you're a thrill-seeker, trying something dangerous could get you off. Then some people just like it really kinky." He looked at Rose. "And what's your thing?"

"Curiosity."

"K. I didn't factor that in."

"It's more common than you think. A lot of women like it from what I've read."

Rose went on to show Taylor what she had researched on the Internet after school. It wasn't about compressing or squeezing the trachea or windpipe; it was about blocking the blood flow to the brain for only a few seconds, which caused light-headedness and could heighten pleasure during sex.

After fully discussing the technique, what to expect, and what do to if anything went awry, Taylor was still visibly worried about attempting this new roleplaying with Rose. She, however, was becoming more and more excited the further they discussed it. Rose placed Taylor's hand over her neck and showed him where to apply the pressure, how long to press down, and the signs for which to look. Repeatedly, Rose went over the technique, explaining what she wanted, when to begin the chokehold, and when to let go. It was only after Taylor felt comfortable that they began their new role playing game.

Rose lay back in bed, ready for Taylor to begin. She would keep her eyes open and tell him when to apply the pressure. As soon as he began to press, Taylor was to count to three and then release his grip. They began gently, looking at each other, kissing, and once again exploring each other's bodies with their hands. This foreplay continued for several minutes until Rose arched her back and let out a loud moan as Taylor entered her. Even though they had had sex hundreds of times, this experience was new and exciting. Rose, who was normally the instigator, was now letting Taylor take the lead. She continued to reassure him that it was going to be okay. At the moment when she was close to orgasm, Rose gasped that she was ready.

Taylor's quivering hand moved closer to Rose's neck, and then hesitated. Rose couldn't feel any pressure. She opened her eyes and saw that Taylor couldn't - or wouldn't - go through with it. She grasped his hand, placed it around her neck, and started to compress it.

"Like this. Hurry."

Taylor found the two landmarks and gently applied pressure.

"Harder. Please," Rose begged.

Taylor applied more pressure. As they had agreed, Rose kept her eyes open, and Taylor slowly started to count. Rose felt an immediate euphoria. Her world became blurred and fuzzy. Images began to swirl in her mind. She could feel Taylor inside of her, and the sensation became more intense with each thrust. It became harder to keep her eyes open, and to focus on what was about to happen. Rose could feel the pressure on her neck building as she lost all other feeling in her body, and then in one sudden, instantaneous moment, Taylor released his grip.

Blood flow returned to Rose's brain, and with her heightened senses, she felt the most intense orgasm of her life. She arched her back and her legs wrapped tightly around Taylor's waist, squeezing and forcing him deeper into her until she let out a wild scream. Rose covered her eyes with her forearm. Her breathing was heavy and her entire body glistened with sweat. She felt tiny tremors of pleasure that continued to flood her body and senses. She jerked as if having a minor seizure, and then relaxed.

Taylor reached around, pulled himself free of her legs, and then stepped back from the bed. His breathing was heavy, and his eyes were wide open and panicked. It was clear that he hadn't enjoyed the experience. He was scared and freaked out after what had just happened. He swiped his hands on his thighs in a vain attempt to wipe away what he had done to Rose. Rose continued to writhe and squirm on the bed as the pleasure inside her continued.

"You okay?" he asked.

"Oh yeah, better than okay." Rose still had her eyes closed.

Taylor left the bedroom, went to the bathroom down the hall, and turned on the shower, setting the water temperature hotter than he usually did. It was their "thing" to shower together after sex, but right now all Taylor wanted to do was wash away the experience he had just had in the bedroom. He soaped up his mother's hard bristled scrubber and proceeded to clean his conscious. Taylor was scared and mortified at what he had done. He was even more afraid that he had agreed to such an act - something that could have killed her.

Taylor finished his shower, dried off, and went back to the bedroom to check on Rose. She was still lying in bed, uncovered and with her eyes closed. She was smiling as her hands slowly roamed freely across her body. Taylor dressed, all the while looking at this girl whom he had known for most of his life, who now appeared like a complete stranger. It was as though he did not know her at all. He remained silent. Rose said nothing to Taylor.

In the kitchen, he got a bowl of cereal, poured the milk, and ate alone. He knew his parents wouldn't be coming home for another few hours. Taylor finished the bowl, poured another, and waited for Rose to come downstairs even though he didn't want to see her at that moment. He powered up his phone and checked his email and text messages. He answered a few messages, finished the second bowl of cereal, and continued to wait for Rose.

When Rose didn't come down, Taylor went upstairs. Rose was still lying naked in bed. He gathered up her clothes, laid them on the foot of the bed, and then sat down beside her. He stroked her hair. Her eyes were still closed, and she smiled as soon as she felt his touch. Blindly reaching over, her hand found his thigh, and she rubbed his leg. This experience had been one of the best of her life, and she wanted to soak up every last moment of it. They were both comfortable seeing each other naked, and Rose didn't feel uneasy lying in bed unclothed with Taylor sitting fully dressed nearby.

"What are you thinking about?" Taylor asked.

"Always the psych, aren't you?"

"You know what they say about answering a question with a question?"

"What do they say?"

The two of them shared a laugh. Taylor finally began to feel a little more at ease.

"You really didn't like it, did you?" Rose asked as she pulled herself up and leaned against the headboard. With both hands, she brushed her damp hair back, pulling it into a ponytail before wrapping it high on her head. Taylor shook his head from side to side, with his eyes downcast.

"I didn't like it at all. I don't like hurting you, and the idea of putting my hands around your neck freaks me out."

"You didn't hurt me. On the contrary, you gave me the greatest orgasm of my life. I swear it lasted for about twenty minutes. Well, it felt that way, anyway. It was amazing, and you did that for me. You didn't hurt me. You gave me a wonderful gift."

"Are you planning on getting dressed at all tonight?" Taylor asked in an attempt to change the subject.

"I was waiting for you to recharge and try it again." Rose rubbed his crotch over his jeans. Taylor stood and jumped back.

"This," Taylor said as he waved his hand over the bed like a wizard conjuring up a spell, "this thing we did, will never ever happen again." Taylor was shaken, and his voice quivered.

"What?" Rose's tone changed from that of only moments ago. "What's the problem? I'm fine, and this thing," she repeated his hand gesture, "was amazing. It's the best experience I've ever had."

"Maybe for you, but it freaked the fuck outta me."

"Oh come on, you big baby. It was fun. Why won't you do it for me?" Rose tried on her best pouty face to get her way.

Taylor went from feeling panic about choking Rose to outright distain. "Don't try that with me. It may have been great for you. But it wasn't for me. It'll never be good for me. It'll never be amazing for me. It'll never do anything but freak the fuck outta me. Got it?"

Rose stood, walked over to Taylor, hugged him, and looked up at him. "I love you, big guy. And if this really does freak you out, then we don't have to do it. There are other things we can try."

"As long as it doesn't involve pain, Shetland ponies, midgets, or bondage." Taylor paused and thought about what he had just said. "Well maybe we can include the ponies."

Rose reached around, grabbed his buttocks, and asked him if he wanted to have a shower with her. Taylor pulled his t-shirt over his head as Rose unbuttoned his jeans.

5

Rose decided that not telling Taylor about her dream and obsession regarding Angela Blunt's death was in her best interest. They showered together,
got dressed, and were watching television when Taylor's parents came home. He
drove Rose home, and they chatted about everything and nothing at the same
time, but the choking didn't come up again. Rose kept touching her neck, and re-
calling how she had felt when Taylor's hand was wrapped around it: the pressure,
and then the intense pleasure. Even though Rose tried to hide her disappoint-
ment in Taylor's refusal to continue with their new experimental sexual technique,
it was evident to him. She told him that she was just thinking about Angela Blunt,
who was so close to her own age and was murdered only a few kilometres from
her own home. It was reason enough to be upset, and Taylor believed her story.

In bed that night, Rose wore her buttoned-up nightshirt and pulled the sheets
up high. Usually, she could fall asleep as soon as her head hit the pillow, but tonight her hand kept reaching up to her neck and gently squeezing where Taylor's
hand had been. Her chest heaved as she thought about him inside her, the passion, and the intense feeling as his fingers tightening around her neck.

Unable to ignore the erotic feeling of strangulation during sex with Taylor,
and how they had mirrored the killings by Marie Ret, her mind was flooded with
images and ideas of asphyxiation. She wondered what it would be like to put her
hands around someone's neck and squeeze. Rose knew that Taylor would never
agree to be chocked, and would probably never choke her again. Rose wanted to
be the dominant one and choke someone. She could only imagine the control that
person must feel as they wrap their hands around someone's throat and block the
airway. Hold pressure for a few minutes, and the person dies; release at the right
time, and the person is in ecstasy.

The room was dark, and she was unable to see anything around her, even
with her eyes wide open. Her bedrooms had always been that way. It was the
only way she could sleep: in total darkness. She touched herself softly. Her hands
started at her hips, slid slowly up to her stomach, paused, and then one continued
to her breast as the other reached around her neck. She found the pressure points
and started to squeeze. She closed her eyes, felt the pressure on her neck, arched
her back, and then abruptly let go. She couldn't go through with it and relaxed
her grip.

She sighed deeply and opened her eyes to complete darkness. Tomorrow she
would have to present what she had uncovered about the story she chose to her

classmates. She didn't have a lot of information yet, but she did have an idea.

*****

Rose's first class of the day was Mrs. Helms' Social Studies and it was Rose's turn to update the class on her topic of choice. Although she hadn't prepared for her presentation in her usual fastidious way, Rose thought that her dream, or nightmare, was a good starting point. Everyone took their seats; the same seats as on the first day of class. Rose sat patiently with her study guide in hand and her notes on her tablet. She wasn't nervous; she was more impatient to tell everyone of her story.

"Okay, everyone. Pipe down," Mrs. Helms said as she closed the door and sat on a stool at the back of the class. The students eventually calmed down, and most put their cell phones away although some continued to text.

"Rose?"

"Yes, Mrs. Helms," Rose answered as she turned to face the professor. "Am I up?"

"You are." Mrs. Helms raised her voice. "Rose volunteered to be the first to present what she has. So, let's see how she does and how well the rest of you do when you come to the front of the class and do your presentations." A collective sigh of displeasure was heard. "And for those of you who didn't get the memo on cell phones in the classroom, if anyone is caught texting, calling, surfing, tweeting, or doing anything else on their phones, I can confiscate them until the end of the year. So," she raised her voice, "I will, and I repeat, will take your precious phone for the rest of the year if I see anyone with it out during class."

Mrs. Helms knew that taking away their phones was an empty threat, but she wanted the students to show respect and keep their phones on mute and out of sight.

The few remaining students who hadn't put their phones away quickly pocketed their devices. Mrs. Helms thanked the class as Rose made her way to the front of the room. She plugged her tablet into the overhead DLP projector and started up her presentation, then began to narrate:

"So, this is the first week of class and I don't have much on this yet, but I'll show you what I do have." She swiped the screen from right to left.

"I found this story in the paper about a young girl, Angela Blunt, not much older than us," she waved her hand back and forth before the classroom, "who was murdered. Funny thing is, not even my parents remember hearing about this when it first happened, and I didn't know about it either until I read that they found the body. There were two other girls who were killed - same approximate age, same type of death - in other parts of the city, but the press isn't sure if they are linked. Police have stated their usual 'No Comment' about the incidents. Personally, I think they are related. I don't have any evidence; just a gut feeling."

Rose swiped again to show a scan of the article she had cut from the newspaper. "Anyway, it seems that Angela went missing and no one knew where she was until her body was found by two young kids. I searched on Facebook, Twitter, and other social sites for more information or details about the murder, and the only thing I found was a tribute to Angela by her friends on Facebook. I joined the Facebook tribute group out of respect, but already the posts seem to be dwindling. It would be nice if each one of us could join the tribute group."

She showed a screenshot of the Facebook page. Not one of her classmates made any note of the page or showed any interest in what she was asking them to do.

"I've been keeping up on the story in print, and there've been a few small articles, but the one thing I've noticed is that electronic media has a much shorter attention span. Something my dad says we kids lack today is the ability to focus." Rose expected some sort of comment or snort from at least one student, but everyone in the class pretended to be interested while their mind was on something else. That was when Rose decided to stray from her planned presentation. She stood up from behind the desk and walked to the front of the class.

"I have a theory." Rose raised her voice, and it rang with confidence and authority. A few of the students who were pretending to pay attention looked up. "I haven't spoken to the police, maybe that's my next step, but I have my own thoughts." She caught the attention of a few other students. Rose pointed at one of the more popular girls in school who was sitting close to the back.

"Ashley, can you help me up front please?"

The girl who Rose had singled out looked at Mrs. Helms and asked, "Do I hafta?"

"You can have Rose help you with your presentation when you're up front."

"Fuck," Ashley swore softly, not realizing that she could be heard.

"What was that?" Mrs. Helms was not pleased.

"Sorry." Ashley walked to the front of the class and glared at Rose.

Rose took Ashley by both arms and turned her sideways. The two of them faced each other; Ashley towered over Rose and gave her the kind of look that only girls can give and understand. Rose brushed it off.

"K." Rose smiled at Ashley. "After reading what I could about the case, this is what I think may've happened." Rose turned Ashley around so that Rose was looking at her back. "Ashley is walking through the park alone. It's late, dark, and you're scared, Ashley. The lamps in the park give you just enough light to see the path and a bit around you. Close your eyes."

"What?" Ashley turned around. "Why?"

"Please."

Ashley closed her eyes. Rose continued. "It's dark, you're alone, and you hear footsteps behind you. The grass crunches with each footstep and you realize you're not alone. The sound echoes in the park, bouncing off of trees and rocks, so you quicken your pace. The sound of the footsteps behind you quickens as well. The breeze is strong and you feel it on your neck." Rose gently pursed her lips and blew on Ashley's neck.

Ashley swatted at the air like she was brushing away a fly. "This isn't funny." Ashley kept her eyes closed but wasn't pleased. A few of the kids in class laughed.

"Shhh." Rose had the upper hand, much like the killer must have had with Angela, and she was enjoying tormenting Ashley, who had bullied her for the previous four years of high school. Rose changed her tone, deepening her voice, and her words were well chosen to achieve the desired effect.

"The killer follows you, Ashley, ducking behind trees or whatever he can find. He's moving quickly to shorten the distance between the two of you. You look back but all you see is darkness. You're not sure why, but you feel his presence getting closer, and that's when he decides he's going to attack. He tackles you, and you're lying face down. He's on top of you, pushing your face into the ground, and you fight back, bucking him off. You jump to your feet and try to race away. He drops whatever he was pulling out of his pocket and gives chase again. He tackles you, pulls his leather belt from his pants, wraps it around your neck, and tightens it."

Rose put her hands around Ashley's neck. Ashley let out a loud, piercing scream that made others in the class yelp in surprise as well. Even Mrs. Helms let out a shriek of her own. Ashley pulled free of Rose's grip, took a few steps forward, turned, and faced her mock attacker. "What the fuck is your problem?" Ashley's face was red, and sweat dripped from her dyed-blonde hairline. She was panting and trying to catch her breath.

Rose smiled. "Imagine how Angela felt when that belt really was chocking the life out of her."

"You're a sick bitch." Ashley stepped up to Rose menacingly. Rose reached out with two stiff arms and pushed her back.

Mrs. Helms said sternly, "Enough, both of you."

Rose held her ground as Ashley went back to her seat.

Mrs. Helms walked to the front of the class down the same aisle as Ashley, who purposely bumped into her. Mrs. Helms took the shoulder bump in stride and let it go, this time. Ashley fell hard into her chair, making the seat screech as the feet dragged on the tile floor.

At the front of the class, Rose unplugged her tablet from the projector and packed up her notes as Mrs. Helms helped coil up some of the cables. Quietly, Mrs. Helms asked Rose where she had learned the details of the crime. Rose explained that she had pieced together the specifics from the articles in print and online.

Taking her seat, Rose noticed that one of her classmates who had also been the target of Ashley's taunts had left a small note on the desk: "*Nice job up there.*" Rose stuffed her tablet into her backpack and used the note as bookmark. She turned and smiled at the girl who had written it. "Thanks," she whispered. Looking past the note writer, Rose noticed that Ashley was talking to her boyfriend, and made out a few words such as "bitch" and "dead." Rose looked right at Ashley and laughed. Not long ago, Rose would have been intimidated by Ashley, but that was in the past.

Mrs. Helms finished the class and thanked Rose for volunteering to be the first to present, but cautioned the students to be less dramatic with future presentations. The comment brought forth a round of laughter from the class, except from Ashley and her friends. Mrs. Helms released the students and they quickly gathered their gear and headed for their next classes.

Mrs. Helms waited for everyone to clear the classroom before she retrieved her cellphone from her desk drawer and placed a phone call.

"Brian Lahey, please. Yes, I'll hold."

A few moments later, a male voice answered at the other end, saying, "This is Brian."

"Hey, big brother. How's Mom's favourite police detective?"

"How's Mom's favourite professor? What's up? You never call during class time."

"I need to speak to you tonight about one of my students. Can you and Marcie stop by for dessert tonight? Say around seven?"

"Sounds good. What's for dessert?"

"Whatever you want to bring."

"Is this serious?"

"Very."

"I'll bring something apropos for serious sister brother talk. Love ya, kiddo."

The line went dead.

*****

Just after seven that evening, Brian and Marcie Lahey arrived at the house of Linda and Eric Helms. Brian carried in store-bought lemon meringue and apple pies and a small container of ice cream. Linda already had a pot of coffee on, and she cut both pies into several pieces while Eric placed a stack of dessert plates and bowls on the table along with forks and spoons. Linda poured coffee for everyone as they chose their favourite slice and topped it with some ice cream. By the time everyone was finished his or her first cup of coffee, Brian had pulled his sister into the living room.

"So what's up?" Brian sat down on the couch. Linda chose to remain standing.

"You still investigating that murdered girl found in the park?" Linda paced around the living room, rubbing her hands together.

Brian patted the cushion beside him, saying, "Sit." He moved over to let his younger sister rest beside him. Linda sat down beside her brother with her hands still clenched together.

"I have this Social Studies class I'm teaching this year and the kids have to pick a current events topic and follow it on social and print media."

"K. Following so far."

"This girl in my class decided to follow your investigation and today she did a presentation that spooked the hell outta me." Linda stood and started to pace the living room again. "How much did you tell the press about the details of the investigation?"

Brian leaned back deep into the couch, crossed his legs, and anchored his feet on the corner of the coffee table. "You know we tell the press nothing. Christ, I don't even talk to Marcie about half the shit I deal with. I tell you more than I'm supposed to. What's gotten into you?"

Linda stopped pacing, sat on the corner of the coffee table, and pushed Brian's feet to the floor. "This girl said the killer stalked the dead girl, attacked her from behind, and choked her with his belt."

Brian sat forward on the edge of the couch and looked at his sister. "Belt - she said belt. How the hell did she know about the belt? No one is supposed to know about the belt. We didn't tell anybody, and I only told you about it because, well, you know."

"There are a million things she could have said in class but when she described the attack, she scared the living shit out of everyone. And then when she said the belt was wrapped around her neck, I almost pissed my pants. How could she have known?"

"How old is this girl?"

"First year, pre-med, wants to be like her parents, if she gets accepted. Smart kid, maybe too smart for her own good sometimes. Rose is a petite little thing, can't be more than a hundred and ten pounds in soaking wet clothes. Good family. Never been in trouble in her life."

Brian asked Linda for all the information she had on Rose Metzel. What little she knew, she told her brother. Linda felt a sense of relief knowing that her brother was now taking control of the situation, the way he had her entire life. She took in a deep breath and felt much more relaxed.

Linda thanked her brother and hugged him before they walked back to the dining room table to finish their pie and coffee.

*****

Rose walked through the park with a flashlight, kicking at the long grass to see if she could find what she was searching for. During her talk in front of the class, she had realized that she had forgotten a very important detail from her dream under the tree. That little detail had slipped her mind until she went through the scenario with Ashley as the victim. Her feet continued to sweep the ground, turning the blades of grass over in the area where she thought the attacker had initially slipped.

After thirty minutes of searching, Rose looked up at her surroundings to make sure that she was in the right location. She closed her eyes and pictured her dream about the attack. She hit the rewind button in her mind and played the entire scene over in slow motion. She would open her eyes to obtain a reference point in the landscape, walk around, close her eyes, and move again. In her mind's eye, she could see the attacker - hood pulled up over his head - following Angela, going from tree to tree, and then making his move and darting after her.

Rose retraced the steps of the attacker where she could remember him walking and hiding. She closed her eyes and could almost instinctively walk in his steps without stumbling. He had tackled Angela and pulled out a long piece of cheap yellow nylon rope. Angela had kicked him off and he had fallen to the ground, dropped the yellow rope, and then taken off after her. Rose blindly took a few more steps and then stopped. With her eyes now open, she continued to sweep the grass with her feet, the flashlight illuminating the ground beneath her. Her right foot swept right, then left, and then back again. The long grass turned upwards and fell back, and bright yellow nylon peaked out from beneath. Rose froze. She knelt down and steadied the beam of the flashlight on the end of the rope.

The end of the rope wasn't tied in a knot, but was melted in a glob of darkened yellow nylon strands that peaked out between blades of grass. Rose couldn't see the rest of its length but knew that it must be under the grass. She pulled leather winter gloves and a plastic bag snuck from her mother's kitchen from her jacket pocket and laid the flashlight on the ground with the beam aimed at the rope. She tugged on the end of the rope, freeing it from the grass. She continued to pull until the entire thirty inches of yellow nylon rope were dangling from her gloved fingers. She lowered the rope into the plastic bag, zipped the seal, picked up the flashlight, and examined the discovery.

Rose had found her prize.

*****

Rose was at home alone at the same time that Brian and Linda were cleaning up the dessert dishes and putting them away. Marcie and Eric had left the brother and sister alone in the kitchen, knowing that when they started talking, it was best to leave them to themselves until they were done. Marcie and Eric watched the eleven o'clock news in silence as the siblings continued to discuss private matters in the kitchen.

As Rose lay in bed, the room dark except for the flashlight beam shining directly on the plastic bag held above her, she tried to deny the excitement she had felt when she had closed her hands around Ashley's neck. A sense of power came over her as she imagined her hands around the other girl's throat, squeezing and holding Ashley's life within them. She imagined that must be similar to the power surgeons feel when they operate. If this feeling was the "God Complex" people talked about, Rose thought, then she surely knew how potent it could really be. Was it the same power the killer had felt when he had wrapped the belt around Angela Blunt's neck and twisted the life out of her? He would have known that he had the power to bestow life or death; if he let go at the right time, the victim would recover and start breathing again, but if he continued to squeeze, then she would die.

Rose wondered if, in some sick way, Angela had felt the same erotic sensation that she had experienced when Taylor had cut the circulation to her brain during sex. Or did it require penetration and the sudden rush of oxygenated blood back to her brain, she pondered. Rose wanted Taylor to strangle her again, but she also wanted to feel the same power that she had felt today when she could have easily choked Ashley to death.

Rose tangled her new prized possession in the air above her head as it twisted and turned before her. In the dim light the yellow rope almost seemed to glow with a neon hue behind the protective plastic. She felt powerful as she held the rope in the bag, but resisted the temptation to open it up and handle it. The more she fondled the rope, the more Rose wanted to be sexually strangled again.

*****

Brian told his sister one more time that he would look into Rose Metzel the next day and see if she knew more about the case than she should, or if she was involved. Linda relaxed, hugged her brother once again, and thanked him for stopping by. They walked from the kitchen to the living room. Marcie and Eric joined them as they strolled out to the foyer. They all said their goodnights, and there were hugs and cheek kisses all around before Brian and Marcie walked out.

The door closed behind Brian and Marcie as they sauntered to their car. Brian sat in the driver's seat and stared forward.

"You okay? Linda seemed really upset tonight," Marcie asked with concern.

"Ever get one of those feelings?"

"The 'hair-on-the-back-of-my-neck-standing-up, spine-tingling, felt-like-I've-seen-it-before' type of feeling?" Marcie was joking with her police officer husband who routinely asked her that same question over and over again. "Is this a bad one?"

Brian continued to stare straight ahead as he answered. "About as bad as I've ever had." He keyed the engine to life. "Did I ever tell you how much I hate my job?"

Brian asked Marcie this question as often as the other. "Yeah, all the time."

Brian put the car into gear and they drove home in silence.

*****

Rose tossed the damp, crumpled tissues into her wastebasket and hid the plastic bag under her mattress. It wasn't as good as being choked, but it was still good. She turned onto her side, bunched the pillow under her head, and fell asleep.

*****

After Marcie was asleep, Brian sat at the kitchen table with his laptop open, connected via a secure login to the police server. His elbows rested on the table, and both hands supported his chin. He continued to stare at the screen, which only showed one thing: a close-up picture of Angela Blunt's neck. The markings were unmistakable: a one and a half inch wide groove with tiny, evenly spaced out holes that could only have been made by a belt. The fourth hole of five - or perhaps it was the second hole of five, depending on which way the belt was placed around the neck - was misshapen from wear. Unfortunately, there was no way to tell the size of the belt that had been used. They were fortunate in another aspect, however; DNA had been retrieved from the wound created by the belt, although it was still too early to have determined any results.

The body had been buried like the other girls', but even though many of the details of the murders were similar, the use of the belt was different. All of the other girls had been strangled with a narrow rope. Was Angela Blunt killed by the same person who had killed the other girls, and if they so, why had a belt been used instead of a rope, Brian wondered. Was it an unplanned, spur-of-the-moment killing, or did something go wrong? Why a belt?

He flipped the picture on the laptop to one of Angela Blunt on her graduation day. Angela was young, smiling, and being hugged by friends who were also graduating that day. She looked so happy, and had so much ahead of her. Angela's haircut reminded Brian of Linda's hairstyle when she had graduated from university. Now, he would do whatever he could for Angela.

"We told nobody about the belt. How could she have known?" Brian wondered. He rationalized that it must have been a guess; nothing but a fortunate, lucky, shot-in-the-dark guess.

He disconnected from the server, powered down the laptop, and put it in his briefcase. As he walked upstairs to bed, he couldn't help but wonder about the girl he would have to interview tomorrow. She was old enough to be considered an adult, but he still hated having to talk to young people. He decided that he would call his supervisor in the morning and see if a female detective could join him to talk to the girl. Either way, with or without a female detective, he planned on talking to Rose Metzel the next day.

6

Brian Lahey sat his desk, waiting for the female detective assigned to him for the interview to arrive so they could leave for the university. He checked his briefcase again to make sure he had everything he required. He was nervous. His first day on the job, his preceptor had told him to make sure he had everything he needed for each shift before he started. "Check it once, make sure you have it, and don't check it again. It shows that you're indecisive," he had said. Brian still remembered being told that, and each time he did something twice, he could see his old friend standing beside him, shaking his head. Checking things multiple times was his nervous tell; he knew it, his wife knew it, his kids knew it, and he was pretty sure the other detectives knew it.

Brian looked at his watch, tapped his fingers on the desk, and checked his cell phone for emails and texts. When he looked up from his phone, he saw a young female in plainclothes walking towards him.

"Sorry for being late. The Chief told me to change from my uniform to plainclothes for the day." She extended her hand. "Sara Milles. It's my first day in plainclothes."

Brian stood, shook her hand, and, without saying a word, started to walk towards the parking lot. Sara quickened her pace and followed close behind. She sensed that her new partner was not very happy. "*Stupid! He hasn't even spoken to me yet. Of course he's pissed,*" she thought. Her mind raced with thoughts of things she might have done. She wondered if she should've stayed in her uniform. Or did he not like women police officers?

The sedan beeped as Brian pressed the remote. He got in the driver's side, started the car, put it in reverse, and waited. Sara finally caught up, jumped in the passenger side, and sat quietly with her briefcase on her lap.

"Seat belt," Brian suggested as he stared forward.

Sara secured her belt. "Sorry."

The drive to the university was uneventful, quiet, and very uncomfortable. Brain wasn't upset; he was nervous. On top of his nervous tell of double checking things, he also became sullen, silent, and very moody. He pulled into the parking lot, killed the engine, and turned to Sara.

"Listen, I'm sorry for starting off on the wrong foot. I'm really nervous right now. Kids, they - well - they freak me out. You got kids?" Brian stepped from the vehicle, slammed the driver's door, and pressed the remote to lock it.

"Engaged. My fiancée and I want to wait until I make detective and get out of uniform." Sara had to walk faster than normal to keep pace with Brian. She looked at him from behind: a short, thin man with thick dark hair and otherwise unremarkable features, he was non-descript in every sense of the word. She could have passed him a thousand times at the station and paid no attention to him. His suit fit him well and he walked with the stride of a confident man, not that of someone who was nervous about talking to a first-year university student.

"Well, I guess after today, you and your boyfriend won't have any excuses not to have kids."

"Girlfriend."

"Huh?" Brian stopped short, almost causing Sara to walk into him. He was wide-eyed and confused. "Huh, okay, girlfriend." He turned and resumed his walk to the school. "I'm getting too old for this job."

"Does that concern you, detective?" Sara's voice showed disdain.

"Not at all. I used to be able to read people just by looking at them, and I was usually right. Now, I can't tell the guys from the girls. Hell, most guys wear makeup and dress to look like girls, and the girls want to look like guys."

"Are you saying I look like a guy detective?"

"Nope, I'm saying I can't tell anymore. I used to have this voodoo thing," Brian spun his hands around his head, "and if I thought about something long enough I would get these, I dunno whatcha would call them, images, premonitions, hallucinations, whatever. Anyways, I could see things that happened or were about to happen. I could see someone and know what they were like. Now, I can't read shit. Lost my voodoo. And reading people is important in this job." Brian's tone changed. "And stop calling me 'detective' for Christ's sake. My name is Brian, not detective, not officer, just plain old Brian. But whatever you do, don't call me Bri."

He pulled the main door to the school open and stepped to the side. Sara smiled and walked in. "Chivalry is still appreciated detect… Brian."

Brian shook his head and muttered to himself, "I'm getting too fucking old."

At the front desk, both Brian and Sara showed their identification, asked to speak to the dean, and were offered seats in which to wait. Sara sat, while Brian stood - another indication that he was uncomfortable.

"What are we doing here?" Sara spoke softly.

"One of the female students here knows more than anyone else about the Blunt murder."

"The girl killed in the park. Is that why the Chief wanted a young woman present during the interrogation; because you want to talk to a young girl?"

"It's not an interrogation." Brian looked down sternly at Sara. "It's an interview to see what she knows."

"How old is she? Do we need her parents present?"

"She's an adult now but I'm making sure the dean will be in the room."

Shortly after, the detectives were escorted down the hall to the dean's office. The name on the office door was "M. Taggart." They both took a seat and sat quietly, waiting for the dean to return. The office was large yet sparsely decorated and contained only a sizeable metal desk and a single book shelf that held merely a dozen or so books on it. There were few items that personalized the office; no photos, no diplomas, and no certificates.

Brian leaned in to Sara and whispered, "Male, older, single; he won't have a wedding ring; he'll be thin; he'll have grey, most likely slicked-back, hair; and he'll be wearing a dark suit, white shirt, and bland tie."

Sara looked at him in astonishment. The office door opened and in walked a tall, thin man who looked exactly as Brian had described him except he was wearing a brown suit, green shirt, and chocolate brown tie.

This time Sara leaned in close to Brian and whispered, "How did you know?"

"His picture was in the front foyer when we walked in. Be more observant," Brian teased.

Brian stood, shook the dean's hand firmly, and introduced himself and Sara. The dean offered them the opportunity to move their chairs in closer to his desk. Mr. Taggart's chair was positioned several inches higher than the chairs in which Brian and Sara sat. Brian didn't like the implication that Mr. Taggart was in charge, but it was his office and his university.

Brian explained that they had received an anonymous tip that Rose Metzel had made some comments in her Social Studies class about a homicide he was investigating, and the person who had provided the tip had made it sound as though Rose knew more than she was letting on.

"Do you think Rose is involved in this crime?" Mr. Taggart leaned back in his chair. It creaked.

"Not at all. We just want to speak with Rose and find out why she made certain comments. No loose ends, as they say." Brian wasn't going to say much more.

"Do you know who provided the tip? Was it one of my students?"

"One of the nice things about anonymous tips, Mr. Taggart, is that - " Brian was cut off.

"That they are anonymous." Mr. Taggart finished the sentence.

"Can we speak to Ms. Metzel, please? And of course, she can have you or any member of your staff present during our talk. Please remember, she is not a suspect in any way." Brian changed the direction of the conversation to show that he was in charge.

"Of course. It won't be but a few moments." Mr. Taggart excused himself and stepped out of the office. Mr. Taggart was a very formal man as evidenced by the way he dressed, spoke, and carried himself.

"Pleasant man," whispered Sara.

"Shh. I wouldn't be surprised if the office is bugged."

Brian took advantage of their time alone to bring Sara up to date on what they knew and what they wanted to talk to Rose Metzel about. They had no video surveillance from any of the scenes, no DNA results, no fingerprints; no real evidence of any kind yet. There were six detectives working on the case and they still had nothing to go on. Brian continued to debrief her for several minutes in the office before the door opened and in walked a petite young woman. Rose Metzel was smiling - almost beaming. The dean motioned for Rose to join them at the desk. She pulled up a chair as Mr. Taggart explained that he would be looking out for Ms. Metzel's interests.

Brian introduced himself and Sara, and told Rose that they had received an anonymous tip that she seemed to know a lot about the Blunt crime scene.

"Was Ashley the one who called 911 to whine about what I did to her in class?" Rose was enjoying her newfound notoriety. She relaxed and slouched in the chair.

"Even if we knew, we couldn't tell you," Sara explained, using a soft, sympathetic tone, trying to relate woman-to-woman with Rose. "I just want to clarify that we don't think you had anything to do with the incident in question. It's just that you seemed very sure of the circumstances of the Blunt incident in class yesterday. That's all we want to talk to you about."

"Is that all?" Rose looked at Mr. Taggart and the two detectives. "I've been researching the 'incident,' as you call it. I've been tracking the story on social media sites, the papers, you know, just like Mrs. Helms asked us to. So anyway, I looked up everything I could find, and believe me when I tell you, there's not much out there. Did you know my parents were okay with me going to the same park at night? I don't think they even know about it. Anyway, I had to present what I had in class, and I sorta made things up as I went along. Why? Is there a problem?"

Sara looked at Brian, silently asking if she should continue questioning Rose. He simply blinked to indicate his approval.

"Is that all you've done, research the attack on social and print media? Nothing else?" Sara asked.

Rose shook her head from side to side.

"Did you know Angela Blunt?" Sara continued.

"Nope." Rose answered quickly and without hesitation.

"I know you had nothing to with the incident, but can you tell me where you were the night she disappeared?"

"At home, with my parents. You can check if you want." Again, Rose replied quickly and confidently.

"No need." Brian made a few notes in his pad. "One more question. Do you know anything about the incident that you're not telling us?"

Without a moment's hesitation, Rose answered, "No. Absolutely not. I think what happened is horrible and if I did know anything, I would certainly tell you." Rose shocked herself at her ability to lie so well. She still had the yellow rope under her bed, she knew exactly what had happened, and she was aware of what the attacker looked like, yet she was able to lie as if she was telling the truth.

Rose looked around the room and asked, "Is that all?"

The three adults looked at each other and nodded in agreement. Rose nodded too and walked out of the office. Brian and Sara thanked Mr. Taggart for his time and he escorted them out to the front door. As Brian and Sara walked to the car, Sara thanked him for letting her tag along and lead the interview.

"No problem. You know she was lying, right?"

"What?" Sara stopped short, grabbed Brian's arm, and spun him around. "You're sure?"

"Is water wet? Learn to read people, Sara. It's what I was talking about. She was lying through her teeth. If Rose Metzel didn't kill Angela Blunt, she knows who did, or knows a hell of a lot more than she's telling."

"How the fuck do you know that?"

Brian looked Sara squarely in the eyes. "If someone accused you of murder, would you not get your guard up, become defensive, or something? All Rose did was smile politely and offer her condolences and assistance. Have you ever accused anyone of doing anything bad? I mean like 'murder' bad."

"No."

"If I accused you of murder, would you politely say 'No,' or become a little pissed?"

"I'd freak all over your ass."

Brian flipped his eyebrows up and down, unlocked the car, started the engine, and secured his seatbelt.

"You up for more detective work?" he asked.

"You bet."

7

It was just after noon when Brian and Sara arrived at Butler Park. Brian parked the car in the lot and they both walked across the grass instead of taking the paths. Brian always enjoyed the walk through the thick grass, and could never understand taking the paved path through the park. Sara was going to take the path but decided to follow her senior partner. Even in the grass, Brain kept a steady pace. Sara continued to walk a few steps behind him, which made Brain feel very uncomfortable. He continued to slow his pace, hoping that Sara would catch up and walk beside him instead of behind him. Finally, Brian stopped and waited for Sara to catch up before asking her why she walked behind him.

"It's not that I want to. I just can't keep up. I'm a slow walker and even your slow pace is too fast for me."

Brian laughed out loud and went back to his regular pace in the grass, and Sara almost started to trot to stay beside him. Even as Sara began to pant, Brian never let up. He arrived at the tree with the memorial to Angela Blunt, stopped about twenty feet away, and stared at the sight. Sara stood beside him, breathing heavily. He crossed his arms and scanned the area from left to right for anything that might catch his eye. Fall was coming; Brian could feel it in the air. He pulled the collar on his suit jacket up high and crossed the lapels on the front.

"What are you looking for?" Sara inquired.

Brian stayed silent and stared straight ahead. He had been looking around the park, but was now fixated on the area around the tree. There was an uncomfortable silence between them as Sara waited for Brian to answer.

"You know, if you answer me, maybe I can help," Sara said with a sarcastic tone.

"I'm waiting for the scene to speak to me."

"Has it ever worked before?"

"Not once. But there's always a first time." Brian turned to Sara, lowered himself down, crossed his legs, and sat in the grass. "What is it about shrines? I don't understand the concept of placing flowers around the site where someone has died. Seriously, if someone dies in a crash, do you start leaving flowers in the middle of an intersection? Maybe I'm old and miserable or just a prick but I. Don't. Get. It ." Brian placed his chin in his hand and laid his elbow on his thigh. Resting his chin in his hand was a habit he had adopted when he was a child whenever he started to think hard about something. It was learned behaviour from his father, and each time he did it, he felt his father watching over him.

The wind picked up and the few leaves that had already fallen blew across the park. All the grass in the park was long, and lying flat for the most part, but some of it would lift with a gust and then fall when the wind died down. Brian looked to the right and something caught his eye.

"I just heard something speak to me," Brian said, never taking his eyes off of the spot that had caught his attention. He stood up and walked over to the spot that stood out. Approximately ten feet from the crime scene was an area that was remarkably different from the rest of the grass. Brian stopped and looked down. Sara joined him.

"Something spoke to you?"

"The scene spoke to me and said 'look here.'" Brian pointed to the area of dirt and grass that had been turned over. The grass was folded back onto itself, and some of the blades stood straight up and revealed a few shoe prints in the dirt where the grass had been scrubbed away. They were predominantly scruffs, but there was one solid shoe print to be seen. Brian got down on all fours and looked closely at the area. It was definitely a shoe print, he thought. Whoever had been here had dragged their foot back and forth through the grass to the dirt below, and then stood in the freshly overturned earth, leaving a fresh print.

"Now why would someone be searching through the grass, here of all places?" Brian turned and looked towards the area where the shrine was erected, then returned his gaze back to this spot.

Sara thought Brian was talking to her and answered, "There could be a number of reasons."

Brian looked up at Sara. "Huh?"

"You weren't talking to me?" Sara looked embarrassed.

"Was I thinking out loud again? I have a tendency to talk to myself. I don't usually have a partner so I talk to myself a lot. It helps get the juices flowing."

Brian got within inches of the footprint and asked Sara to join him. He pointed to the shoe print in the dirt. "Notice anything?"

Not wanting to embarrass herself, Sara thought long and hard as she examined the print carefully.

"Good edges, lots of detail, deep groves, soil must've been moist when it was made. We can get a good cast."

Brian looked disappointed. "Go beyond the obvious."

Sara looked again. "Go beyond the obvious. Okay!" Sara put her mind into overdrive and ran several ideas before it finally clicked. "Son of a fucking bitch. You're right. Rose was here."

*****

Rose sat in class wondering how the police knew about her presentation the day before. She looked straight ahead at the professor, but her mind was lost to the discussion going on around her. Her teachers had become accustomed to Rose not always being the most involved, but she always ended up at the tops of her classes. The professor paid little attention to Rose as she simply followed the class with her eyes and nothing else.

"*Who could have called the police? And why? Did I raise any further suspicion, or lay it to rest?*" Rose's mind raced with question after question. Each answer was the same: "*How could they think I was involved?*" Class ended at the top of the hour. The other students packed up their bags and exited the class, leaving Rose alone. Slowly, she stood, closed her books, and stuffed them into her backpack.

The professor noticed Rose taking her time. She was still gathering her books as the students for the next class started to file in.

"Rose?"

She looked up from her desk. "Yes?"

"Are you okay? You seem a little spaced out today."

Rose walked past the other students as they entered and stopped beside the professor's desk to speak with him.

"I'm just a little scatter-brained today. A lot to think about."

He nodded. "If you need anything, let me know." It was always easy to speak with Rose. When the professors got together, they talked, mostly about their students, and mostly about the bad ones or the exceptional ones. It was the first week of school, and already Rose was known as a model student. She had a reputation as a hard worker, had never been in trouble in high school, and her past grades would give her a pass on minor infractions that would get other students noticed.

Rose thanked her professor, hugged her backpack close to her chest, and walked out of the room to her next class. As she walked down the hall, she passed the main entrance, stopped, turned, and decided to go home instead.

*****

The investigative unit had secured the area of the park around the shrine and the new print found in the dirt. Technicians scanned the grass in and out of the secured area with metal detectors. Several technicians were busy taking pictures of different areas of the park, and one of them had carefully cut the long grass with scissors around the shoe print and poured white liquid plaster into a cardboard box frame around it. The plaster was then levelled across the entire surface.

Pictures had already been taken of the footprint before the casting, and measurements had been carefully collected. Back at the station they would input the tread pattern to see if they could match the boot to a manufacturer.

Nothing new had been found in the park. Brian sat in the grass with his legs crossed, feeling the coolness of the earth on the seat of his pants. His pants had been stained green from kneeling in the grass. His chin rested in his hands again, and his elbows on his knees. Sara already recognized this posture as a habit of Brian's that he tended to repeat when he was in thought. This being her first day working with him, Sara stood behind Brian silently, not wanting to get in the way of the technicians or her new partner. She found it odd that someone of Brian's age would sit on the ground like a child, but kept her thoughts to herself.

Brian remained silent and unmoving, like a stone. He watched the technicians do their job, not wanting to interfere. He absorbed all the events before him and made mental notes, oblivious to everything other than the actions of those responsible for collecting evidence. His cell phone buzzed several times but he ignored it completely.

"You're sure the footprint is that of Rose Metzel?" Sara asked, breaking the tension.

"Is the sky blue? Is water wet?" Brian answered without moving. "Did you notice the size of the shoe? Rose is petite and the imprint was that of a small boot."

"I thought that as well, but it could have been a little kid turning the grass over, looking for something."

"Think, Sara. What was special about the shoe? Yes, it's small, but how many kids wear boots with high heels?" Brian pushed himself up, brushed the dirt from his pants, and squared his shoulders, causing his neck to crack audibly. "The print has a pointed toe and a space between the ball of the foot and the small, deeper section of the heel. The print clearly shows a number 'five.' That's a small woman's shoe size. And the clear and distinctive tread pattern is unworn, indicating that the boot is new. It's the first week of September. Every kid in elementary school, high school, college, or university buys new clothes, shoes, boots, laptops, cell phones, and shit at this time of year. And that," Brian paused and pointed at the cardboard box on the ground that held the plaster in place, "is the print of a brand new boot of a small woman."

*****

Rose lay in bed, alone. The house was quiet; her parents were still at work. Rose had decided not to tell Taylor that she was going home. He would have asked to stop by for a load of "laundry." Laundry was not on her mind. Rose couldn't get the thought of the two police detectives talking to her out of her head. The more she thought about it, the more incensed she became. She had done nothing wrong and yet they had still wanted to speak with her.

As she lay there, she imagined straddling the male detective, his arms handcuffed behind his back, her hands around his neck. What would it feel like to choke a person, knowing full well that you weren't going to let go until they were dead? How long would it take to choke someone to death? Three minutes? Longer, she thought; surely it must take longer for the body to use all the stored oxygen in the lungs. Then panic would set in as the body tries desperately to bring in fresh oxygen, but the hands around the trachea prevent any air exchange.

Then when the male detective was dead, she would take her time on that prissy little female detective. Rose thought she was trying to be the good cop to his bad cop. She saw right through the charade. Rose would gently put her hands around the female detective's neck and apply pressure, watching as the life slowly ebbed from her pretty little body. The detective would look up to see Rose smiling. Her fingernails would dig into the back of the detective's neck, her thumbs pressing down hard on the front of her throat.

Rose would watch as tiny vessels in the eyes would burst as she squeezed. Each time a vessel burst, a little more of the detective's life would slip away. Rose thought about kissing the detective in the last moment of life. She would then look down on the limp body of the dead female detective and see what she had done. Rose felt jubilant to think that she had just killed two cops - detectives, nonetheless.

Rose realized this scenario may have been fantasy, but she had never wanted anything so badly before. Having the power to kill or to spare lives; surely that was what doctors must feel like. You could save a patient or secretly nick a blood vessel and let them bleed out and die.

She retrieved her phone and texted Taylor, "Laundry?"

*****

The man sat alone in the restaurant enjoying a bowl of chicken noodle soup and garlic toast. He was young, clean-shaven, and good-looking. As he leaned forward to sip his soup, his dark hair fell forward over his forehead. With his free hand, he brushed it back. He finished his soup and toast, sat back, and wiped the butter from his thin lips.

The server stopped by his booth and asked if he had enjoyed his soup.

"If I didn't like the soup, Stella, would I stop by every day and order the same thing?" He laughed.

"You want your water topped up before you head out?"

"Nah. All done. One day I'll find out how you guys make the soup and stop coming here."

"Back to work?" Stella asked.

"Dollar store first. I have a few things to pick up."

Stella laughed and walked away, thinking that one day she might tell him that his beloved meal was canned soup that the chef liked to tell everyone was homemade.

He didn't need a bill; it was the same every weekday. He left a ten-dollar bill on the table to cover his meal and tip. He gulped down the last of his water, waved to Stella, and left the restaurant to go back to work. He always ordered the large bowl of soup and garlic toast, and he felt the meal settling in his stomach. He adjusted his leather belt and ran his hand around his waist. The memory of how the belt had been used made him feel good. No, it made him feel alive.

Two blocks south of the restaurant, he walked into a dollar store. He knew exactly what he wanted and where it was located: down the centre aisle, immediately beside the tarps, was the yellow nylon cord. Cheap, sturdy, and almost impossible to track down. He chose a package of fifty feet of bright yellow nylon rope packaged in a clear plastic wrapper. He flipped his purchase in the air as he walked to the cashier, paid for it in cash, and left the receipt on the counter.

He walked back to the insurance company where he worked, pulled the bottom drawer of his desk open, and placed the bag with the rope behind some files.

"Good lunch, Jeff?" his boss asked as he walked passed his desk.

"Always good, boss. Thanks."

Jeff answered the ringing phone and went back to work.

8

Rose told her mother she wasn't feeling well, skipped dinner, and stayed in her bedroom. It was hard to lie about her health with two parents for doctors, but she had learnt at a young age to keep her ailments vague, non-descript, and not too serious. She never told her parents that she had a headache; that led to too many possibly serious conditions. She knew never tell them that her chest was sore or tight, either; that elicited the same type of reaction. Now she simply told them that she felt a little achy and tired.

Rose lay on her back in bed, held the plastic bag with the yellow rope in her hands, and felt elated and excited as she looked at it. She spun it around, examining it closely, and failed to note anything special about the rope. The more she examined the rope, the more motivated she became. She rubbed her thighs together and became more aroused as a thought came to her mind. She texted Taylor again to see if he was free to do "laundry." He replied that he was bogged down with homework and asked about the next night. Rose told him that her cell phone was almost dead but that she would love to meet after dinner tomorrow. She plugged in her phone even though it was almost fully charged, hid the plastic bag under her mattress, and raced downstairs to the basement with a basket of her dirty laundry.

Rose passed her mother, who was surprised to see her daughter up. "Feeling okay, honey?"

She smiled at her mother. "Might as well clean my room instead if of just lying in bed," she answered, and continued to the basement.

Rose dropped the basket of laundry in front of the washer, then went to the back of the basement and started to rummage through the tote boxes of old clothes. Her mother wasn't a neat freak or a pack rat, but she liked to keep things tidy. All of her old clothes and shoes were in clear totes, clearly labelled. Rose found an old pair of shoes, pants, a shirt, and a hoodie. She went to the laundry room and did a small load, putting all of the items into the washer with two full caps of laundry soap. Rose was hopping with anticipation.

Rose took the stairs two at a time and ran through the kitchen as her parents were sitting down to tea and shortbread cookies. She grabbed a biscuit off the plate, kissed her mother on the cheek, and started to make her way back upstairs.

"Feeling better, honey?" her mother called.

"Much!" Rose replied.

Rose found an old bra and pair of panties that she didn't want anymore, changed into them, and threw her used ones in the hamper. She put on an over-sized sweat suit and waited for the load to finish its cycle, then placed her clothes in the dryer.

While she waited for the clothes to dry, she felt like her old self again. She finished her homework then went downstairs, put her clean clothes on under her sweats, and told her parents she was going out for a walk.

In the backyard, she removed her sweatpants and sweatshirt, put on a pair of leather gloves, removed the yellow rope from the plastic bag, and stuffed her clothing into it. She hid the plastic bag under her father's boat trailer, which was now winterized for the season. The yellow rope went into her hoodie pocket along with an old pocket knife and a small plastic bag, and she held on to both items tightly, making sure they didn't fall out and get lost. She flipped the hood over her head and started to dart from one backyard to the next.

Rose ran to the centre of town, ducking between houses and down alleys, before she stopped to catch her breath. She was excited, and she couldn't believe what she was doing. She crouched down beside the side of a strip plaza in the shadows. Only one road ran past the plaza, and the security lights didn't illumi-nate the area well at all. Beyond the plaza, a low-rent housing project surrounded the south side of the area. Streetlights that had burnt out long ago had gone unchanged. It was sad that the city hadn't bothered to repair the streetlights, Rose thought, but this oversight now made for the perfect spot to hunt her prey. Rose wasn't sure exactly what she was looking for, but she knew she would know it once she saw it. Her chest heaved as she breathed deeply. The temperature of the night air was starting to drop, and it was cooler than normal for early September.

A group of children walked past. Most of them were texting, and no one was speaking to anybody. Rose let them walk by, and they continued on in silence. Now she saw what her parents kept talking about. Rose thought that she could have been lying in the shadows, dead or hurt, and the group of kids wouldn't have noticed. They were too busy with their cell phones to even look up or talk to one another.

As she waited, her excitement waned, and Rose began to wonder if what she was planning was a good idea or better left as a fantasy than turned into reality. She sat in the dark for over an hour before a lone figure approached from the north, heading south towards the apartments. The person walking was definitely a young girl, Rose thought; small enough that if things went wrong, Rose could run away. She fit the profile of the other dead girls from what Rose could see, and she was pretty and had long hair. Rose stood, and felt that her leg muscles had tensed up. She rubbed her thighs to work out the kinks in her legs.

Rose casually started to walk behind the girl with only a slightly quicker pace. Looking down, she watched her old shoes step forward and then disappear beneath her as she followed her prey. Rose looked up every few moments to see how much farther the girl was in front of her. She then pretended to be texting, and held the pocket knife like a mobile phone.

Rose kept an eye on the girl in front of her as she calmly walked up the street. Rose hummed a tune, and laughed as if she had just read something funny on her imaginary pocket knife phone. At one point, Rose laughed out loud, and the girl in front chuckled. *"Good,"* Rose thought to herself. *"The girl is relaxed, so her guard is down."*

Up the street, Rose noticed a section of sidewalk that was darker than the rest. Two consecutive streetlights were out, and she hadn't seen a car drive past since she had started to stalk the girl. As they approached the darkened section, Rose picked up her pace and pocketed the knife. When they were hidden by the shadows, Rose struck.

Rose pushed the girl from behind. The girl had her hands tucked inside her jacket pockets and fell forward, flat onto her face. Rose stepped up to her and kicked her hard, repeatedly, anywhere and everywhere. Rose aimed for the girl's stomach, and her foot found its mark several times. The girl on the ground curled up into the fetal position, trying to protect herself. Her legs covered her stomach, and her arms protected her face and head. She tried to scream, but she couldn't speak or yell. The repeated kicks to her stomach had caused all the air to escape her lungs, and yelps and moans were all that the girl could muster.

Rose didn't stop the barrage of kicks. The girl on the ground rolled away from her attacker in an attempt to escape, but her strategy only sent her farther into the darkness where she was more deeply hidden from the street. Rose continued to kick her as she rolled away. The girl, weakened by the barrage, let her arms fall to the side. Her leg muscles, too weak to protect her stomach, simply collapsed.

From the repeated blows to the head, both of the girl's eyes were already swollen shut. Rose was confident that the battered girl was unable to see her and had not glimpsed her during the attack. Rose picked up the girl by the wrists and dragged her behind a clump of trees before letting her arms drop. The weakened girl made a feeble attempt to scream for help, but a pitiful squeak was all that she could muster. It was enough to send Rose into a rage. With adrenaline pumping, Rose swung her leg back, and with all her force, kicked her in the stomach. The girl curled up from the impact and vomited on the grass. She was defeated. Rose was breathing heavily and could hardly contain herself.

Rose stepped over the girl to roll her onto her stomach and stepped in the vomit, causing her foot to slide in the grass. Rose stumbled but caught herself before she fell. She regained her footing, grabbed the girl by the waistband of her pants, pulled up swiftly, and rolled her onto her stomach. Rose sat on the small of the girl's back. With one hand she pulled the girl's head back, and retrieved the yellow cord from the plastic bag with the other. The girl gasped, and Rose could smell vomit on her breath. She coiled one end of the rope around her palm, grabbed the other end, and wrapped the cord around the girl's neck.

Rose pulled hard on the yellow cord like the reins on a horse bridle. The girl coughed, made a sickly gurgling sound, and clawed at the rope around her neck. Her fingers dug deeply into her own neck as she tried to loosen the grip of the rope, and her nails cut into her skin. Blood started to flow around the yellow nylon rope. Rose saw the girl trying to defend herself, and pulled higher and tighter. She twisted the rope for only a few seconds more before the girl lost consciousness and collapsed.

Rose stood over the unconscious girl, breathing heavily, her chest heaving. Rose had thought that she was going to be more nervous. Instead, she was excited, and the attack left her wanting more. She pulled the glove off of her right hand and checked for the pulse in the girl's neck like her parents had taught her. She wasn't moving, but she was breathing normally and had a steady pulse. Rose put the leather glove back on and knelt beside the girl.

Satisfied with the results, Rose tossed the rope to the ground. She reached into her pocket, pulled out her pocket knife, and flipped open the blade. Rose grabbed a handful of the girl's hair from the back of her head and began to sever clumps, watching it fall onto the victim's own back. Rose scattered some of the loose hair on the ground and stuffed a handful into the plastic sandwich bag. She checked the girl's pulse again; it was steady and strong. Her breathing was regular. Satisfied that the girl's condition was stable, Rose casually stood, and made certain that she had the pocket knife and the hair in her pants pocket. She purposely left the rope behind and then ran into the darkness and disappeared.

Back at the house, Rose stripped down, put her old clothing and shoes in the bag, donned her clean clothes, and hid the bag in the same spot. Rose was so excited that she could barely contain herself, as evidenced by her soaked panties. She paced back and forth in her backyard, wondering what to do next. She was almost giddy and felt exhilaration she had never felt before. When her excitement abated, Rose took a few deep breaths and decided it was time to go back inside. In the distance, Rose could make out sirens racing to a scene somewhere.

Inside, Rose's parents were in the living room. Her mother was reading and her father was watching the television as Rose rushed in, kissed them on their cheeks, and ran upstairs without saying a word. Rose closed her bedroom door, tore off her clothes, tossed them in the hamper, put on her nightshirt, and jumped on her bed. She sat crossed-legged and powered up her phone to text Taylor. She started to message him, stopped, and erased what she had typed. She realized that she was still too excited to start texting, and that she might say something wrong inadvertently. Instead, she powered up her tablet and started to stream the local news. Nothing was being reported about the attack. She checked the homepage of the online newspaper, and again, she found nothing. *"Maybe it's too soon,"* she thought. She searched every news site in the region and didn't find a single mention of the incident. Rose even Googled "police and ambulance broadcasts," but discovered nothing.

Rose thought about the story that she would read tomorrow in the print paper. She wanted to see the print paper, more so than reading it online. She was beginning to understand why the old print newspapers were so important to some people. After wrapping herself in a thick terrycloth robe, Rose went downstairs to find her father asleep in front of the television and her mother at the dining room table researching a case for one of her patients on her laptop. Rose grabbed a glass of water for herself and one for her mother. She placed one glass to the right of her mother's computer, pulled a chair out from the table, and sat down beside her. Her mother stopped what she was doing, closed the laptop lid, and took a sip of water.

Although she knew Rose had outgrown it long ago, Mrs. Metzel wanted to stroke her daughter's hair, and she couldn't resist. Rose leaned in and closed her eyes just like she had when she was a child. It felt good.

"You haven't joined me at the table in years. What's up?" Mrs. Metzel asked as she took another sip.

"Just thinking about the old times."

Mrs. Metzel laughed out loud. "You're still so young. You don't have old times yet."

"It's all relative, Mom. You've been working since before I was born. Your career doesn't seem that long to you, but for me, it's been a lifetime."

"You're pretty smart. You must get that from me. Certainly not from your dad."

"Whatcha working on?" Rose changed the subject.

"I have a patient with a weird skin condition and I can't figure out what it is. Thought I would do some research before sending her to a dermatologist. Nothing serious. How's school?"

"Actually, I did some research myself tonight for my Social Studies class. It was pretty exciting." Rose smiled behind the glass as she took a sip.

"What kind of research?"

"Field."

"Have I mentioned how proud I am of you and your brother?"

Rose laughed, took another drink of water, and answered, "All the time, Ma."

Rose stood, walked behind her mother, and watched her continue to work on her computer. She rested her head on her mother's shoulder and felt a familiar gentle hand rise from the keyboard and stroke her hair. Rose continued to silently watch her mother work for a few minutes, then raised her head without saying a word, kissed her on the cheek, walked over to the couch, and kissed her father on the head. He didn't move or wake up. Mrs. Metzel watched her daughter run upstairs, and then went back to researching skin diseases for her patient.

*****

The man bolted up in bed, breathing heavily and drenched in his own sweat. He ran his hand through his wet hair and it felt as if he had just gone for a swim. He swung his legs over the edge of the bed and sat for a moment to catch his breath. The images in his head were too vivid to have been a dream. But he had been asleep when he had seen them, so it had to have been one. What else could it have been?

He had seen the entire event through the eyes of the person who had attacked the young girl, choked her, cut her hair, and left her unconscious in the grass. It was only after the assault was over that he had somehow moved out of the attacker's body, and was able to float around and see the face of the person who had pretended to be him. The image that he couldn't shake was that of someone else using the yellow nylon rope he had lost. He was then able to follow her back to her own home, and had watched her change and enter the house; he had even seen her interactions with her parents.

He couldn't take the chance that what he had seen wasn't a dream. If anyone found the rope and the cut hair, the police may try to blame him for this one. And the last thing he wanted was more attention - or potential clues that may lead the police back to him.

He got dressed and knew exactly where to go. And after he was done, he would drive by the house he had seen in his dream and find out if that pretty young girl really lived there.

*****

Brian continued to look over the plaster cast photos taken earlier in the day. He had them laid out on the kitchen table. He pushed his laptop aside to concentrate on the pictures. He would look at one and then toss it onto the table, making it spin in the air before it slid across. Brian took notes of even the most insignificant details in his pad and circled areas of interest on the pictures with a coloured marker. He kept going back to the one picture that clearly showed the sole of the size five boot. As he had noticed at the crime scene, the treads were new, with no discernable marks, no wear patterns, and nothing stuck in the grooves. It was almost as if the boot had been taken right from the store shelves and used to make an imprint in the moist earth.

Marcie pushed the pictures aside and placed a cup of coffee on the table. It was Brian's favourite mug: a large ceramic one in the shape of Spiderman. Brian picked up the mug, blew across the top to cool the coffee, and took a sip. He pulled back quickly and grimaced.

"Seriously, after all these years, you can't wait for a few minutes for the coffee to cool? You burn your tongue every single time. You never learn," Marcie said as she pulled a chair from the table and it screeched across the tile floor. "You never stay up this late unless you can't figure something out. What's got you so dumbfounded?"

"Dumbfounded?" Brian looked at this wife. "Dumbfounded?"

"Okay. What's got you so perplexed?"

Brian looked up at Marcie again, who was smiling from ear to ear. "You want anything with that coffee?" she asked.

"How about a thesaurus so I can learn what the hell you're saying. That and a rice crispy treat would be nice. Thanks. Oh, make it two. Those damn packages are small." Brian went back to looking at the photos on the table while Marcie went to the kitchen.

From the kitchen, Marcie yelled out, "Okay hon, what's got you so confused?"

Brian organized the photos into three piles: the first murder, the second murder, and then the third. He then put the photos in each pile into some form of chronological order.

Marcie walked out with a cup of coffee for herself and a handful of silver foil-wrapped treats. She dropped a few in front of Brian, saved one for herself, took a seat, and held her cup with both hands. "Okay, what have you got so far?"

Brian held up the first two stacks of photos. "Each of these girls was attacked and strangled with what we think was cheap nylon rope. The attacks came ninety days apart. Not ninety-one, but ninety days exactly. The attacker cut each girls' hair and left 'em for dead out in the open." He moved the first two piles of photos to the side.

Brian then held up the third pile of photos. "These were taken again exactly ninety days after the second attack. The girl was also strangled, and her hair was cut off, but she was strangled with a belt. And for some reason, she was buried in a shallow grave." Brian placed the pile of photos down and away from the first pile. "The rest of the guys on the team think the third girl is a copycat, but I say it's the same killer. It's like a game of Survivor. We've got Tribe One Killer and Tribe Two Killer. Hell, I flip-flop between the two camps almost every day. I can't seem to make up my mind."

Marcie took a sip of coffee, moved her cup away from the area in front of her to avoid spilling anything on the photos, and asked to see the first pile. She flipped through them, examining the crime scene photos carefully, not really sure what she was looking for, but thinking that perhaps an untrained eye could spot something her husband and the police couldn't. She looked at each photo before slipping it to the back of the pile until she got through all of them. As Marcie examined each print, she thought that she should be more affected by the dead girls lying in the grass. Instead, she rationalized that it was a case, just like the dozens before that she had helped talk her husband through in the last twenty years he had been on the force. She shut off her emotions to stay focused on the task at hand, knowing that she would cry in bed later as she thought of what she was now looking at.

After placing the first pile on the table, she picked up the second, and examined those photos with the same degree of scrutiny as the first. After finishing her examination of the third pile, she took in a deep breath, sipped her now-cold coffee, and stated, "These three girls are definitely connected."

"Why?"

"All three girls look so much alike they could be sisters. That's not a mistake and couldn't be a coincidence."

Marcie grabbed a picture of each one of the three girls that showed the ligature mark. "Your killer is right-handed. He holds the left side of the ligature more horizontal and pulls back and up with his right dominant hand." Marcie pointed at the pictures that showed the marks on the girls' necks. "I see what you mean that the first two girls were killed with a rope. You can actually make out the rope pattern around the two girls' necks. But the third girl has a flat indentation around her neck." Marcie looked to Brian. "You said the third girl was strangled with a belt."

Brian pointed to the area at the back of the neck where there were multiple, tiny, evenly-spaced holes visible. "Forensics counted five complete holes and possibly one partial. If it is a partial hole, the thinking is that the person must have lost a lot of weight and added a few more holes to the belt."

"How do you know that?" Marcie held up a finger. "Wait, most belts have five holes. Any more were probably added afterwards to accommodate the weight loss."

"Very good. We got that, too. But are you sure it's a 'He'? None of the three girls were raped."

Marcie paused, thought about it, and said, "If it is a guy, the attacks aren't sexual to him; it's about power. If it's a girl doing the attacks, it's about control. My guess, it's gotta be a guy."

Brian asked very softly, "Why?"

Marcie explained that the three girls looked very much alike; they were average-looking, not beautiful, and certainly wouldn't stand out in a crowd. Each victim was probably stalked beforehand. He chose the girls based on appearance, maybe because they reminded him of someone that he really wanted to kill but couldn't. Marcie went on to say that if the attacker was a girl, she would most likely be killing girls who had scorned her. Marcie told Brian that when she was in high school, some of the girls had formed a small group and would taunt less popular girls. And they could be very cruel. This girl may have been taunted and pushed, and these actions were her way of fighting back.

Marcie asked to see the autopsy reports on the three girls. Brian pulled them from the file, and after Marcie read them she pointed out that all three girls were approximately the same weight and height, give or take a few pounds and inches.

"We got that, too."

Marcie took another look at the photos and after examining them again, she turned them over and looked at her husband. "It's the same guy who did all three. I'm sure of it."

"Explain."

"Look at the placement of the ligature marks around the necks. They're almost exactly in the same spot on all three victims. The girls are all pretty much the same height, which means the attacker repeated the same method on all three girls. I accounted for the width of the belt too, before you ask." Marcie smiled coyly at Brian and took another sip of cold coffee.

Brian had already finished his coffee. "After hearing it from you, I'm convinced that it's just one attacker. But why ninety days apart, and why these girls? What is it about the way these girls look that makes him want to kill them? And why use a belt on the third?"

Marcie got up from the table, grabbed her mug and Brian's, and headed to the kitchen. "Those questions are best left for the men and women of law enforcement. I'm just a store manager and in a different pay grade. You're not even supposed to be showing me those photos."

"It's good to get a different perspective. You're my conscious, my sounding board."

"Whatever I am, you make sure you put that shit away before you come to bed, hon. I don't want to have to clean your mess in the morning." Marcie placed the mugs in the sink. "I'm tired and have to work in the morning, big guy. Don't be too late." Marcie went upstairs, leaving Brian to work things out in his head. She and Brian had been going over crime scene photos and details for years. For them, it was a game - a very serious game - but it kept them close, and they both enjoyed working out the details of a difficult case.

Marcie went to the bathroom, brushed her teeth, and started to disrobe as she walked to the bedroom. She tossed her clothes into the hamper, put on her thick oversized sweater, crawled into bed, and started to cry. The images were now stuck with her forever, and in a very small way, she hated Brian for involving her in crimes like the one at which she had just finished looking. She wiped her tears with the back of her arm, turned off the bedside lamp, pulled the sheet up high around herself, and hoped that she wouldn't have nightmares if she managed to sleep.

9

Rose woke up the next morning and, before even getting out of bed, grabbed her phone off the nightstand and began searching for tweets or Facebook posts in her news feeds about the attack the night before. She scrolled through different local news sites and became annoyed when she couldn't find anything mentioning an attack on a young girl.

She ran downstairs to the kitchen. Her mother and father were already up, dressed, and sitting down at the dining room table having breakfast. She aimed the remote at the television on the kitchen counter and flipped through the channels until she found the local morning show.

"Well, good morning to you too," Mr. Metzel said with his mouth full.

Rose chose to ignore him. She was lost in her own world.

"Hey!" A more aggressive greeting from her father jolted Rose back to reality. She turned to see her mother and father at the table.

"I'm sorry."

"What's so important?"

"Remember that Social Studies class I told you about? Well, I'm trying to see if there is any news for my assignment. That's all." Rose flipped through the channels, paused on each news broadcast, watched the ticker tape news feeds at the bottom of the screen, and failed to see anything about a young girl being attacked the night before. She dropped the remote on the counter and ran upstairs without saying another word.

Rose checked her phone again to see if she had missed any texts or messages, but the only new text was from Taylor telling her that he missed her, loved her, and would see her in class. Something inside Rose began to boil over, and she felt the tension building inside her. She wasn't mad; she was livid. She wasn't even sure why it upset her to this degree. Looking at the text from Taylor only enraged her more. She gripped the phone tightly and flung it onto the bed. It bounced off the mattress, hit the wall, and fell to the floor. Rose simply turned away and went to the bathroom to get ready for school.

*****

Brian was already at his desk when Sara walked in wearing her old uniform blues. Brian didn't even look up from the same photos that he and Marcie had debated over the previous night. He tossed a file over to the corner of his desk and asked her to take a look at the lab reports and the photos of the shoe cast.

"Ah, maybe I shouldn't." Sara's voice was subdued.

"Why?" It was only then that Brian looked up and saw Sara wearing her uniform. "Get the hell outta that thing, we have work to do today."

"I was only allowed to work with you yesterday because there weren't any other female detectives to assist you at the school when you interviewed Rose Metzel. I'm back on the road today." Sara sounded apologetic.

"Bullshit. I'm heading back to the school today to see Rose and if you had to be there yesterday, you have to come with me today. Go get changed and I'll clear it with the shift commander."

Sara was beaming as she left Brian's office, and he picked up the phone to demand that Sara be assigned to him for the balance of the investigation. There was some friendly arguing between old friends, and before the conversation was finished, Brian had a new full-time partner until the case was solved.

Brian was lost in thought again when Sara walked in wearing a pair of jeans, a button-up dress shirt, and a denim jacket.

"Not exactly detective apparel. But I'll dress more appropriately tomorrow." Sara tugged at the base of her jacket to hide the gun clipped to her belt. "I'm ready whenever you are."

Brian asked her to take a look at the photos of the cast and the rest of the pictures taken the previous day.

"Oh, take a look at this." Brian flipped her a sheet of paper with the incoming call logs from the last week.

"What am I looking for?"

"I'm testing your powers of observations, detective."

Sara glowed when Brian called her "detective." She scanned the photocopied sheet of names and followed her finger down the list until she stopped short. Sara looked up from the sheet to see Brian grimacing.

"The notes say she called to get information on the Angela Blunt murder. But we asked her if she had researched the incident on anything other than social media. And she said she hadn't. She lied again," Sara said, surprised by what she had read.

"Semantics. Technically, they didn't put her call through to anyone, but you'd think she would've said something about that. Do you believe in coincidences?"

"Like Karma, what goes around comes around, shit like that? And I mean shit." Sara looked very serious. "You make your own luck. I hate whiners who complain that some people have all the luck but won't go out and make things happen for themselves. In the case of our friend Rose, I'm betting she knows a lot more and is more involved than she lets on." Sara grabbed the portable radio from Brian's desk and clipped it to her belt. "Let's go ask her just what the fuck she really knows."

*****

He woke up, still tired from the activities of the previous night. He had to call in sick before going back to bed, knowing full well that he never could've gone to work. He was exhausted, dirty, and pissed. Walking to the bathroom, he couldn't rationalize how he knew what he knew. He braced himself on the bathroom vanity and stared at himself in the mirror in disbelief. He had seen things the night before. In his mind, he saw a girl attacked, strangled, and left unconscious. It could've been a bad dream, but he saw the face of the person who attacked the girl, saw the victim's hair being cut, and, most importantly, saw the yellow nylon rope he had lost being dropped beside the girl lying unconscious on the ground. He saw the exact location and knew where it was.

The timing wasn't right; it was too soon between girls. He had to go and clean things up. He had to finish what was started - what was left undone. He had buried the body away from anywhere he had buried any of the other bodies. She wasn't even the right type, but there were too many similarities between his work and the attack the previous night. He had been so careful in the past. How had anyone known about all of the details, including the rope, he wondered? He had specifically chosen that rope because there were so many styles and brands that were not only close, but next to impossible to match, or so he had thought. Someone had found the rope he had lost, or discovered the exact rope used, and that rope had to be found. He had searched frantically for the rope when he had lost it in the park, but couldn't find it in the dark. It wasn't the police who had found the rope; it had to be her. She had found the rope he had lost, had used it last night, and he had seen her face in his dream. She was young, and very pretty. Regardless of the fact that she wasn't his type, she was marked. She was dead.

*****

Brian and Sara pulled up to the university they had visited the day before, put the car in park, and walked to the front entrance. Brian held the door open for his new partner who graciously accepted the offer and walked past him into the foyer. She stopped before the print of the dean, Mr. Taggart, that Brian had noticed the day before.

"I noticed this time."

"A little advice: when you walk into a crime scene - well, pretty much anywhere - don't stare at your shoes. Your feet know where they're supposed to take you. Look above, around you, and ahead. It may save your life someday, and you can learn something, too." Brian stopped, stood beside Sara, and looked at the framed pictures of Mr. Taggart and the rest of the faculty. "If I looked like that guy there," Brian pointed, "no way in hell would I let them hang a picture of me in the lobby." He turned and walked towards the front office with Sara following closely behind, again trying to keep pace with his stride.

Brian introduced himself to the same receptionist, who once again asked them to take a seat until Mr. Taggart was ready to see them. They sat for only a few moments before the door to the dean's office opened and a frustrated-looking Mr. Taggart emerged. This time there were no pleasantries, just a hand movement gesturing for them to enter his office. Brian turned to Sara, smiled as he stood, and repeated Mr. Taggart's gesture, allowing Sara to enter before any of the gentlemen.

Mr. Taggart fell into his chair, obviously upset. The stern look on his face did nothing to hide his displeasure at a repeat visit from the detectives.

"What now?"

"We need to see Rose Metzel again, please. Just a few more questions are all we have. If you don't mind," requested Sara.

"I have to object to this – "

Mr. Taggart was cut short by Brian. "It's only going to take a few minutes of her time and yours. We just need to have – "

"Have what? A few more minutes of her time, and my time. For what? This investigation of yours doesn't concern me, this school, or– "

"Doesn't concern you or this school? Are you fucking kidding me?" Sara reached out and placed a gentle hand on Brian's shoulder as he continued. "Three girls have been killed, maybe more, and you think it doesn't concern you. What kind of sick bastard are you?"

Mr. Taggart stood up from behind his desk. "You listen here, detective. I strongly object to you coming in here to bully - "

"Well, I don't give a rat's ass to your objection. You listen here; I will get a search warrant to talk to every student, every professor, every teacher's assistant if I have to. I'll look in every single closet and classroom and storage locker, disrupting your whole school day, and making you look like the jackass who asked for the search. I'll do what I need to if it's in the best interest of the public." Brian stood and made his presence known to Mr. Taggart.

The dean sat back down, weighed his options, stood again, and left the office without saying a word. Brian sat back down as well. He held up his hand; it was shaking badly. "Flashbacks to my high school days. Always wanted to tell off my old principal. I thought I had bigger balls than this. Thought I was gonna piss my pants for a second there."

Sara squeezed her partner's arm for support and thought it best not to say anything. They both sat quietly until the office door opened. Rose Metzel followed closely behind Mr. Taggart. The dean took his chair. Rose sat in the chair in front of Mr. Taggart's desk and turned it to face the two detectives.

"Hi Rose. Remember us?" Sara asked.

Rose simply nodded in agreement and smiled politely.

"Can we ask you a few more questions about the incident in the park?"

Rose thought it was funny how they kept referring to the killing as "the incident." She also noted that they didn't mention anything about the girl from last night. Rose remained silent and nodded in agreement again.

Basic psychology was always taught to new police cadets, and Sara knew the art of mimicry. Scratch your nose and the person across the table will often scratch their nose. Place your hand on your chin and the person opposite you will do the same. Sara opened her notebook and crossed her legs. She paused for a few moments, pretending to read the notes in her book. Shortly after, Rose crossed her legs as well. Sara scribbled a few lines and let her pen fall to the carpet below. She bent forward, picked up the pen, and looked at the soles of Rose's running shoes. On the bottom of the shoe that dangled in the air, Sara noted an upside down number five.

Sara sat upright in her chair, pulled a large manila envelope from her bag, drew out a photo taken of the plaster cast, and handed it to Rose.

"Do you own a pair of shoes or boots that match that tread pattern?" she asked. Rose took the photo and studied it.

"The funny thing is, when I buy a pair of shoes or boots, I don't buy them based on their tread. So to answer your question, no, I don't recognize the tread pattern." Rose's voice was filled with disdain for the detective.

"Did you notice the size of the shoe in the cast?"

Rose looked closely at the picture. "Size five. Again, so?"

"You wear a size five, don't you?" Sara looked directly at Rose.

"If you took a poll of this school alone, I bet you would find close to a hundred girls who wear the same size. Why don't you round up every girl in town who wears a size five and question them?"

"But how many of them were at the park and left this print?"

"And you think I was there because someone with the same size shoe left a print?"

Mr. Taggart slammed his hand flat on the table. Everyone in the room turned to see Mr. Taggart as he demanded that this meeting come to an end. He stood before he could get a rebuttal from either detective, grabbed Rose by the arm, and escorted her from his office. Before leaving, he turned to the detectives and said, "You know the way out. Next time you show up to my school, bring that fucking warrant."

Brian looked at Sara. "Guess we wore out our welcome here."

Mr. Taggart walked beside Rose down the hallway. Rose didn't appear at all upset about the visit from the police. The two remained silent as they made their way to Rose's class. Finally, the dean asked Rose why the police were so interested in her.

Rose explained that she had become overly fascinated by the latest homicides in the city for her Social Studies class, and may have crossed the line by calling the newspapers and police, and going to visit the scenes of the attacks as part of her research. She went on to claim that the reason she had done that was to maintain her grades for med school, and that she felt ashamed that she had become over-zealous in her research.

When they arrived at Rose's classroom, Mr. Taggart held the door open for her as she passed by. Everyone in class turned to watch Rose walk back to her desk. For only a brief moment, Mr. Taggart wondered if someone so small, with such a bright future ahead, could really have been involved in any way with what the police claimed. He dismissed the thought as Rose took her seat and chatted with her classmates before the professor asked everyone to settle down.

As he returned to his office, Mr. Taggart felt pleased with himself for standing up to the police the way he had. It wasn't often that he had the opportunity or the will to do what he had done, but he had enjoyed it. He decided to make a short detour to the professors' parking lot, and made sure no one was around to see him before he unlocked his car, sat in the backseat, and lit a cigarette.

*****

The man with the upturned nose travelled to the Metzel residence. He was amazed that he knew exactly where to go. It was as if a beacon had been turned on inside his head and pinged the location of the house. He parked his car a few blocks away and walked to the house he had seen in his head. The image of the house was fuzzy and grainy, like a black-and-white photograph that was decades old. He turned a corner and saw the house before him, no longer blurry or in his mind. He knew the house, and as he got closer he could see the inside: the layout of the dining room, kitchen, and upstairs bedrooms. Most importantly, he could see the bedroom of the girl wearing the hoodie whom he had watched attack the female victim. Her bedroom was clear, vivid. He thought he must have been inside that room, but knew that was not possible. He knew the family from long ago. His sister had babysat for the Metzels. He wondered, in a world of coincidences, how this happenstance could be.

He approached the house, glanced at it only momentarily, and continued to walk past. He also looked around at the surrounding houses to see who might be outside, which houses faced the Metzel house, and if any of the trees and shrubs offered any kind of late-night coverage. The Metzel residence was as standard and non-descript as they come: two-storey brick and cheap, white, fake alumini-um shutters screwed in beside each of the street-facing windows. The front door was centred in the façade, and tall bushes were situated on either side of the door and under the windows.

He paused for moment, and then bent down to untie and retie his shoelaces as he scanned the side of the house. From the neighbour's property line to the

Metzel house, the yard was well treed, with more bushes and shrubs scattered throughout. The bushes would make it easy to hide to the side of the door, under the windows, or in the yard. None of the outside lights appeared to have motion sensors attached to them. *"Don't these people ever watch TV about how to crime proof their house?"* he thought to himself. He stood, tucked his hands in his jacket pockets, and made no attempt to look like he didn't belong on the street. A woman walking a dog turned the corner and strode towards him. As they approached he bent low to greet the dog, petted him, smiled at the lady, and continued to walk past.

"This is going to be easy." He stuffed his hands back into his jacket and continued to walk down the street.

*****

Back at the station, Brian was typing a search warrant request he knew would be refused. He painstakingly described the scene at the park where the last victim had been found, the circumstantial evidence discovered afterwards, the way Rose Metzel had described the attack in class, the shoe cast; everything of relevance. He knew the evidence he had proved nothing, and if he got a search warrant, a good lawyer would quash any evidence found, but he had nothing else to go on.

Brian finished the search warrant request form and hit "print." The laser printer hummed to life and spewed out a sheet of paper. The request for a warrant was based on, in his opinion, "Fucking nothing!" He pulled the request from the printer's paper tray, looked at it, crumpled it into a ball, and tossed it into the shredding pile.

"Why'd you toss the request?" Sara walked over and retrieved the paper from the bin. She unfurled it, placed it on the table, and pressed out the wrinkles with the palm of her hand. She held it up and read the request. After she finished reading it, she crumpled it back up into a ball and tossed it back in the bin. "We have shit, don't we?"

Brian nodded in agreement, put his feet up on his desk, and interlaced his fingers behind his head. He let out a loud moan, closed his eyes, and appeared to be taking a nap. Sara walked around the desk, kicked his feet off to the floor, and pulled his chair away. "Giving up?" she asked.

"Not at all; there's a subtle difference between giving in and admitting defeat."

"Pay attention, old man. I said 'giving up,' not 'giving in.' Subtle difference: 'giving up' means you're gonna stop investigating because we aren't having any success. 'Giving in' means you're gonna stop trying to solve this thing because you ran out of lead. So in essence, 'giving in' is admitting defeat."

Brian stood and laughed out loud - louder than he had in weeks. "Give in. Give up. Who the fuck cares? I'm at my wits' end. I can't get an angle on this guy

141

or girl. Look at me. Yesterday, I couldn't even tell that you were a... well, you know."

"Say it: I'm a lesbian. There's nothing wrong with it. It's who I am."

"I used to be able to see someone and read them and know who and what they were before they even knew I'd done my voodoo on them. I've lost it. I couldn't read you, and I can't read this case." Brian was pacing around the room and jamming his index and middle fingers into his temple. "I need my voodoo thing. It's who I am."

Sara sat Brian back down, lowered her tone, and spoke to him softly. "Close your eyes. Let's try to reclaim your voodoo." Brian took in a deep breath and closed his eyes as Sara walked around behind him and began to speak in his ear. "You see the victim walking in the park. Someone is behind her. Stalking her. What do you see?"

Brian smiled. "This isn't what I do or how I do it, but okay. Just let me do it my way."

*****

Rose came home from school, left her bags at the front door, and went straight to her room. She heard someone moving about downstairs in the kitchen - most likely her mother had come home early and was making dinner. She was hungry, and thought about going to join her downstairs, but was too upset about the police to eat.

She checked the news feeds again on her tablet, turned on the television in her room, and tuned it to the twenty-four-hour all-news channel. There had still been nothing reported on the girl she had attacked the night before. She checked the police Twitter feed, but there weren't any reports of injured or missing persons. The more she searched, the more frustrated she became.

A million thoughts burst into Rose's brain in a single moment. She wondered if the girl had simply woken up and went home. Maybe the girl herself had been doing something illegal and didn't want to be caught. Maybe someone had found her and taken her to the hospital and her identity was still unknown. No, she thought. That couldn't have happened. The press would've been all over a story like that. Maybe she had died, and then what? What would she have done? Maybe some stranger had found her and brought her home to help her recover. No one would do that anymore. Rose paced her room, anxious, upset, and, more than anything else, confused at the fact that she didn't know what had happened to the girl.

Rose kept replaying the scenario over in her head: how she had stalked the unwitting stranger, followed her, and, when the time had been right, pounced for the kill like a lioness. She understood the euphoria the killer must have felt when he actually went all the way and killed those girls. Or was the "he" a "she"?

Even Rose wasn't sure anymore. The feelings she had experienced immediately afterwards were almost too complex to explain. She had thought that there would be remorse and guilt for what she had done, but she was void of any of those emotions. The only thing she knew for sure was that she wanted to experience those emotions again. With the police questioning her, Rose knew that any further attempts would have to involve better planning, and she would have to learn patience. Know who and when and where to strike.

The television stations still hadn't reported anything about the missing or injured girl, so Rose decided to join her mother in the kitchen. Walking down the stairs, she heard voices: her mother's and a voice she didn't recognize. She turned the corner from the hall to the kitchen and stopped short.

Standing beside her mother was the man with the upturned nose from her dreams. The man in her dream who had killed the girl in the park

10

"Honey, you'll never guess who I bumped into at the grocery store today!" Rose's mother was jubilant. "Do you remember Gregory?" She held her hand out in his direction.

"Greg, please." He extended his hand to Rose. "Nice to see you again, Rose. What's it been; ten, no, twelve years?"

Rose took his hand and Greg squeezed hers hard - hard enough to cause Rose to grimace in pain. Rose and Greg locked eyes and stared at each other. Rose instinctively knew that Greg was fully aware of what she had done the previous night, and that he was responsible for the deaths of those girls. Why and how they could read each was a mystery to Rose, but she didn't care. She knew, and she was certain he knew, too. That was all that mattered.

"Honey, you remember Gregory's sister - sorry, Greg's sister - Samantha, who used to babysit you and Adam?"

Rose forcibly pulled her hand free from Greg's grasp. "I do, Mom. You're home early. Where did you say you bumped into him again?" Rose walked backwards, away from Greg, until she bumped into the counter. She knew exactly where she was in the kitchen and slid sideways to the right, where her mother had always kept the knives.

"No patients this afternoon. Gave the office staff the rest of the day off. You'll never believe it, hon; I turned the corner at the grocery store when I was picking up stuff for dinner and Greg's cart bumped into mine. He recognized me, we got to chatting, and since Greg didn't have any plans for dinner, I invited him to join us. Found out that Samantha got married and moved to Elmsdale, and Greg is still working in IT . After all this time, I just thought it would be nice to catch up. Isn't that wonderful?"

"It's great..." Rose's voice trailed off. Behind her back, her fingers found the drawer she was looking for and slowly started to pull it open.

"I can't believe my luck, Mrs. Metzel, seeing you after all these years. It's too bad your dad won't be joining us tonight, Rose; he has to work late I guess." Greg took a few steps closer, while Rose silently closed the drawer and moved away from him.

"He won't be late, Greg. He always gets home at the same time," Mrs. Metzel said. She turned to Rose. "Greg can't stay late so I decided we would eat a little early. Your dad'll join us after he's done."

"That's great, Mom." Rose never took her eyes off of Greg. The two of them played their game of chess in the kitchen. For every move Greg made, Rose countered in the opposite direction, making sure he kept his distance. Rose's mother had her back to them as she peeled carrots in the sink. "Ma, do you think we should eat out tonight? That way you don't have to cook." Greg was only a few feet away from Rose as she made the suggestion.

"Don't be silly. I think Greg would appreciate a home-cooked meal." Mrs. Metzel looked up from the sink as Greg turned away from Rose and walked towards the dining room. "Greg, could you set the table please? The forks and knives are in that drawer." She pointed with the peeler. "Honey, can you help him please with the place mats and napkins?"

"A home-cooked meal that I don't have to heat from a can sounds great, and setting the table is no problem." Greg walked over to the drawer that held the cutlery. Pulling it open, he saw the silverware on the right and the large kitchen knives neatly stored on the left. He picked up a large carving knife as Mrs. Metzel turned to see him hold it up.

"Not those, Greg. We're having pork chops. Just get the steak knives beside the regular ones, please." Mrs. Metzel pointed with her chin this time.

Greg put the carving knife back in its cradle and pulled four forks and five steak knives from the drawer, sliding one of the knives into his pocket as he followed Rose to the dining room and watched her lay the place mats. Rose never took her eyes from the houseguest. She blindly laid each mat down, and then stepped around the chairs to the next place setting. Greg followed her around the table, laying the silverware down on the place mats. Rose stared at the man only a few feet away from her. She recognized his face, his features, the very way he moved. It wasn't a dream she'd had of Greg, it had been as if she really was there watching him. And she wondered how Greg knew her and what she had done. The way he glared at her made her more certain than ever that he knew she had found the yellow nylon rope and attacked the girl. Suddenly she realized that Greg was the reason the girl hadn't been found. At the last place setting, Greg held up the steak knife and pointed it at Rose before placing it on the table beside the fork.

Rose bolted around the table and back into the kitchen, and stood beside her mother. Mrs. Metzel had the carrots and turnips boiling on the stove, and asked Rose to trim some of the fat from around the pork chops. She handed Greg a large head of lettuce, tomatoes, cucumbers, and green peppers, and asked him to prepare a salad. Rose and Greg stood at the counter on either side of Mrs. Metzel. Greg washed the lettuce and vegetables at the sink and dried them as Rose carefully trimmed the fat from the chops. Greg looked down and shuddered when he saw the skill that Rose possessed as the razor-sharp knife cut through the fat and curved around the frame of each chop.

"You handle that knife pretty well," Greg said without looking up from the sink.

"My dad's a surgeon. He taught me how to handle a knife like a scalpel as soon as the baby rattle left my hand." Her tone was almost threatening.

"Greg, I hope you like mashed carrots and turnips? I know it's not for everyone but it's one of my favourites. Once we have everything ready, we can go and sit down while the carrots boil," Mrs. Metzel piped up.

Rose finished trimming the pork chops, rinsed them under the running water, and covered them with plastic wrap, all the while keeping an eye on the houseguest. Greg had the lettuce torn apart and the vegetables cut up, and he added them to the bowl. Mrs. Metzel placed both the plate of pork chops and the salad in the fridge and invited Rose and Greg to the living room to catch up.

Rose washed her hands after trimming the meat as Greg kept his eyes on her. Neither one wanted to be the first to walk out to the living room, leaving the other person to walk behind. Mrs. Metzel called out from the living room asking where they were, and came back into the kitchen to find Rose and Greg staring at each other.

"Honey, I think Greg might be a little old for you. And besides, what would Taylor say?" Mrs. Metzel said jokingly.

"Sorry, Mrs. Metzel. Haven't seen Rose in so long, it's hard to imagine her all grown up." Greg turned towards the stove. "Let me just check on the carrots." He removed the lid, grabbed the handle, stirred the water, and then picked up the pot and swung it at Mrs. Metzel. Boiling water splashed over his hand and along the wall, pieces of carrots and turnips flew across the kitchen, and the base of the hot pot struck Mrs. Metzel on the right temple. A wound opened up along her hairline, and blood splattered in the air as she fell to the ground, unconscious.

Rose reacted immediately, grabbing the knife she had been using from the sink and slashing it across Greg's right forearm. The blade cut deep through the skin and into the muscle. He screamed in pain as the skin gave way to the blade. Greg dropped the pot and a hollow sound echoed across the kitchen as it bounced off the floor. He covered the laceration with his left hand as Rose swung the knife back again, catching him along his right shoulder and cutting open his shirt. Blood flowed from the wound and Greg fell to his knees.

Rose stepped forward and held the knife up high to plunge it into Greg's back. Greg picked up the pot, swung it around, and connected with Rose's right knee. She felt the bones shatter and her knee bend inward at a grotesque angle. As she fell to the floor in pain, the blade missed its mark. Impulsively, she released her grip on the knife and reached for her fractured leg. Her head hit the tile floor as she collapsed and started to scream in agony.

Her eyes were already filled with tears as she looked up to see Greg struggling to get to his hands and knees. He braced himself on his left hand. Instead of the pot, he was now holding the knife Rose had just dropped in his other hand. Rose pushed back with her left leg and both hands on the cold tile to distance herself from Greg. Unable to use her injured leg, she simply dragged it along the floor. She continued to claw her way backwards until her back hit the kitchen cabinets. She began to sob uncontrollably and scream at Greg to stay away. "Keep your hands off of me, you sick bastard! If you hurt my mother, I swear I'll kill you!"

Greg simply smiled, but he could feel himself getting light headed. The amount of blood loss from the two deep lacerations was more than he had imagined. He knew he had to finish her off quickly, before he passed out. As he raised the knife to strike, a loud pop rang behind him, and the cabinet door beside Rose exploded into a million slivers. Another loud pop sounded. A searing pain burnt through his neck, and Greg saw blood and tissue splatter across Rose's face. The bullet entered the left side of his neck and ripped through his trachea and larynx, severing his right carotid artery before exiting the right side of his neck and lodging in the cabinet door. His breathing instantly became laboured.

Greg dropped the knife and rolled sideways onto the blood-soaked tile floor beside Rose. He grabbed his throat to stem the bleeding, but the blood broke through his fingers like a leaky dam, rolled down his neck to his chest, and saturated his shirt.

Brian and Sara stood before him in the kitchen. Brian was still pointing the gun at the wounded man, and he surveyed the scene before making his next move. He saw Rose sitting beside the man he had just shot, crying, her right leg severely angulated in a horrific manner. Tears rolled down her cheeks and she was breathing heavily. He knew that asking the wounded man not to move was a little ridiculous, considering his injuries. Instead he opted for something more direct.

"Did you kill those girls?" Brian asked.

Greg simply nodded that he had.

"Where's the girl from last night?"

Greg shook his head from side to side, then looked sideways at Rose. Rose began to cry uncontrollably, her face covered in Greg's blood and white soft tissue.

"I'll call EMS," Sara offered.

Without taking his eyes off Greg, Brian reached down and felt for the pulse in Mrs. Metzel's neck. She moaned loudly. Her pulse was steady and strong.

Brian stepped forward, leaving his footprints in the blood. He held the gun high, and aimed at Greg's head as he leaned in. He kicked the knife on the floor out of Greg's reach. The knife slid in the dark red blood, leaving a twisted trail in the crimson fluid. Greg's eyes became heavy as the blood drained from his body. Brian opened up two cabinet doors, placed one handcuff around Greg's left wrist, pulled his arm away, and locked the other cuff around the centre post between the two doors. Brian had no desire to stem the flow of blood oozing from Greg's wound, and knew that EMS wouldn't arrive in time to save his life. If Brian didn't make it look like an attempt had been made to help the injured man, however, it could look very bad for him. Brian patted Greg down for hidden weapons, and only felt comfortable when he knew that his suspect was unarmed. He pulled a tea towel from the oven handle and wrapped it around Greg's neck. The makeshift dressing did little to control the bleeding. Rose continued to cry and scream as Brian ignored her.

"Did you attack the girl last night?" Brian asked Greg.

Barely conscious, Greg made a slight nod from side to side. He again looked at Rose, and then closed his eyes as his breathing became laboured, his chest began to heave, and the demand for more oxygen increased.

"Did you have anything to do with her disappearance?"

Greg mouthed the word "Yes," but no sound came forth.

Sara entered the kitchen, saying, "EMS is on the way. I asked for three rigs."

"We'll only need two. Check on the mother." Brian pointed towards Mrs. Metzel, and then turned his attention back to Greg. His head had dropped to his chest, and the hand he had been using to hold the dressing around his neck now rested on the floor. Brian checked for a radial pulse in Greg's cuffed left wrist, and found nothing. His index and middle finger jumped around the area of the artery and found no pulse there either.

"Is he dead?" Rose screamed.

"Yeah." Brian was matter-of-fact about it. He stood and walked over to Mrs. Metzel.

"What about me? My fucking leg is broken. You should be helping me," Rose sobbed.

"I tried helping you. You lied and laughed me off. Now sit your privileged ass there, and shut your fucking mouth while I check on you mother."

Brian looked up to see Sara attempting to stifle a chuckle. "I'll check on her," she offered. She holstered her semi-automatic handgun and went to Rose's side. Sirens could already be heard in the distance. Sara felt for a pulse behind Rose's ankle.

"Your leg is broken but you still have a good pulse. You'll be fine."

"What? You a fucking doctor now?" Rose was howling at the top of her lungs.

Sara smiled, stood, and walked away, not wanting to have any more to do with Rose. Mrs. Metzel was starting to regain consciousness, moaning, and attempting to move. Brian whispered in her ear, and she relaxed and remained motionless.

The front door opened, and in walked two uniformed officers leading the three teams of paramedics into the house. Brian and Sara removed themselves from the kitchen and sat down at the dining room table. Rose screamed and cried as the paramedics treated her severely fractured leg. Mrs. Metzel was quiet and co-operative as the second paramedic crew treated her. The third crew assessed Greg and left him as they had found him, assisting with the other two patients instead.

Mrs. Metzel was treated and taken away first. When Rose's injuries were sta-bilized, she was placed on the cot. The paramedics were rolling her through the house to the front door when Brian asked the lead medic if he could have a moment with her in private. The medic checked the IV and cardiac monitor for Rose's vitals and quietly stepped aside.

Rose held up her wrist, showing the cuff that was locked firmly to the stretch-er rail. A uniformed officer had cuffed Rose after she had been loaded onto the stretcher. "Is this really necessary?" she demanded.

"You're a suspect in a murder case. So yeah! The cuffs are necessary. You have a problem with that?"

Rose shot Brian a look that he had seen numerous times from every suspect that he had cuffed as they protested their innocence. Brian was used to seeing that look, and it failed to impress him or evoke any emotional response from him.

"So your mother is already on her way to the hospital and we sent a few officers to speak to your dad. He's being told everything we know as of now, including our suspicions of your involvement in the attack on the girl last night."

"Can I see my mom?"

"Actually, we asked if you could be sent to another hospital so that you can't see your parents until we get a statement from them and you. That officer," Brian pointed to a female officer standing at the front door, "will be with you every minute until she's relieved and another officer takes her place."

"Why?"

"Well, for one, I know you attacked the girl last night. I'm just not sure if you had anything to do with her death yet. And believe you me, even if you didn't kill her, I'll make sure you get charged with accessory to murder or just for being a royal pain in my ass."

"You have nothing on me. You can't prove a thing."

"Yeah well, little missy, I'm going to have to beg to differ on that one." With a gloved hand, Brian held up the plastic bag that Rose had hid her clothing in after she had attacked the girl. "Wanna bet I'm going to find a whole lotta shit in here that says I'm right?" He placed the plastic bag back in a brown paper one.

Rose's face went pale and blank, and she started to cry. Brian waved to the medics, thanked them for their co-operation, and told them he was done with the patient. Brian watched as Rose was wheeled out the front door. He stood in the living room, silent and unmoving. Sara walked up and stood beside her partner, who was looking at the open front door. "What's up?"

"Nothing." He turned to Sara. "Thanks for helping me get my voodoo back."

"That's what partners are for. You ever gonna to tell me how you put all this together?"

"Nope. My voodoo is my secret."

"You're one spooky guy detective."

"Been called worse."

THE END

HIGHWAY 7

1

It had been some time since Sandra and I had last seen each other after she decided she needed time apart. Sandra packed up her things, along with my infant son Sam, and moved to London to be closer to her parents. Her mother had a severe stroke last year and her elderly father wasn't up to the daily care her mother required since she had come home from the rehabilitation hospital. It was decided that Sandra would move back in with her parents and help care for her mother. Well, to be truthful, she decided it would be best if she moved back to her parents'. We had been drifting apart; not an easy thing to admit, but I wasn't surprised by her move. We never should have gotten married to begin with.

After weeks of phone calls and texts and countless invitations to come down for a visit to see Sam, the time had come for me to drive to London and see where our relationship was headed. I reasoned that as long as Sandra and I hadn't official separated, there was still a chance of salvaging what we had.

I had given Ben Fyne, my work partner, a key to my house years earlier when Sandra and I were still together, and he would be staying at our house for the weekend to care for our dog, Tyler. My work wasn't very demanding; I did more volunteering than actual work, so it was about time I went to London. I figured Sandra and I would have almost a day and a half to discuss what needed to be said.

I still had no clue how to operate the GPS on my phone, and had a hell of a time trying to buy an "old fashioned paper map." Sandra emailed me directions from my house in the west end of Ottawa to her parents' place in London. I asked for two options: south on Highway 416 then west on Highway 401, and the longer, quieter route along Highway 7. I opted for the slow drive from Ottawa along Highway 7. Highway 7, also known as the Trans-Canada Highway, banked west off Highway 417 and snaked its way through several small towns, changing speed limits along the way. This stretch of the Trans-Canada highway is a two-lane road with several sections that expand into three lanes, offering travellers the option of passing slower drivers in safety instead of waiting for an opening in the oncoming traffic.

My plan was to take Highway 7 from Ottawa, and accept the slower speed limits and twists and turns, until I arrived in Peterborough. South of Peterborough, I would take Highway 115 to the 401. This route would add hours to the trip, but with my used car, a Dodge Neon, I would feel safer driving a little slower for as long as possible. I had called my cellphone provider and was assured that there was coverage along the entire planned route, but knowing the reception I get just outside of Ottawa sometimes, I doubted the sales rep who cheerfully answered all my questions and thanked me for being a customer.

I woke early Friday morning, took Tyler out for a walk, changed his water bowl, added extra hard food to his dish, and then unceremoniously dumped in a large can of the moist food that he preferred over the dry anyway. The patio door leading to the fenced-in yard would remain ajar. Tyler could roam the yard and come and go as he pleased until Ben arrived.

I had a quick shower, ate breakfast, spent as much time with Tyler as he would tolerate, loaded the car, texted Ben that I was leaving, and hit the road. Ben would arrive some time on Friday and stay until Sunday afternoon. My plan was to make it home before dinner on Sunday night. As I found out, however, plans seldom ever go according to, well, plan.

For late October, the sun was low, just above the east end of Ottawa. I wiped the frost from my windows with my arm, and then brushed the moisture off my jacket sleeve. I let the car warm up for a few minutes. Despite the frost on the cars and the grass in the front yard, I could feel heat on the back of my neck as I made my way west on the Queensway. I would travel only a few minutes on the Queensway, past Canadian Tire Place - formerly Scotiabank Place, formerly the Corel Centre, formerly the Palladium - before taking the off ramp to Highway 7. Even though I lived not far from the arena, I still cheered for the Toronto Maple Leafs. My dad was a diehard blue-and-white Leafs fan, as was his dad before him.

I made the turn from the Queensway to Highway 7 and increased my speed to ten kilometers over the posted limit to match the speed of most of the traffic heading out of Ottawa. I turned up the radio and began to enjoy the ride. I realized I needed a new car, which was something I had known for a long time, but I always felt that cars were such a waste of money. On long trips, we would always take Sandra's new car. Since she left, I had no choice but to drive the Neon everywhere I wanted to go. I missed the new car smell and control of her vehicle.

Driving the Neon was more of a chore, but knowing that in a few hours I would see my son Sam again after so long apart made it worthwhile. I had nothing ahead of me but a beautiful clear sky, open roads, and the radio. I pressed one of the tiny station buttons on the radio that I had pre-set to CHEZ 106, and a loud crackle of static erupted from the speakers. I turned the volume down so that the static wouldn't burst my eardrums and pressed another pre-set station button. Static. Another button; more static. I changed from the radio to a CD, and was met with more static. Great, I thought; my stereo had died. That meant a silent six-hour trip. I remembered that Ben had loaded music onto my phone, since I hadn't mastered the art of downloads yet. Now I needed to remember how to turn the music on.

Fumbling for my phone on the passenger seat, I blindly swiped up, down, and across, then pushed an icon. Nothing; wrong icon. Again, more swiping and icon pushing, but still no music. I'd read about more accidents than I could count where the driver was distracted by a cellphone, either texting, answering or making a call, or doing something idiotic like I was doing now. I decided to forgo music and tossed my cellphone onto the passenger seat. I passed the speedway on my right and knew that Dwyer Hill Road was approaching.

I rolled down my window and let the cool, crisp fall air rip through the car and keep me awake. I would enjoy the silence for a change, or so I thought. After fifteen minutes of wind whistling past me, swirling loose papers in the back seat, I was craving sound. The radio continued to play static on every station, regardless of which button I pushed. I looked across the seat and realized I must have tossed my phone too hard, as it wasn't on the passenger seat. It must have slid across and onto the floor. That was probably a good thing, or I might have ended up in the ditch. Wind it was.

I kept pace with the few cars travelling west. Traffic was much heavier on the east lanes going into Ottawa. For those working Monday to Friday, it was the end of the work week. When I was in college, I had worked at a small factory pulling twelve-hour shifts. I preferred shift work, since it gave me more time off to study and the shifts were flexible enough that I could keep working all though school.

Even on the four-lane divided highway, as cars approached, they made the familiar "swooshing" sound as the passed me in the east lanes. Sandra and I used to play the "Slug a Bug," or "Punch Buggy," game. Now, even alone, I still slapped the passenger seat every time a VW Bug passed. A bright yellow VW Bug approached and out loud I screamed, "Slug a bug," and slapped the seat beside me. I looked and swore I saw Sandra sitting there, laughing.

Sandra and I had been married for almost three years before she decided to return to London. It was the first real relationship I had ever had. It had been going good - more than good, great. Sandra was the first thing on my mind when I woke up in the morning and the last thing when I went to bed at night. It was an unhealthy obsession, I realized that, but in every way conceivable, in every possible facet of life, I thought she was "the one." Apparently, I totally misread the entire relationship. I've never been great at understanding women. What I thought was a symbiotic relationship, where we fed off each other – no, grew with each other – was actually so much more. More often than not, we only seem to remember the good stuff, and the bad memories get washed away in the ocean surf of the mind. I honestly can't remember anything negative of my time with Sandra other than the pain when she left. She was the most beautiful woman I'd ever seen at that point in my life, not that I ever told her that.

A transport truck passed me on my left. The wind almost took my sunglasses along for the ride and brought me back to reality. I refocused my attention on the road and straightened up in my seat.

The large green sign indicating the exit to Dwyer Hill Road approached and disappeared as I drove past. The road ahead was quiet as I banked to the left.

I was now alone on the highway and matched my speed to the posted limit. Even with the sun rising behind me, the air seemed a little cooler than before. I rolled up my window and remembered why I always turned up the volume on the radio. The seal around the window was worn, and the air would whistle through the rubber and became increasingly irritating the faster I drove. I tried the radio again and static burst forth. Irritating whistle it was.

After twenty minutes or so, the divided highway merged into a joined two-lane highway as I drove into Carleton Place. Stores lined the north and south sides of the road, not like they do in Ottawa or other large cities, but the way they did fifty years ago before big box stores took over. I expected to see an old general store with a wooden veranda and an old man sitting in a rocking chair, wearing worn-out jeans with suspenders, a pocketknife in hand, and making splinters of a small twig. I was a little disappointed to see that a Home Depot had sprung up since the last time I was here. It was nestled in with the old-style stores and open spaces between businesses. Progress even comes to rural Ontario, I guess. I was sad to see a big box store here, but I would still be using a VHS machine and rotary phone if I could. For me, progress peaked with the microwave pizza.

Even after hitting every red light in town, I was through Carleton Place in less than five minutes and continued west on Highway 7. I crested a hill and Carleton Place was gone, replaced with new urban development that rivalled any city. Instead of in a quaint town, frozen in time, I could have been anywhere. I rounded another bend and was back in forest and farmland. Taking Highway 7 was so much better than taking Highway 416 to the 401; this was a picturesque drive that captured my attention instead of forcing me to speed down from one highway to the next with nothing to see. Not having the radio wasn't so bad.

In an attempt to quiet the whistle, I tugged hard on the window crank, hoping it would silence the high-pitched banshee scream that toyed with my sanity. That didn't work. The sun was midway up over Ottawa now and cast a long shadow before me. Taking that as a sign of warmer weather, I rolled the window down until the whistle was replaced by an alternating wind hum. Much better.

As I continued my drive, I rounded Mississippi Lake and headed straight south to Perth, an even smaller town than Carleton Place. Highway 7 turned and headed west for the lonely two-hour drive to Peterborough.

Suddenly, the Neon bucked forward then back, then continued on as if nothing had happened. I looked down at the dash, trying to diagnose the problem. The few gauges the Neon had all showed normal: gas full, engine temperature within the operating specifications. None of the lights were illuminated, so I rationalized that it was just some bad gas. I had the car serviced before leaving and everything had checked out fine.

I reached behind the passenger seat where I had put my cooler with a couple of sandwiches, a few granola bars, a banana, and my travel mug of coffee. With my eyes still on the road, my hand patted the floor, but felt nothing. I reached behind my seat, but again came up empty-handed. I tilted the rear-view mirror down and looked along the length of the back seat. My overnight bag sat comfortably alone in the middle of it. My work cooler wasn't anywhere I could see. I must have packed the cooler, put it on the counter, poured my coffee into the travel mug, crammed the mug between the sandwiches and the granola bars, went to the bathroom, and left the house. Shit, I thought to myself. I had left the cooler on the counter.

With nothing to eat or drink, and with no radio, I decided that I would stop at the next town I came upon for lunch.

The car was travelling over one hundred and ten kilometers per hour and decided to buck again, throwing me forward until the seatbelt snapped and then held tight. It dug into my neck, and then sent me back into my seat. The jolting was extremely annoying. I would have to get that checked as well when I stopped. I hoped that the town would at least have a garage where my car could be repaired quickly. I rubbed the dash and spoke to it nicely, asking that it not break down in the middle of nowhere. If it got me to the next town, I promised I would fill the gas tank with super unleaded instead of regular gas as a treat. I didn't want to refer to my old Porsche, thinking the Neon would take offense and stall out, leaving me stranded.

I set the cruise, and the speedometer needle held steady at just over one hundred. The cruise control was one of the only features in the car that still worked. I prayed that it would continue working until I got home on Sunday night.

Every few kilometers, the Neon would hiccup, tossing me back and forth in the driver's seat. I became adept at stiffing my arms just as the car would decide it wanted to try and throw me into the air. I was unwilling to take my hands off the steering wheel, and I decided the next town - any town - would be great for a pit stop, something to eat, and getting the Neon looked at.

It was at times like these that I realized how much I missed Sandra. I hadn't renewed my CAA membership in years. She was the one who purchased the CAA membership and kept up on the dues. My card had probably expired more than a year ago.

The road seemed to go on forever, bending slightly every few kilometers; just enough to keep drivers awake. With the window down, no radio, and no music, I was being hypnotized into a light sleep. My eyes became heavy and my mind foggy. Coffee, tea, or anything at this point, was needed to keep me awake.

The car bucked hard once again. A loud metallic sound, like two empty oil drums smashing together, came from beneath the floorboards. All of a sudden my foggy mind and heavy eyes were gone. I looked behind me in case the transmission had been left on the road, and was relieved to see nothing in my wake.

As I made the turn around a large tree-covered field, a small town became visible in the distance. My decision had already been made to stop there regardless of what services they offered. The car bucked again. This time, it didn't jolt quite as aggressively, and no sound was emitted.

A small wooden signpost on the side of the road proclaiming "Bakers Corner" lay at a slight tilt. It wasn't your usual sign indicating the town that lay ahead, I thought to myself. This relic was something left over from the 1950s. Some local farmer had probably found it in the hay field and decided to put it back where it rightfully belonged. I could envision him freeing the signpost from the weeds, brushing off the mud, digging a new hole, and securing the post in place. He then stood up, pulled up his pants, tilted his thread-worn ball cap back, and smiled at the nostalgic remnant he had erected before climbing back on his tractor and returning to ploughing or tilling or mowing the fields - or whatever farmers do on tractors. Man; driving without a radio or any distractions is difficult, I realized.

The car continued to tell me how irritated it was with me, and showed me more and more often as I got closer to Bakers Corner. The highway narrowed from four lanes to two less than a kilometer from the town line.

The speed limit slowed from one hundred kilometers to seventy, then to fifty as I entered the town. Small, wooden homes that had been painted over several times - the older paint peeling beneath the new like suntanned skin shedding itself - lined the highway on either side. The spaces between them grew smaller and smaller as I drove farther into the town of Bakers Corner. The homes here looked newer than the ones on the outskirts, but still held their quaint, 1950s appearances. Manicured lawns, white wooden fences, and small single-family homes seemed to be the norm on the main street. The few people who were outside as I drove past simply turned and looked at me, then went back to their business.

A few streets branched north and south from the main road. As I looked down each street, I noticed that the town seemed to have a basic building code for their homes. Each house looked similar to the others with only slight differences appearing between them: possibly the owners' personal touches. I assumed that any service centre would be on the main street through town so that it could sell gas and do minor repairs for travellers. Not a block farther down the street a weathered, wooden, hand-painted sign hung out from at building, "Lucious' Auto Service" written upon it. I had expected a chain service centre, and suddenly realized that I hadn't seen any chain stores, convenience stores, or big box stores.

Nothing! Lucious' Auto Service fit right in.

The car bucked again as if on cue to remind me to pull into the service centre and have it checked. The two service bay doors were pulled up high to reveal cars inside, not on hoists like I had expected to see, but with the mechanics working on them from pits below the vehicles. A few cars were parked along the east side of the lot with plastic flags strung from their antennas and large "For Sale" signs on their dashes. I made some mental notes on the prices and options of the cars for sale in case my Neon repair bill was too expensive.

I pulled up to the gas pumps and heard an ancient, familiar "ding" in the distance. I must have run over a black hose that had caused the bell to ring inside the office. I hadn't heard a service centre bell in years. An older black man walked out from the open office door, wiped his hands, and stuffed the rag in his back pocket. He adjusted his oily ball cap and slowly walked over to greet me. My Neon was idling like it was fuel-starved and would die at any moment.

"How y'all doing today?" His smile was as wide as the street and his teeth as white and as perfect as any I'd ever seen. His greeting was sincere and he seemed genuinely pleased to see me. "Sounds like your ride is givin' you some attitude."

"Well, I'm doing fine, but my car decided to have a mind of its own today. I didn't know where to park. Your lot's pretty full. Do you have someone who could take a look at this for me?"

"Well you just leave that car right there. We don't get hardly no business through here so I be doubting that anyone will want this spot." More of the whitest teeth I've ever seen. "Leave that car running and go inside and get yourself a Coke, and I'll take a look under the hood for you."

"Thanks. Have you got a washroom too?"

"Around back. It's pretty greasy. Don't get too many people other than me and my brother using it so long as you don't mind."

"I'll stand." I smiled back, and realized that my grin was nothing like the one beaming back at me.

There was no key to unlock the painted grey wooden door of the washroom. The stench was pretty powerful, and assaulted my senses as I opened the door. As I stood above the toilet bowl, I realized that Mr. White Teeth hadn't been kidding when he had said the washroom was dirty. The porcelain bowl may have been white the day it was installed, but I doubted that it had been cleaned since. Even the sink itself wasn't much better than the toilet. I decided the hand sanitizer in my car was a better choice than the sink.

As I walked around the building, I saw Mr. White Teeth backing my Neon into the far bay. His brother was getting out of the car he had pulled out to free the bay for my car, and he threw me a polite wave before he crawled back into the mechanics' pit.

Mr. White Teeth slammed my driver's door and met me inside the office. It was a tiny little room with a rounded desk and an antique cash register. Along the wall, cans of oil stood beside each other, with gas treatment and other additives lining the shelves. In the corner, a banged-up and scratched red-and-white Coke cooler hummed away. He lifted the lid of the metal cooler and pulled out two glass bottles. He had to use the bottle opener on the side of the cooler to pry the caps off of the bottles, and then handed me one of them. The cold glass felt good in my hand and across my forehead as I ran it over my brow.

"No Diet Coke?" I asked.

"Diet?" He tilted his head back and finished half the bottle. "Diet? Who the hell drinks diet? You so skinny anyway, a few pounds couldn't hurt."

I lifted the bottle to Mr. White Teeth to thank him and took a mouthful. "Wow! That's sweet."

"A little sugar never hurt no one." Mr. White Teeth laughed and finished his bottle. "Your car is fuel starved." He pointed to the garage where the Neon was now parked. "That's why it's talking back to you. I'm gonna work on it 'til close but I think I can get you on your way first thing in the morning."

"Morning?" I wasn't upset; I had just planned on being in London in a few hours.

"If we need parts, especially for these foreign cars, we have to order them in and that can take time. If we don't need no parts, I can get 'er going later this afternoon."

"It's a Dodge," I offered.

"Really?" Mr. White Teeth looked at the car. "Looks foreign to me. But all cars work the same; just the way they get put together is different. Nothing wrong with foreign cars, but being North American means they are just simpler to fix." He grabbed another bottle and took a big drink. "And those foreign cars have the nerve to break down more often, too."

"When will you know how long it will take to fix?" My expectations weren't too high that I was getting out of Hicksville tonight.

"Take a walk around town, come back in a few hours, and I'll know for sure." Mr. White Teeth smiled, trying to provide reassurance that he knew what he was doing. "I'm the only service centre in town and I fix pretty much everyone's car in Bakers Corner, so I must be pretty damn good, if I do say so myself." He pointed his second Coke bottle at the sign out front. "That's my name on the sign and I don't want no one calling Lucious King nothing but the best mechanic in town. And my brother is a close second."

"Well," I smiled back, "aren't you two the only mechanics in town?"

Lucious "White Teeth" King smiled his million-dollar smile and laughed. "Ain't no one ever put it quite like that before. That Coke you just had is on me."

He pulled another bottle out of the cooler, pried the cap off, and handed it to me. "One for the road." Lucious smiled. "Head over to Annabeth's Counter and have a nice lunch."

"Annabeth's?" I looked out the front office window.

Lucious stood beside me and pointed to the centre of town. "Annabeth has a little diner called Annabeth's Counter. Everything's home cooked from Annabeth's recipes and she's been running that place since she was just a youngin'. You tell her that I sent you over and you want the Lucious special." He turned to me. "You got a hunger on there, Skinny?" It was fair, I thought. I was secretly calling Lucious "Mr. White Teeth" and I had just picked up a new nickname, "Skinny."

I rubbed my belly. "I could eat."

"The Lucious special is four eggs over easy; four slices of toast, one for each runny egg; bacon; sausages; pancakes; and home fries. Can you handle that, Skinny?"

"Dan, not Skinny." I extended my hand. I was a little underweight; I had lost quite a few pounds since my wife had left. It's not that I didn't eat - I just nibbled. I tilted the bottle back and took a mouthful of Coke.

Lucious grinned an even bigger smile, and his eyes widened. He wiped his hand on his pants, which, if the dirt on his pants indicated anything, didn't do anything to clean it, extended it, and shook my hand so hard that my arm swung up and down.

"Head down past McKinnon Street and on the north side of the road you'll see the diner. Remember, tell Annabeth you want the Lucious special."

"So have lunch, take a walk, and come back. Do you want my cellphone number in case you need me?"

"If I need ya, I'll ring Annabeth's."

"Do you have a number I can call?"

Lucious turned to show me the antique black bakelite wall dial phone. "The number's on the phone."

In the centre of the rotary dial was a small circular piece of paper with the phone number on it. I entered the number into the "Notes" on my cellphone. After I finished, I noticed that I didn't have a cellphone signal, just a red "X."

Lucious laughed out loud. "Our town's a little forgotten. I'll call you at Annabeth's. K?"

I nodded in approval, opened the front door, and headed west toward Annabeth's while sipping from my second bottle of Coke.

2

Highway 7 cut right through the middle of Bakers Corner. Most of the homes in the town lined the highway a few houses deep on either side. Every building was a single level family home - no duplexes or apartment buildings to be seen. Small, well-groomed front yards, with flowers or shrubs lining the borders with the neighbours' properties, acted as a greeting for visitors. The houses looked almost identical to one another, and I began to wonder if the front doors were even locked.

As I walked past several houses, the occupants in the front yards waved politely, smiled, and then went back to their business. I smiled and waved back. As I walked along the sidewalk, I tested my cellphone carrier's ability to keep me connected. I waved my phone back and forth, scanning the airwaves for any type of signal. I held the phone up higher, stretching my arm as far as it would extend, all the while looking at the screen to see if I could capture any bars. Nothing. When Lucious had said Bakers Corner had been forgotten, he had meant it. I had no cellular signal at all.

A square wooden sign that bore the name of the diner below swung softly in the breeze. The rusted metal hooks squeaked with each pass. The white painted wood entrance was narrow, and two large windows flanked the frame and glass door in the centre. I walked up the two creaky steps, pushed the door inward, and heard the soon-to-be-familiar single chime of the bell that hung above the door. The aroma of grease, eggs, toast, and home cooking made my mild hunger turn ravenous. The sound of friendly conversation humming, ceramic dishes clanging, and forks and knives scraping dishes echoed in the narrow diner.

"Annabeth's Counter" was true to its name. There were no tables. The entire diner was no more than fifteen feet wide and featured one long counter that ran from the front door to the kitchen at the back. All the swivel stools placed before the counter were occupied, and every single person in the diner turned to look at the stranger who had just entered. No sooner had they greeted me with their looks than they turned and continued eating and talking. A woman worked behind the counter, pulling plates when the customers were done eating while taking orders and barking to the cook at the far end.

There must have been a row of two dozen gleaming silver stools that spun. On the wall behind the woman, glass shelves held tumblers, coffee cups, plates, and bowls. The entire diner was painted white with only a splash of red here and there to break up the monotony.

The woman behind the counter had a tea towel over her shoulder, and she swung the rag at one of the patrons, giving him a loud "GIT! You're not eaten' anyway." The heavy-set man with his shirt half pulled out of his jeans got up using the counter as a crutch and walked down a few stools before stopping to stand between two other patrons.

She looked at me and I swear time froze. She smiled an honest smile. Her hair was pulled back around her left ear and dropped down just past her shoulders. Her eyes were dark, and set deep, and they seemed to smile just as brightly as her mouth. She wore a flannel shirt tucked into faded jeans. I stood motionless, stunned, unable to move, and the sounds and smells of the diner disappeared as I stared.

"...well?"

I closed my eyes to reboot my brain. "Sorry. What was that?"

She smiled again and my mind went blank.

"From the city, aren't you?"

"I am. How can you tell?"

"Bakers Corner is pretty small. Anyone who lives here knows everyone else. And you, I don't know. Yet!" She wiped the counter area where the farmer had sat and walked a few stools down, her eyes never leaving mine. Was I imagining that? Probably, I thought. I've never been the guy who girls look at.

I took my seat as she handed me a menu. The stool was still warm from the previous customer. It was a simple hand-written menu on card stock, black ink on white. Coffee and food stains covered the front and back.

"'Scuse the menu. Been meaning to change those for years."

"Years?" I looked up at her.

"Everyone knows what we have. Don't need to show the regulars my menu. Don't get many strangers stopping by."

She walked away smiling. There wasn't much on there to choose from. Everything on the menu was designed to keep cardiologists employed: fried eggs, bacon, home fries. Scanning the entire menu, I remembered what Lucious had said.

I placed the menu on the counter and slid it away from me. She walked back with a glass coffee pot in hand, placed it on the counter, and asked what I wanted.

"I was told to ask for the Lucious special."

"Your car broke down, didn't it?"

I nodded. She poured coffee into the cup she had placed before me. "I assume you drink coffee?"

"I do."

"Well, that explains why I've never seen you before. One Lucious special coming up." She leaned in close as she placed a few creamers beside the cup. "I hope your car can't be fixed for a few days," she murmured. Then she stood up, yelled at the cook, "Gimme a Lucious will ya," and walked away without looking back.

My eyes followed her down the counter and watched as she topped up the coffee cups of the other customers. I was about the turn away when I caught her giving me a momentary gaze. It was only a fleeting glance but I saw the look; the way her head turned for just a second before her attention returned to her customers. I smiled. I thought of Mr. White Teeth and how I didn't have the same smile, but I grinned anyway. It's amazing how something so small can have such a huge impact.

*****

I pushed my plate to the edge of the counter, leaned back, and moaned. Annabeth came over and asked if I was done.

"Done, full, take me out to pasture." I crumpled up the napkin, tossed it onto the plate, and moaned again. "I can't believe how much food that was. Well, that and the calories and fat."

"So you enjoyed it. Looks like you could use a few pounds," she commented.

"I did. I'm gonna have to thank Lucious when I see him. And your cook."

"Are you heading out soon?" She swung the tea towel over her shoulder and placed her hands on the counter.

"Soon as my car is fixed. Lucious told me it would take a few hours. I'm hoping it was nothing too serious."

"I was kind of hoping your car wouldn't be fixed at least until tomorrow." She pulled the coffee pot from the hot plate and offered me a refill. I covered the cup with my hand.

"I think I'm coffeed out. Thanks. I've got to get to London to see my family."

"Too bad." She put the coffee pot back.

"That I don't want any more coffee or that I have family?"

"That you have to leave. You're a little thick, aren't you? Can't you tell when a girl is hitting on you?" Her eyes lit up again as she pulled her hair back behind both ears and stood tall. Her flannel shirt was unbuttoned and revealed a little cleavage, and I found my eyes drifting lower to sneak a peek. When I looked up again, she had noticed what I had done and smiled.

"Sorry, Annabeth. That was rude."

"Oh, you know my name. I'm flattered."

"Every customer was yelling your name any time they wanted something. Kinda easy."

Someone called out her name again, asking for a coffee refill. "Be patient. I'll be right there," she hollered over her shoulder. Then she pulled the coffee pot from the hot plate and looked at me.

I looked around the diner and found that it had emptied while I was focused on finishing my two thousand calorie meal. Only a few customers remained, and they had all finished their food and were just chatting with each other. Annabeth walked around the counter and came over to sit beside me. I spun on my stool and our knees bumped. We laced our knees between each other's to sit closer.

"Let's make this formal." She extended her hand. "Pleased to meet you, I'm Annabeth Anderson. And you are?"

I held her hand gently; held it instead of shaking it. "Nice meeting you, Annabeth Anderson. My name is Dan Grewal." I continued to hold her hand without realizing it. We just stared at each other.

"You're not married, Dan Grewal. At least you don't have a ring or a mark, and the tan on your hand doesn't show you were wearing a ring." She gripped my hand tighter.

"Was. Not anymore. Well, technically still married, but separated. Living in two different cities. Long story. I can tell you about it one day over coffee." She laughed as I stumbled for words. "You?" I asked.

"Nope. Never was. Don't plan on it. Never lived with a guy either." She was still holding my hand but pulled it down so it was resting on her lap.

"I can't believe someone like you was never serious about a guy."

"I'm not a virgin, Mr. Grewal, but I'm not easy either." Her thumb started to roam across the back of my hand. "Just haven't met the right guy yet. I'm almost forty. I'm not dead."

One of the remaining customers yelled out, "Not like we haven't tried, huh, Annabeth?" He bellowed at his own comment.

"Maybe if you didn't smell like cow shit every day, Robbie, a girl might look your way." Annabeth's eyes never left mine as she spoke. "All the men around Bakers Corner are like brothers or cousins. I'm like the local bartender. They tell me everything and sometimes it's too much information."

The man I assumed was Robbie walked past and slapped me on the back, saying, "Maybe you got a better chance with Annabeth than any of us ever had." He bellowed again. And he did smell like cow shit.

The afternoon lunch crowd was now gone, and the cook yelled from the back that he was turning off the grill and fryer until dinner and would be back in a few hours.

Annabeth stood, looked out the front door, and turned the sign from "OPEN" to "CLOSED." She didn't bother locking the door and sat down beside me. We were now sitting with our elbows on the counter, sipping regular Coke; they didn't have diet because a little sugar never hurt anyone.

Annabeth told me her life's story. She had been born and raised in Bakers Corner, had inherited the diner from her mother when she had retired, and would live out the rest of her days here. Never married, no serious relationships, worked a lot - sometimes too much, she thought. She spent every Sunday with her parents; Sunday was for family, she explained, and was the only day she closed the diner. Although I didn't really know Annabeth, I thought I saw a little resentment in her eyes. I wondered if she begrudged her mother for giving her the diner. It may have trapped her in Bakers Corner instead of allowing her the freedom to move away.

"And what about you, Mr. Grewal?" I noticed that she enjoyed flirtatiously calling me "Mr. Grewal." "What do you do for fun? Drink, party, pee and not flush the toilet?"

"Don't party much. Can't hold my liquor. Sometimes, in the middle of the night, when it's cold and dark and there's no one around, I don't lift the toilet seat and don't flush. I'm a wild man."

She chuckled. I went on to tell Annabeth that after graduating from the University of Ottawa with a degree in finance, I had gotten a job with Revenue Canada. Before I could continue, she told me she pays her taxes on time. I smiled and didn't have the heart to tell her that was one of the clichéd comments I always got when I told people where I'd worked. I'd hated the job with a passion, so I'd quit and started a very small, very non-profitable book keeping business. I was much happier in my new job, but my wife had preferred the money I had made when I had my government job.

Annabeth stood up, went to the fridge, removed an apple pie, and cut one large slice. "Ice cream or cheese?"

"Really? After that meal?"

"Ice cream or cheese?"

"Would you be upset if I said neither?"

"Thinking outside the box, and the best choice of all." She opened the door of the warming oven and set the plate inside. "Only way to enjoy apple pie is hot and on a warm plate to keep it smelling good. If you would've said cheese, I would've shown you the door. No one, and I mean no one, puts cheese on my mama's apple pie."

After a few minutes, she reached in with her tea towel, pulled out the pie, and placed it between us. Annabeth had placed only one fork on the plate, and she grabbed it and took a bite. I didn't expect her to feed me, but apparently that was her intention. "This is my mama's apple pie. If you like me, you will love my mama's pie." She was laughing. "Even if you think it smells and tastes like Robbie." Cow shit.

I opened my mouth and the warm pie tasting of nutmeg, caramel, apples, and brown sugar hit my taste buds. "Oh my lord!" I was speaking with my mouth full. "This is amazing."

"I think we're destined to be together, Mr. Grewal."

She cut another piece for herself.

I didn't serve myself any of the pie. Annabeth fed me each bite, and it was more than a little erotic. I was beginning to have feelings for this girl whom I had only met a few hours earlier, and already they were stronger than those I had ever felt for my wife.

The fork sat on the empty plate, and a few crumbs from the crust lay on the counter. Two tall glasses of Coke were emptied, refilled, and emptied again. I had eaten more that afternoon then I had consumed in the previous two days.

We sat facing each other again, Annabeth's legs between mine, hands held, leaning close. Conversation went from relationships, to children - she asked a lot about my son - to my business, if I could call it a business. I told her that I volunteered helping people on social assistance balance their budgets, teaching them how to put money aside for emergencies. I found it ironic, because while I was telling people how to save, I was barely scraping by myself. Instead of volunteering, I should have been taking more paying clients, but I truly enjoyed helping people.

She pulled one hand from mine, placed it on my cheek, leaned in, and kissed me softly on the opposite one. "You've got a good heart, Mr. Grewal." She was about to lean in again when the phone rang. Startled, I jumped back.

She laughed. "You can still hear that thing ring over all the chatter when the place is packed."

Annabeth stood and answered the phone. She covered the mouthpiece, yelling over the invisible crowd for effect, "It's for you, Mr. Grewal."

She stepped forward, let the hand piece dangle, and spun it around. I took the phone and leaned against the wall, watching Annabeth as she cleaned the counter and put the plate in the grey plastic bin of dirty dishes.

"This is Mr. Gre... Dan."

"Well you must have put quite the spell on little Annabeth, Skinny. I been hearing from everyone that Annabeth is treating you something special."

I chose to ignore the comments. "What have you got for me, Lucious?" I was secretly hoping that my car had caught on fire and was now just a mass of burnt and charred metal.

"Good news, Skinny." Shit, I thought. "It's nothing serious. Your fuel filter is plugged solid with crap, and your gas tank has got more dirt in it than a crop field. I've gotta drop your tank and clean it out, and I ain't got no filter to fit your foreign car. I'll soak the filter to clean it and order another one just in case."

"That's great, Lucious. Thanks."

"'Thanks?' You gone loco, boy? I just told you that your car won't be ready until..." His voice trailed off. "Annabeth, right, Skinny?"

"Lucious." The strong tone of my voice indicated I wouldn't discuss this matter with him.

"Sorry, Skinny. Just that Annabeth ain't had no boyfriend for as long as I can remember. You break her heart, Skinny, and I swear I'll break you." His voice was firm. At this point, I knew he wasn't showing his broad white smile.

Lucious was being very protective of the girl cleaning her diner as I spoke on her phone. "Don't worry about that, Lucious. She's a big girl and I think if any heart is gonna get broken, it'll be mine."

"Skinny, she may come across as a tough girl, but deep down, she's fragile. She's never had no one serious-like. You know what I mean."

"I'll keep that in mind. What time tomorrow?"

"Any time after ten. I pulled your bag out of the trunk and have it in the front office. I close at five. Better be here, Skinny, or I'll leave your bag outside the front door." He hung up.

Annabeth had finished putting the dirty dishes in the sink and was wiping down the prep area. "Problem?"

"Car won't be ready until tomorrow."

"That's great." She threw the cloth in the sink. "It is great, right?"

"It is, actually. Just direct me to the town hotel, motel, inn, manager; whatever you've got here in Bakers Corner."

"Well, Mr. Grewal," she said as she walked closer to me, "we don't have any hotels, but I do have a plan."

My mind began to race as I tried to guess what she had in mind.

"My ma and pa have a huge house and I'm sure they wouldn't mind taking you in for the night. Well, by 'huge' I mean it's just me and them and an extra bedroom."

"You still live with ma and pa?"

"Don't make fun of me. I'm a busy girl. I run this place six days a week and barely have time to sleep."

"What do you do for fun?"

Annabeth pulled her black hair back and used an elastic band to make a small ponytail. She twisted her neck and I heard it crack. "Sleep."

I sat back down on the stool and retrieved my phone from my jeans. I swiped up and unlocked it before handing it to her with the wallpaper on the screen. I had it set to a picture of my son sitting in a wagon being pulled by my wife.

"What a darling. How old is he?"

I swiped the screen to the left and tapped the "Pictures" icon, and the screen flooded with more pictures of Sam. She giggled at the sight of him doing all the things babies do.

"Sam is two now. His mom left when he was just over a year old. I've only seen him a few times since."

She asked how to move the pictures on the scene and make them bigger. Annabeth was fascinated by the images on my phone. I thought it was odd; it truly seemed as though she had never used a touchscreen device before. I showed her the basics and she caught on quickly. She explained that since Bakers Corner was in a deep valley and had such a small population, technology just kept passing them by. She said they were lucky to have a regular telephone line, even if it didn't always work.

Annabeth placed my phone on the counter and walked back to make a call from the phone on the wall. She had her back to me, and I stared at her and followed the lines down to her jeans. She crossed her legs, leaned against the wall, and flipped her ponytail between her fingers. I took in a deep breath and looked long and hard. I'd met this girl only a few hours earlier, and already these feelings were stirring up inside me. I heard her mumble, laugh, and then hang up the receiver.

"It's all set, Mr. Grewal. You'll stay the night with me and my parents. My pa said that you better be on your best behaviour or he'll teach you some manners." She laughed as she walked behind the counter.

"Did he really?" I was nervous that she might actually be serious.

Annabeth wiped down the length of the counter, pushing any debris to the floor. She lifted each of the items on the counter, wiped beneath them, and then replaced them. I was surprised at the cleanliness of the lunch counter. "As soon as I'm done, I'll walk you over to my parents' to introduce you and get you set up. Do you have a suitcase or anything?" She continued to clean as she spoke.

"I have a bag in my car. But I feel like I'm imposing. Are you sure there isn't any place for me to crash tonight?"

"Don't think you're getting off easy, Mr. Grewal. You'll be working the dinner crowd tonight to pay me back. Besides, it's not every day I bring someone home to my parents." She looked up long enough from her work to flash me a smile.

"What?" I was stunned.

She reached under the counter and tossed me a white apron. "I could use the help clearing dishes and bringing out the orders. Can you handle that, Mr. Grewal?"

I held up the apron. "I've never waited tables before."

"Just don't break anything and you'll do fine." She tossed the rag under the counter. "All done. Come on. Let's go pick up your bag, then off to my parents'." She grabbed my hand, closed the door, and led me back to the garage where my day in Bakers Corner had begun.

3

Annabeth was clearly enjoying her time away from the diner. She walked down the street, her face pointed toward the sun, her eyes closed, holding my hand. Her arms were completely outstretched like wings, following my lead. The sun was blazing down through a cloudless sky.

"I don't get to do this very often," she confided.

I'm sure if it had been raining, her tongue would have been stuck out, trying to capture raindrops.

"What do you usually do when you close the diner between lunch and dinner?" I stretched out my arm farther and let her have her freedom as she glided on the sidewalk.

Her eyes were still closed. "Clean, wash dishes, prep some of the food, call some of the locals to bring me my orders. Boring stuff like that." Annabeth quickened her pace, skipped a few steps, and then settled down to let me lead her. "I need a vacation."

We walked in silence back to Lucious' garage. There were a few people on the street who turned to watch. Those that did, laughed, and Annabeth wiggled her fingers in their direction to acknowledge them.

Lucious saw us coming, stepped from the garage, lifted his oily ball cap, wiped his hands, and smiled his Mr. White Teeth smile. As we approached, Annabeth skipped a few steps ahead and gave him a big hug. His brother was working on another car from inside the pit; he looked up and went straight back to work.

"Watch yourself, darlin'. You be getting your pretty outfit all dirty." That didn't stop Lucious from giving Annabeth a big squeeze, picking her up, and holding her tightly. He let Annabeth down slowly until her feet were on solid ground again. I was curious. Lucious had a drawl; not quite a southern US drawl, but he certainly could be mistaken for a southerner. The more he spoke, the more I could detect a trace of Mississippi, Alabama, or Georgia in him. He certainly had the southern hospitality down pat. And I had never known a "Lucious" in my life.

"You two know each other?" Annabeth looked at both of us.

Lucious still had his wide smile set to full brightness. "We do, darlin'."

I spotted my bag just outside the front door, went over, and picked it up. "Thanks for pulling my bag out of the trunk, Lucious." I heaved it up high as if to emphasize to what I was referring.

"I'll have your car ready for you in the morning, Skinny. Have one of Annabeth's breakfasts before you leave. It'll keep your gut full until night."

I rubbed my "gut" and told him I was still full from the lunch and apple pie. I didn't think I would be hungry again until next week. Annabeth kicked my soft luggage bag. "If I have my way, Lucious, Skinny here may be sticking around for a while. What's it gonna take for you to sabotage his car so it takes a few more days to fix?"

Lucious told me that the problem was not complicated, just that my "foreign" car was old and needed to have the fuel system cleaned more often. He apologized to Annabeth, who gave him a pouty look and stuck out her lower lip to show her displeasure.

"I finally find a nice guy and you're sending him away. I think you want me for yourself, Lucious." Annabeth hugged him again, saying, "Off to Mama's now." She kissed him on the cheek and yelled out to Lucious' brother Willie who was still working in the pit. Willie waved back, saying nothing.

"Lucious?" I stayed behind as Annabeth walked away.

Lucious put his hands on his hips and waited silently for what was to follow. "Is she always like this?"

"Not since I known her, Skinny. You gave her something bad, that's for sure. She's acting like a sixteen-year-old with her first serious crush. I think she's been stuck here with us old town folk far too long. She's never had no real man in her life and you may just be what the ol' doc ordered. You better be on your best behaviour."

Annabeth turned and saw us talking as she walked ahead. I gave Lucious my best and ran to catch up, then followed a few steps behind. Her pace was quick, probably from the years of running behind that counter. For a girl "almost forty," as she had told me, she didn't act it or show it. I caught up, a little winded, and kept pace with my tour guide. She turned to look at me. "You are skinny."

"Not skinny. Slender. Or too tall for my weight."

"I can fix that." Annabeth's smile, like the one Lucious had, was wide and infectious. "Where do you live, anyway, Mr. Skinny Grewal?"

"Dan." I hit her butt with my bag. Annabeth purposely stumbled into my shoulder and smiled. I couldn't help but smile back. "Ottawa. Actually, not that far from here. I could start making regular trips if you keep serving me lunch, or take you to the city for dinner and have someone serve you for a change."

"I'd like that."

The rest of the walk to her parents' house was quiet but filled with subtle touching and hip checks. When we arrived, Annabeth ran ahead up the walk of the pale blue house with wood siding and large windows on both floors facing the road, and bounded up the front steps. She opened the door and entered, returning with an elderly woman she held closely just as I arrived at the front door. I let my bag fall to the walk and extended my hand.

"Ma'am."

The elderly lady was stern and showed no emotion. She stood very proper-like with her arms crossed, her shirt buttoned up high, her long sleeves closed at the cuffs, and her full-length pants reaching to her sensible shoes. She was very unlike her daughter standing beside her, who did look and act like a sixteen-year-old. "Mom, this is Mr. Dan Grewal from Ottawa."

My hand was still extended, left hanging in the air. If there was ever an awkward moment in my life, this was it. I'm sure it was only a second, but it felt like hours. Between the two women, a man who had a warm smile like Lucious broke through, and he grabbed my hand and shook it firmly.

"Rick Anderson, Dan. Pleased to meet you. It's not too often Annabeth brings a guy home. So I figure you must be pretty special." He looked at his wife, who was still standing rigidly beside Annabeth. "Mama, don't be showing your tough side and trying to intimidate our guest."

Rick showed me the wicker chairs on the porch and offered me a seat. "Mama, if you're gonna scowl, go inside and git everyone a beer."

"No thanks, Mr. Anderson. It's way too early for me. But I could go for a glass of water please," I said quickly.

Mrs. Anderson and Annabeth left without saying a word. My bag was still sitting where I had dropped it. Two Andersons down, one to go, I thought. Rick was now more relaxed, and he leaned back in his chair and looked out over the street. "Don't worry about Mama. She hated me for the first ten years of marriage. Actually, I'm still not sure if she likes me." Rick laughed out loud. I smiled politely. "Don't say anything, but she's the reason Annabeth hasn't gotten married. Mama hates everyone and has no compunction telling you just that. All the guys git scared of her and figure Annabeth will end up just like her mama."

I smiled again, but honestly, who says "compunction" anymore, I wondered.

"I've never heard of Bakers Corner before."

"Up until the highway went through, we were so far off the beaten path, no one knew we were here." He shifted in his chair. "I think it was a curse when they built that road through town. I remember the old days when we were lucky to see a car come through once a week. Now that cursed highway does nothing but make noise, scare the horses, and force us to welcome technology." Rick's mood had changed the instant he mentioned the highway.

I wanted to change the mood back, and fast. "What was it like before?"

Like a switch, Rick's face relaxed and his eyes squinted, showing the lines around both his eyes and across his forehead. He leaned back again, and I could imagine the memories flooding into his mind. "Quiet." He leaned forward and slapped my knee. "Enough of the past; tell me about yourself."

Compunction and knee slapping, all in a few minutes; I really was in Hicksville. If Annabeth and her mother had come back with freshly squeezed lemonade, the scenario would've been complete.

"Not much to tell really." I went on to convey to Rick the exact life story I had relayed to Annabeth only a few hours earlier. Rick listened intently and made me feel like he was genuinely interested in my life. Annabeth returned with two beers and a glass of water, - no lemonade - pulled up a chair, and joined in the conversation. Her mother stayed in the house and didn't come out to join us. I felt a little uncomfortable knowing she was inside, probably plotting my murder while I slept in her house, and wondering if I had touched her daughter yet. Part of my mind was wondering what Mrs. Anderson was doing while I sat and spent the afternoon talking with Annabeth and her father.

Rick moved on to his second beer as we sat on the front porch and talked about nothing. I was working on my second refill of ice water when I had to excuse myself to use the washroom. Annabeth showed me the washroom on the main level. To avoid making any noise in case Mrs. Anderson was close by, I chose to sit. As I did so, forcing myself to be quiet on the pink toilet, I noticed the vanity and tub were also pink. The lace valance above the window and lace shower curtain also indicated that Mrs. Anderson was in charge. I was having flashbacks to my grandparents' home that I had visited when I was just a kid, and feeling very uncomfortable.

After completing my task, I washed my hands and found only two bath towels; no hand towels were present to dry them with. Holding my hands in the air like a sterilized surgeon, I looked around and found no extra towels anywhere. Waving my hands back and forth in the air to dry them, I decided to use my jeans to finish the job. Another one of the reasons I always felt uncomfortable in other people's homes; sometimes even the most mundane change can cause severe stress.

Returning to the porch, I found that Mrs. Anderson had decided to join us. She sat the farthest away from me, followed by Rick, and then, immediately beside me, Annabeth. She and Rick were smiling, while Mrs. Anderson scowled and looked more than a little stressed. Her arms were crossed over her chest, and she looked down with her legs together and her feet flat on the ground, refusing to make eye contact. My glass of water had been refilled and Rick and Annabeth each had a fresh beer.

Annabeth sat on her chair with her legs folded beneath her. She was the opposite of her mother. She leaned into me, beaming the entire time. Annabeth took a sip of beer directly from the bottle and wiped her lips with the back of the hand. She must have seen me smiling at her actions because she winked back. I found it refreshing to see a woman comfortable in her own body and not caring what others thought.

The conversation between Rick, Annabeth, and I continued for several hours. Mrs. Anderson refused to join in or make any contribution. Empty beer bottles stood on the patio deck under their chairs, and my glass of water was refilled one more time.

I checked the time on my phone and realized I should have been in London by now. Since I didn't have cellphone coverage, I asked the Andersons if I could use their phone and reimburse them for the long distance charge. Rick laughed it off and told me not to worry about the expense.

Annabeth took my hand and led me to the den. Like the phone in the diner, this device was an old model Nortel bakelite desktop phone with a rotary dial.

"No cordless phones." I lifted the handset and was amazed by the weight of it alone.

"Too modern for Bakers Corner, Mr. Grewal." Annabeth left me alone to make my call.

Even after all this time, I had to look up my wife's home telephone number, as I couldn't use my cellphone and simply tap and swipe for a few moments to call her. I inserted my finger into the circle under the number "one" and rotated the clear plastic dial to the stop. The sound the phone made as it returned to the start position each time I rotated the dial reminded me of my childhood.

A familiar voice answered on the other end. "Hello."

"Sandra, its Dan."

"Where are you? You okay? Call display is coming up as number unavailable." Even though we were separated, our relationship was still friendly, and I could recognize the concern in her voice.

"My car broke down in this tiny town; not even a town, really, more like a few houses and a stable. Some really nice people offered to let me crash at their place until tomorrow when my car gets fixed."

"Strangers are letting you stay at their house! Really? Who does that anymore? That's sweet."

I was thinking that Lucious, Annabeth, and Rick cared about strangers, but Mrs. Anderson certainly didn't exhibit the same friendly attitude Sandra was asking about.

"I met some really nice people in town. I should be on my way tomorrow morning. Just didn't want you to worry."

"Thanks for calling. I was beginning to wonder what was going on." Sandra paused. I had been expecting something more like anger for not showing up on time again from Sandra; it had been a common accusation during our marriage and then through our separation. "Well, let me know if you're going to be late tomorrow, okay?"

We chatted about Sam, her parents, and what time I should be in London, then hung up.

The hinges creaked and the low-hanging spring slammed the wood screen door behind me as I walked back out onto the porch. Rick and Mrs. Anderson were arguing quietly and Annabeth sat silently ignoring them. They stopped suddenly when I returned.

Rick was all smiles again and asked if everything was all right. I gave him a briefing of my conversation with Sandra. He laughed loudly, and made a comment about how difficult women could be, which made me feel more than a little uncomfortable. He looked over to Mrs. Anderson, who, without having to say a word, made it clear to her husband that she didn't appreciate his comment.

Annabeth excused herself, explaining that she always had a shower between the breakfast/lunch rush and dinner. The screen door slammed again as she left me with her parents. An excruciating silence that last several minutes followed, until Mrs. Anderson simply stood up and went inside. Rick breathed a sigh of relief and exclaimed, "Thank God. That was painful." I couldn't help but chuckle a bit myself.

"So are you going to help out Annabeth with the dinner crowd tonight?"

I shot him a surprised look. "Yeah, of course. How did you know?""

"I figured you'd wanna help out with dinner tonight."

I gave Rick a broad smile. "Yeah, sure. I can't even carry more than one dinner plate at a time. Can't imagine what I could help out with but I'll do my best. Maybe dishes?"

"Annabeth will tell ya she doesn't need the help but you insist, my boy. She's as stubborn as they come and just as hard-headed. Besides, if you're gonna stay the night and eat the food, you earn your keep." He picked up all the empty beer bottles from the floor and started to walk past me.

"Actually, Rick, we already agreed I'd help out at the diner tonight," I informed him.

Rick stopped short and laughed out loud. "Late enough for a beer now, Dan?"

"Definitely. Can I help?"

"Stick to helping Annabeth at the diner. Mama will kill ya if you go into her kitchen."

After Rick and I finished our fresh drinks, he showed me to the guest room immediately beside the master bedroom. I opened my bag and laid my clothes out on the bed. Pulling out a lighter pair of pants and a dark T-shirt, I changed before my first shift as the new local diner dish-washer. Annabeth met me on the porch, and kissed her parents before we walked to the street and headed toward the diner. It was a silent walk. Not awkward - not the type of silence that two people experience when they don't have anything to talk about - but rather a comfortable silence wherein nothing needed to be said.

Annabeth was proving to have an aggressive nature that I enjoyed. She knew what she wanted and went after it. On the walk, without looking down, she reached across, grabbed my little finger, and held it tightly. Then she added the ring finger and then the middle finger, followed by the whole hand. She held on firmly and swung.

She looked over at me once, then turned back to watch where we were going.

"Just making sure you're okay with this?" Annabeth asked as she squeezed my hand.

"Very." I squeezed back. "I'm just not sure where this may lead and what you expect."

"I'm almost forty; I'm not some teenager with a crush who'll cry my eyes out tonight if we don't see each other again. I'll be disappointed as hell, Mr. Grewal, if you never call me again, though." She never looked at me.

"I'll call. I'm just not used to a woman being the aggressor, but I gotta tell you, it's a nice change." Annabeth squeezed my hand again. Even from the side, I could see that she had a broad smile on her face. I was a little uncomfortable having feelings so strong so quickly for someone new. Regardless of your age, when you get that feeling in your stomach, when you palms sweat when the other person takes hold of your hand, when your heart races and you feel like a kid again, it's new and wonderful and it feels even better to know you make someone else feel the same way. There was nothing but silence between us for the few blocks left to her diner.

The front door to the restaurant was already unlocked. Annabeth pushed it in and the tiny brass bell above the door chimed. The man whose face I'd only partially seen stuck his head out and waved. "Hey, Annabeth. Ready for the night crowd?"

"You bet, Gus. Meet our help for the night."

Gus walked out from behind the counter and looked completely different from what I had imagined. I had caught glimpses of the man behind the counter cooking the orders, but that was all. Now, a small man - maybe five feet, two inches tall - stood before me, with his hand outstretched in greeting.

I took his hand and he shook it firmly, which seemed to be the norm in this town, then dropped it just as quickly. Gus had arms like a trucker - thick and solid - and his tiny, bald head sat on huge square shoulders. He had a thick nose but thin eyes and lips. Although his chest was flat, a perfectly round belly protruded with his pants tucked up high beneath it.

"Hey Gus. Pleased to meet you. Annabeth couldn't tell me enough about your cooking today while I was at her parents'."

Gus looked at Annabeth with inquisitive eyes. The glance spoke volumes without saying a word. Annabeth stared back. It was like an entire conversation was occurring telepathically without my involvement.

Finally, Gus looked back at me. "Actually, people come here for Annabeth's charm and my cooking. Don't you forget that." He cast me a disapproving look, turned, and went back to the kitchen.

"Did I say something wrong?" I whispered.

Annabeth leaned in close. "Gus is very private and the thought of other people talking about him gives him the willies." She pulled me behind the counter. "Come on. This is your job tonight." She led me to a large double porcelain sink. The size of it reminded me of the massive concrete washtub in my parents' basement beside the old washer and dryer.

Annabeth hung a clean, thick white apron around my neck, stepped in close, reached around, and tied the strings behind my back. We were only inches apart. When she finished tying, she looked up and paused. My breathing had stopped and my heart had ceased beating. Time stood still. I was staring into these beautiful dark eyes, and I could feel her breathing on me but I have no recollection of my own breath. Her arms reached around and pulled me in tighter. I responded in kind, and placed my hands on the small of her back. Our entire bodies now touched. I took the lead and leaned in and kissed her. The kiss was soft at first, then she tilted her head and opened her mouth.

The goddamn fucking bell chimed above the door and Robbie walked in. I could smell the shit that the breeze picked up from his clothes and gently passed by me.

Annabeth pulled away, put her head down - embarrassed, I think - and asked Robbie what she could get him.

Robbie smiled; he, too, was embarrassed, and simply extended a large ceramic mug. "Coffee please. Got a long night in the barn."

"Put a fresh pot on for you now. Grab a seat. It'll be few minutes." Annabeth took his mug.

Robbie dropped onto the first stool and looked at me. It was like I had been caught kissing his girlfriend. He didn't seem too happy to have walked in and seen Annabeth and I doing what we had been doing.

"Did I disturb ya?" he asked.

"Sorta." I thought it best not to engage him further.

"Good." His voice was stern and loud. He wanted it known that he wasn't happy to have caught Annabeth with another man.

"Robbie! Are you ever gonna wash this thing? It's disgusting. It's blacker than the pit in Lucious' garage." Annabeth was yelling from the porcelain wash station.

"It keeps the flavour strong when I don't wash it." Wash came out as "worsh."

"Come here, Mr. Grewal, and earn your keep." I walked over and Annabeth handed me the mug. "See if you can clean this for Robbie." She leaned in close. "We'll finish that thing later."

Robbie's cup was scrubbed, cleaned, and handed back to Annabeth. She looked inside before filling it with coffee and then glanced back at me. The dark stains remained for the most part. Dish soap and a soft dishcloth were not what I needed. It would have been better to have tossed that mug in the garbage and gotten Robbie a new one.

The brass bell above the door chimed again as Robbie left. Annabeth was already getting the silverware ready in grey plastic bins spaced evenly under the counter. I offered to do that so she could concentrate on other things. I asked if they had any specials that night. All I heard was Gus laughing from the back.

"Same thing every night, Mr. Grewal," Annabeth told me. "We have the same clientele, and the same food on the menu. It's what everyone wants when they don't want to cook at home. Remember the menu?" She pulled a menu out from beneath the counter and tossed it to me like a Frisbee. "Same thing, every day and every night. And if someone wants something different, Gus will cook it up for them. Won't you, Gus?"

A loud "Yup!" came from the kitchen.

An hour later, every stool was full. The tiny diner was noisy with the sounds of chatter, forks and knives scraping porcelain plates, and me splashing away in the double washbasin. Every time I turned to observe the customers, they were talking to one another and to Annabeth, or yelling back at Gus with Gus yelling back. It was like a large family dinner at the counter.

Occasionally, I would turn to look at Annabeth, and she would catch me watching her and give me a quick smile back. She never had time to speak to me, but would casually touch me as she walked past. When I finished one load, she would refill the counter with more dishes. It was a never-ending cycle. Wash the dirty dishes in the hot water, let them dry, and put them under the prep table. Then Gus would fill another order and back out they went.

As Gus cooked up the food, he often didn't even need to hear what was being ordered. He looked over to see who had come in, and would start their usual meal before Annabeth even took the order. He turned to me while he was cooking. "Thanks for helping out. Before you came along, me and Annabeth both had to do the dishes on a busy night."

"You mean there isn't a regular dish washer?"

"Look behind you, man; we have enough dishes to get us through three days without washing one plate. You're just making our work easier at the end of the..." His words were cut short.

Tires screeched, and the sound ended with a loud thud. All the dinner chatter and plate banging came to a sudden stop. Everyone in the diner turned and looked out the window to the street. I ran from the kitchen and pushed my way to the door.

The sun sat low in the sky and cast long shadows from the west. Bright orange light burnt down and ran along the highway that cut through Bakers Corner.

Out front, a car had come to a stop twenty or thirty feet past the diner. Directly in front of the building, a young child, maybe five or six years old, lay on the road with his legs bent at grotesque angles. A small puddle of blood had formed near his head and was getting bigger. Skin had pulled away from his forehead and was flapped to one side. Just below his hairline, the open wound revealed the white bone beneath. He lay unmoving on the pavement like a rag doll discarded and tossed to the road. An adult, seemingly paralyzed with fear, stood over him, simply looking down. I assumed they were father and son.

I looked directly at Annabeth, yelled, "Call nine-one-one," and broke through the restaurant crowd, throwing open the door and running to the street.

I knelt beside the boy. He had a soft round face, which was now scarred from the asphalt and darkened by the blood that smeared his skin. His eyes were closed, and he looked peaceful, not injured or hurt. I reached down to where his pulse should have been in his neck. My fingertips slid along until I found what I wanted. The pulse was thready, weak. When I looked at the wound on his head, the gentle, sudden spurts of blood emanating from it were perfectly synchronized with the pulse I felt in his neck. I pulled hard on my apron, ripping the strings from around my waist and neck. I balled up the white cotton material and gently placed it on his head. Blood found the cotton and spread crimson across the lower section of the apron. I placed my hand on his chest and felt a slow, steady rise and fall. He was still breathing.

The driver of the car came running over, stopped short, and fell to her knees in tears. The father standing over the boy was still motionless as he stared at his son.

The victim lay immobile; one arm was underneath his torso, and the other arm lay straight down beside him. Other than a few abrasions, his arms didn't appear injured. I looked at his pants: the material was completely twisted around like someone had rung them out to dry with the boy's legs still in them. Both of his shoes lay where he had been hit. I pulled down one of his socks and felt for a pulse on the top of his foot. I couldn't locate it. I tried the other foot. Nothing. Shit, I thought.

The female driver who had possibly hit the young boy was crying hysterically. She was screaming at God, and yelling at whomever would listen about the boy running across the street. I heard her but I blocked out her screams. The father was still silent, remaining oddly quiet. I thought that if it were Sam lying there I would be freaking out, not simply staring, but everyone reacts to trauma differently.

I looked up and found Annabeth standing off to one side. "Did you call nine-one-one?"

A hand was placed on my shoulder. I turned to see Lucious standing over me. "Skinny, come on. Git up."

"What did the nine-one-one operator say? How long for the ambulance to get here?" I was looking at Lucious, wondering why everyone was so calm.

"Come on, Skinny, git up here and let us handle things."

"We have to keep him stabilized until the medics get here. His legs are badly fractured and the pulse is comprised."

He looked me straight in the eyes and spoke in a low, steady, calming voice. "Git up, Skinny. We can handle this." He placed his hand under my arm and helped me up. I stood before Lucious, turned, and saw that the woman driver was also being escorted away.

The crowd around the boy grew larger. Annabeth was among the group and paid no attention to me as Lucious tugged at my arm to keep me away. I turned, twisted, and forced myself free to return to the boy lying in the street. The crowd surrounding him stood firmly and refused to let me pass. I stepped from side to side, trying to find a break in the crowd that would let me in.

Lucious grabbed me once again, spun me around, and pulled me to the diner. He pushed open the door and threw me inside. I landed on the diner floor and slid into a stool. Plates, cups, and glasses on the counter toppled over or banged together. My head hit the metal seat and I instantly felt the warmth of blood flowing from the wound that had opened on the back of my head. When my vision cleared, I looked up at Lucious, and he wasn't Mr. White Teeth anymore. He stood tall before me with his arms crossed over his chest, staring at me. His strength surprised me. He wasn't an old man anymore. Lucious may have looked weak and frail, but he had the strength of a much younger man. I felt the warm fluid running down the back of my head and past my collar, and ran my hand along the injury. I looked at my hand to see a mixture of hair and blood covering it.

Lucious picked up a cloth from the counter and tossed it at me without saying a word. I pressed the cloth against my head to quell the bleeding. I pulled myself up between two stools, bent my knees, hoisted myself upright, and looked at Lucious.

"Next time I tell you to do something, Skinny, don't be giving me no lip."

I stood up and let my spinning head settle. I still felt a little dizzy but I wanted to walk to the door and see what was happening outside. I stumbled, grabbed the counter for stability, regained my balance, and made my way to the front door. Lucious blocked me, preventing me from leaving. I couldn't put up much of a fight in my condition, so I looked over his shoulder to see the crowd outside. The driver and her car had disappeared and the father of the child was nowhere to be seen. The crowd surrounding the scene formed a tight circle around the young boy lying on the ground.

I waited for sirens but heard nothing. There was little movement from the crowd. The circle remained tight. I searched the mass and found Annabeth. Her back was to me and she seemed to be one with the crowd, not moving unless the entire group did.

I backed away from Lucious and thought about trying to get past him. His arms were crossed, he looked larger than I remembered, and I didn't want to test his strength again. The wound on the back of my head had stopped bleeding so I tossed the rag to the floor. I attempted to lean around Lucious and get a better look, but he stood his ground and made a threatening move.

The crowd slowly started to part and disperse, and I saw the father stand, holding the broken body of his son in his arms. His face was emotionless: stoic, brave, no heavy breathing. He wasn't exhibiting any emotion at all. He started to walk away, up the road and away from the scene of the accident, while carrying his son. No one followed, and no attempt was made to stop him. The boy hung loosely in his arms, and blood still dripped to the pavement as he carried the broken body away. The father just strolled like a man carrying groceries from the local market. The crowd broke up and diffused into the neighbourhood.

Lucious turned and saw that the group was beginning to disperse, and relaxed his stance. His arms loosened, he pushed his cap back on his head, and he stuck his hands deep in his pockets. Mr. White Teeth had returned, and he slapped me on my shoulder. "Sorry about your head, Skinny." He laughed. "Some things are just meant to be private."

The bell above the door chimed and the customers filled back in, taking the same seats they had occupied before they had gone outside. The bell continued to chime over and over again and the conversations started up where they had left off. I didn't overhear one comment or remark about the incident outside. Gus walked past on his way to the kitchen.

Annabeth walked past me as well. She didn't even glance at me or comment about my blood-soaked hair as she took her place behind the counter. She simply cleaned up the spill I had made when I had been tossed to the floor by Lucious. She put the toppled glasses and coffee cups in the grey dish bin, laid out clean ones, and refreshed the spilled drinks.

Lucious asked Annabeth for a coffee to go. She filled a paper cup with coffee, black, and left it on the counter. Lucious added his sugar and cream, picked it up, and raised the cup to me as if in a toast. "Don't forget, Skinny, your car'll be ready first thing in the morn." I heard the familiar chime as he let the door close behind him.

I looked around the diner. The same customers who sat and chatted about farm work, crops, and their animals continued the talk as if nothing had happened. Turning around, I wondered if I had imagined the whole thing. I ran my fingers through my hair and jumped when I hit the open wound in my scalp. Pulling back my hand, I saw that my fingers were again covered in hair and blood. I wasn't imagining the event that had just occurred. Spinning on my heels, I stalked to the front door and gazed out to where the boy had been hit. A man with a wheelbarrow full of dirt and a water bucket scoured away at the dark stain on the asphalt, then covered it with fresh dirt and patted that into the road. When I turned back, Annabeth was leaning low on the counter, talking to one of the locals who had been part of the circle. No one - not one person inside the diner - paid any attention to the man outside.

Annabeth noticed me staring at her. "So, Mr. Grewal, you gonna come back and start washing the dishes to earn your keep?"

I felt light-headed, and my mind was swimming with the details of the events that had just unfolded before me. I couldn't comprehend what had happened. I looked out the door again as the man with the wheelbarrow pushed the shovel into the remaining dirt, lifted the handles of the contraption, and wheeled it away with no sign of emotion. When I turned back to Annabeth, she smiled and winked at me.

"What's up, Mr. Grewal? You gonna do the dishes or do I hafta fire you on your first day on the job?" She was beaming, and continued to smile as she tossed me a clean apron.

4

I was silent for the rest of the shift. Dirty dishes piled up, got washed, and were put away, while counters got wiped and cleaned. Annabeth would look my way and smile at me, and I would smile back to avoid a confrontation.

Just past seven, I took a bathroom break and sat on the toilet with my head hanging low, cradled in my hands. The light was off; I needed the darkness to think. The wound on my head still reminded me that the events upon which I was fixated had happened, and I wasn't imagining them. I ran the tap to drown out the sound of the chatter in the diner. I played the series of events over in my head, forwards, backwards, sideways, and then back again. Regardless of the way I reviewed the events, nothing seemed to make sense. Maybe this indifference was some weird country way of dealing with things, like the way a farmer will tie a rope around a dead cow's leg and drag it to a huge hole, drop it in, and bury it.

The people of Bakers Corner had been isolated for so long, they may have traditions and their own cultural ways foreign to the rest of the province, I rationalized. My thoughts went back to the driver of the car that hit the child. What had happened to her? Were the police even called? What had happened to the boy who had been carried away by his father? Why did the diner guests act as if nothing had happened after they returned? These questions were all still unanswered. I wanted explanations, but what authority did I have to pursue the situation with a girl I had only met that morning?

Even though I didn't use the toilet, I flushed, washed my hands, dried them on my apron, and exited the bathroom. My head was down and I almost bumped into Gus. Looking up at him, I noticed that his apron was covered in red stains - I hoped that they were tomato-based and not blood from the boy - and grease.

I didn't mean to say anything, but it just came spewing out. "That was some commotion out there, wasn't it?"

"Huh?"

"The boy!"

"Yeah. Gotta piss." He pushed past me, slammed the door, and locked it.

I wasn't sure if it was my imagination or his lack of reaction, but I couldn't help but sense that even Gus didn't feel any true remorse for the young boy hit by the car. As I walked back to the dining room, I was still in a daze about everything. Suddenly, Annabeth jumped up, put her arm around me, and kissed my cheek. A bright flash bulb went off, temporarily blinding me. White burn marks in my eyes blinked away like stars on a dark summer's night. Even with my eyes closed,

I could feel Annabeth's arm wrapped tightly around my neck.

"You sure you can get me a few copies of that by breakfast tomorrow morning?" I overheard Annabeth ask.

When the flash burns in my eyes finally disappeared, I looked up and saw a man with a camera walking out of the diner. "Who was that?" I asked.

"That is our resident photographer, Alan. He takes pictures of everything in town. I wanted a picture of us to mark the day we met. He said he should have the film developed and a few prints made before you leave."

I looked at Annabeth, puzzled. "Developed? I can use my phone to take a picture and email you a copy. Wait, did you say he takes pics of everything?"

"Yeah, he walks around with that camera around his neck all the time."

I pulled away from Annabeth's grip and took off after Alan. I stepped on something and felt it shatter under my foot. Looking down, I saw an old flash bulb flattened by the weight of my step. I thought of how Lucious called me "Skinny;" at least I could flatten an old-style flash bulb.

I burst out the door and caught Alan on the sidewalk outside the diner, grabbing his arm to make him stop. He turned around and bright lights burnt my eyes again. Alan had set the flash off as he had spun around and activated it only inches from my eyes.

"I'm sorry. You scared me. I didn't mean to do that." I could hear Alan speaking but my eyes were awash in super bright white light. Even with my eyelids closed tightly, it was like staring at the sun.

I held out my hand and Alan grasped it. "Do you really take pictures of everything around town?" My head was down as I waited for the light to clear again.

"Yeah. That's right. Why? You got something going on ya want pictures taken of?"

I still couldn't see Alan as he held on to my outstretched arm. "Did you get any pictures of the accident today?"

"Accident? What accident? Shoot, did I miss something?"

"You didn't hear about the little boy killed by the car only a little while ago?"

"Nope, and news travels fast around these parts." Alan saw that I was having trouble with my eyes and led me back into Annabeth's Counter. I heard the doorbell chime as we walked in and he sat me down on one of the stools.

I thanked him for his time as he gently placed me on the stool, and overheard him tell Annabeth what he had done. I blinked a few times to help my eyes refocus, but it didn't do much good. I heard Annabeth ask if I was okay. I shook my head and told her it would only take a few more minutes of keeping my eyes closed for me to recover. Alan said he was going to leave again, and Annabeth reminded him that she wanted a few stills of the two of us by breakfast.

Keeping my head down, I opened my eyes and realized that the flash burns had subsided, but played as if I was still blinded by the light. I hoped to catch someone in the diner doing something unusual or letting something slip, thinking I was still without sight.

I saw feet pass close to mine as I looked down and heard the regular conversation continue. My rouse was all for nothing as everyone finished their meals and no one said anything of the incident in the street.

Annabeth brought me a cold cloth that I put over my eyes, and in a few minutes I told her I was fine and could finish my shift washing dishes. She joked that I was dogging it and pushed me toward the sink.

There were only a few people left in the diner and it wasn't long before Annabeth went to the front door, locked it, and turned the "OPEN" sign to "CLOSED." It was now only Annabeth, Gus, and I left in the restaurant.

I finished washing the dishes, stacked them where I was shown, and cleaned my hands on my wet apron. I untied it and hung it on a hook in the kitchen before walking out into the diner and finding Annabeth and Gus sweeping up and wiping down the counter.

"All done?" I asked.

"Almost." Annabeth was all smiles. Gus continued to work.

"Hey, I have an idea. Gus, come here." I waved him over. He reluctantly walked around and joined Annabeth and myself.

"What?"

I guided him to where I wanted him. "Annabeth, could you hop up on the counter, and Gus, stand beside Annabeth, will ya?" Annabeth was beaming, and Gus was sour. I pulled my phone out, unlocked it, and activated the camera. I pointed it at the two of them and crowed, "Smile!" Annabeth was still grinning widely, while Gus looked miserable.

"Gus," she said as she pushed him away from the counter and toward me, "would you please take a picture of Mr. Grewal and myself?" She reached for me.

"How do I work this thing?" Gus held my phone like a grenade.

"Turn it this way," I explained as I positioned the screen before him, "and tap the screen when you get the picture you want."

Annabeth, still sitting on the counter, pulled me in front of her, wrapped her arms around me, placed her head on my shoulder, and told Gus not to take the picture until it was perfect. The flash went off and burnt my eyes again. Gus handed me the phone, and I showed Annabeth the two pictures. She laughed and asked for a copy when I got them developed. Developed?

I asked her to get behind the counter and lean forward, and I took a few more shots. Gus was being grumpy and moaned, "When are we going to close?"

"In a minute," she barked back.

Annabeth played model while I snapped away on my phone. Then she walked up, took the cellphone from my hands, and gave it to Gus, saying, "One more Gus, please, and we can leave."

Gus aimed the phone at us as Annabeth walked slowly toward me. She held both my hands tightly, leaned in, and kissed me. The flash went off and we continued to kiss. No flash burn this time; my eyes were already closed and I was lost.

Gus put my phone on the counter. "Now!"

Annabeth pulled away. "Okay, Gus, we're leaving."

I pocketed my phone and walked out of the diner with Annabeth and Gus. Gus said goodnight, walked around the building, and disappeared. Annabeth and I stood outside the diner beside each other, and I looked past her to the still-dirty patch of earth on the roadway. Annabeth grabbed hold of my hand and pulled me toward her house. I planted myself and refused to budge.

"Doesn't it bother you?"

"What?"

I pointed with my head. "The young boy who died. Well, I think he died. I don't know. No one wants to talk about it."

Annabeth started walking toward the house without saying a word about the accident. She looked up into the sky. The sun was setting in the west, where I should have been that night with my son instead of in Bakers Corner. Over London, the sun was a brilliant yellow, orange, and white light sitting low in the sky and shooting rays of sunshine upwards. Annabeth stared westward as she walked alone on the sidewalk toward her parents' house.

"Are you coming?"

She refused to answer any questions about the accident. I jogged to catch up and walked beside her. There was no handholding and no small talk as we walked leisurely from the diner to the house. The pace was slow and deliberate; I didn't want to have to deal with Mrs. Anderson or with what had happened. The few people we passed on the street waved, nodded, or offered a "good night." But by now, Bakers Corner was getting ready to roll up the streets, turn off the streetlights, and tuck itself in for the night. I assumed from the rural farming that everyone must go to bed early and wake up with the sun.

We walked up to the porch, where Rick was resting in the same chair in which he had been sitting earlier. Mrs. Anderson hadn't joined him, thank God. Annabeth sat beside her father and took a sip of beer from his bottle as Rick asked if we wanted to join him. This time, after what I had seen a few hours earlier, I agreed. Annabeth went inside to get the beer.

"Rick, did you hear about the incident that happened just outside the diner tonight?"

"Yeah. I heard. What of it?"

"You don't think it's weird?"

"What's weird?" Questions answered with more questions. I used to play this game with my father when I got in shit for something I shouldn't have done.

"No one called nine-one-one. No ambulance. No police. The father just carried the dying boy away." I tried to word it as a comment instead of a question.

Rick sat forward, placing both elbows on his knees. "Dan, ya gotta realize we think a little different than they do in the city. We don't fear death. It's a part of life here. Things die all the time. Sure we're sad, but freakin' out and fallin' down and rollin' on the ground ain't done anyone a bit o' good far back as I can remember."

"But to simply gather around, watch, and do nothing. You gotta admit, even for country folk, it's a bit on the odd side."

"Odd to you. Normal to us. Don't talk about this in front of Annabeth; she does get freaked out by this stuff." He pursed his lips and held his index finger up to them. Odd, I thought; Annabeth had been in the crowd and hadn't seemed the least bit fazed when she had come back after the father had carried away his child.

Annabeth returned with two open bottles of beer, handed one to me, kept the other, and sat beside her father. She rubbed the bottle between her hands, tilted it back, and took a long, slow drink. When she pulled the bottle away, more than half its contents were gone. While she drank, Rick gave me that look. It was the quiet, telepathic look that re-enforced his comment about not speaking about the incident with Annabeth.

The next few hours on the front porch were filled mostly with idle chit chat about country life versus city life; how dark it gets in the country without the lights from the big city, the lack of stress, and how time has little relevance in Bakers Corner. I wanted to bring up Lucious' behaviour, but my unspoken agreement with Rick not to discuss the incident any further kept me silent.

I put my empty beer bottle down on the table and noticed that I had drunk one beer to Rick and Annabeth's two each. My head was beginning to swim again. I gently put my hand over the cut on my head.

"You're looking a tad bit oozy there, Dan. That beer hit you hard or what?"

I chose not to mention how I had banged my head, lying instead. "I whacked my head pretty bad at the diner. Cut myself good. I don't think drinking this beer after banging my head so hard was such a great idea." I sat upright and felt like I was going to lose my balance and fall right off the chair. "I think I'm gonna throw up."

I fell to my knees from the chair and kept my head low. I crawled over to the edge of the porch and hung my head over the shrubs in case I did vomit. I made some guttural noises and heaved my back a few times but nothing came out. My whole body felt like it had been beaten to within an inch of its life. The little reserve of strength I had was depleted and spent.

"Maybe you city folk can't hold you beer, young man." Rick laughed. If I had possessed the strength, I probably would have punched him. Instead I turned, looked up at him, and smiled sickly. I used the porch post to pull myself up and excused myself, asking Annabeth if she would help me upstairs to the bedroom. She wrapped one of my arms around her neck so I could use her as a crutch, opened the screen door, and let it slam behind us as we entered the house. I didn't realize how loud the door was, and how much it echoed, until just then. I held the bannister tightly and took one step at a time until I made it to the top of the stairs, then limped slowly to the bedroom. I was just happy that Mrs. Anderson hadn't seen me like this.

I faced the bed, Annabeth released her grip, and I fell forward onto it. My face hit the pillow and that is all I can remember until I woke up to the feeling of my bladder straining for relief.

5

I awoke facedown on the pillow. Turning over, I didn't notice any more light in the room than I could detect while looking into the soft sheets. The bedroom was black; the kind of black you only see outside the city where the electric lights haven't polluted the night sky with their glow. My memories of where I was were confused and jumbled with thoughts that travelled through my brain faster than the speed of light. I had flashes of driving, the garage, this girl; what was her name? Annabeth, I thought. I was at a diner - why was I cleaning a kitchen and doing dishes - and then the sight of the young boy, a halo of blood around his head, his legs twisted and deformed. People gathered around him. What were they doing? The images were coming and going faster than I could process and catalogue them. Even in this mire of darkness, I covered my eyes with my forearm. Then I was faced with a new problem: my bladder was screaming for relief. If I moved I might pee the bed, but I knew I had to. I couldn't remember where I was - a hotel, or a bed and breakfast? The scents made it clear it wasn't home; not my home, nor my wife's. So where was I, and more importantly, where was the bathroom?

I stood carefully, feeling for the walls and sliding my feet along the floor. My shoes were off, and my socks slid along the slippery hardwood. My arms waved slowly back and forth like those of a blind man trying to find his way. In this case, the saying was literally true.

I didn't know where I was or which way I had to go to get to the bathroom. My right hand felt a wall. I walked sideways, still sliding my feet along the floor. I ran my hands farther along the wall and tried to distinguish what I was feeling. My hand distinguished a ninety-degree corner to the right, so I turned and went along in the new direction. It wasn't long before I felt something familiar: a door hinge. I ran my hand down and found the doorknob.

I opened the door and a window at the end of the hall allowed some light from outside to penetrate the blackness inside the home. I was now able to see a few doors down the hall but it still didn't look familiar to me. I opened each door and looked in, trying to find the bathroom. I had success with the fourth door. Even the dim light from the hall illuminated the white porcelain of the toilet. My bladder was straining. Without closing the door, I dropped my pants, fumbled to lower the seat, and sat down. My head was still reeling, but slowly Annabeth, Rick, Bakers Corner, the boy, Lucious - they all started to come back. I continued to pee. I didn't think it would ever stop.

I tapped my pockets, looking for my cellphone to see what time it was. Then it hit me: I should have used the flashlight app instead of fumbling in the darkness. I felt my front and back pockets, but found nothing. I patted myself down from head to toe but couldn't locate my phone. I leaned back and felt a sharp, sudden, electric pain course across the back of my head. I reached up and felt the open wound, suddenly remembering the stool incident. Everything was coming back in bits and pieces. I was in Annabeth's parents' house.

I finished peeing, pulled up my pants, and searched for a light switch without success. At least the sink was where it was supposed to be. I washed my hands, dried them on my pants, and went out into the hall. The solitary window at the end permitted only a small amount of light to penetrate the darkness. I went to the window to see what the light source was. I bent low and looked out into the night.

I was looking out into a farmer's field of wheat, or grass, or something grass-like. A large fire, maybe half a kilometer away from the house, was burning high into the night sky and casting long, dark, human shadows behind the crowd encircling the flames. I was too far away to distinguish who was standing around the fire, but the size of the crowd was substantial; it looked to be a hundred or more people from this distance.

I called out to Annabeth and didn't get a reply. Then I tried Rick's name, but again, I received no answer. I opened each door and found myself entirely alone. I went back to my room, found my shoes, and ran downstairs, through the kitchen, and out the back door. Standing in the doorway, I could see how big the fire was. The flames licked up high into the night sky, and the crowd surrounding the fire simply stood around it. Even from this distance, I could hear the fire as it cracked and popped. Embers floated up into the air like fireflies dancing in the wind.

I called out to Annabeth again and was met with the same vacant quiet. I jumped from the back door onto the grass and started to make my way toward the fire. I stumbled and fell more times than I can remember, and my head was still foggy. I rationalized that it must have been a concussion from hitting my head on the stool, and then having alcohol before bed. My lack of coordination, mixed with the ruts and furrows in the field, made it hard to walk in a straight line at night without a flashlight. Damn, I thought; I should have brought my phone.

Walking toward the fire, I could see my breath in the chill of the night air. Mosquitoes buzzed around my head, and a few found their mark and began to feast on my blood. The nearer I got to the fire, the fewer mosquitoes attacked me as the chill gave way to the warmth of the flames. The light from the fire cut through the darkness and revealed the people surrounding it. Not a single person was wearing clothes. Every person around the fire was naked - no shoes, no pants, nothing. I crouched low, and silently made my way toward them.

When I was less than one hundred feet away, I laid down in one of the furrows and crawled nearer to the group. I used my elbows and feet and pushed and pulled my way closer, keeping my head down but my eyes up. The ground was damp and cold. I could feel the muck sticking to my pants and shirt and filling my shoes. Above, heat from the fire caused my back to grow warmer the closer I got to it, but the lower half of my body was freezing as I crawled in the muck. I shivered as goose bumps appeared on my arms and legs. I stopped when I was within twenty-five feet of the crowd and spotted Annabeth. I looked at her body - slim, beautiful - and I found it difficult to tear my eyes away from her naked form.

She stood naked, silent, and unmoving. Beside her, Rick and Mrs. Anderson, naked as well, stood looking into the fire. Scanning the crowd, I recognized faces from the diner: Gus, Robbie, and then Lucious. Every single one of them was naked, silent, and staring into the fire. One section of the circle was broken, and a lone male figure stood there looking into the flames. The crowd gave him an unrestricted view of the burning structure. I peered into the fire to see what he was staring at, and as the flames jumped around, they revealed that on which everyone was focused. Something wrapped in a blanket or cloth was barely visible and lying atop the burning wooden structure.

It looked to be a large wooden pyre, made of logs and timber. On top, fully engulfed, a small body - that of a child - was burning. It must have been the boy, the one who had died earlier in the day. Was this the way the people of Bakers Corner dealt with the dead? I had no way of knowing how long they had been there, standing quietly before the fire. I couldn't begin to understand a ceremony wherein everyone in town undresses and stands naked before a huge fire while the body of the deceased is burnt to ashes. Was this some pagan ritual, something carried over from long ago? I felt like a coward hiding in the dirt, intruding on their private grieving process. But I also couldn't pull myself away. This ceremony was unlike anything I had ever heard of or read about.

I stayed low in the furrow, watching as the fire grew in intensity and listening to the crackling of dry timber in the flames. One of the pyre supports buckled and the entire structure collapsed, sending the body and wood to the ground. Those standing close to the area where the structure had fallen weren't concerned about the rogue flames, but still gave them a wide berth. The circle surrounding the pyre opened up to accommodate the new size of the fire. I lost sight of the body, and everyone began to look at the ground where I assumed it was now burning, hidden from my view.

I waited for something, anything, to happen: a chant, a song, a dance, maybe a flask of magic elixir passed around. Instead, everyone from the town simply stood around the bonfire, naked, focused on the flickering orange glow. As I lay there, my body began to protest against the contrast of heat and cold; my belly was freezing, while my back was beginning to sweat. I wanted to crawl away from the fire and get back to the house, but I also desperately wanted to see what everyone was going to do. My head was less foggy and my sense of balance seemed more stable. My thoughts didn't seem as jumbled as they had been earlier, either.

My hands were covered in the cold wet earth and my fingers were beginning to wrinkle. I brushed my hands on the back of my pants to clean off the muck, and then held them up high where the air was warmer. Crouching low, I continued to watch the silent crowd. I must have stayed in that furrow for an hour or more before the first person broke away and walked from the fire. Minutes later, another few left the group. That was all I needed; the show was over. I reversed my crawl, never taking my eyes from the group, and using my feet and elbows to put distance between Annabeth, her parents, and myself.

I felt comfortable when I no longer suffered from the heat of the fire and the chill returned to the night air. I stood and half ran back to the house, slipping and tripping on the sticky earth beneath my feet. I looked back; the crowd was less than half the size it had been when I'd decided to leave, and maybe a dozen or more dark forms were walking in my direction. Before entering the house, I sat down, pulled my shoes off, removed my pants and shirt, and balled them together. I then ran upstairs to my bedroom, hoping that I wouldn't bang into or break anything. Retracing my steps, I made my way to my bedroom, closed the door tightly, fumbled for my bag, pulled out a new change of clothes, and stuffed the dirty ones to the bottom, covering them with other loose pieces.

I heard the back door open and close and the sound of steps echo through the house. I let myself slowly and quietly down onto the bed, pulled the sheets up high, closed my eyes, and pretended I was sleeping. I strained to hear any sounds coming from Annabeth and her parents. Doors opened and closed, and they didn't make any attempts to disguise their footsteps or silence their movements.

Fear came over me as I lay in bed, in total darkness, realizing I may have violated something they held extremely personal and sacred. Could this ceremony be a secret they didn't want revealed, I wondered? For the first time, I recognized I might be in danger. In my mind's eye, I followed the noise, and could see Annabeth and her parents cleaning up and walking down the hall. I heard doors opening and closing, and the sound of bed springs squeaking under the weight of the person lying down on top. After I heard the sounds of three distinct squeaks, I felt more comfortable, and let myself relax. There was now only silence in the house. No movements; no sounds of any type.

I thought sleep would come easily but my mind was racing with what I had seen. I rolled over, pulled the sheets up high under my chin, and rubbed the back of my head where the wound reminded me that this experience was all real. I looked into space and even in the total darkness I wasn't able to differentiate the difference between that which I saw with my eyes open or closed. Even though I was completely freaked out by what I had seen, my mind kept going back to the sight of Annabeth naked in the field, standing by the fire. I became extremely aroused at the thought of this beautiful woman, and began to imagine her in bed with me. Even with the oddities of life in Bakers Corner, I thought about life with Annabeth, and what it could be. Then my mind went to the sight of her father and mother standing naked beside her, and I suddenly lost the sensation.

A bedspring squeaked and I jolted upright. I closed my eyes and strained my ears to hear every little nuance the house might reveal. I heard footsteps, an old doorknob turn, more footsteps that sounded as if they were getting closer to my room, and then another doorknob. I opened my eyes to see if it was my door, but in the darkness, I saw nothing. Then there was the sound of the door closing, and the unmistakable noise of someone urinating snapped me back to reality. Again, I was being irrational. I heard the toilet flush, the taps run, and the reverse sounds of doors opening and closing, footsteps, and bedsprings.

Tomorrow, I would pick up my car from Lucious, drive to London, and leave Bakers Corner behind. But what of Annabeth; could I abandon her so easily? Honestly, the feelings I had were too strong to ignore. Could I stay in Bakers Corner with Annabeth? I shook my head. This was probably all just a fling with a guy driving through town. Once I left, she could forget me, or refuse to return my calls. I was that skinny guy, as Lucious had so eloquently pointed out. There were women who had a thing for guys in prison, bikers, or bad boys, but I don't ever recall beautiful women being into short, skinny, average guys with no money. I can't imagine a woman saying, "Oh, I have to get me some of that short skinny guy. Maybe I could get him to grow, buff up, and get a better paying job. Then would he ever be a catch." Sure, Annabeth was a few years older, but she was in a class by herself compared to me. No woman who looked like that had ever hit on me so quickly or showed me so much attention without an ulterior motive. So what was up with Annabeth? Better I leave for London and put her out of my mind. I decided that was what I was going to do.

I woke up looking at the ceiling. The room was brilliantly lit as the sun broke through the lace curtains in the easterly facing window. A large fan hung in the centre of the room with an ornate pull cord to activate the light dangling from it. Damn it, I thought; that's why I couldn't find a light switch.

I stretched my arms wide to shake the sleep, sat up, and scratched my head, and pain once again shot through my scalp. Looking at my fingers, I saw dark dried blood under my nails. I shoved the bed sheets aside, pulled on a clean pair of pants and shirt, opened the door, and peeked in both directions down the hall. The house was silent, with no movement apparent anywhere. I stepped out into the hall, closed the bathroom door behind me, and sat on the toilet. On the vanity rested two towels and a face cloth, and a note was partially tucked between the towels.

Good morning Mr. Grewal.

Mom and Dad have already left to visit the neighbours and I left at 6:00 for the diner. Meet me there for breakfast.

Annabeth

No comment about the event in the field. I hadn't been killed in my sleep, so that was good. As I sat there holding the note, I tried to understand what it was I had seen. Had I even really seen it? These were questions best left for when I had someone who could give me answers.

I flushed, set the water temperature, and had a long, relaxing shower. After drying myself off, I hung the towel over the shower curtain rail, draped my face cloth over the side of the tub, and made sure everything was as it had been before I arrived.

When I checked my phone, the time showed "6:22" and the battery indicator was red, revealing less than ten percent battery reserves. I really should have plugged it in, I realized. I decided I would ask Annabeth to use the rotary dial phone at the diner and leave a few bucks for the long-distance charges. After packing up all my clothes, I stopped at the front door, debating whether or not I should lock it by pushing in the centre lock button before closing the door. I had to ask myself if people in these parts still left their doors unlocked. I surprised myself at how long it took for me to decide to lock the door.

My stomach was rumbling, so I bypassed the garage in favour of breakfast with Annabeth. The sun was coming up behind me in the east and it looked like a clear day, perfect for the rest of the drive to London. The front yards were busy with homeowners gardening, and this time I even received a few waves and smiles from the locals. A few of the faces I recognized from the previous night, and I felt a little embarrassed at having seen them naked.

I pulled the door to the diner open and heard that familiar bell chime. From within the kitchen, this beautiful, dark-haired girl came bounding out to greet me. I let my bag drop to the floor just as she wrapped her arms around me and kissed me softly on the cheek. Annabeth pulled back, still hugging me, and smiled a Mr. White Teeth Lucious smile. My mind flashed with images of her naked body the night before as she had stood by the fire. Where I lack tone and shape, Annabeth had it down perfectly, and as I looked at her only inches away, I envisioned her naked again. I smiled my version of the Mr. White Teeth smile, too.

"Are you really leaving me today?"

"I have to see my son but I plan on coming back." I was lying. I wasn't sure if I could or should.

"Soon? Yesterday was fun, Mr. Grewal, and I would like to see if there might be something more for us. If that's what you want?"

Before I could answer, my stomach rumbled. She loosened her grip from around my neck, bolted for the kitchen, and asked what I wanted for breakfast. I took a stool at the counter.

"Anything really. I'm not that hungry."

"That's why you look like you should be holding yourself up on a stake in Robbie's field scaring away birds." She laughed at her own comment. "Really, you need a little meat on those bones."

All I could think of when she mentioned the scarecrow analogy was the huge burning pyre with the body on top. Then I began to convince myself that she had seen me and was making vague references to the event, trying to trick me into tipping my hand.

"Scrambled eggs and sausages or oatmeal? Or both?" She stuck her head around the corner. "What about pancakes? We don't sell a lot of those here. Most of the guys who come in here want their daily intake of fat and cholesterol. White toast I assume?"

"That's more food than I usually eat all day. How about toast and a coffee?"

Annabeth pulled herself from the back, walked around to her side of the counter, planted her elbows firmly before me, and rested her chin on her closed fists. She looked at me seriously for a few moments, and then smiled. "Really, Mr. Grewal? Toast and coffee? This isn't some diner in the big city. Besides, I'm not letting you outta here without enough food to get you to…" She paused.

"London."

"I'm not letting you outta here without a good meal to get you all the way to London." She leaned in and kissed me, then went back to the kitchen.

"I've been meaning to ask you a very personal question," I called.

"Yeah?" she screamed from the back.

This was a face-to-face type of question. I walked to where I had been doing the dishes and leaned against the wall.

"You're getting a three egg omelette with white toast. You want home fries or bacon?"

"Bacon, please."

"So what do you want to ask?"

Best to get it out quickly, using the BAND-AID approach, I reasoned. "Why me and why so fast?"

Annabeth cracked the eggs in a bowl, tossed the shells in the trash, and then stood before me. Her demeanour had changed immediately, and she looked angry. "So if a good looking girl pays you attention, and doesn't go at your pace, you think there's something going on. Is that it?"

I was taken aback. "No, that's not it. I mean that you're not just a good looking girl; just the opposite."

"So you're saying I'm not good looking." She put her hands on her hips and stepped a little closer.

"No. Crap. No, I mean, you're not good looking. Crap, you've got me flustered." I began to feel the sweat form on my brow. "I mean, you're gorgeous, Annabeth. You could have any guy in town and I show up yesterday and you're all over me."

Her voice went up an octave. "I've lived here my entire life. If any of these shit-toting rednecks were attractive, I would be hitched to one of them. Did you plan on staying any longer than you had to before you met me? Probably not, right? So a girl can't find a guy attractive and show him how she feels." Annabeth backed away. She looked angry - no, pissed.

"Look at me. Skinny, short, I have no money, and you hardly know me."

"So you're saying I'm easy?"

"No, but me. Seriously? Me?" I looked down and presented myself to her.

"Yes, you! I'm looking at you and I like what I've seen so far. A - as you say - gorgeous girl can fall for a guy she finds attractive, and who gives a shit about money anyway. There are more important things than money." Her voice was firm, and her eyes focused; they did not blink or waver from mine.

I suddenly felt very shallow myself. I kept my head low and couldn't face her.

"So you want bacon then?"

When I looked up she was back behind the grill and winked. "Don't worry, Mr. Grewal; I don't give up that easily."

Annabeth made two breakfasts and sat beside me at the counter. The bell chimed above the door and Gus walked in, grunted at Annabeth, and ignored me, thank God; I could still remember seeing him naked.

Annabeth elbowed me and leaned in close. "I think he's jealous of you. Good thing I made your breakfast; he probably would have poisoned you. Eat up. Place opens at eight. The boys get all their morning chores done on the farm, then come here for breakfast or a coffee and to chat."

Gus started making noise - pans banging against each other, utensils clinking into the sink - in an attempt to drown out our conversation. It wasn't long before I heard food sizzling on the grill.

"I'm really proud of you. You've done an amazing job here. I thought I worked hard in the city but I could never do what you do," I told her as we ate.

"It's not that hard when you love what you do. I'm used to getting what I want. And Dan," she called me "Dan" for the first time, "I really want to get to know you better. You're unique and not like the other guys around here." She tore off a strip of her toast and ran it through the egg yolk.

"I'd like that a lot. There's nothing more that I want right now than to see more of you."

The bell chimed and a few of the local farmers entered. The stench of their work followed them into the diner. As one of them slapped me on the back I heard a reference to "Skinny," and wondered if this attention was their way of tolerating me. Was I being accepted because of Annabeth, or because they knew I had seen the ceremony?

I carried our empty plates to the sink, washed them, and asked permission to use the phone to call Sandra. While I was calling London, more of the stools became occupied, and the noise level grew. Sandra answered the phone and I told her I would be there in a few hours once I picked up the car. She asked if everything had gone okay the night before, and for a moment I thought about telling her about what I had witnessed, but decided that would remain a secret, for now. The bell chimed again, and Alan, the resident photographer, entered the diner, waved to me, and walked directly to Annabeth. I finished with Sandra, hung up, and went to join them.

Annabeth was pinning a black-and-white picture of the two of us directly on the wall in the kitchen. "This is all I have of you until you come back, so you better make another appearance soon." She waved a white envelope in the air. "This is your copy."

I pulled out my wallet and presented a twenty-dollar bill to Alan for the pictures.

"Twenty? Wow. I would have been happy with a two spot." Before I could retract my offer, Alan snatched the bill from my hand and offered to take more pictures if and when I needed them.

"I have to use the bathroom. Could you put my copy in my bag for me, please, so I don't lose it?" I asked Annabeth.

I closed and locked the door behind me. Sitting down, I felt an immense wave of happiness fill my entire body. The events of the previous night now seemed distant and of little relevance to how I was feeling. I decided I would ask Annabeth if she would be all right with me seeing her again so soon if I stopped by on the way back from London. I washed up, exited the bathroom, and watched her serving coffee and chatting with the customers. I just observed, and after a few minutes she caught me staring, walked over, and inquired if there was a problem. I asked her if I could return tomorrow night on my way back to Ottawa.

"If you didn't, I would be very disappointed in you, Dan."

She pulled me into the kitchen, away from Gus, pushed me up against the wall, and gave me a kiss the likes of which I haven't had in years. It was passionate and real. I wanted more, and hoped that when I returned from London there would be more - lots more.

Annabeth pulled herself away, licked her lips, and looked at me. I knew the diner was packed and Gus was only a few feet away working at the grill, but I wanted to take her, now. At that point, I didn't care who saw, who knew, or what they thought. The only thing that mattered was Annabeth, here and now.

Annabeth turned on her heels and headed back to the counter. I was left in the kitchen with Gus, standing there in unmistakable discomfort, unable to go back out for a few minutes. Gus looked up from the grill, shook his head in obvious disgust, and went back to cooking. I cleared my throat, straightened my back, and walked out into the diner. Annabeth gave me a silent, wicked look, and never missed a beat with her customers.

As I picked up my bag from behind the counter, I looked outside, and dropped it where I stood. Across the street, the same man from the day before who had knelt before his dying son - the man I had seen naked watching his neighbours burn his son's body atop the pyre - was holding the same son's hand as they walked down the street.

I didn't say anything; I bolted from the diner, looked up and down before crossing the street, and ran up behind the man. He was less than one hundred feet away from me, but I was breathless when I caught up to him. Grabbing his shoulder, I managed to gain his attention. Calmly, he turned, faced me, and asked if he could help. He was definitely the same man with the cold stare I had witnessed the day before. I was facing that stare now.

"Your son." I was breathing heavily.

"Yes, this is my son."

"I was here yesterday when your son was killed." I motioned to the boy standing between us, who looked up at his father and asked what was happening.

"Sir, I don't know what you're talking about. My son isn't dead, as you can see."

"A twin. The one who died yesterday, this is his brother?"

"I only have the one child, no twins. No one died yesterday."

I reached out, clutched the man's arm, and squeezed it tightly. "I saw," I turned and pointed to the spot on the road, "right there." I jabbed the air with my finger. "Right there."

Annabeth and a few of her customers came from the diner and stood on the opposite side of the street, watching me grill the man about what I had seen. Unlike the day before, no one came by to encircle the man and child or push me away from the scene. Instead, I had to motion for Annabeth to join us.

"She was here. I saw her stand over your son."

"Daddy! What is this man saying?"

"Don't worry. He isn't from here and has us confused with someone else."

"Dan, what's going on?"

"Sir, I saw you carry your son away. He was dead."

"Daddy?"

"Dan, stop this. You're frightening the child."

"Annabeth, I saw you and the others." I pointed across the street. "Those guys too. They were here. They all saw what happened."

"Sir, nothing happened to my son yesterday."

"Dan, this isn't funny. Stop it."

"Your son was dead. I saw you carry him away. Then last night, I watched you," I turned to Annabeth, "and you, and the others, stand around a huge bonfire and burn something."

"A fire. Dan, there wasn't a fire last night. No one stood around a fire."

"There was a fire, a huge fucking fire. I left the house in the middle of the night and crawled like a dog through the mud to get close and watch as each and every one of you in town got naked and you burned something. It was wrapped up but it looked like the body of a small child."

The man pulled the child around behind him to protect him from me. "I would never burn my child. He didn't die. And what fire are you talking about?"

"Dan, I think I would know if I was outside last night at a big fire, naked, with a bunch of guys no less." Annabeth squeezed my arm tightly, digging her fingers into my skin as she attempted to pull me back to the diner.

"I know. I know what I saw. I saw most of the town standing around a huge fire and in the centre of the fire was a wood... a wood whatever, and the wrapped body of a young child. And you were standing there with everyone else, naked."

"Really! When was this?"

"After I went to bed."

Suddenly, a smile came across Annabeth's face. "Dan, you aren't going to like this. You looked exhausted last night. I slipped one of my mom's sleeping pills in your beer. You probably hallucinated or dreamt the whole thing. I'm so sorry. I never should have done that without your permission."

Annabeth faced the father, reached out, and held his hands. "I'm sorry, Mac. Dan is a friend and stayed over at my parents' last night. He was having a bad day yesterday, and he looked so tired. I just wanted to help."

Annabeth turned to me again, saying, "Dan, I'm sorry. This is all my fault." She placed the palm of her hand on her chest. "Giving you medication that wasn't prescribed to you was wrong. And now this whole thing - seeing everyone naked, watching us burn a body, a boy dying - it was all a dream or a nightmare.

And it's all my fault."

The father looked relieved, thanked Annabeth, and held out his hand to me. I shook it and apologized for traumatizing both him and his son. "No harm," he told me, and walked away.

"No harm," I thought. No harm! There was no way I dreamt that whole thing the night before. I kept my disbelief and anger to myself.

Annabeth faced me, placed both hands on my cheeks, and looked into my eyes. "This is all my fault. Mine. I'm the one responsible for what happened." She hugged me, wrapping her arms around my waist and placing her head on my shoulder. "Come on back inside."

The diner guests had already lost interest and returned. I bowed my head and followed Annabeth into the diner. As I walked past the row of stools, I overheard conversations between customers, and it was all about ploughing, seeding, barns, animals, and the weather. No one, not one single person, made a comment about my outburst; there were no snickers, and no chuckling. Either Bakers Corner was the friendliest town in the world, or everyone had something to hide.

Annabeth handed me my bag and yelled at Gus that she was walking with me to the garage. She held my hand and guided me back outside to the sidewalk. There wasn't much conversation between us, and at this point I preferred it that way. Annabeth continued to act as if nothing was wrong; as if my outburst was nothing more than getting upset over burnt toast or spilled milk.

As Annabeth held my hand, her fingers played with mine, twisting, rolling over, and squeezing my hand as we walked. For a woman of almost forty, she looked younger, acted younger, and made me feel younger. If not for the lies, the possible drug overdose, and the naked ceremony in the middle of the night, she would have been perfect. Despite those flaws, however, I couldn't help but feel something strong, almost powerful, about this girl. Her thick, black, wavy hair bounced as we walked and I noticed that it was shiny, almost glistening in the sunlight. I reasoned that she must colour her hair to make it look that way, but then I spotted a rogue, single strand of grey in the back - only one hair, mind you. So much for the colouring theory, I realized.

"What?" She had noticed me looking at her.

"Just admiring the view." A good come back, I thought.

Not much more was said during the walk from the diner to the garage. When we arrived, Willis was still in the pit, and he waved silently to Annabeth. Lucious came out from under the hood of a pickup and wiped the grease off his hands with an equally dirty rag. He tilted his cap back and smiled, showing his Mr. White Teeth persona.

Annabeth leaned in, greeting him with a kiss on the cheek. His smiled never dimmed. Lucious then stuffed the rag in his back pocket and pulled my keys from another.

"Well, Skinny, your car is all set and ready to go. I dropped the tank, drained the gas out, soaked and cleaned the fuel pump, changed the filter, and made sure you had plenty of pressure in the gas lines. I even changed your plugs, oil, and air filter. You do know they have a thing called regular maintenance, or preventative maintenance, huh? Your oil was thick like molasses in the winter. When was the last time you changed the oil?"

"I added a litre of oil before I left the house."

"I'm not surprised she decided to give ya trouble. Now, she's purring like a kitten on your lap after being fed by Mama. I added windshield washer fluid just to be nice. Well it's on the bill, anyway. So maybe not so nice." He pointed to the back of the lot. "She's right over there. I'll meet you inside to square things up." Lucious walked back to the main office, leaving Annabeth and I alone.

"So, Mr. Grewal, you leaving me?"

"Only for a day. I'll stop by on my way through tomorrow. It'll be late but I promise I'll stop, even if it's only for a few minutes."

Annabeth picked up my bag, walked to the car, dropped the bag by the trunk, turned, and leaned against the driver's door. She kept her head down, looking more like a sixteen-year-old worried that her new boyfriend would find another girl once he left town than a grown woman.

I walked slowly over to her and moved in close, and all those fears I had about the overdose and burning suddenly seemed of little relevance. We were now touching. I fell into her, and she spread her legs and placed them on either side of mine. Our bodies pressed together tightly, the car door holding her up. Annabeth put her hands on my waist, and my hands rested on the glass behind her. She looked up at me and rubbed her hands on my hips. "You are a boney little man, aren't you, Mr. Grewal?"

"My cooking sucks." I moved in and kissed her, my hands gently cradling her head as we continued to force our way closer to each other.

"Why me?" I had to ask her again before I left.

"Why not you? I sense a good soul in you, Mr. Grewal. And that's what counts." She pushed her lips to mine again. I felt her arms move across my back. Her hands finally came to rest on my butt cheeks, grabbing them firmly and forcing me hard into her. Her head tilted back, and she let out a soft moan.

"It's been so long. You better hurry back tomorrow because I can't wait." I could feel her moving her pelvis against me as she pushed into me again.

"Hate to disturb you, Skinny, but I gots your bill ready and I gots to get back to work."

I looked up and there was Lucious, grinning as wide and as white as could be. He was holding the office door open as an invitation for me to join him inside to settle my debt.

I pulled back; Annabeth licked her lips, reached up quickly for another kiss, and then let me go. I walked carefully and slowly to the main office to join Lucious.

As I walked in, Lucious embarrassed me by exclaiming, "You're showing, boy!"

"Thanks, old man. At least I still have a reason to, well, show."

"That you do."

I looked at the bill, and was surprised by the low total. I lay down cash on top of the handwritten invoice, and left a handsome tip to ensure his discretion. "Keep the change, Lucious, and don't be telling tales."

"About what?" Lucious never stopped smiling. He should've been in politics. I shook his hand and felt the grease transfer from his to mine, but it didn't matter. "Been a pleasure, Skinny. You coming back soon?"

I smiled my version of the Mr. White Teeth smile, proclaimed, "I most certainly am," and walked back to the car where Annabeth was waiting. She opened the door, and I fell into the driver's seat, locked my seat belt, and started the car.

"You want a ride back to the diner?"

"I need the walk to cool down." She slammed the driver's door. I manually rolled down the window, and Annabeth peeked her head in. "I'll be waiting, Mr. Grewal. Don't leave me in anticipation for long. I might forgot all about you." A broad smile appeared. "Tomorrow?" she asked.

"Tomorrow," I confirmed.

"I'll be here." I started the car; it did indeed purr like a kitten on my lap. I dropped the car into gear and drove away slowly, watching Annabeth in my rearview mirror. She stood there, alone. I pulled onto the main street and accelerated, and she disappeared from view.

The small town of Bakers Corner was behind me. The time on the radio flashed four zeros. Lucious must have disconnected the battery to work on the car. I plugged the power cord into my cellphone, the screen lit up, and the time showed "10:24." I noticed five ascending bars in the top right corner of the screen and realized that I had cell reception again. The power disruption had also cleared my pre-set radio stations, so I found the stations I wanted, set the radio to all 80's music, and tapped the steering wheel as eastbound traffic flowed past. The roads were clear, the sky was cloud free, and I figured I had a five or six hour drive before I arrived in London.

The wind whipped through the open window and tousled my hair. I licked my lips and still tasted Annabeth. My heart raced and I felt that rush that only happens when the relationship is new.

Song after song went by on the radio, but I couldn't have recalled a single one if the DJ had broadcast my name personally and offered me a million dollars to call in the song title. I was lost in thought. Unable to pay attention to the road, the last few kilometers were also a blur.

"10:53."

I was only half an hour outside of Bakers Corner. I could call Sandra, tell her the car wasn't ready, and that I would come down next weekend, I thought. It sounded plausible. After all, not all of it was a lie. Sam was too young to know if the visit was this weekend or next, and my time with him this weekend would be limited anyway. A full weekend of planned activities next week would be better. It didn't take much self-convincing before I knew I would turn around. I'd call Sandra from Annabeth's diner when I got back into town, I decided. I licked my lips again and Annabeth was still there. Settled!

"10:55."

At the next off ramp, I took the exit, spun around, and headed back east on Highway 7. I accelerated above the speed limit, turned off the radio, and noted the time. I'd be back in Bakers Corner before 11:30.

My heart raced, and the pulse in my temple throbbed in anticipation of seeing Annabeth again. I couldn't sit still because I was so excited. I kept looking at the time on the radio that seemed to stand still. A minute seemed to take two, and five minutes felt like ten.

"11:23."

The area seemed familiar; I had passed it only an hour earlier. I knew I would be in Bakers Corner any minute.

"11:35."

I'd been driving faster on the return trip than I had been while leaving, but I still hadn't arrived back in town. The area with its farmland was now beginning to look just like the last ten kilometers had: green pastures, a few cows, a silo every now and then, and a fence running on the north and south sides of the road.

"11:42."

I knew I was well past Bakers Corner. Something was wrong. I asked myself, did I take a wrong turn, or take an off ramp by accident? I passed a sign indicating that I was on Highway 7, and a distance sign showed that I was getting closer to Ottawa.

"11:45."

At the next exit I slammed on my brakes and took the turn, leaving a trail of rubber behind me. I merged onto the highway and floored the gas pedal. Just as Lucious had promised, the car not only purred, but now it roared. The engine revved high and dropped down a gear, and I quickly hit the marked speed limit but didn't let up on the accelerator.

"11:59."

By now all the fields on both sides of the highway looked identical. I couldn't tell where I was. Pulling to the shoulder, I unplugged my cellphone and loaded the map app. It only took a few moments before a pin showed my exact location. I swiped the screen left, and then right, but there was no town listed on the highway for kilometres in either direction. I expanded the screen, found a few towns, and tapped on them, but none of them were Bakers Corner.

EPILOGUE

The Ontario Provincial Police officer read the report, closed it, held it high, and looked over the sheets of paper at the man, then placed it before him on the desk.

"Is this your signature?" He tapped the bottom of the last page.

"Yeah."

"Your name is Dan Grewal?"

"Yeah."

"And your story is that you visited a town and that town just disappeared?"

"Yeah." Dan Grewal hung his head low, almost embarrassed by what he was asking the police officer to believe.

The officer flipped through the pages again. He looked at Dan, and then focused his attention back on the report. He picked up a highlighter and stroked neon purple through various sections that he thought deserved attention. Every few moments the officer would look back up at Dan before returning to the report.

"Bakers Corner? You're sure?" the officer asked Dan as he tapped on the keyboard at his desk.

"Yeah."

The officer turned the monitor around and showed Dan a picture on Google Earth. The image was a wide view of Eastern Ontario. On the right side of the monitor, the west edge of Ottawa could be seen, and the left side expanded to Peterborough. The officer handed Dan a pen and asked him to point to where Bakers Corner was located.

Dan followed Highway 7 from Ottawa along the path he had driven the previous day before his car had broken down. He stopped where he thought the town was located and tapped the screen. The officer confirmed his location and zoomed in to an area approximately twenty kilometers wide. After the program refocused on the area, the screen showed nothing but green pastures and fields.

"Are you sure this was the location?"

"It looks different on this thing. I'm pretty sure it was around there. Really, I was there," Dan said, trying to convince the office of his story. "Maybe it was a little farther east." The officer clicked the mouse and dragged the cursor along the highway, moving the image left. "Maybe west." Dan sounded unsure of the location.

"Okay, let's try something different." The officer stood, left, and returned with a large printed map. He unfolded it and placed it before Dan. "Here, take your time and see if you can tell me where you think Bakers Corner was located. Are you sure you were on Highway 7?"

"I don't appreciate your condescending tone," Dan exclaimed.

"Sorry, but you gotta admit, a whole town going missing is not something we get asked to look into every day." He tapped the map, indicating that he wanted Dan to show him the approximate location of the town.

Dan studied the map closely, closed his eyes, and tried to imagine his drive into town. The officer watched Dan turn his head as his memory recalled his location when he had stopped to speak with Lucious about his car trouble. Dan opened his eyes and looked down at the map, slid his fingers along Highway 7, and stopped. With his free hand, he pulled a pen from the desk, marked a large "X" on the map, and circled the area where he thought Bakers Corner should have been.

"There. Right there." Dan tapped the map where he had placed the "X."

The officer pulled the map toward him and turned it around so he could see it. "Here?" He put his finger over the spot. "Right there?" Dan nodded.

The officer ran his finger along the highway and up a side road, and drew a smaller "x."

"This is where I live. Probably no more than one or two clicks away from your 'X.' I drive past this area twice a day when I work and at least a few times on my days off to go into Ottawa and back. Not to mention when I patrol that section of the highway." The officer was growing impatient with the man across from him. "So you're telling me either I'm blind and haven't noticed an entire town, or some Hollywood production company dropped in a town for the day just to play with your mind."

"What about the lady who killed the kid? Did anyone report an accident?"

"Nope."

Another officer walked over and joined them, whispering into the officer's ear. He excused himself and left. Minutes crawled by painstakingly slowly. Dan sat alone, looking around with detachment at the institutional wall colours, metal desks, and bland décor, and wondered if the setting accounted for the officer's demeanour. He looked back and saw the two men discussing something in the far end of the office. The officer who had taken his statement returned with a few papers and sat down.

"Okay. You know we ran you, right?"

"Me?" Dan was puzzled as to why the police would run his name through CPIC, the Canadian Police Information Centre. "Why me?"

"Well, you came in with this cockamamie story, so we checked to see if you're out on a day pass from the psych hospital. Turns out you're a nobody; we couldn't even find an outstanding parking ticket, and that's a good thing. But this town, Bakers Corner; there's only one Bakers Corner in Canada. And it's located in northern Manitoba."

"What? That's impossible. I was there. I slept there, ate there, met the people there, and now the town is gone!" Dan was becoming excited, and his voice rose in frustration.

The officer disregarded Dan's outburst and instead read silently from the sheets he had brought back with him. Dan stared at him, waiting for him to say something. "Bakers Corner was a farm town that closed in the sixties. The main feed company, - hang on, here it is - Parkmain & Prowell, just couldn't make a profit in a small town, so they decided to pack it up and hightail it outta there. The town tried to stay alive but everybody pretty much called it quits eventually and the town was deserted by 1964."

To prove his point, the officer tapped a few keys on the keyboard, moved the mouse, and then turned the monitor so that both he and Dan could see it. Dan pulled his chair closer and leaned in.

"What am I looking at?"

The officer tapped the monitor with a pen. "This, Dan, is Bakers Corner, according to Google Earth. A tiny deserted little butt-fuck of a town in the middle of nowhere northern Manitoba." The officer zoomed in and the overhead view began to tilt, showing the buildings at a more direct angle and bringing them into focus. As the screen resolution adjusted, Dan recoiled in his seat, and the metal chair's feet grated against the industrial tile flooring. The officer looked up to see Dan staring, eyes fixed, unmoving, his skin flushed, tiny beads of sweat forming instantly on his forehead.

"What did you see?"

Dan pointed at the monitor, and the officer zoomed in as much as the program would allow. He immediately realized why Dan looked the way he did, and he felt his own heart skip a beat and his palms become wet. The pictures on the screen Dan was pointing at were described perfectly in his statement, and were now coming to life on the monitor.

"If you researched this town and you're pulling some type of bullshit prank and wasten' my time, I'll lock you up and forget about you for the rest of the weekend."

Dan didn't hear what the officer said; instead, he was looking at the faded and peeling sign of "Lucious' Auto Service." The white painted background had almost completely peeled away, revealing the wood beneath, and the black letters that spelled out the name of the garage were still visible. The building had long since been vacated; vegetation had overtaken the front, windows were broken, one of the bay doors was open, and all the cars that had been for sale were long gone. In his mind's eye, Dan could still see the inside of the garage where Lucious and Willis had been working.

"Zoom; move the view down the street!" Dan didn't so much as ask the officer to do it as order him.

The officer moved the mouse and the view began to change. "No!" Dan screamed. "The other way!" The officer complied and dragged the mouse, and the image on the monitor began to move down the street. Dan recognized the houses; he had seen them only a few hours prior. But then, the houses had been pristine, people had still lived in them, and the lawns had been maintained. The images on the monitor showed houses long since abandoned. The manicured lawns Dan had seen that morning were now nothing but waist-high weeds. Dan's hand slapped the desk in a nonverbal gesture, asking the officer to rush what he was doing.

When Dan saw what his wanted to see, he demanded loudly for the officer to stop. Without asking permission, he grabbed the monitor and turned it so only he could view it. He stared and he didn't blink, hypnotized by what he saw. The entrance to "Annabeth's Counter" frightened him.

The white paint around the windows and door had peeled back like scales on a fish from hard cold winters, humid warm summers, and decades of neglect. One of the side windows was shattered, and the sign that had been hanging above the door only the day before was now gone.

"This is - was - the diner I wrote about. This was Annabeth's Counter. I had breakfast there this morning before leaving. I worked there washing dishes last night. Damn it, I could draw out the layout of the diner and tell you where everything is. That would prove that I was there." Dan pulled his eyes from the monitor, pleading with the OPP officer. "I really was there." Dan almost started crying. He could feel his eyes welling up, and he put his head down and wiped at them. If he had let himself, Dan would've had a full-blown meltdown.

The officer looked across the desk at the man who couldn't contain himself any longer. He thought to himself that if the man was faking his story, he was a great actor. The officer pulled a box of tissues from his drawer and slid it across the desk. Feeling too embarrassed to let the officer see him crying, Dan kept his head low and pulled a tissue from the box. He realized that Annabeth was either a figment of his imagination, or something else.

Dan wiped his eyes with the tissue and whispered, "I was there."

The officer heard him, and said, "I believe you." He left the box of tissue on his desk.

"Wait!" Dan jumped from his seat and started patting down his pockets until he located his cellphone. "Remember I said we took pictures at the diner of Annabeth and me?" The officer nodded. "I have them here."

Dan took his seat, swiped up, unlocked his phone, moved the screen until he located the "Pictures" icon, and tapped it. The folders appeared and he selected the one marked "Camera." All of the pictures Dan had taken with his cellphone appeared, and he scrolled down to the bottom where the most current pictures were. When Dan saw what the images on his phone depicted, the officer could read the horror on his face.

"What?"

Dan couldn't say anything. He sat, frozen in disbelief, and then handed the officer the phone. The last few frames that should've shown Annabeth and Dan together were now only flashes of white light. The officer tapped the frame and enlarged the picture, but the large image didn't offer any more detail than did the preview frame. He slid from one white frame to the next until he found pictures of Dan's son. He swiped back and the white frames returned. The officer handed the phone back to Dan.

"The ones that look like they were over-exposed are the ones that should be of me and Annabeth," Dan explained. "That's not supposed to happen with a phone camera. I've never seen a picture over-exposed on a phone before."

Dan pocketed his phone. He realized he had no evidence to prove his story, and nothing to back up the claims of his experience. Other than lost time and the fact that his car was running better than it ever had, Dan had nothing but his word and details of a deserted town thousands of kilometers away.

The OPP officer completed his reports, made a copy, and placed the paperwork in an envelope after Dan had signed acceptance. Dan was certain that the report would be shelved, only to be pulled out every now and then so that the officer could have a good chuckle. What more could they do, he thought. He gathered up his things and was escorted from the detachment to the parking lot. The officer extended his hand, and Dan shook it.

"If it means anything, I believe every word of your story. Sometimes, you just have to take things at face value." The OPP officer continued to shake Dan's hand, and then relaxed his grip and stepped to the side as Dan opened the driver's door.

"I wish I was as sure as you are." Dan started his car, pulled out of the parking lot, and headed west on Highway 7. The area along the highway seemed all too familiar now.

Dan drove for a minute or so and then pulled onto the shoulder, killed the engine, and exited the car. He looked north across a field, closed his eyes, and tried hard to imagine himself in Bakers Corner. He opened his eyes and saw a huge fire burning with naked people standing around it and a small body on top of a wooden structure within. The body was wrapped in cloth or a blanket but it was a body, the body of a small boy. This location was the spot. He was certain of it.

Dan set the hazard lights on his car, locked the doors, and walked west along the highway. He pulled his cellphone from his pocket, unlocked it, and noticed that he had no cell coverage. Using the phone as a Geiger counter and looking up to watch the terrain, he continued to walk along the highway. He was more certain than ever that he had found the spot. He walked for over half an hour until the phone registered a single bar. He drew a line in the dirt on the shoulder and continued to walk west. The phone signal continued to improve: two bars, three, then full strength, 4G. He drew another line in the dirt. Looking back, he noticed he had walked less than twenty feet. He had gone from no signal to full strength in twenty feet.

Dan retraced his steps, walking back to the first line. As soon as he crossed it, the signal disappeared. To test his theory, Dan activated the camera on his cellphone and took pictures of the fields on the north and south sides of the highway from where he stood. He then walked back to the second line and aimed his camera at approximately the same locations. Dan closed his eyes, held his breath, and activated the "Pictures" app. The pictures he had just taken showed vivid green fields, rusty red barns, and baby blue skies. He swiped the images back to reveal picture after picture of over-exposed frames.

He smiled, let out a little scream, and knew Annabeth was there. He ran back to his car and stood outside, holding the phone up high. It didn't register a single bar of cellphone coverage. Behind the car, in the dirt of the shoulder, Dan spelled out the words "I love you" with the heel of his shoe. He was the happiest he had been in a long time.

Dan sat in his car. He knew he wasn't crazy, and that everything he had experienced had been real. He flipped through the pictures, and when the first over-exposed frame came up he felt a warmth penetrate his body. No one would believe him, but he was sure that within that solid white over-exposed picture was Annabeth. He turned off his phone, started the car, said his goodbyes to Annabeth, and drove away.

*****

Later that night, Dan spent a few hours with his son and had a nice chat with Sandra, but failed to mention anything about what had transpired. Sandra had prepared a meal that the three of them shared and reminded Dan of when they had still been a family. There had been an uncomfortable strain between them since he had arrived at Sandra's house, however. It was nice to see her and his son, but he suspected that there might already be another man in her life. She was polite, but didn't show any of the warmth she usually did. He had been greeted with a kiss to the cheek, but she had leaned in, keeping distance between them. That was a gesture he remembered from his high school days when kissing a girl good night. If she leaned, there was nothing. If there was body contact, there was a chance.

Since he was certain that he and Sandra would get a divorce, Dan decided that any mention of a disappearing town might impact his visitation rights with his son. He helped with the dishes, cleaned up the kitchen, and put Sam to bed. He sat in Sam's room, watching him sleep. The chair was uncomfortable; a good thing, he thought, as it kept him awake to watch Sam. When Dan decided he could no longer stay awake, he left his son's room, closed the door behind him, and walked down the hall. All the lights were off, Sandra's door was closed, and no glow came from beneath it.

Dan tried his best to keep the noise down as he made his way to his room and closed the door behind him. He unzipped his travel bag and pulled out his shaving kit, and a pair of muddy pants slipped to the floor. Startled, he looked at the dirty pants piled at his feet. He reached into the bag and pulled out an equally dirty shirt - dirt from the field where they had the fire. Dan's mood changed. He reached in and began pulling clothing out and dropping it to the floor. He found what he was looking for: a plain white envelope, which he treated like a renaissance masterpiece. He flipped the lid over carefully, opened the body of the envelope, and peered inside.

Dan pulled out a small black-and-white photo of Annabeth and himself at the diner. His hands shook as he held it. He saw the face of the woman with whom he had fallen in love; a woman he assumed was long dead. Across the bottom, Annabeth had scribbled a short note in pen: *"To My Biggest Fan. Annabeth."* The blue ink stood out in stark contrast to the black-and-white print.

Dan sat on the edge of the bed, cradling the picture in two hands, scared to touch the emulsion in case it disappeared. He placed the photo on the end table, found his cellphone, took a picture of the black-and-white photo, double checked that this time he was able to capture the print, and saved it. To be certain, he emailed the picture to his personal and work email accounts. After he sent the email, he carefully placed the photo back in the envelope, closed the flap, and positioned it on the bottom of his travel bag.

Dan placed his ear to the bedroom door, and hearing nothing, he opened it carefully. He looked both ways down the hall, and now seeing nothing, he crept down the stairs to the living room. Sandra's laptop was still on her desk; he powered it up and the lock screen appeared. He tried her password from when they were still living together - "bubblebutt," a reference to her backside - and the system started up. "Some things never change," he thought to himself.

A quick Google search on *"Bakers Corner"* revealed the exact search results he had seen at the police station. He scrolled through the various results, and clicked on the link that indicated the town in Manitoba. Dan read through the information listed on the town, discovered nothing new, and went back to the Google home page. He entered "*Annabeth Anderson,*" held his finger over the "Enter" key, and looked at the screen. Part of him wanted to see the results, and part of him wanted to keep things the way they were. The conflict of whether or not to hit the button wrestled inside his head. His index finger hung over the key, his eyes unmoving from Annabeth's name on the screen. Slowly, his finger moved down and tapped the key, and almost instantly the search results changed from "*Bakers Corner*" to "*Annabeth Anderson.*"

Dan moved the cursor from "Web" to "Images" and the screen filled with pictures of women. Most of the images were in full colour, but a few were in black-and-white, and as he scanned those pictures his eyes stopped on one he recognized. A portrait of the girl he knew as Annabeth Anderson was shown on the third row. He scrolled down the page but failed to see any more pictures of his Annabeth. He went back to the top, moved his cursor over the picture, and clicked on it, enlarging the image.

Dan stared at the picture. The woman he was looking at was the girl he had spent a day with. The description of the picture claimed that it was of Anna-beth Anderson, owner of Annabeth's Counter in Bakers Corner, Manitoba, born 1923. If she was alive today, Annabeth would be around ninety years of age, not the beautiful woman of forty he had fallen for, Dan thought. It didn't matter how old she was or what she looked like; he had to find her.

Dan searched through every obituary search engine he could find but un-veiled no reference to an Annabeth Anderson. If she had gotten married, her new surname could be anything. It was getting late, his mind was spinning with what he was seeing, and he was about to give up when he decided he would try one last search. Dan typed in a different name and the very first result displayed exactly what he was looking for. He clicked on the link to "Annabeth Grewal" and his mind cleared when he read what he had found. The page had been written by Tabitha Grewal as a tribute to her grandparents, Annabeth and Dan Grewal, who had died only hours apart on June 6, 2009, in a Winnipeg nursing home.

Dan was now wide awake, his head clear of cobwebs, and he concentrated on what he read in the dedication to the couple known as Annabeth and Dan Grewal. The couple had married in 1964, and Annabeth had died at the age of eighty-six, Dan at the age of eighty-four. They had three children, and seven grandchildren. After the feed mill had closed, the only thing left had been local farming, and that hadn't lasted too long. Their three children, all born in Winnipeg, eventually moved on and had families of their own. Nothing more was mentioned of Bak-ers Corner. At the very bottom of the article, a series of black-and-white pictures showed Dan and Annabeth in the early years of their marriage, progressing to grainy, blurry, and full-colour photos of them with their children at various ages.

It was like looking in a mirror. The man in the photos from the sixties through the millennium was himself. He was still skinny. Some of the photos showed them working in the diner, and others with some of their neighbours, including one man with a wide smile full of white teeth that even in black-and-white photos was unmistakable. Lucious had his hat pulled back on his head, a rag in one hand, and an arm around Dan's neck. The two of them were smiling at the camera and in the background sat Dan's Neon that was now parked in Sandra's driveway. The Neon in the black-and-white photograph had seen better days. Rust had taken hold around all four wheel wells, and the driver's side mirror was taped in place. The Neon in Sandra's driveway had nowhere near the amount of rust that was shown in the photo.

Dan couldn't explain what he saw. He couldn't understand how or why the Dan in the photos had died an old man in Manitoba when he had been living in Ottawa, working and married to Sandra, at the time of his own death. He had lived his life with Annabeth; he couldn't recall the memories of their lives together, but he had three children and seven grandchildren he didn't know anything about. His own children would be about the same age or older than he was. He had grandchildren, he thought to himself. "I have grandkids," he whispered. The names of his children and grandchildren were all listed at the bottom of the article.

Dan opened up another page on the browser and started another Google search for his eldest son, Ben Grewal. Only one result appeared and he switched the screen to show the images produced by his search. A tall, skinny man appeared in the photos, the likeness with himself too apparent to dismiss. The face of Ben Grewal, Dan thought, showed what he had looked like as a child. Dan rubbed his own face, feeling the features he saw on the son he had never met. Dan now knew he had to contact his family. A family he had known nothing about until only a few minutes prior, but for whom he already felt a sense of responsibility. He wanted to contact them tonight, immediately. He didn't care what time it was, he had to talk to them, meet them.

He scrolled down a few lines of pictures and what he saw made him stop dead. One of the pictures showed a Ben Grewal with grey hair and a receding hairline. The lines around his eyes and across his forehead showed the kind of life he had. Ben had died in 2012 of cancer. Dan felt pressure in his eyes, and tears formed and rolled down his cheeks. He felt remorse for losing the woman he loved and never having the chance to really know her, and for losing a son who was actually older than he was and not having the opportunity to know him at all.

His mind swirled, trying to keep everything in order. If he did contact his children and grandchildren, how would he explain the events, his age, and the fact that he was alive and younger than his own children? How could he explain to his children and grandchildren that he was the same man they had known growing up?

Dan tried to explain and rationalize how these things he was seeing could be real, and prove that he wasn't imagining them or making them up. He had doubts as to whether science could even explain to him what had happened. Perhaps there were things best left unexplained; not everything needed to be answered. He looked at the pictures of Annabeth, his children, and his grandchildren one more time, and went back to the picture of him and Annabeth. He stared at it, never wanting to forget her. He could only imagine the times they had spent together.

Dan copied the pages, emailed them to himself, cleared the browser history, shut down the laptop, and went to bed.

THE END

ABOUT THE AUTHOR

Perry Prete is a Canadian crime writer and paramedic. His first novel, All Good Things, introduced us to Ethan Tennant, a City of Ottawa paramedic who looks at crimes from the medical perspective.

Perry continues to work full-time as a paramedic and uses his thirty plus years of life changing and sometimes dramatic experiences to bring realism to his gripping medical novels. His other works include, The Things That Matter Most and All Good Things.

He is also a business owner, specializing in the pre-hospital care field. His company sells medical equipment across North America, primarily to EMS agencies.

A native of Sudbury, Ontario, Perry, graduated from Fanshawe College in London but now lives and works in Brockville, Ontario.

HIGHWAY 7

4 DARK TALES

*From award-winning author
of the Ethan Tennant Series*

PERRY PRETE

THE REUNION EPILOGUE

Wanda MacLean finished wiping down the counter, tossed the wet cloth into the sink, and started to refill and arrange the sugar dispensers, salt, and pepper shakers. She refilled the forks, knives, and spoons in the large grey plastic bin under the counter. She pulled the dishes out of the dishwasher and stacked them neatly by the warming tray for the next morning.

She wanted to go to the new bar in town with many of her friends and members of the Sanburg clan, but she had to keep the diner open. Saturday night, after all, was her best night of the week. Even in small towns, a Saturday night dinner out was still popular. It had been a good day for business. The Sanburg family had stopped by all day from the reunion and bought food or supplies from the general store.

As Wanda walked past the cooler, she saw herself in the glass door, stopped, and admired her reflection. She had done well; she owned the diner outright, no bank loans, nothing. She pulled her shoulder-length hair around her ears, turned left then right, and wondered what she would look like with short hair. Maybe a pixie cut, something easy to take care of. Her husband loved her long hair but he didn't have to wash it, blow dry it, set it, colour it. He was balding, and kept his hair short. He hadn't used shampoo in years.

Her husband had closed the general store section of the business promptly at six. He usually stayed with Wanda from six until closing, but they had an agreement. On Friday and Saturday nights he was permitted to leave at six when he closed the general store. Tonight he had gone straight home to watch the baseball game from the west coast on TV. She was sure he was already asleep after having a few too many beers, but it was his night.

Wanda looked up at the clock: 10:22. Confused, she looked at her watch: 11:51. She walked over to the plastic clock on the wall and tapped it. The second hand moved once, then stopped. "*Needs a new battery*," she thought. "*Something for Monday morning when we re-open*." She was tired and wanted to get home, and maybe have a beer herself if her husband was still up to discuss her haircut.

She grabbed her purse and sweater, and dug out her keys from the bottom of her bag. As she walked past the last stool at the counter, she sat down and, using her tip-toes, she slowly spun around in circles. Wanda had gone through this routine the very first day she bought the diner and every night since. She loved working here. It was hard work, but it was her work and her money.

Wanda stepped outside, heard the brass bell chime above the door, closed it, and locked up. She pushed/pulled it several times to make sure it was locked. She didn't think they needed a security system at the store; no one had one in town. A locked door still told people to stay away. She bunched her sweater under her chin against the night air. Pointing her remote at her car, she pressed the button to start it and warm it up. She always started the car as she left the diner. There weren't any streetlights in the lot, and the only lights in the area came from her car.

She looked up at the night sky and saw millions of stars. There wasn't a cloud in the sky. "*Starry night, sailors delight,*" she thought. "*Maybe one day, I'll get a boat.*"

As she walked to the car, she suddenly smelled something foul and heard a noise coming from the side of the building. The car's headlights illuminated the front of the store but cast an eerie shadow to the side where the large metal trash bin was located. She looked around and noticed that one of the two metal lids was open.

The cook loved to leave the lid off for the raccoons at night and let them eat the leftovers that were tossed in the bin throughout the day. Wanda knew he loved raccoons and continued to feed them despite the fact that Wanda and her husband told him not to. He had even set up a wooden pallet so they could easily climb in and out without too much trouble.

"Fucking raccoons," she said out loud.

Walking towards the trash bin, she picked up a large stick and started yelling, "Hey. Hey." When Wanda was beside the trash bin, she began to bang the stick on the outside of the metal container. She heard rumbling and the sound of little paws attempting to escape the bin that held the nightly feast. She saw two large, well fed, and healthy raccoons climb over the edge and down the pallet, and waddle their way into the woods behind the diner.

"Man, I hope my ass isn't as big as yours," she yelled to the raccoons, grabbing her own ass and giggling.

Wanda was only mildly upset and also loved the critters, but didn't want to see them trapped inside.

She climbed the pallet and was reaching up to close the lid when she heard a low, deep, throaty growl coming from behind her. She turned to her right, expecting to see one of the larger raccoons attempting to argue its way back into the dumpster, but saw only the large paw of an animal she didn't recognize.

Wanda froze in place. Her pulse quickened and she found herself unable to move. The growling increased and the stench became unbearable. Her eyes had adjusted to the dim light and she saw that the paw of the beast was injured and bleeding freely.

She still had the stick in her hand, the car was unlocked, and the engine had already been started. Wanda moved quickly. She swung the stick blindly behind her and felt it hit something solid, then jumped down from the pallet. The wooden pallet flipped over and landed on the injured paw of the beast, and it howled in pain.

Wanda didn't look back. *"They always look back in the movies, trip and fall, and get caught,"* she told herself. *"Don't look back."* She ran as fast as she could. It was less than thirty feet from the trash bin to the car, but tonight it felt like she was setting the world record for the hundred yard dash. She reached the car, pulled the door open hard, jumped in, and slammed the door. It was only after she had locked the car that she dared look outside.

Wanda saw nothing at the trash bin. The pallet was knocked over, but she couldn't see any animal in the glow of her headlights. The beast could've been hiding in the shadows and concealed from sight. She slowly turned her head to the right, then the left. She saw nothing. She finally felt comfortable enough to breath.

Wanda inserted the key in the ignition, turned it to disengage the auto-start, put the car in reverse, and twisted to look out the back window. Wanda screamed. The entire back window of the car was covered by the furry beast that was standing immediately behind it. She floored the accelerator and aimed the car at the beast. The car should've hit the animal, but instead she drove backwards from the parking lot onto the dirt road. She slammed on the brakes and the tires slid in the dirt. She looked out the windshield and saw nothing in the bright lights of the car. This time she looked around the car and held her breath. There was nothing in the night.

Wanda was putting the car into "drive" when the driver's side window broke inward and a large claw reached in and grabbed her shoulder. Searing pain shot throughout her body as the claws dug deep into her flesh. She could feel the warmth of blood flowing out of the wound. With her right hand, she grabbed the claw that held her shoulder and tried to pry herself free. The claws dug too deeply and were too tightly embedded in her flesh, so she decided instead to shake the beast from the roof of her car. She floored the accelerator and aimed it at the trash bin.

The car's tires spun, dug into the dirt, and then propelled the vehicle like a bullet into the trash bin. The thick metal of the dumpster bent inward as the car's front end collapsed from the impact. Wanda was thrown into the steering wheel and the windshield fractured, the radiator burst, and steam flowed upwards.

The next morning, the police examined the scene and found Wanda's car melded into the dumpster. The driver's side window was shattered inward, and blood covered the seat. Tiny pieces of clothing had ripped and been left dangling from the car's glass when Wanda had been pulled through the window.

The police and search-and-rescue teams followed the blood trail and distinctive paw prints from the car and around the trash bins to the edge of the woods. As they surveyed the scene further, they were unable to track the prints or blood into the forest.

Wanda MacLean was never seen again.

THE END